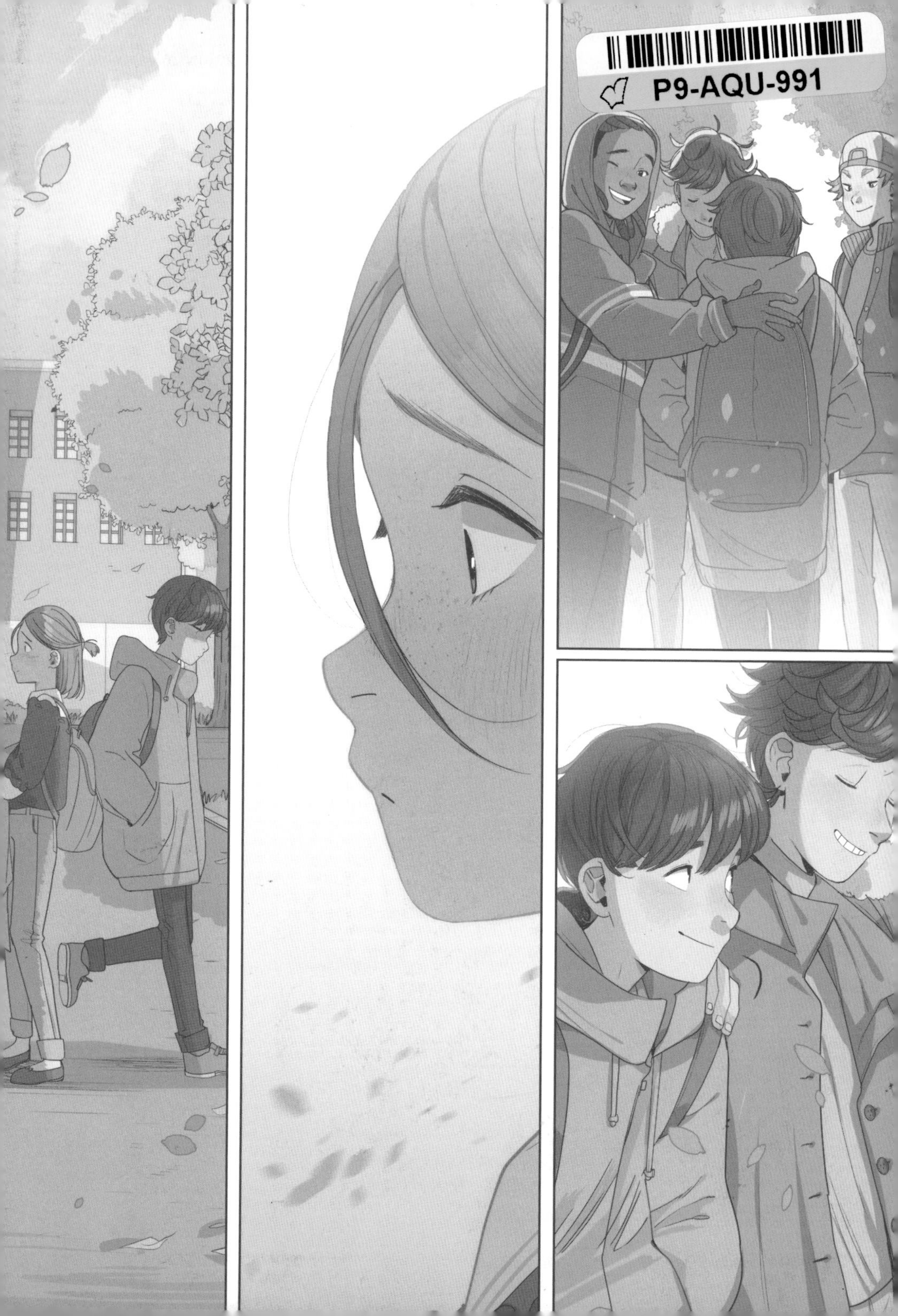

THE LOVE REPORT

Thank you to Maya for trusting us
with her first book in French.

—Caroline and Bertrand BeKa

Many thanks to BeKa for believing in my abilities
and for their incredible enthusiasm throughout
the project. Thanks to Daniele for encouraging
me and helping me day after day.

—Maya

Text by BeKa, art by Maya © 2021, 2022 by Dupuis
Originally published in French as *Coeur College 1: Secrets d'amour* (2021) and
Coeur College 2: Chagrins d'amour (2022) © 2021, 2022 by Dupuis. All rights reserved.
English translation pages 4–101 by Jessie Aufiery © 2023 by Dupuis
English translation pages 102–189 by Ivanka Hahnenberger © 2023 by Astra Publishing House

Hippo Park

An imprint of Astra Books for Young Readers, a division of Astra Publishing House
astrapublishinghouse.com
Printed in China
Library of Congress Control Number: 2022946883
ISBN: 978-1-6626-4040-7 (hc)
ISBN: 978-1-6626-4041-4 (pb)
ISBN: 978-1-6626-4042-1 (eBook)
First U.S. edition, 2023
10 9 8 7 6 5 4 3 2 1
Design by Mary Zadroga
The text is set in Good Dog New.
The titles are set in Scandiebox Four.
The illustrations are done in Photoshop.

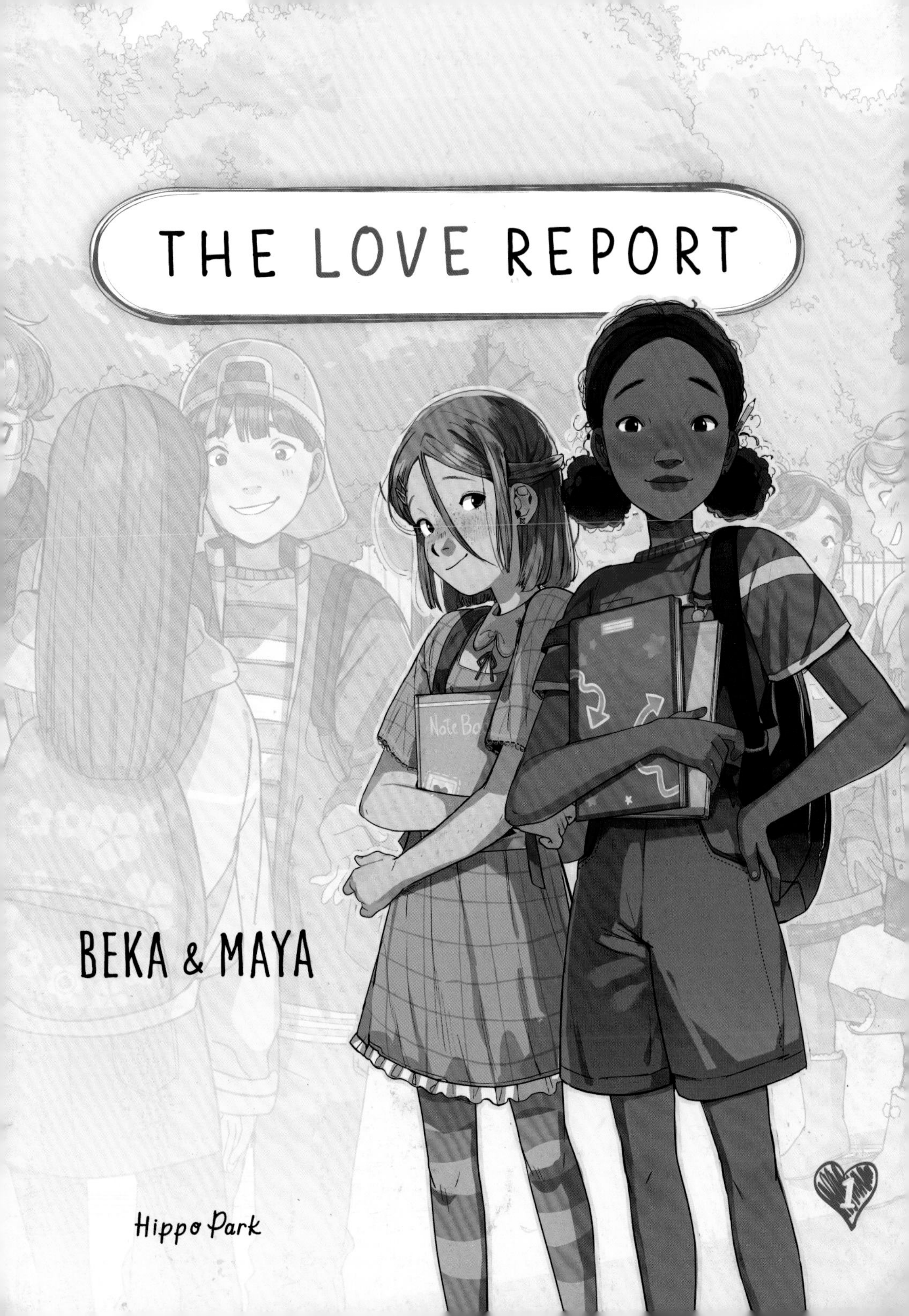
THE LOVE REPORT
BEKA & MAYA
Hippo Park
1

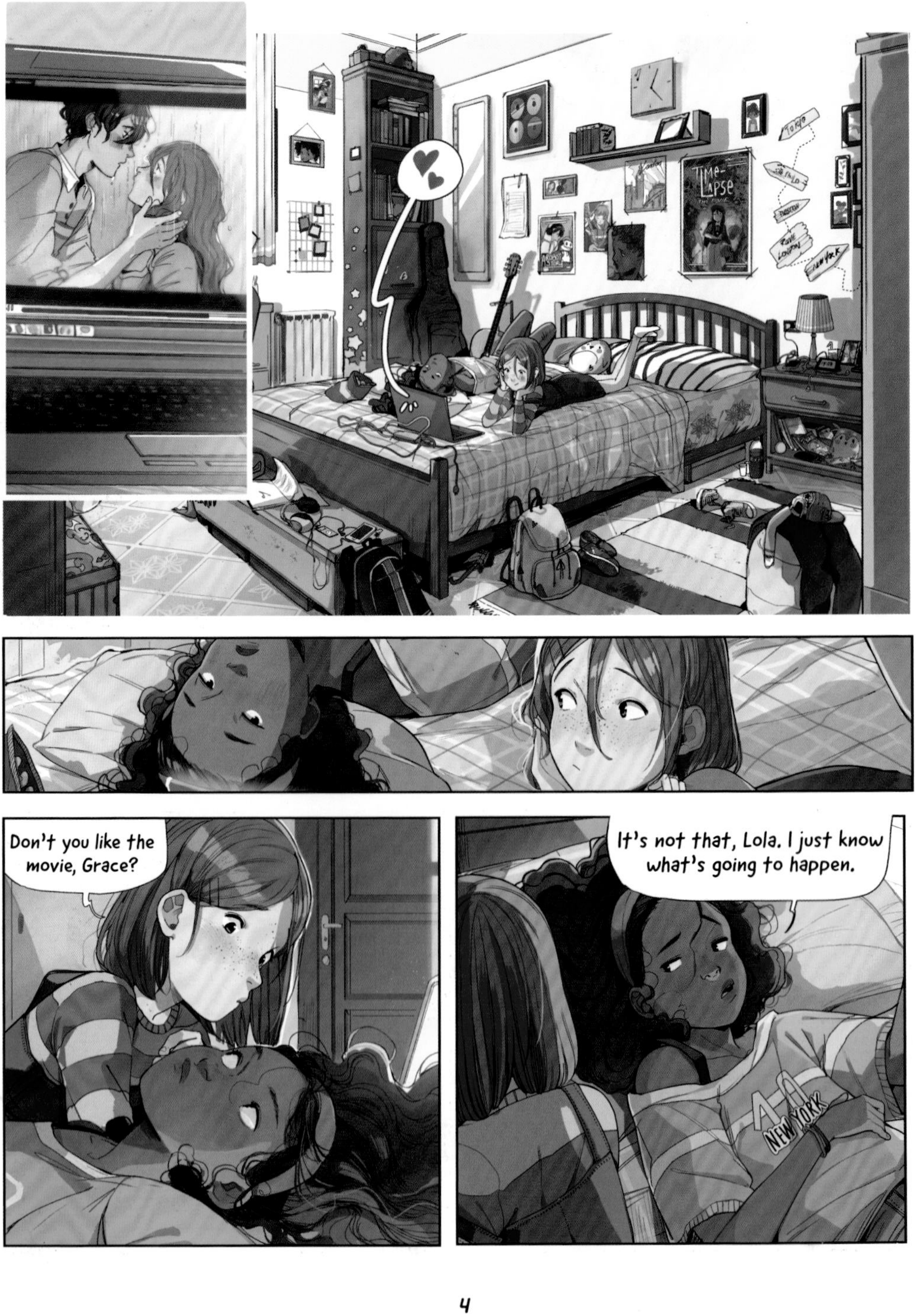
Don't you like the movie, Grace?
It's not that, Lola. I just know what's going to happen.

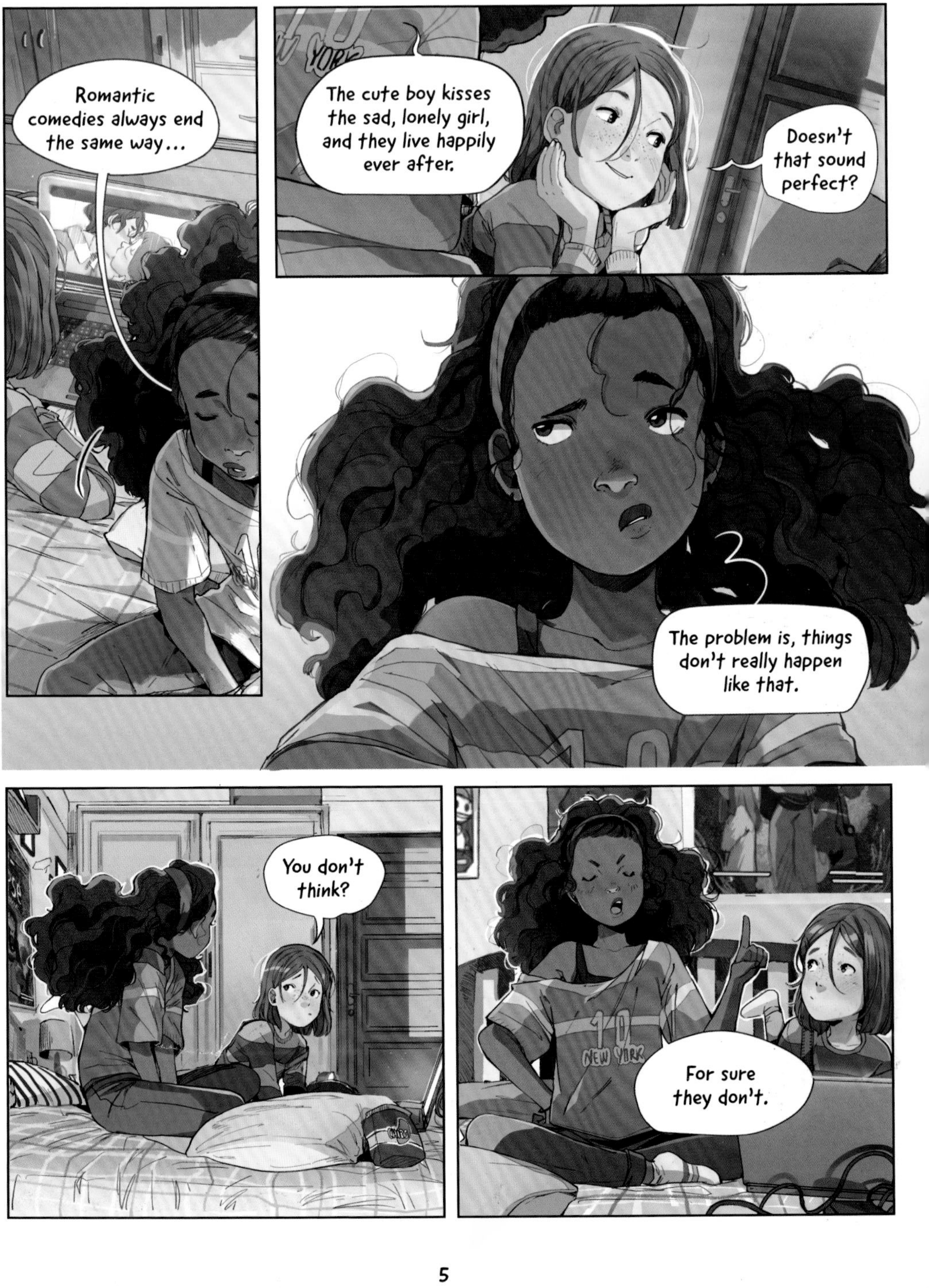
Romantic comedies always end the same way...
The cute boy kisses the sad, lonely girl, and they live happily ever after.
Doesn't that sound perfect?
The problem is, things don't really happen like that.
You don't think?
For sure they don't.

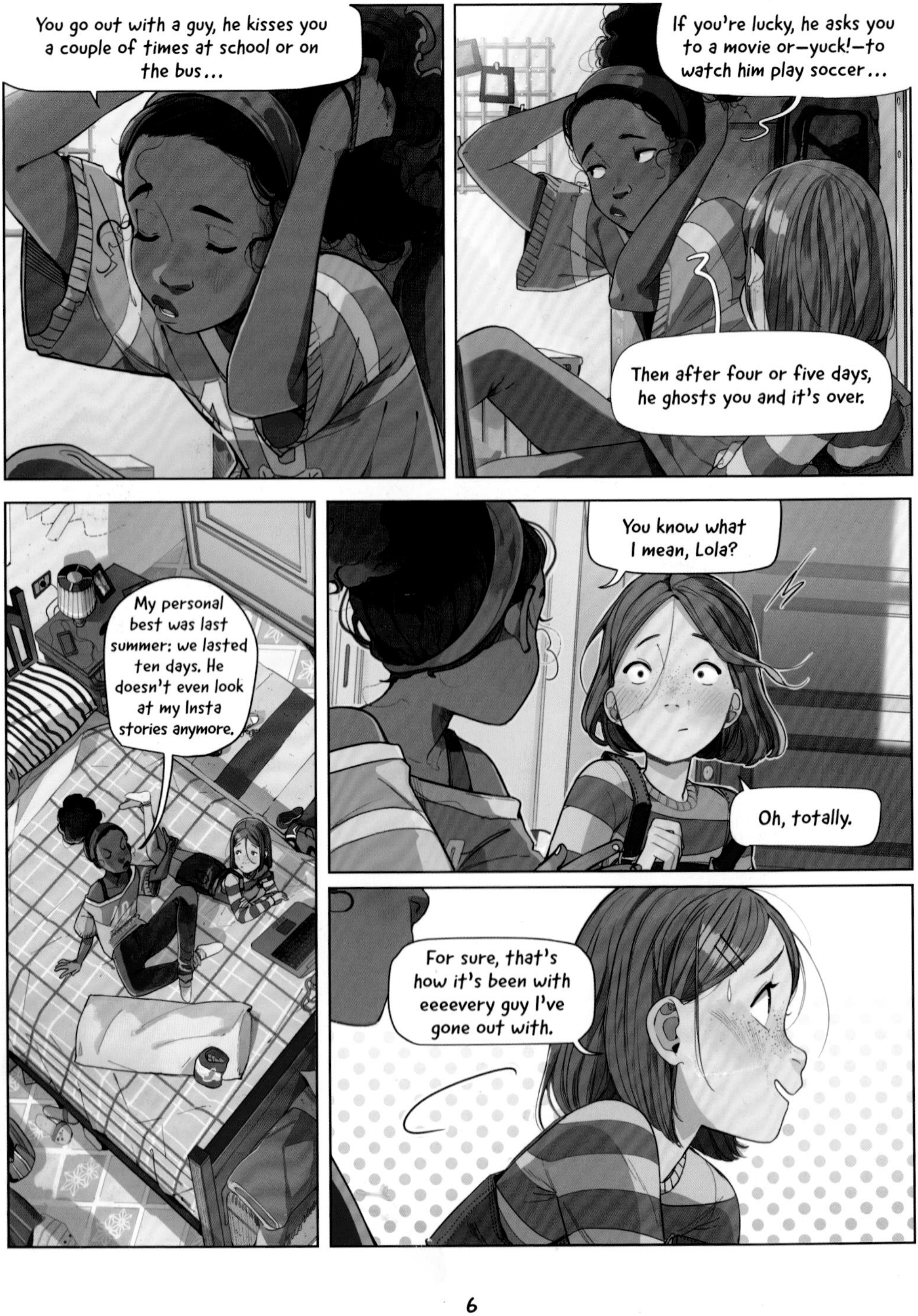
You go out with a guy, he kisses you a couple of times at school or on the bus...
If you're lucky, he asks you to a movie or—yuck!—to watch him play soccer...
Then after four or five days, he ghosts you and it's over.
My personal best was last summer: we lasted ten days. He doesn't even look at my Insta stories anymore.
You know what I mean, Lola?
Oh, totally.
For sure, that's how it's been with eeeevery guy I've gone out with.

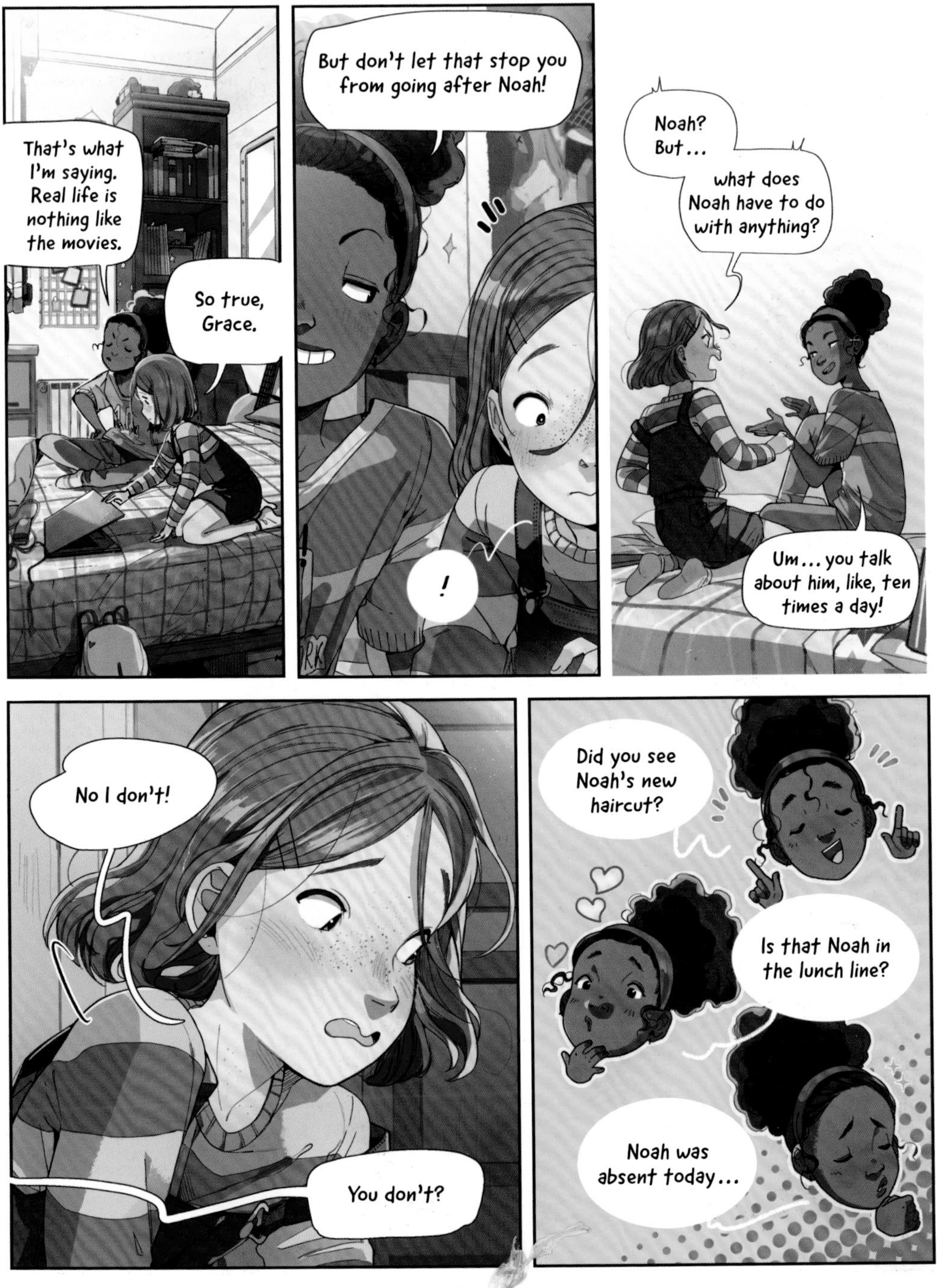
That's what I'm saying. Real life is nothing like the movies.
So true, Grace.
But don't let that stop you from going after Noah!
!
Noah? But...
what does Noah have to do with anything?
Um... you talk about him, like, ten times a day!
No I don't!
You don't?
Did you see Noah's new haircut?
Is that Noah in the lunch line?
Noah was absent today...

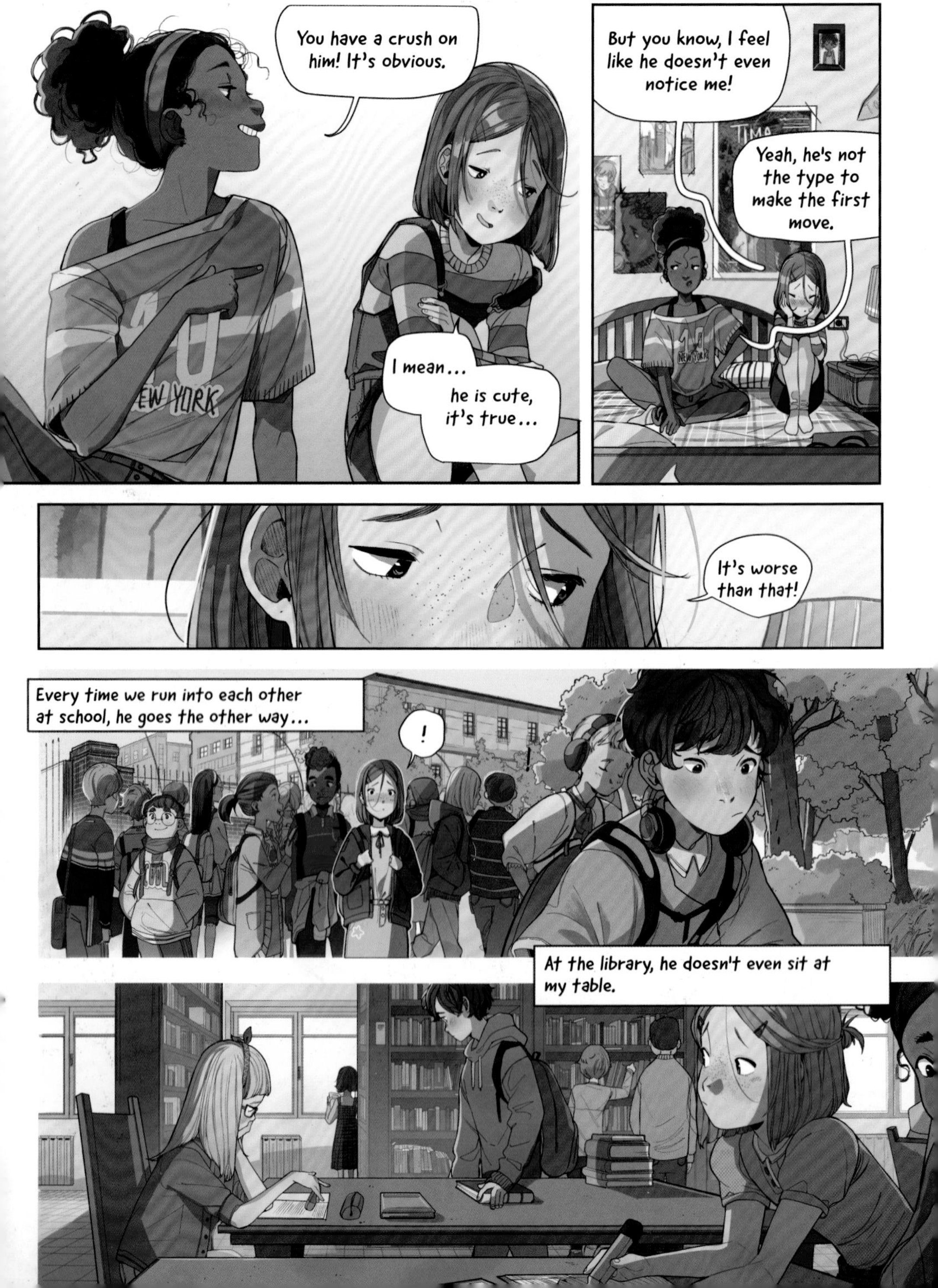
You have a crush on him! It's obvious.
I mean...
he is cute, it's true...
But you know, I feel like he doesn't even notice me!
Yeah, he's not the type to make the first move.
It's worse than that!
Every time we run into each other at school, he goes the other way...
!
At the library, he doesn't even sit at my table.

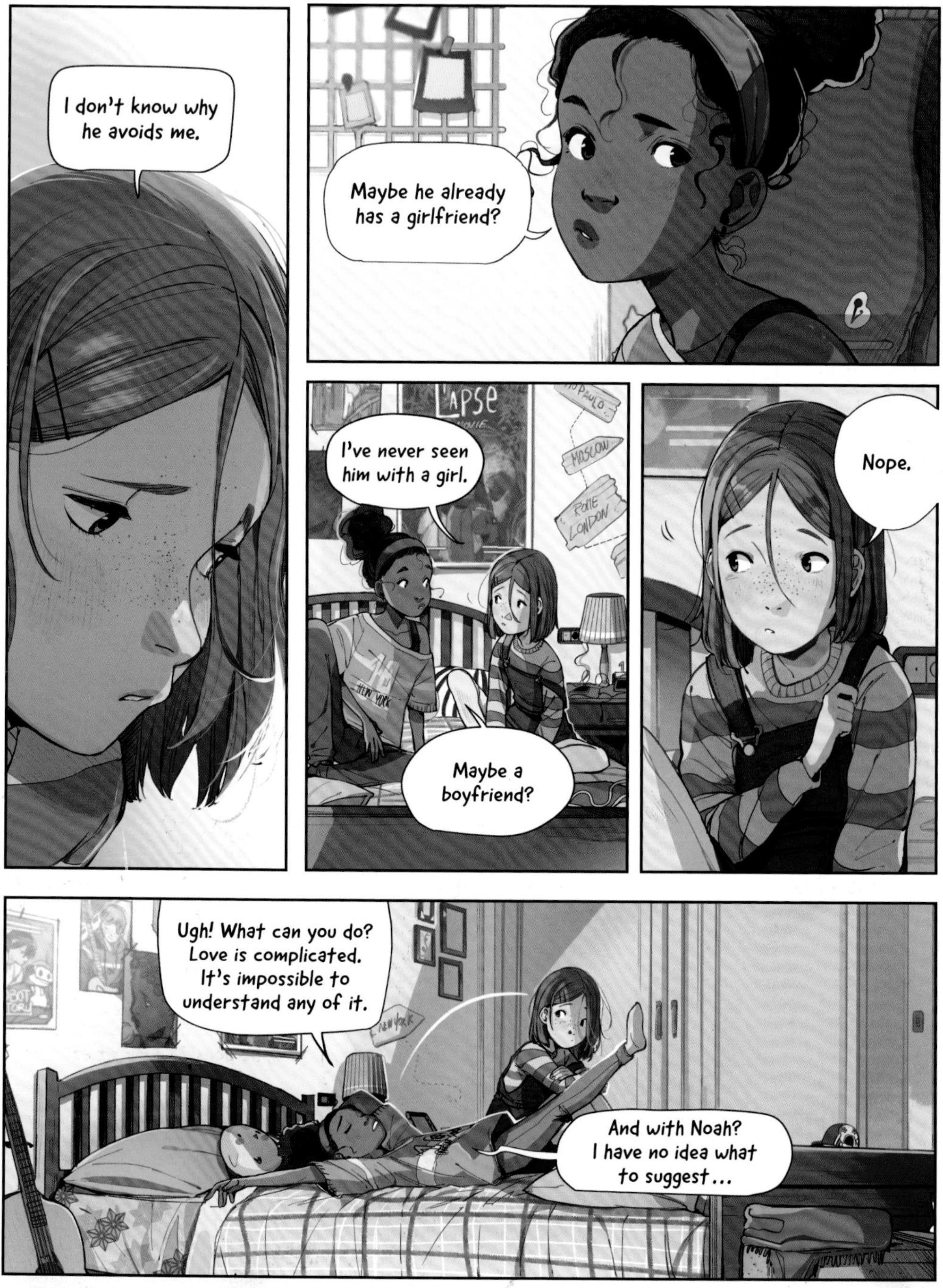
I don't know why he avoids me.
Maybe he already has a girlfriend?
I've never seen him with a girl.
Maybe a boyfriend?
Nope.
Ugh! What can you do? Love is complicated. It's impossible to understand any of it.
And with Noah? I have no idea what to suggest...

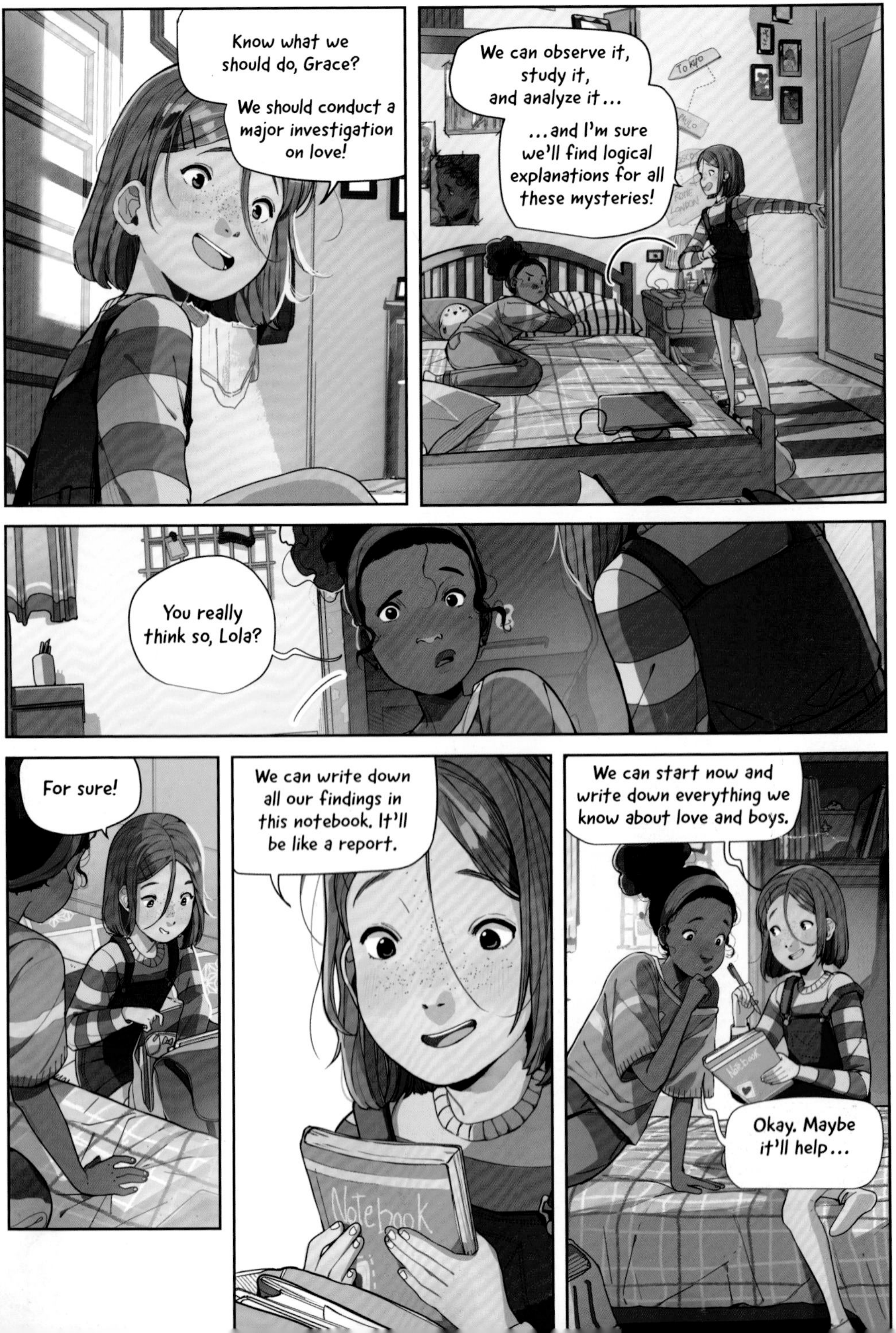
Know what we should do, Grace?
We should conduct a major investigation on love!
We can observe it, study it, and analyze it...
...and I'm sure we'll find logical explanations for all these mysteries!
You really think so, Lola?
For sure!
We can write down all our findings in this notebook. It'll be like a report.
Notebook
We can start now and write down everything we know about love and boys.
Notebook
Okay. Maybe it'll help...

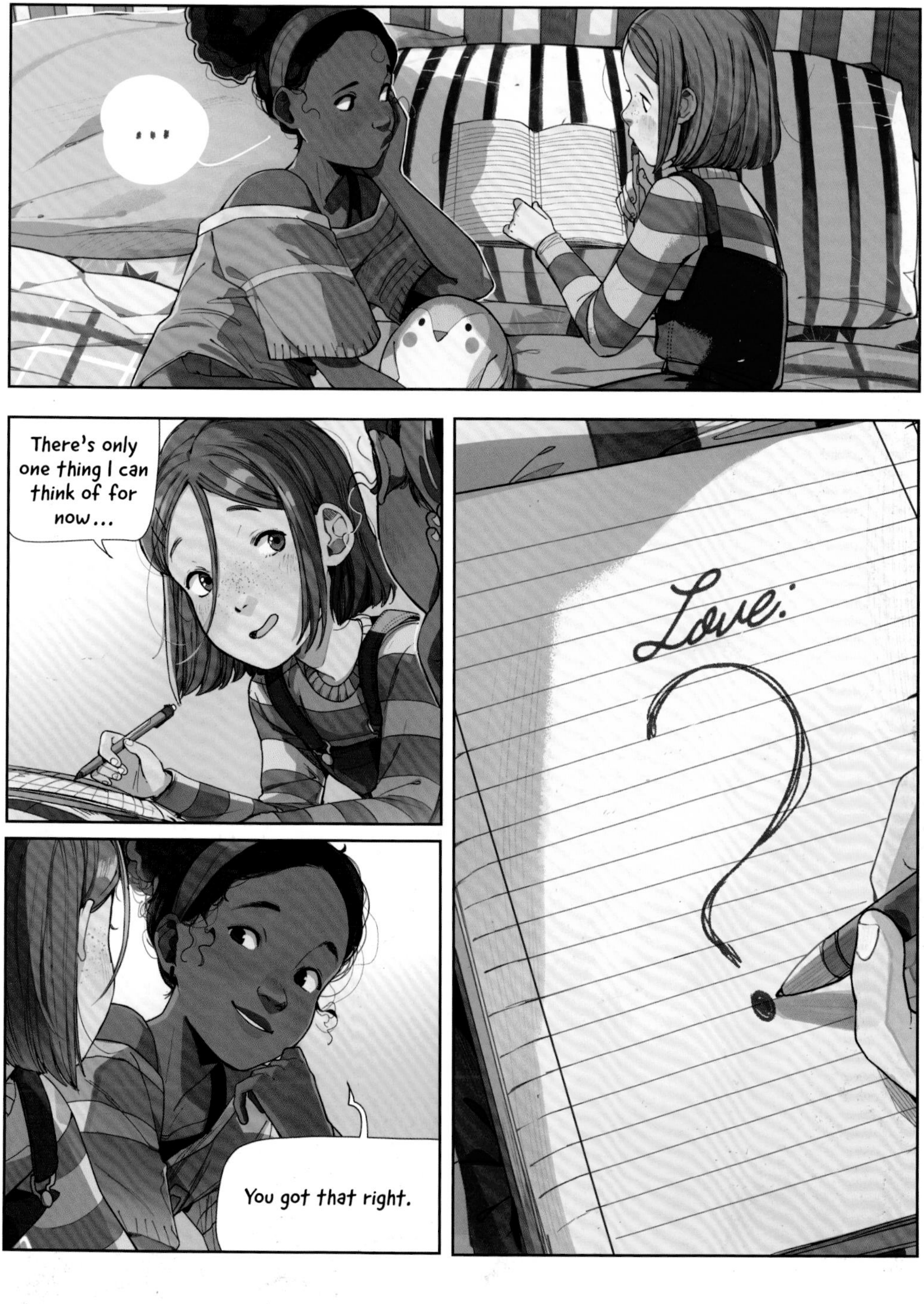
...
There's only one thing I can think of for now...
Love:
You got that right.

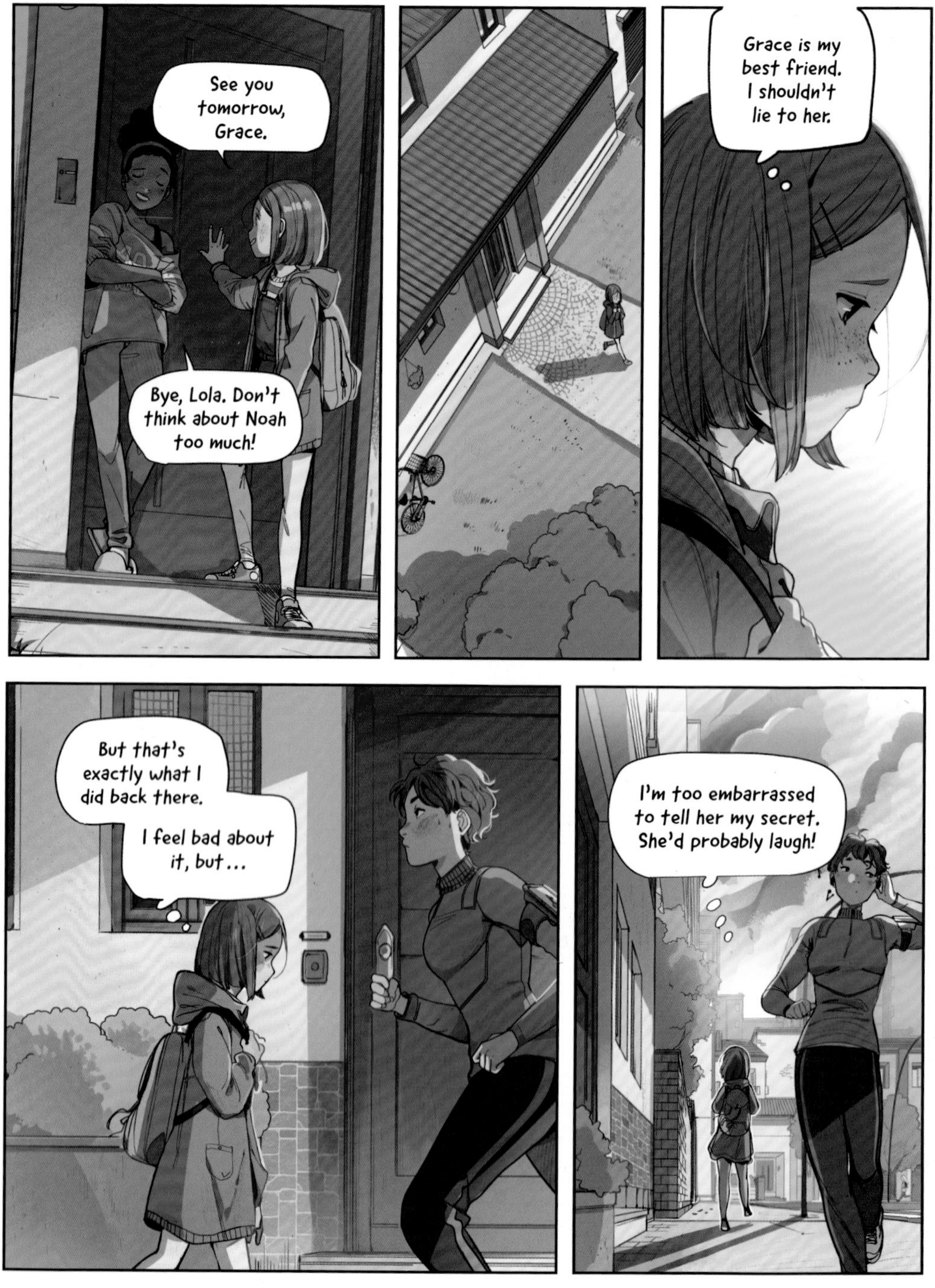
See you tomorrow, Grace.
Bye, Lola. Don't think about Noah too much!
Grace is my best friend. I shouldn't lie to her.
But that's exactly what I did back there.
I feel bad about it, but...
I'm too embarrassed to tell her my secret. She'd probably laugh!

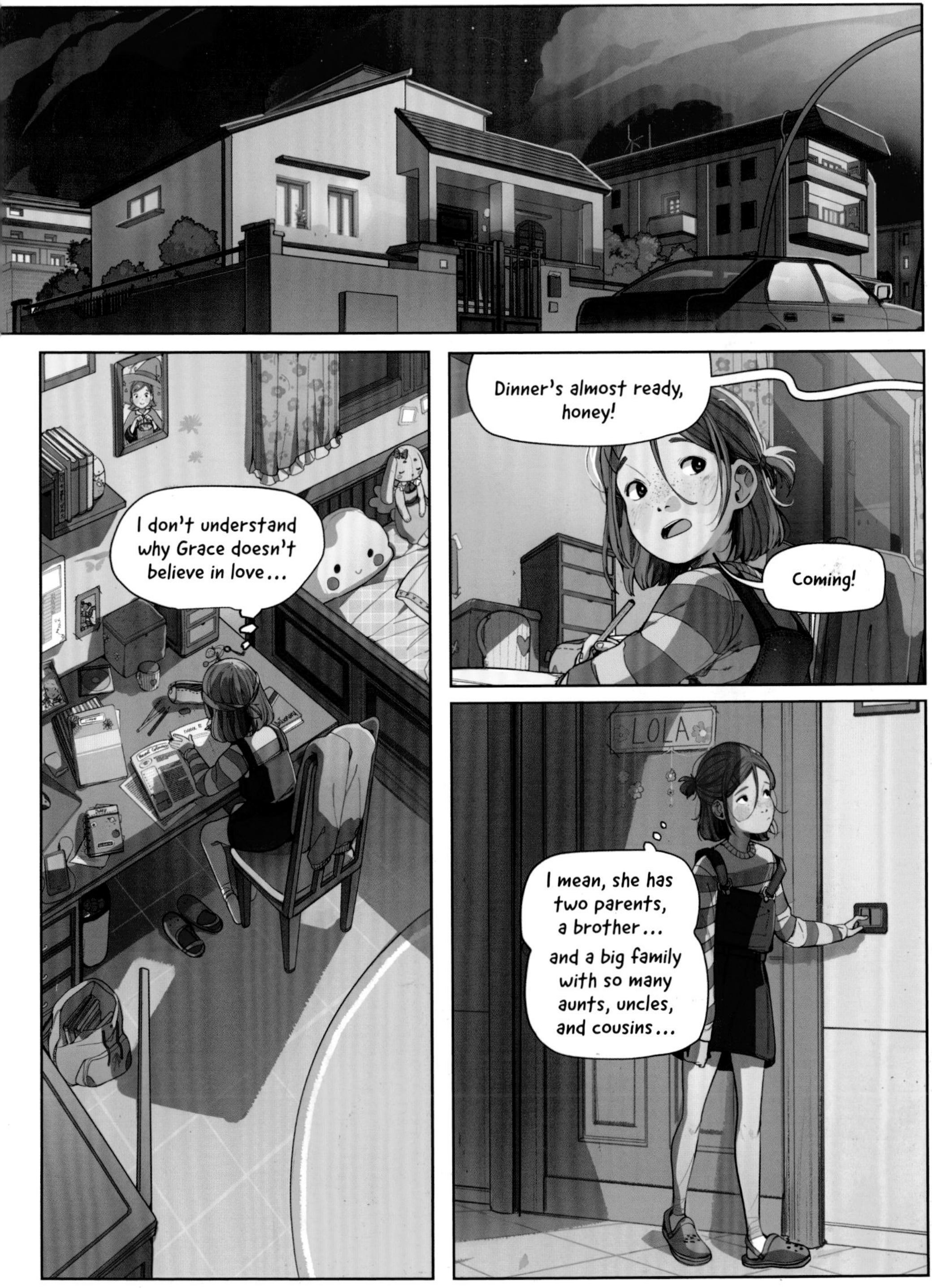
I don't understand why Grace doesn't believe in love...
Dinner's almost ready, honey!
Coming!
LOLA
I mean, she has two parents, a brother...
and a big family with so many aunts, uncles, and cousins...

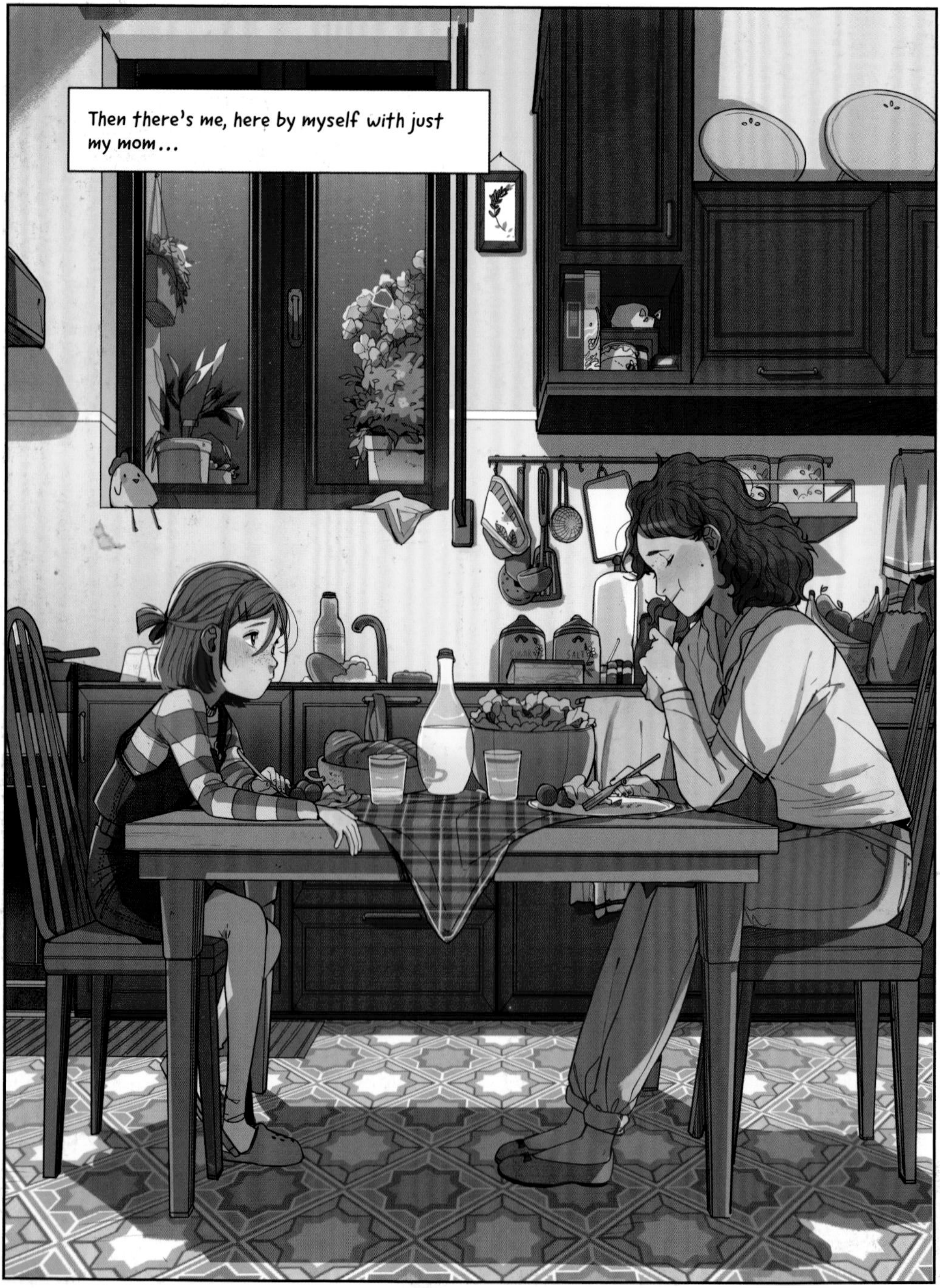
Then there's me, here by myself with just my mom...

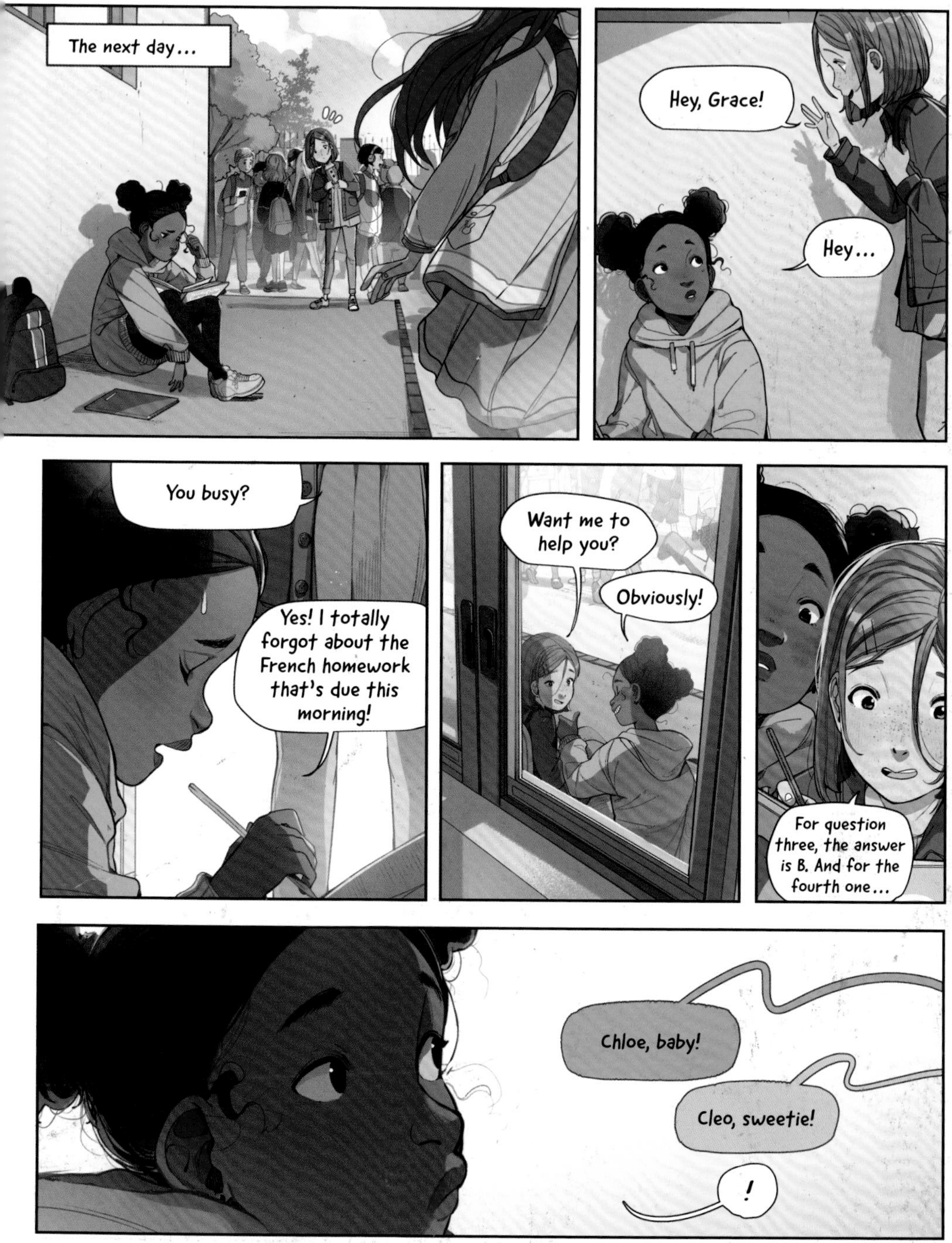

The next day...
Hey, Grace!
Hey...
You busy?
Yes! I totally forgot about the French homework that's due this morning!
Want me to help you?
Obviously!
For question three, the answer is B. And for the fourth one...
Chloe, baby!
Cleo, sweetie!
!

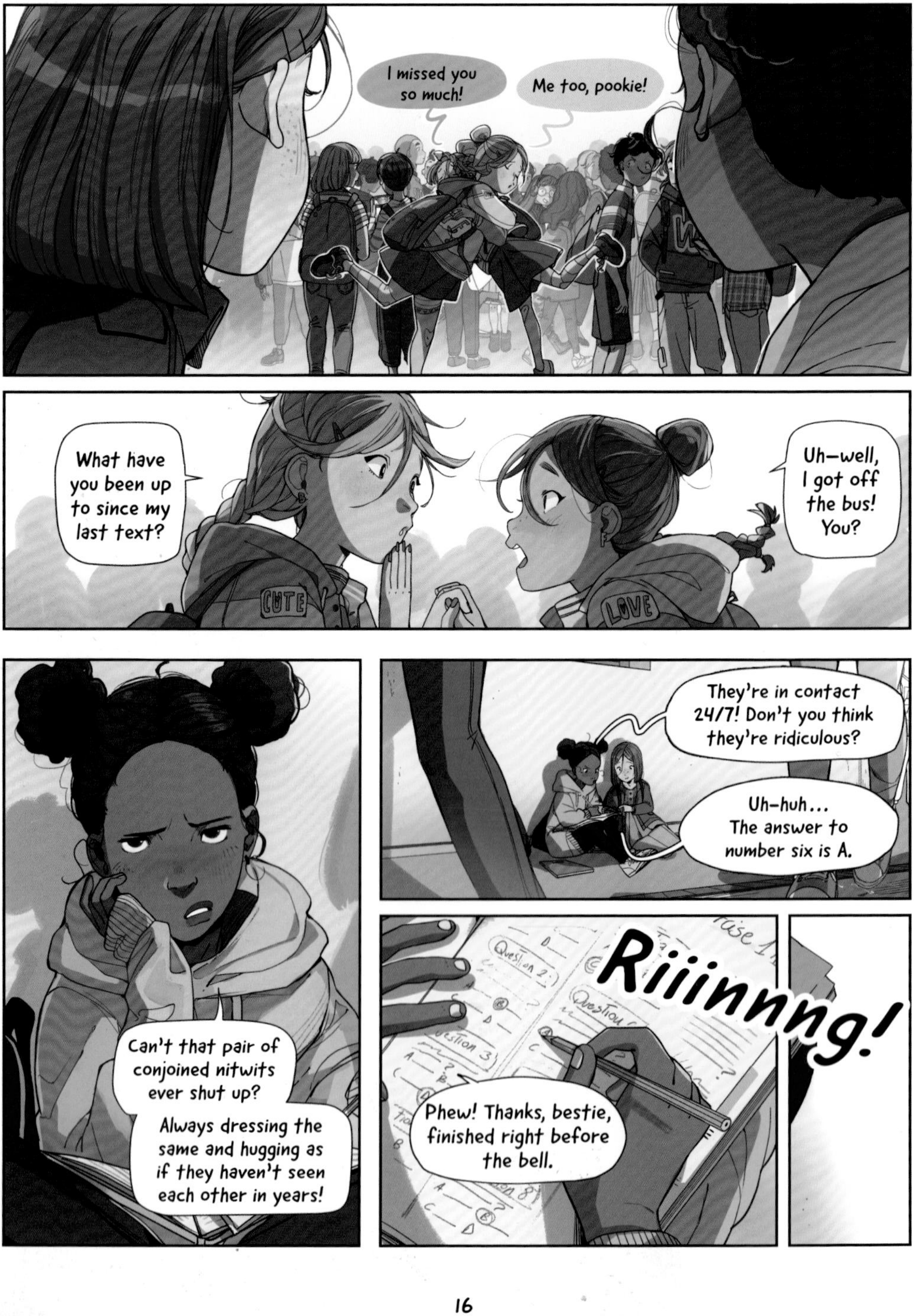
I missed you so much!
Me too, pookie!
What have you been up to since my last text?
Uh—well, I got off the bus! You?
CUTE
LOVE
Can't that pair of conjoined nitwits ever shut up?
Always dressing the same and hugging as if they haven't seen each other in years!
They're in contact 24/7! Don't you think they're ridiculous?
Uh-huh... The answer to number six is A.
Riiinnng!
Phew! Thanks, bestie, finished right before the bell.

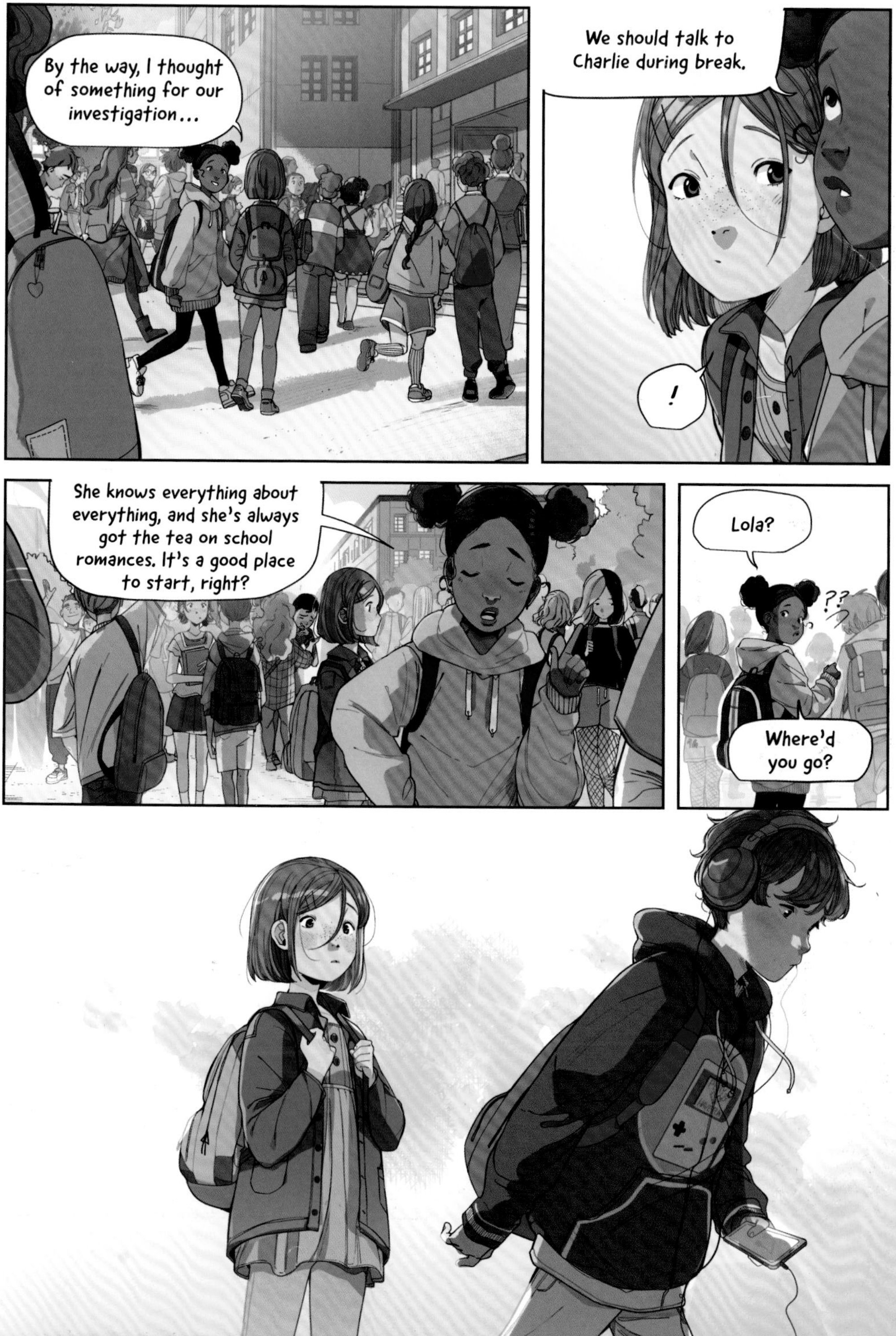
By the way, I thought of something for our investigation...
We should talk to Charlie during break.
!
She knows everything about everything, and she's always got the tea on school romances. It's a good place to start, right?
Lola?
??
Where'd you go?

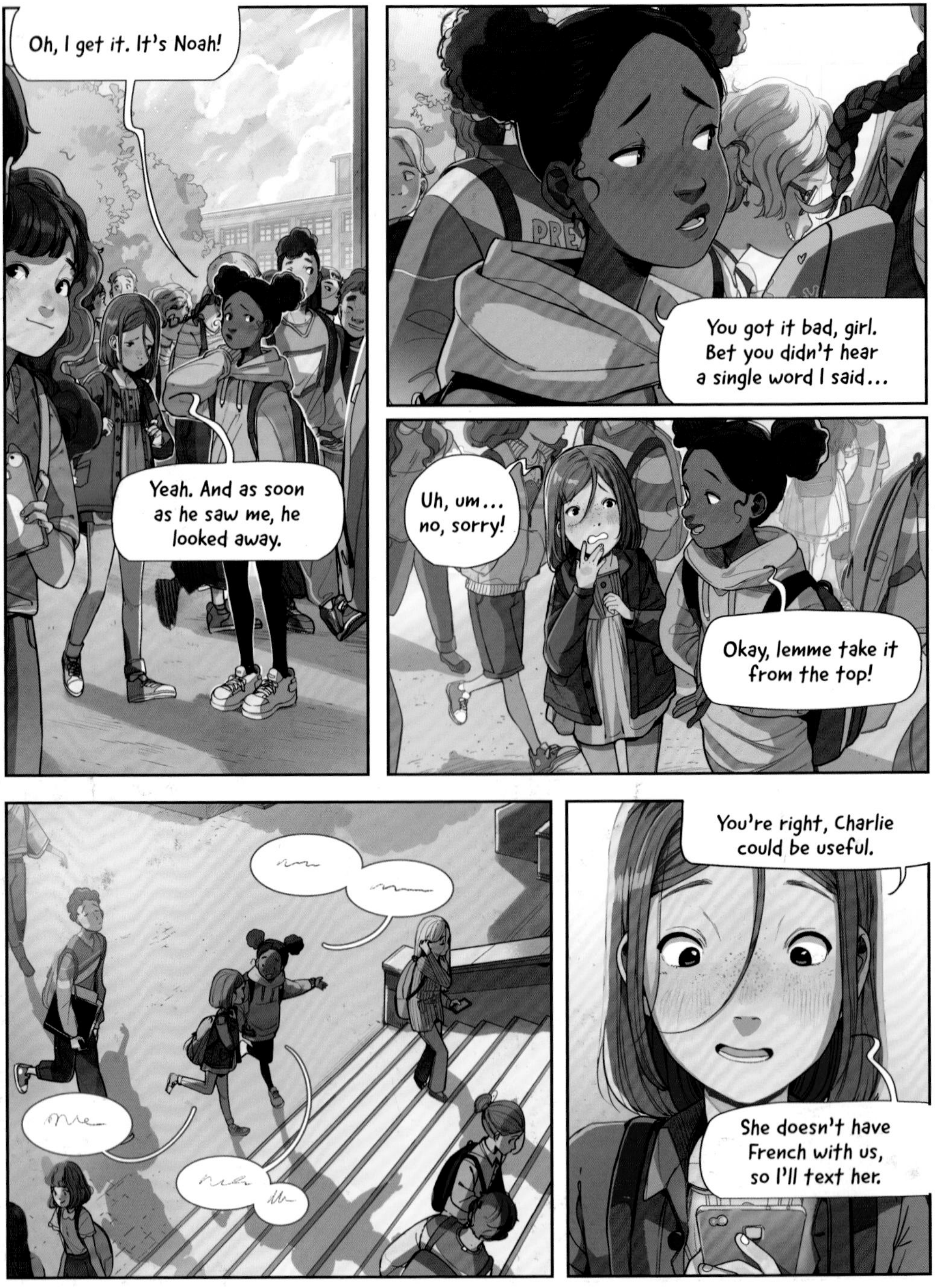
Oh, I get it. It's Noah!
Yeah. And as soon as he saw me, he looked away.
You got it bad, girl. Bet you didn't hear a single word I said...
Uh, um... no, sorry!
Okay, lemme take it from the top!
You're right, Charlie could be useful.
She doesn't have French with us, so I'll text her.

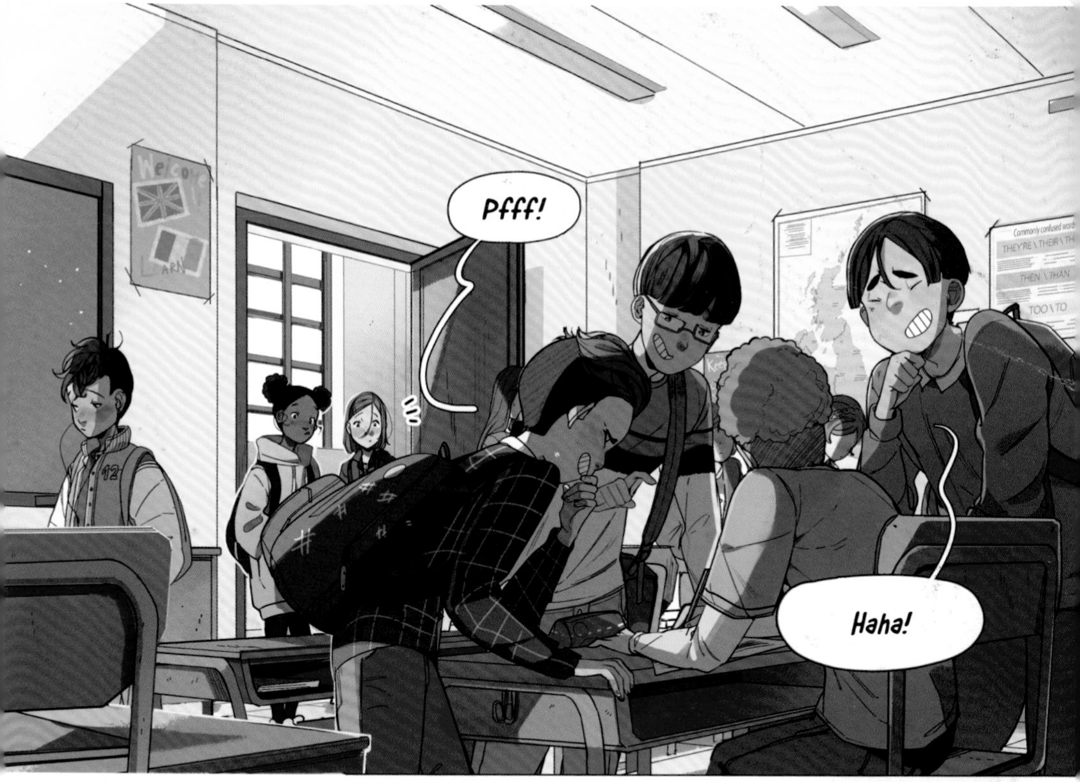
Pfff!
Haha!
Commonly confused words
THEN \ THAN
TOO \ TO

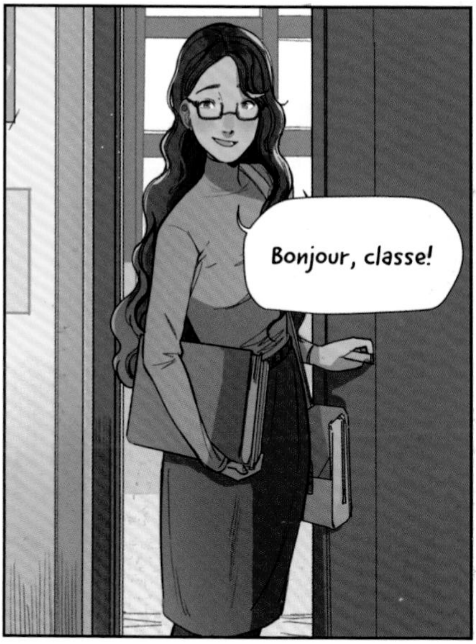
Bonjour, classe!

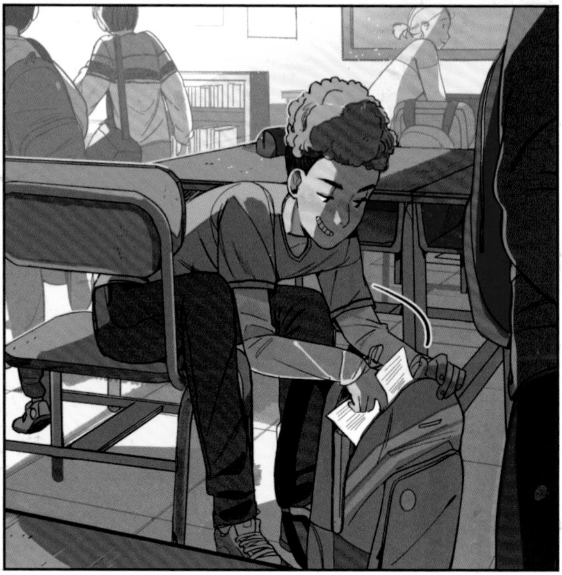

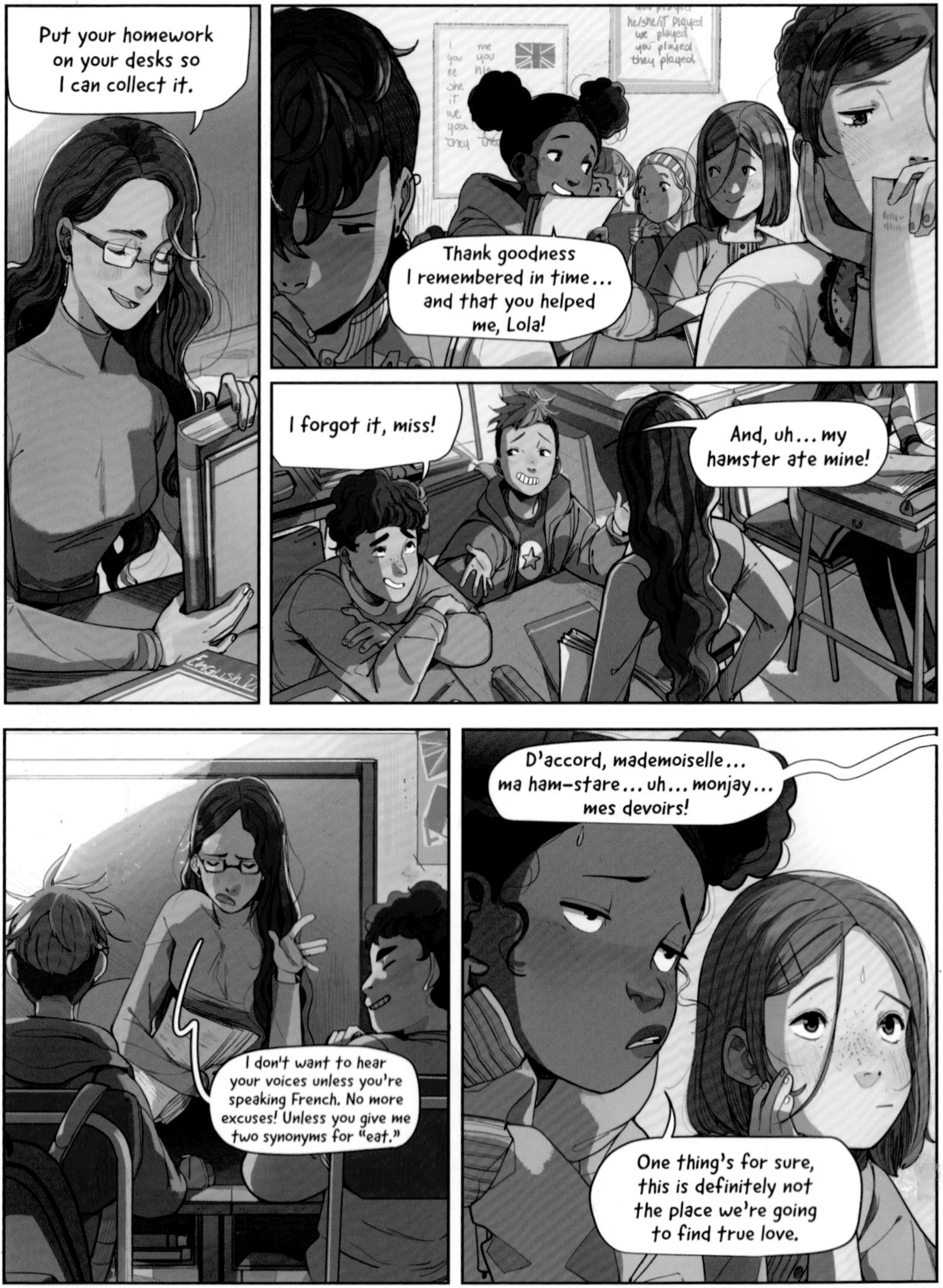
Put your homework on your desks so I can collect it.
he/she/it played
we played
you played
they played
Thank goodness I remembered in time... and that you helped me, Lola!
I forgot it, miss!
And, uh... my hamster ate mine!
I don't want to hear your voices unless you're speaking French. No more excuses! Unless you give me two synonyms for "eat."
D'accord, mademoiselle... ma ham-stare... uh... monjay... mes devoirs!
One thing's for sure, this is definitely not the place we're going to find true love.

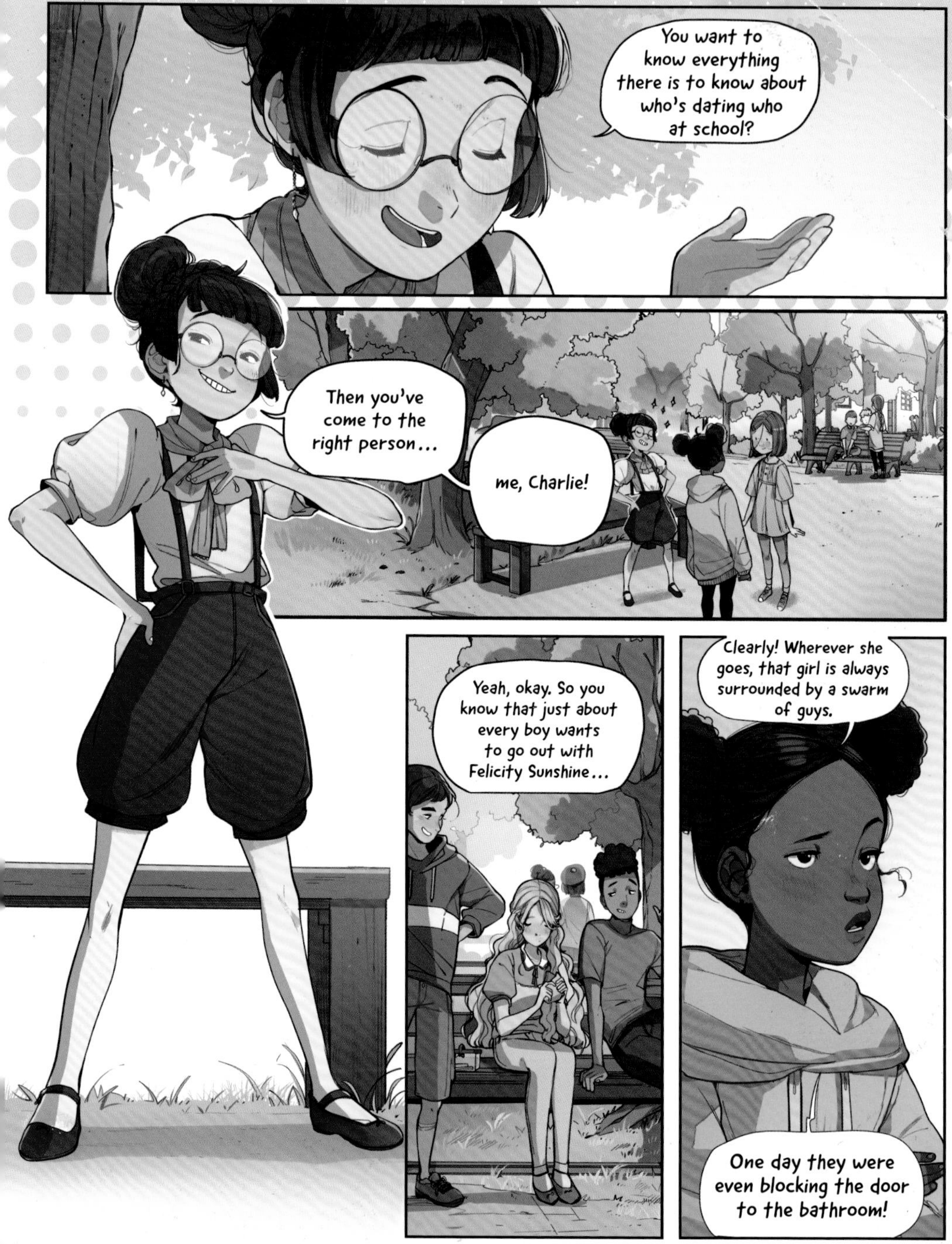
You want to know everything there is to know about who's dating who at school?
Then you've come to the right person...
me, Charlie!
Yeah, okay. So you know that just about every boy wants to go out with Felicity Sunshine...
Clearly! Wherever she goes, that girl is always surrounded by a swarm of guys.
One day they were even blocking the door to the bathroom!

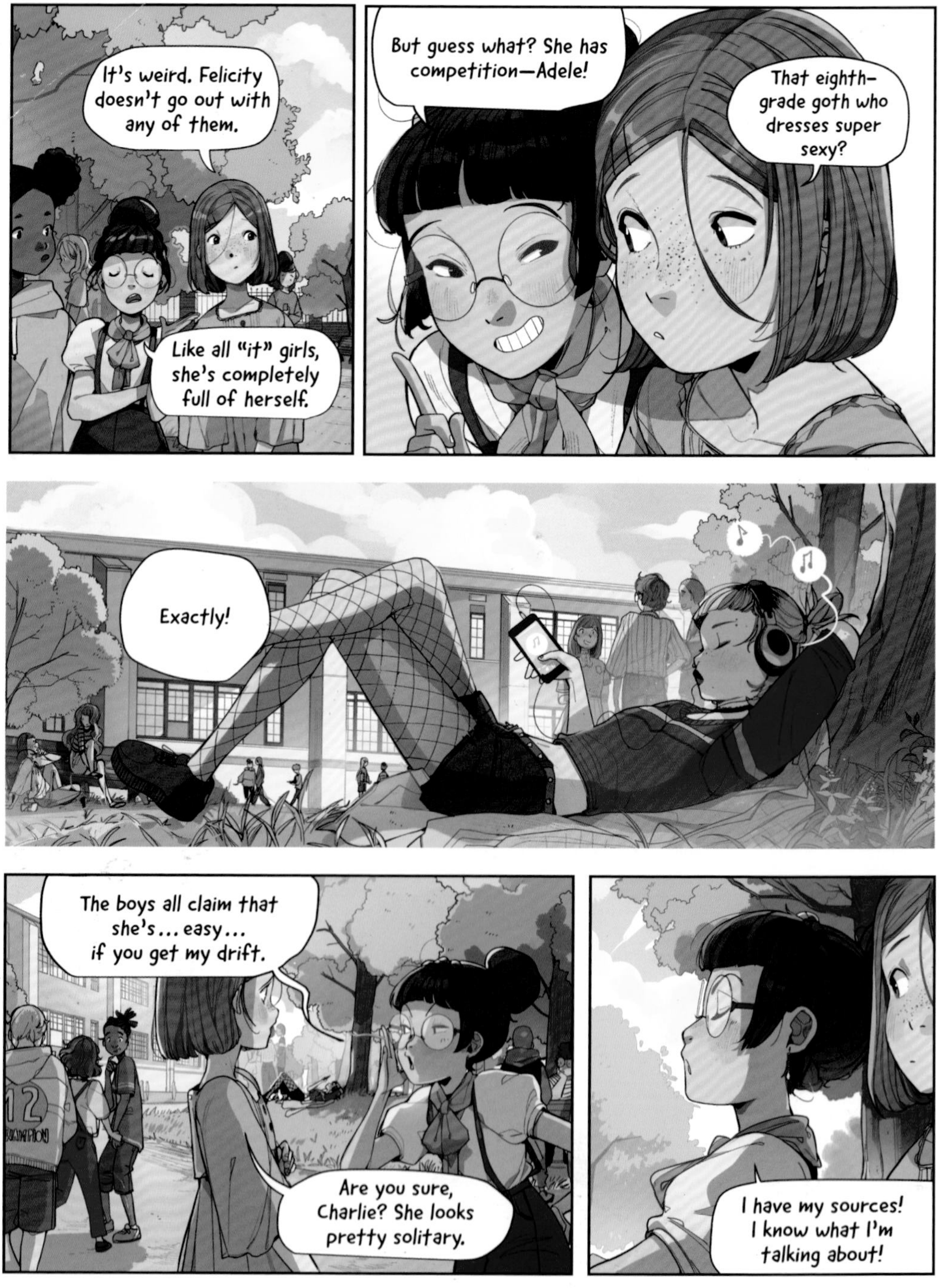
It's weird. Felicity doesn't go out with any of them.
Like all "it" girls, she's completely full of herself.
But guess what? She has competition—Adele!
That eighth-grade goth who dresses super sexy?
Exactly!
The boys all claim that she's... easy... if you get my drift.
Are you sure, Charlie? She looks pretty solitary.
I have my sources! I know what I'm talking about!

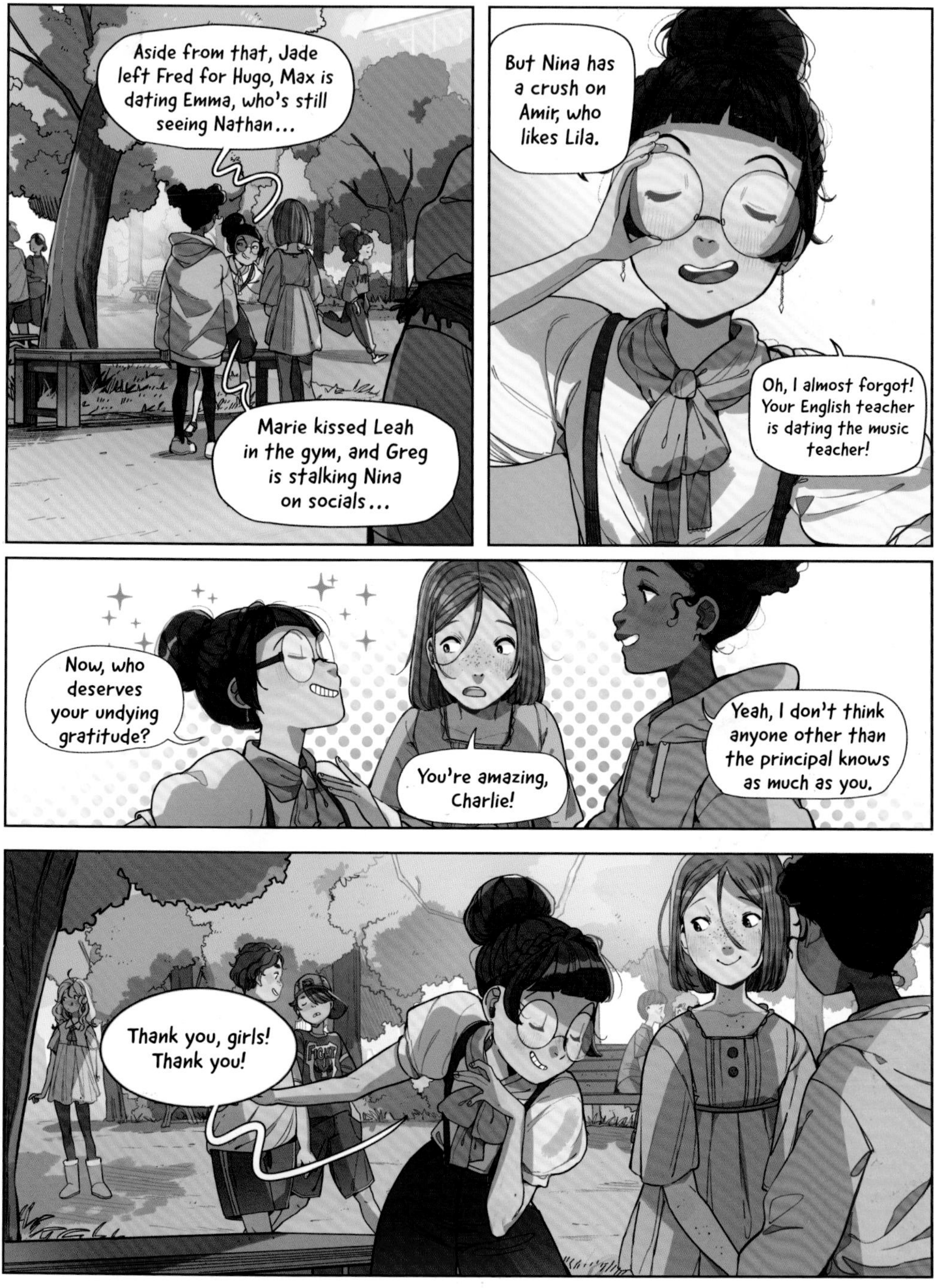
Aside from that, Jade left Fred for Hugo, Max is dating Emma, who's still seeing Nathan...
Marie kissed Leah in the gym, and Greg is stalking Nina on socials...
But Nina has a crush on Amir, who likes Lila.
Oh, I almost forgot! Your English teacher is dating the music teacher!
Now, who deserves your undying gratitude?
You're amazing, Charlie!
Yeah, I don't think anyone other than the principal knows as much as you.
Thank you, girls! Thank you!
FIGHT

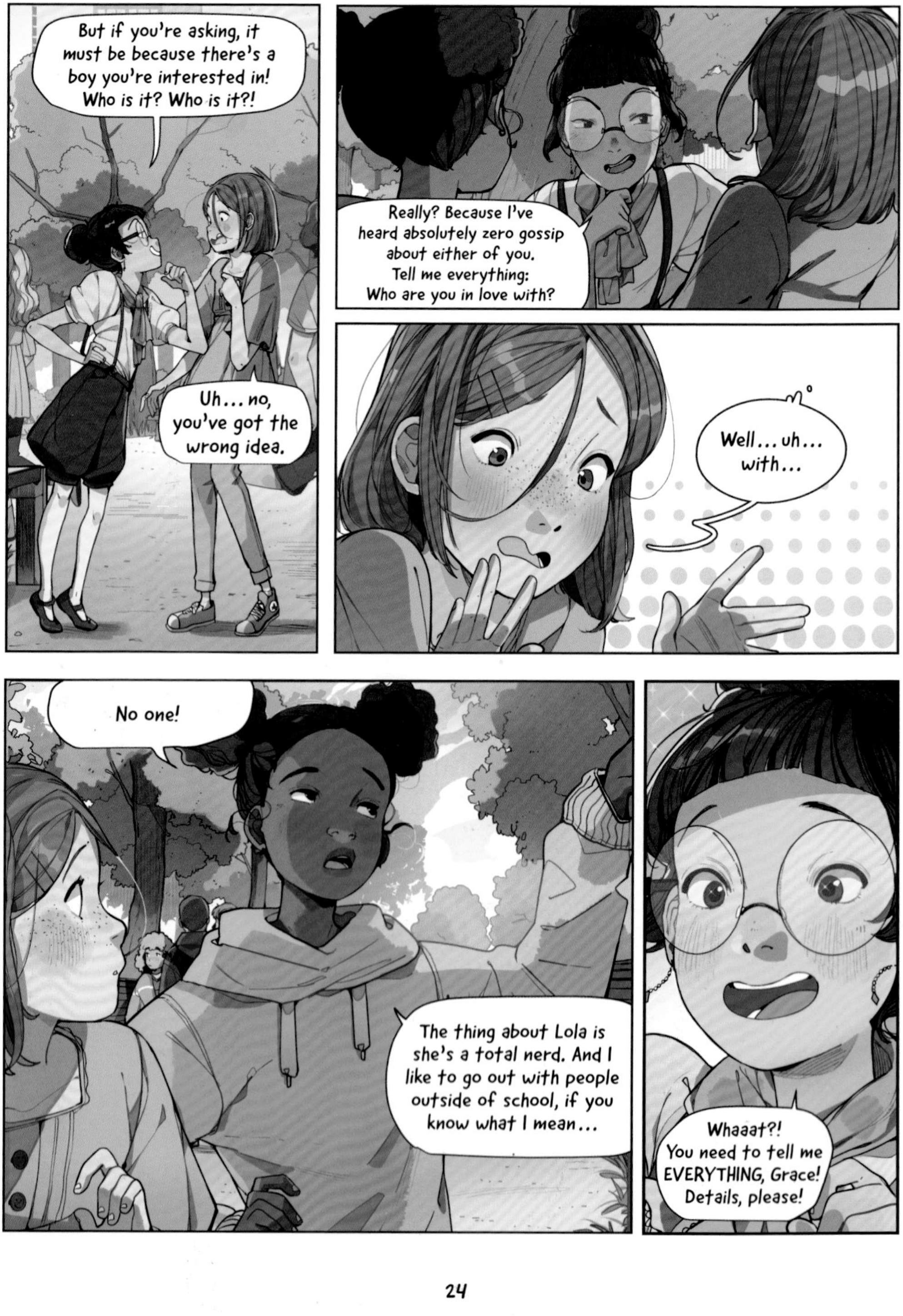
But if you're asking, it must be because there's a boy you're interested in! Who is it? Who is it?!
Uh... no, you've got the wrong idea.
Really? Because I've heard absolutely zero gossip about either of you. Tell me everything: Who are you in love with?
Well... uh... with...
No one!
The thing about Lola is she's a total nerd. And I like to go out with people outside of school, if you know what I mean...
Whaaat?! You need to tell me EVERYTHING, Grace! Details, please!

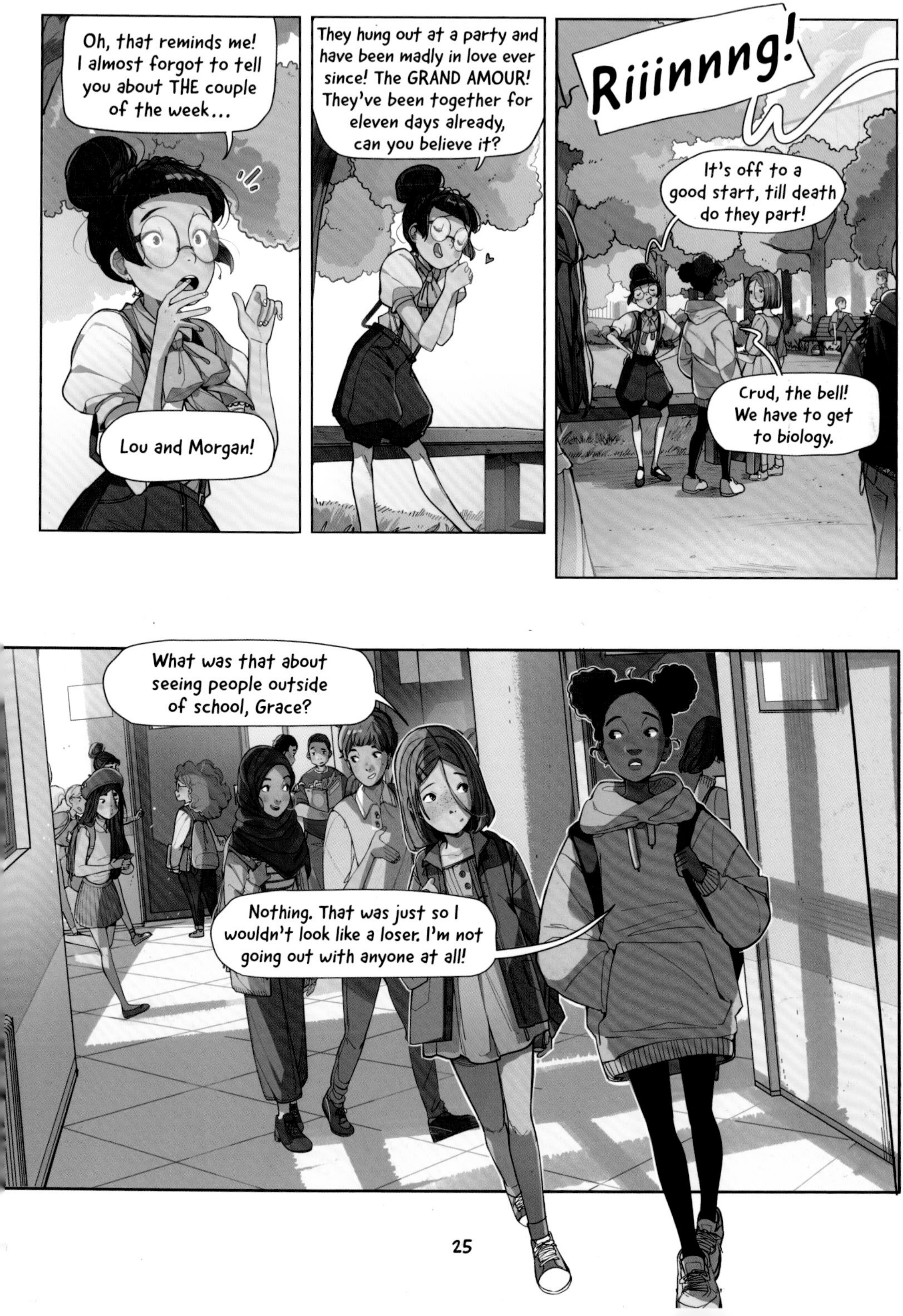
Oh, that reminds me! I almost forgot to tell you about THE couple of the week...
Lou and Morgan!
They hung out at a party and have been madly in love ever since! The GRAND AMOUR! They've been together for eleven days already, can you believe it?
Riiinnng!
It's off to a good start, till death do they part!
Crud, the bell! We have to get to biology.
What was that about seeing people outside of school, Grace?
Nothing. That was just so I wouldn't look like a loser. I'm not going out with anyone at all!

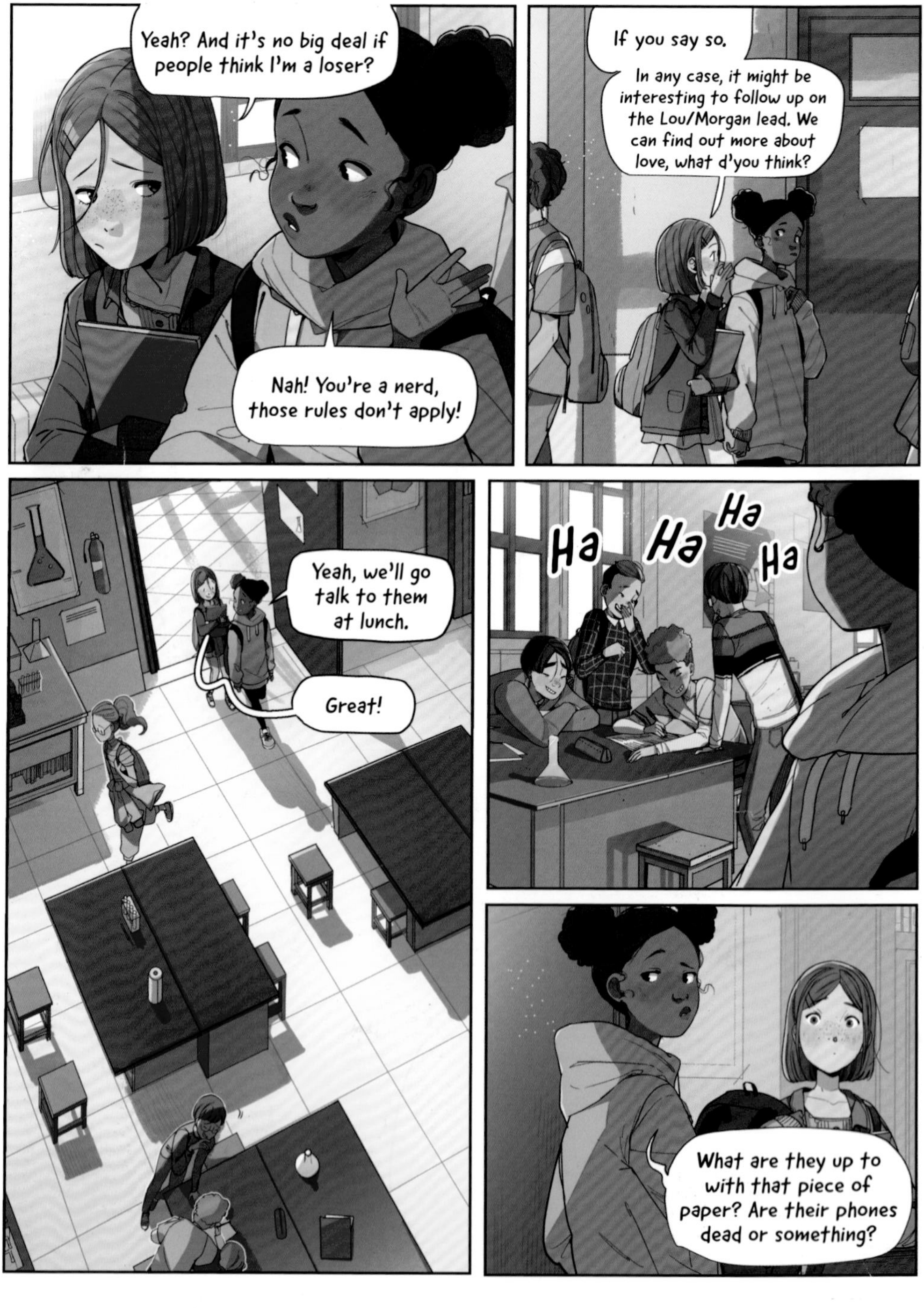
Yeah? And it's no big deal if people think I'm a loser?
Nah! You're a nerd, those rules don't apply!
If you say so.
In any case, it might be interesting to follow up on the Lou/Morgan lead. We can find out more about love, what d'you think?
Yeah, we'll go talk to them at lunch.
Great!
Ha Ha Ha Ha
What are they up to with that piece of paper? Are their phones dead or something?

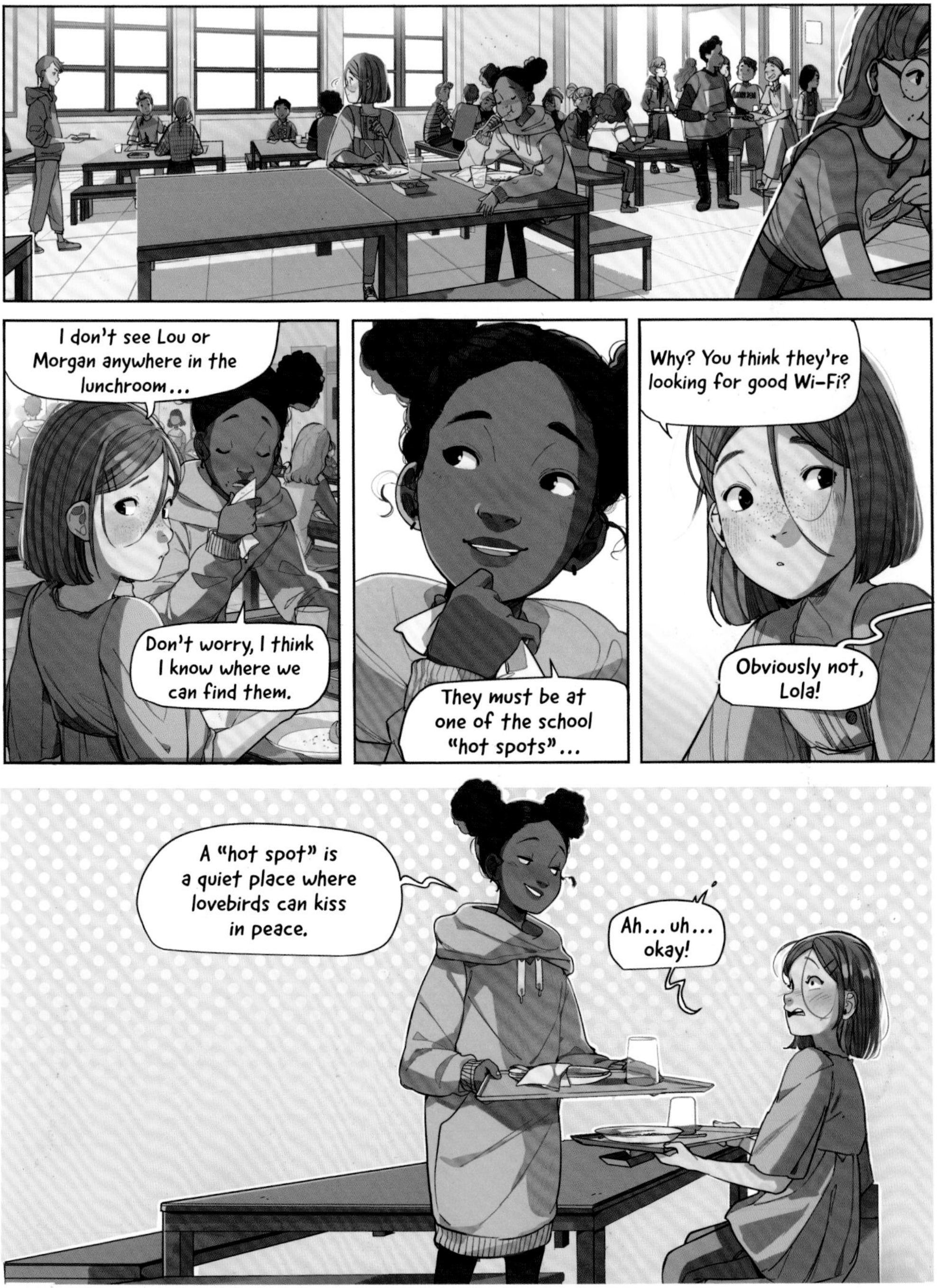

I don't see Lou or Morgan anywhere in the lunchroom...
Don't worry, I think I know where we can find them.
They must be at one of the school "hot spots"...
Why? You think they're looking for good Wi-Fi?
Obviously not, Lola!
A "hot spot" is a quiet place where lovebirds can kiss in peace.
Ah... uh... okay!

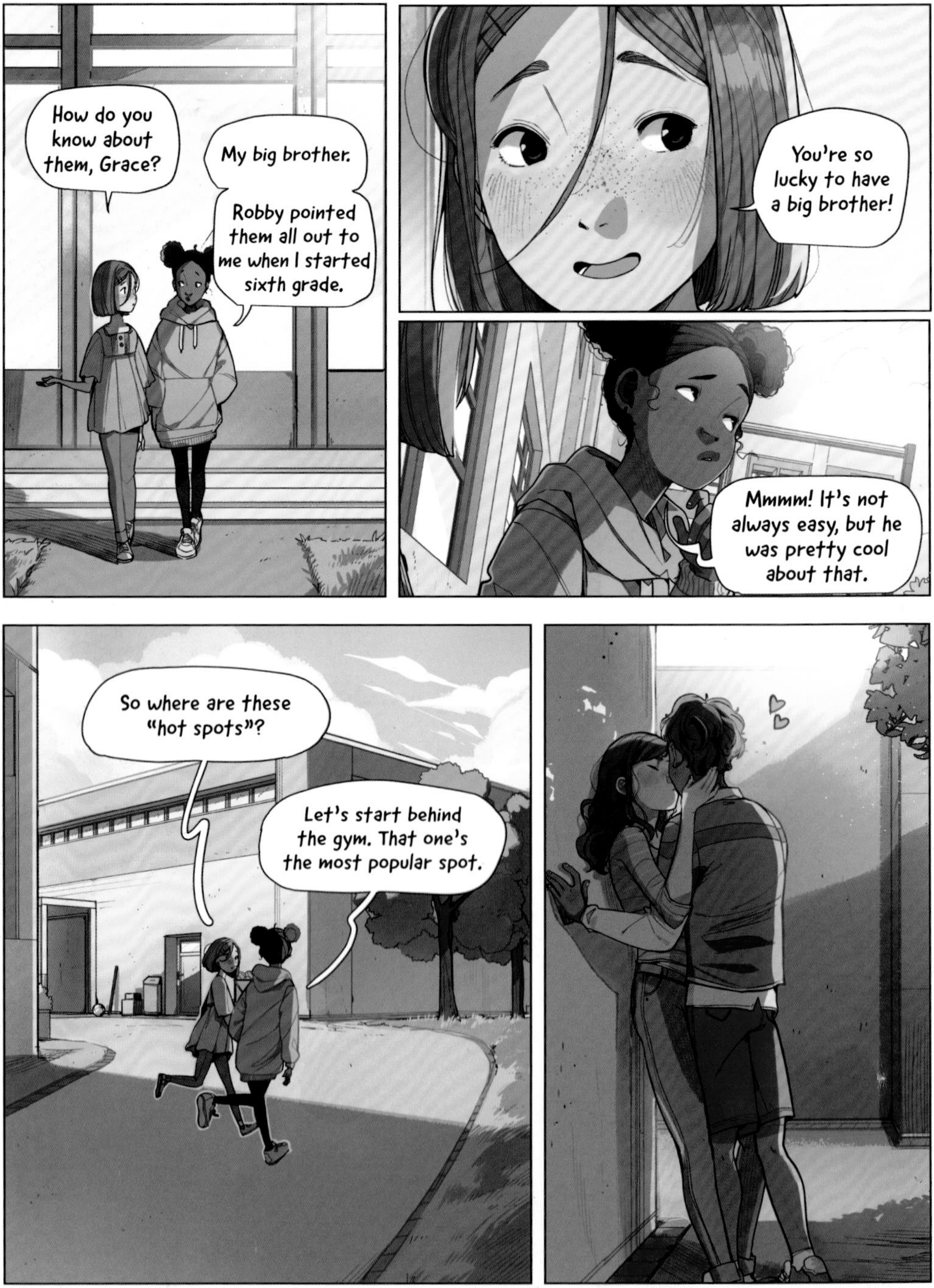
How do you know about them, Grace?
My big brother.
Robby pointed them all out to me when I started sixth grade.
You're so lucky to have a big brother!
Mmmm! It's not always easy, but he was pretty cool about that.
So where are these "hot spots"?
Let's start behind the gym. That one's the most popular spot.

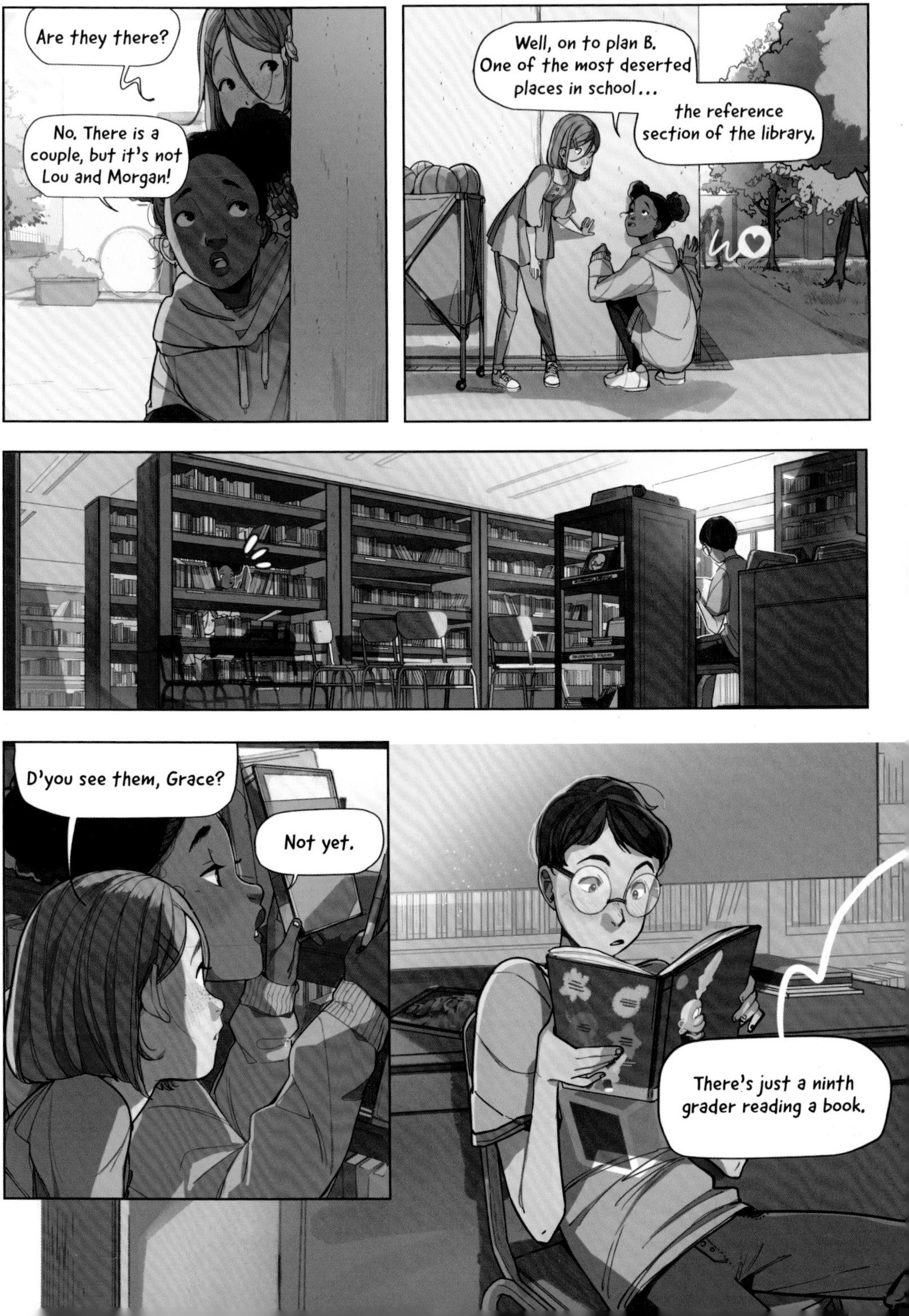
Are they there?
No. There is a couple, but it's not Lou and Morgan!
Well, on to plan B. One of the most deserted places in school...
the reference section of the library.
D'you see them, Grace?
Not yet.
There's just a ninth grader reading a book.

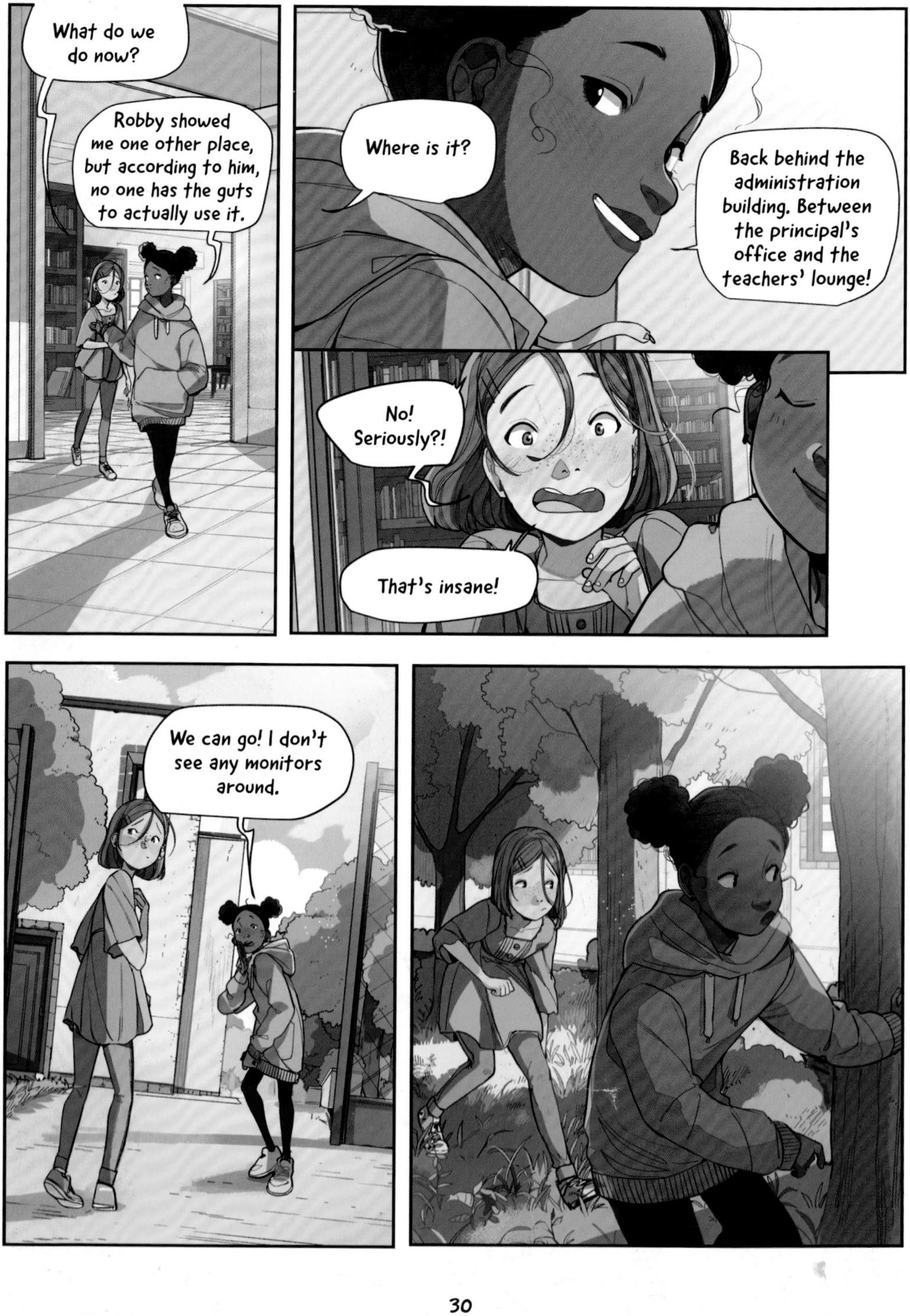
What do we do now?
Robby showed me one other place, but according to him, no one has the guts to actually use it.
Where is it?
Back behind the administration building. Between the principal's office and the teachers' lounge!
No! Seriously?!
That's insane!
We can go! I don't see any monitors around.

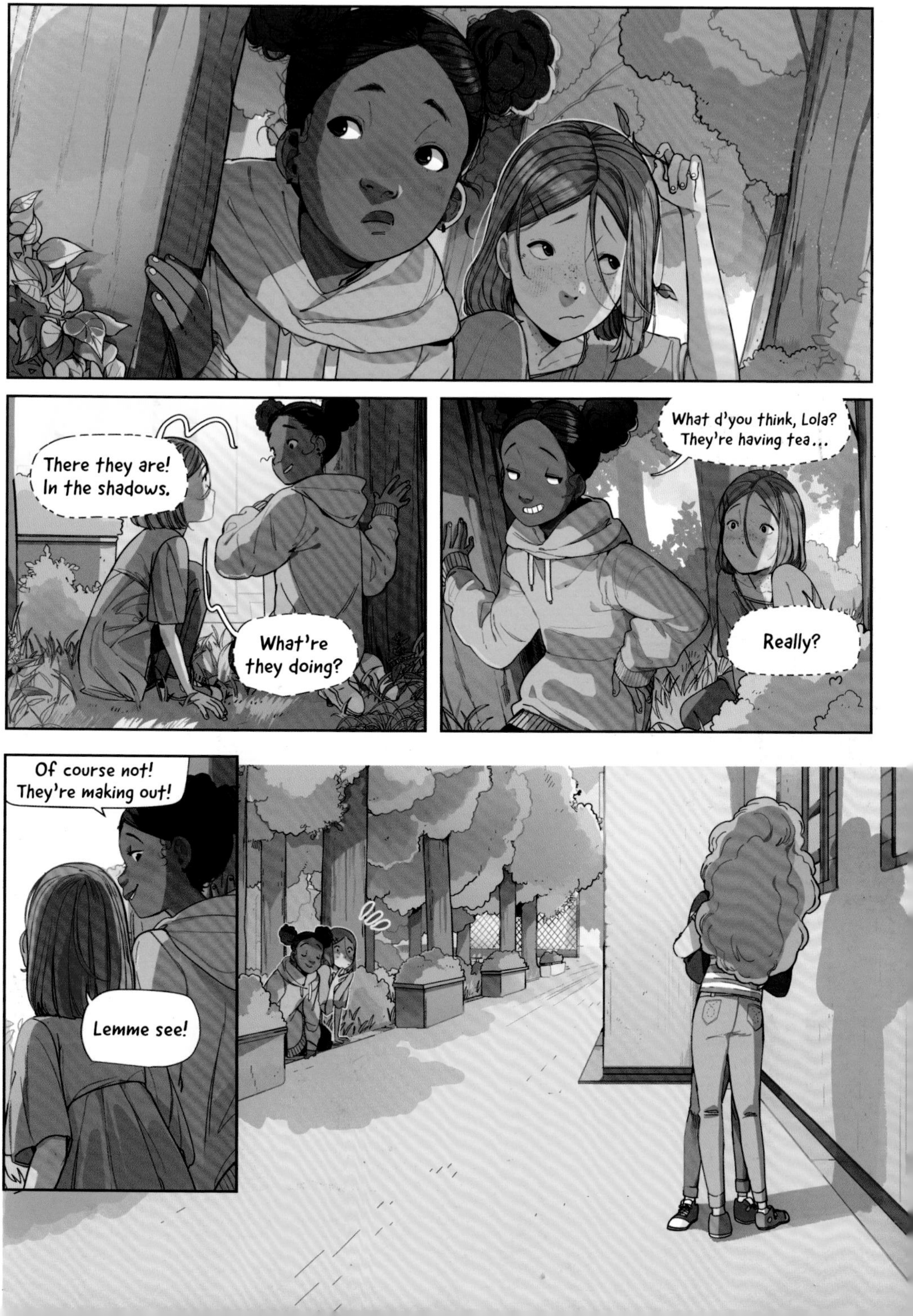
There they are! In the shadows.
What're they doing?
What d'you think, Lola? They're having tea...
Really?
Of course not! They're making out!
Lemme see!

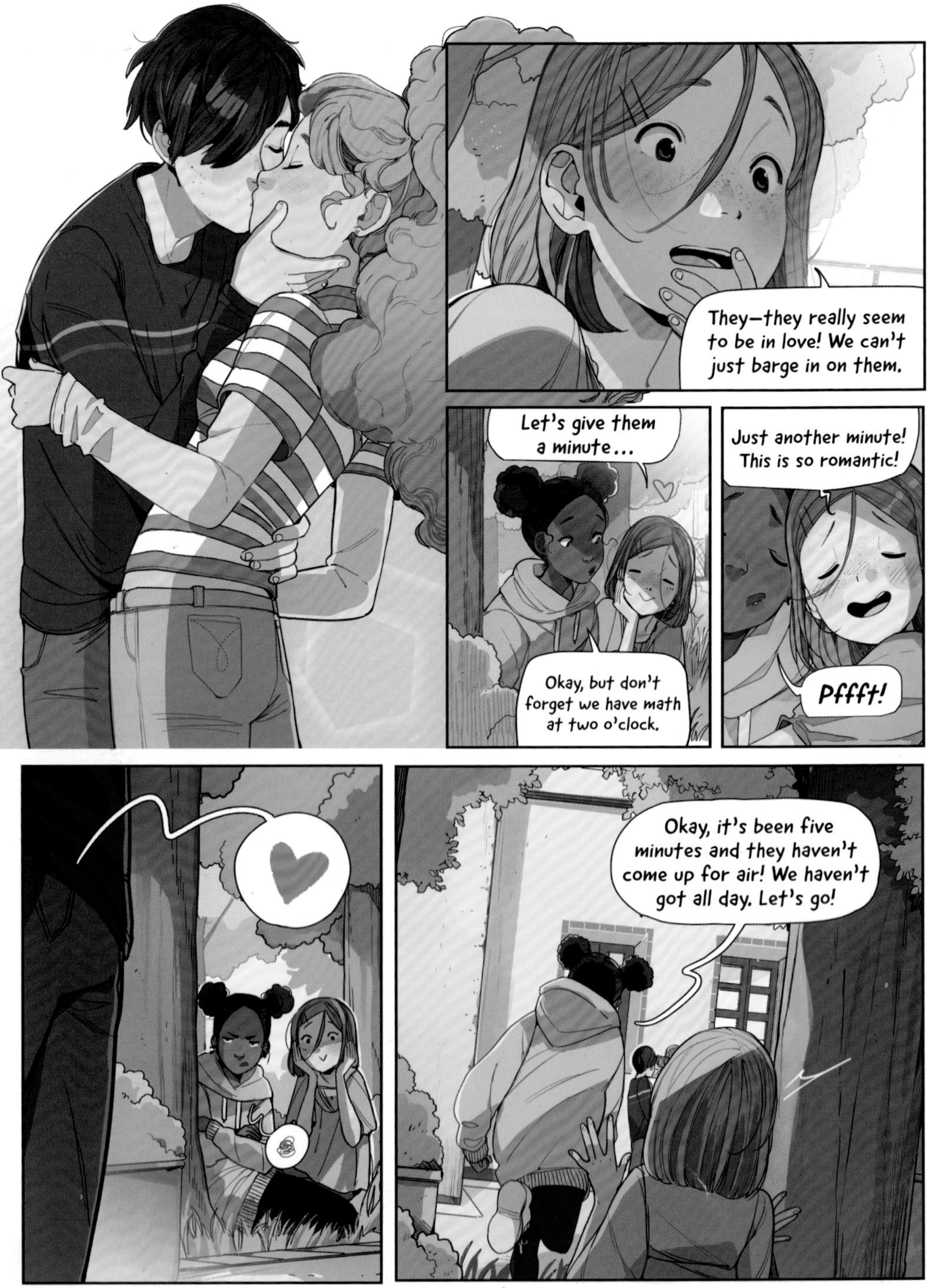
They—they really seem to be in love! We can't just barge in on them.
Let's give them a minute...
Okay, but don't forget we have math at two o'clock.
Just another minute! This is so romantic!
Pffft!
Okay, it's been five minutes and they haven't come up for air! We haven't got all day. Let's go!

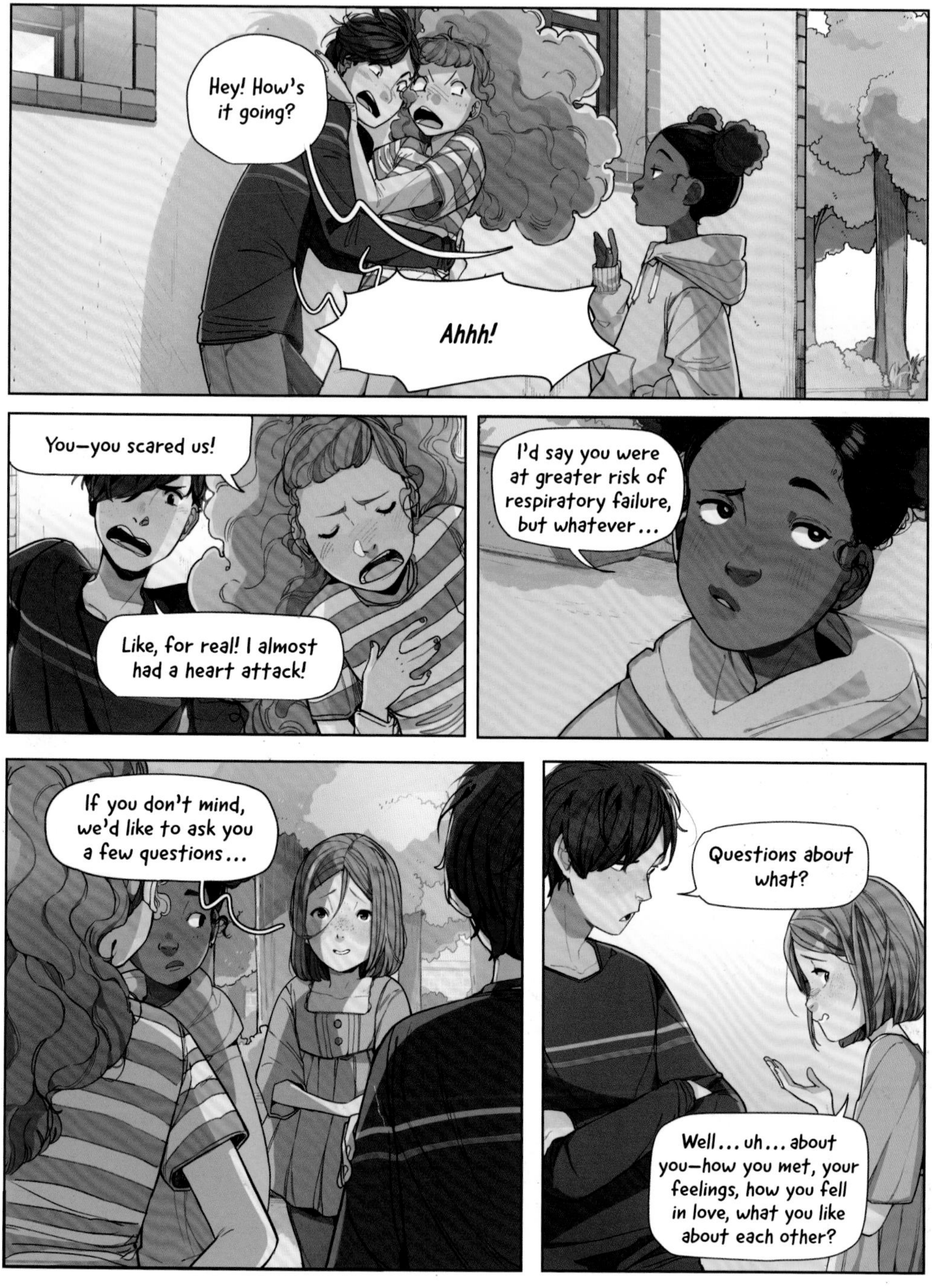
Hey! How's it going?
Ahhh!
You—you scared us!
Like, for real! I almost had a heart attack!
I'd say you were at greater risk of respiratory failure, but whatever...
If you don't mind, we'd like to ask you a few questions...
Questions about what?
Well... uh... about you—how you met, your feelings, how you fell in love, what you like about each other?

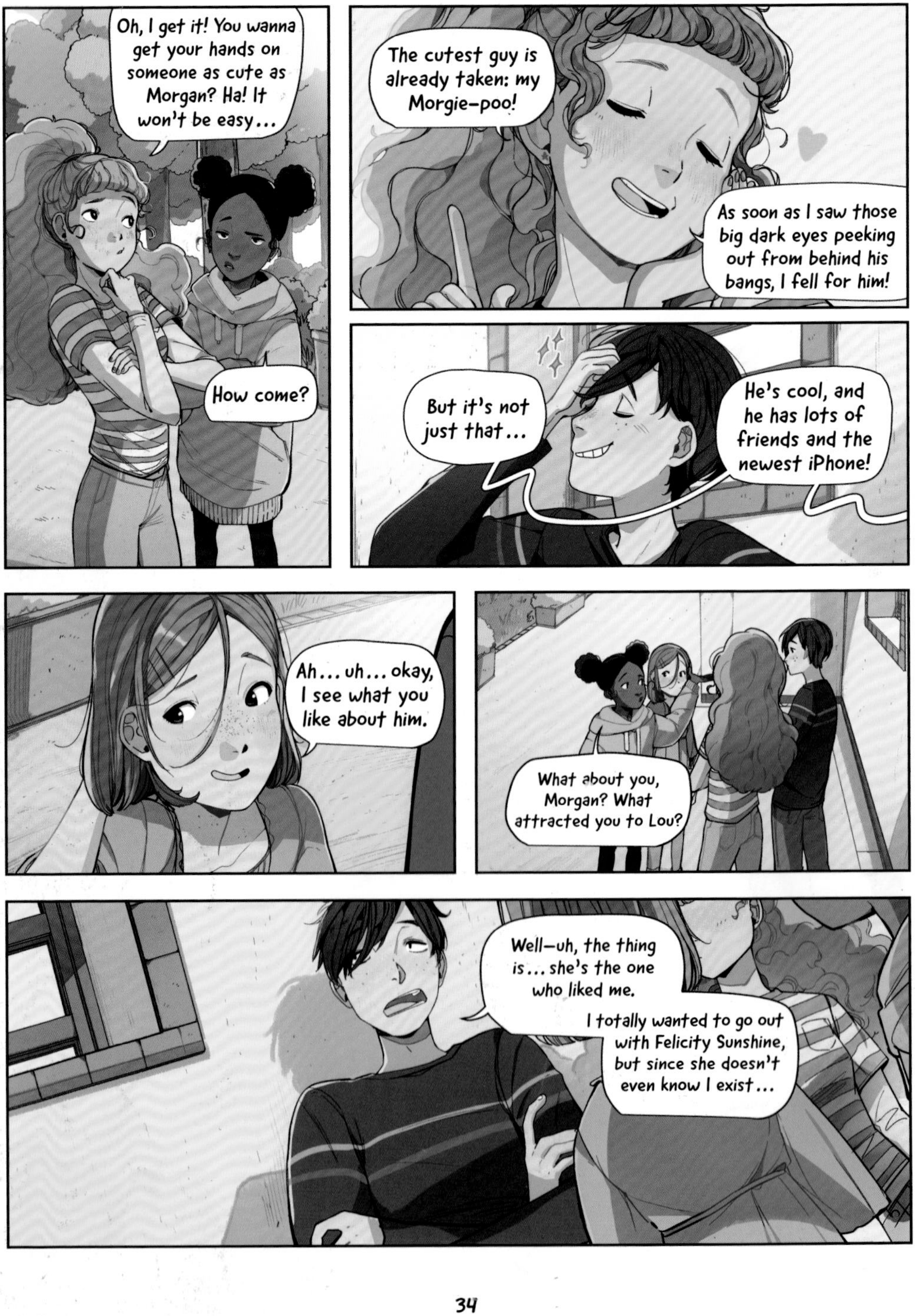
Oh, I get it! You wanna get your hands on someone as cute as Morgan? Ha! It won't be easy...
How come?
The cutest guy is already taken: my Morgie-poo!
As soon as I saw those big dark eyes peeking out from behind his bangs, I fell for him!
But it's not just that...
He's cool, and he has lots of friends and the newest iPhone!
Ah... uh... okay, I see what you like about him.
What about you, Morgan? What attracted you to Lou?
Well—uh, the thing is... she's the one who liked me.
I totally wanted to go out with Felicity Sunshine, but since she doesn't even know I exist...

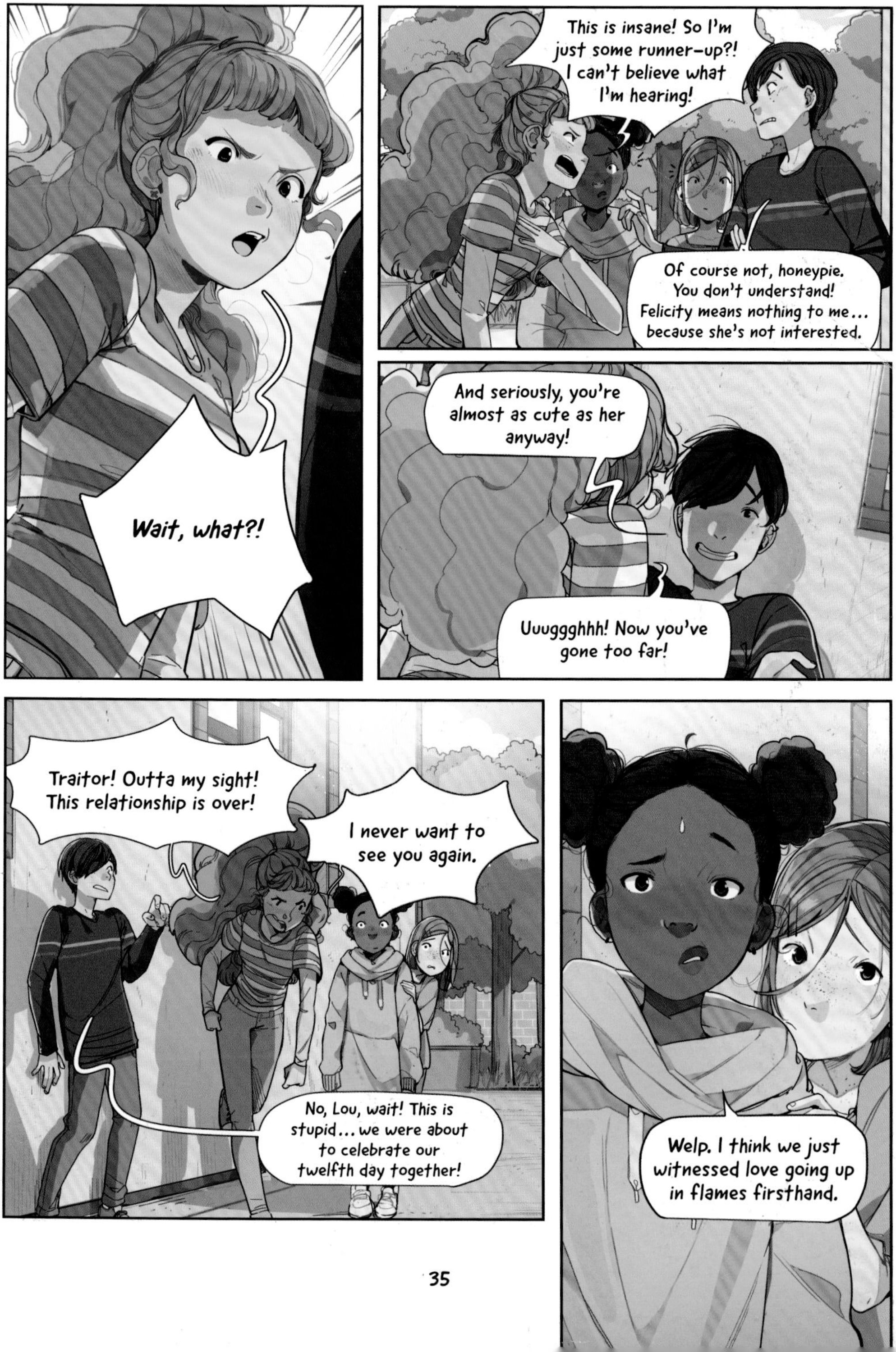

Wait, what?!
This is insane! So I'm just some runner-up?! I can't believe what I'm hearing!
Of course not, honeypie. You don't understand! Felicity means nothing to me... because she's not interested.
And seriously, you're almost as cute as her anyway!
Uuuggghhh! Now you've gone too far!
Traitor! Outta my sight! This relationship is over!
I never want to see you again.
No, Lou, wait! This is stupid... we were about to celebrate our twelfth day together!
Welp. I think we just witnessed love going up in flames firsthand.

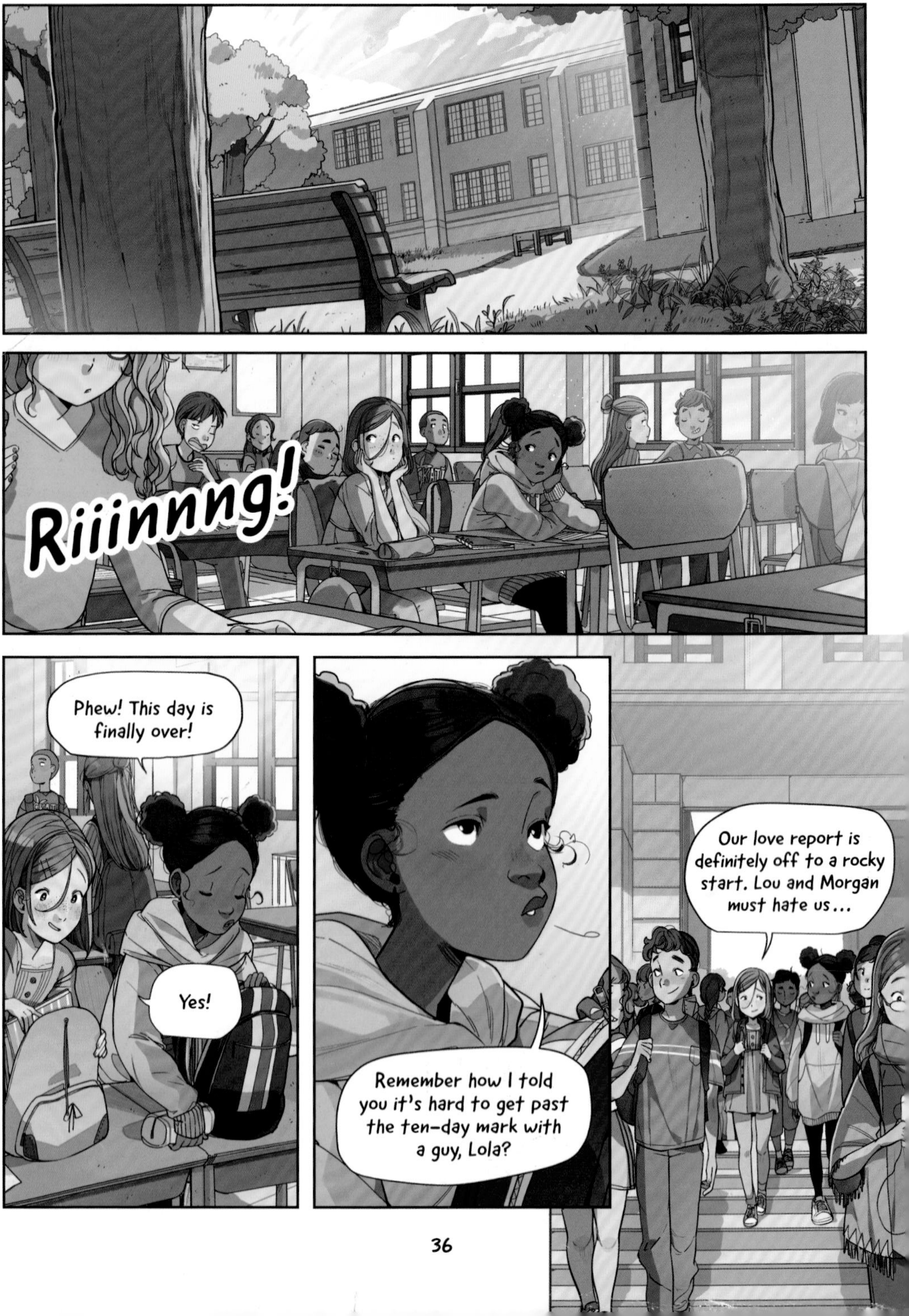

Riiinnng!
Phew! This day is finally over!
Yes!
Remember how I told you it's hard to get past the ten-day mark with a guy, Lola?
Our love report is definitely off to a rocky start. Lou and Morgan must hate us...

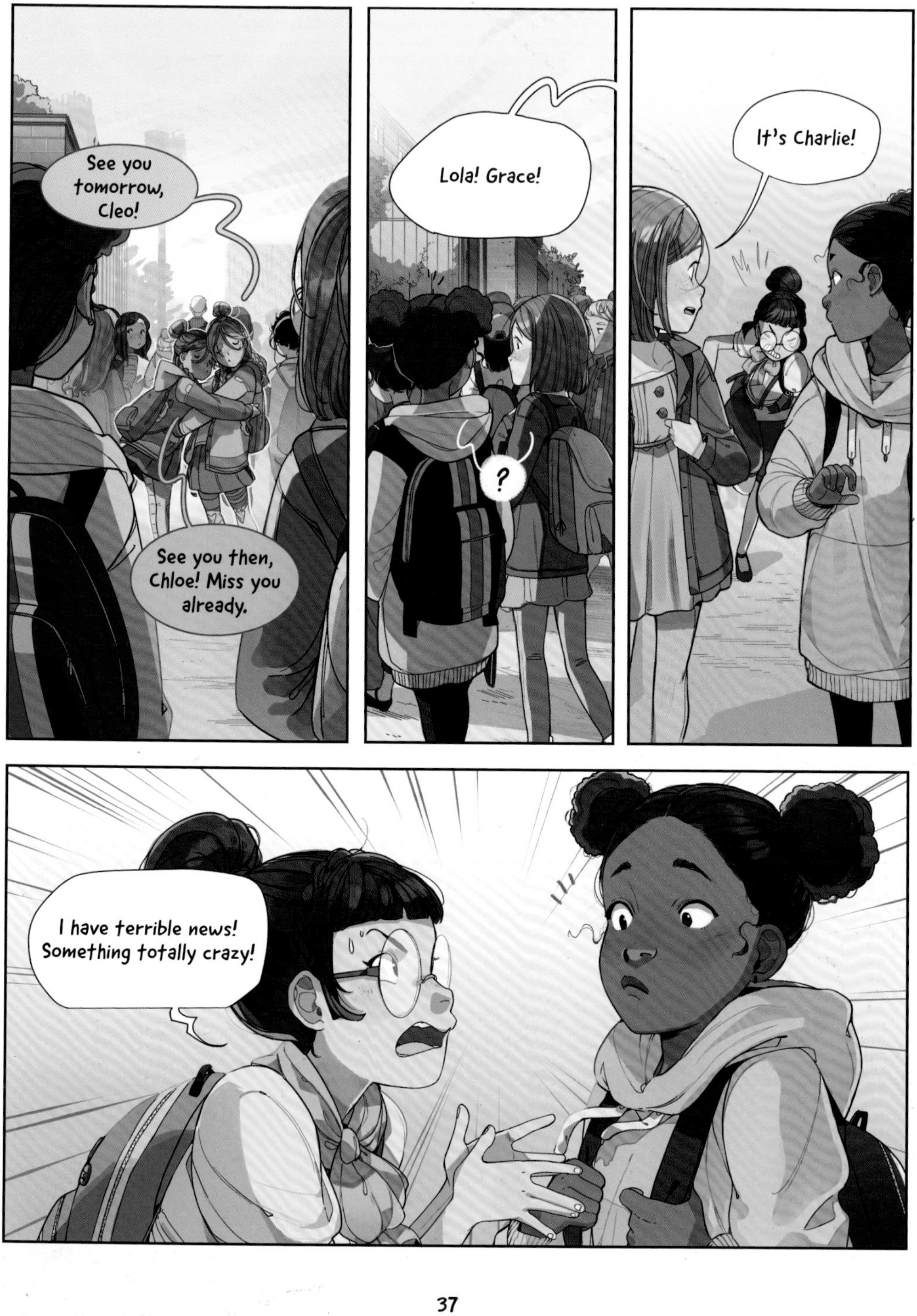
See you tomorrow, Cleo!
See you then, Chloe! Miss you already.
Lola! Grace!
?
It's Charlie!
I have terrible news! Something totally crazy!

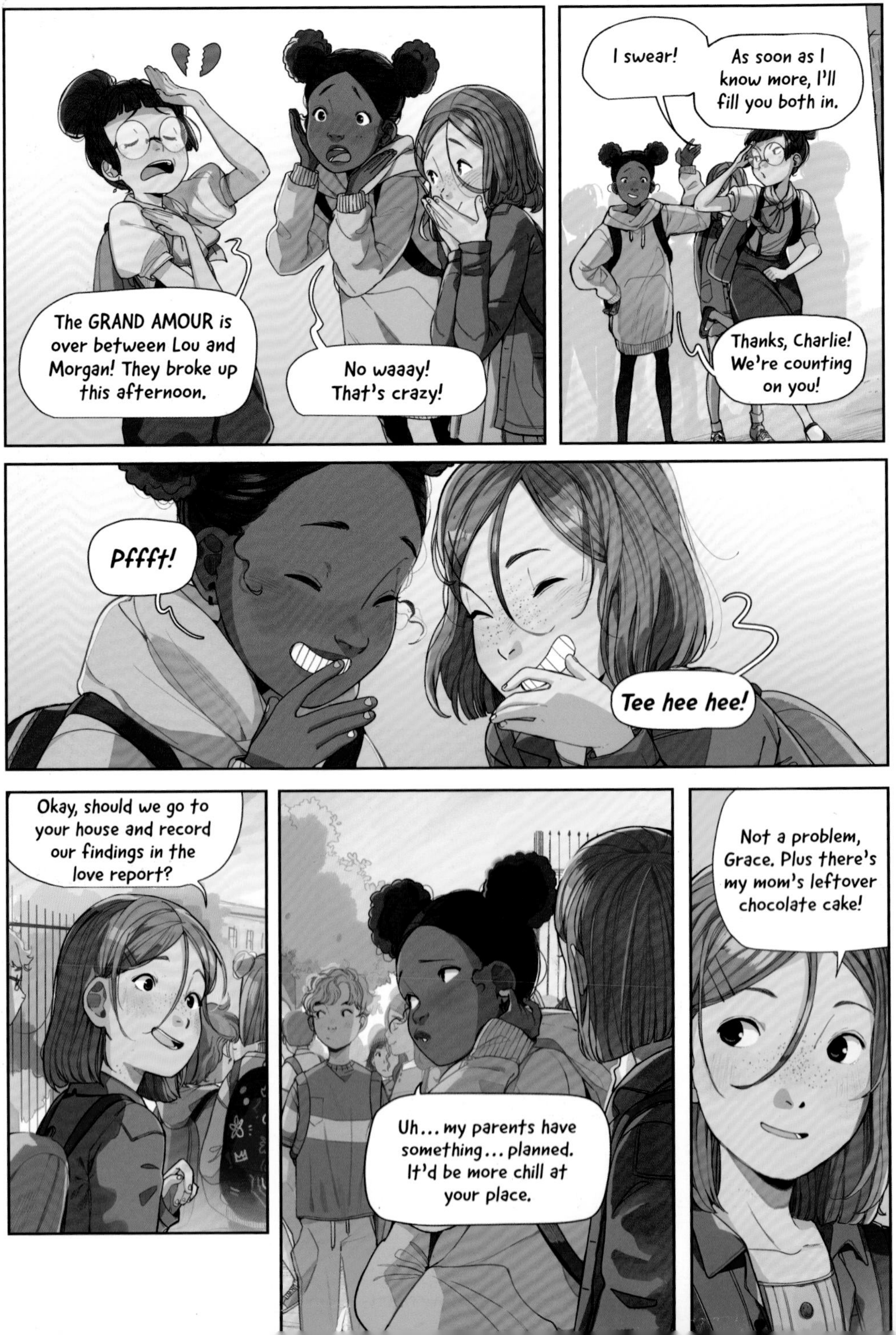
The GRAND AMOUR is over between Lou and Morgan! They broke up this afternoon.
No waaay! That's crazy!
I swear!
As soon as I know more, I'll fill you both in.
Thanks, Charlie! We're counting on you!
Pffft!
Tee hee hee!
Okay, should we go to your house and record our findings in the love report?
Uh... my parents have something... planned. It'd be more chill at your place.
Not a problem, Grace. Plus there's my mom's leftover chocolate cake!

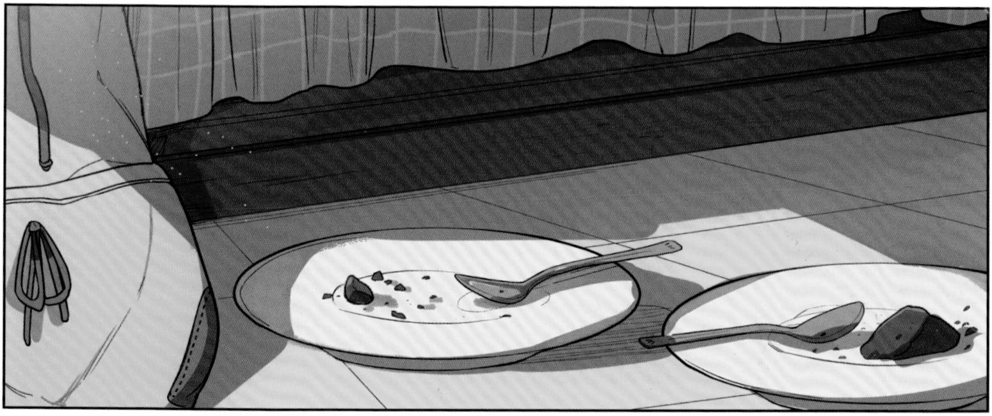

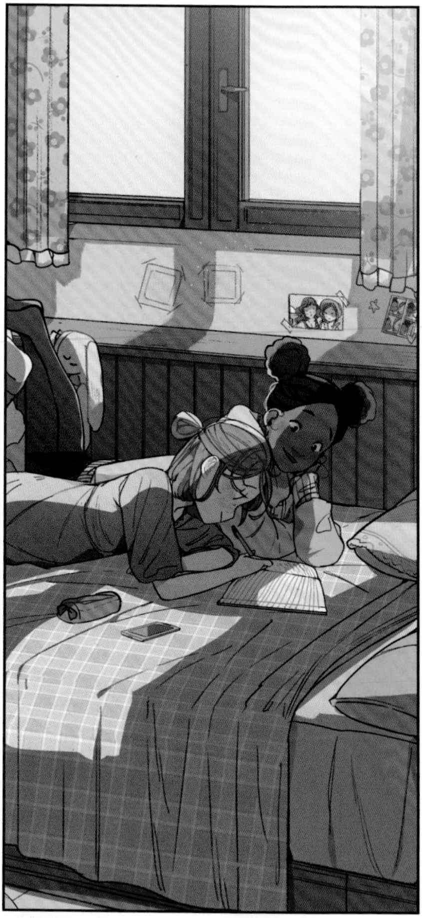

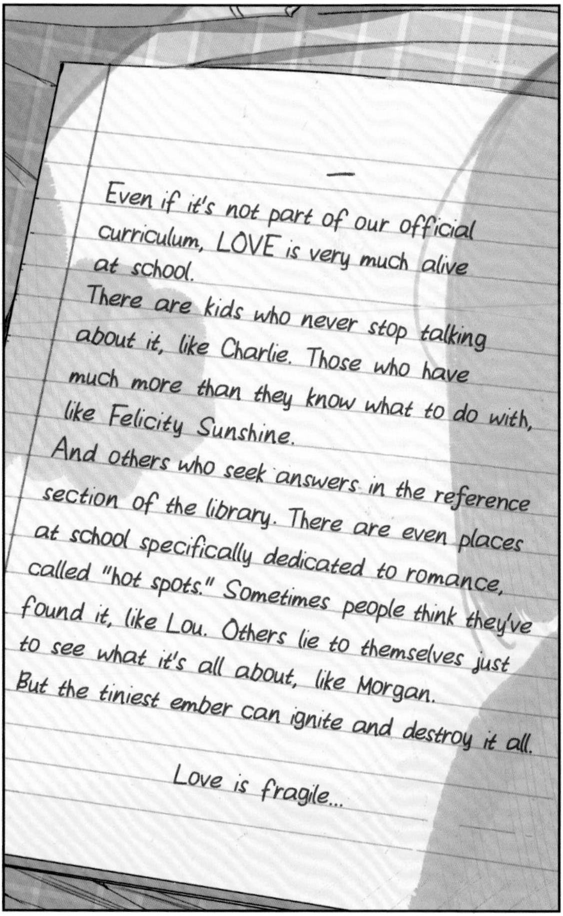
Even if it's not part of our official curriculum, LOVE is very much alive at school.
There are kids who never stop talking about it, like Charlie. Those who have much more than they know what to do with, like Felicity Sunshine.
And others who seek answers in the reference section of the library. There are even places at school specifically dedicated to romance, called "hot spots." Sometimes people think they've found it, like Lou. Others lie to themselves just to see what it's all about, like Morgan.
But the tiniest ember can ignite and destroy it all.
Love is fragile...

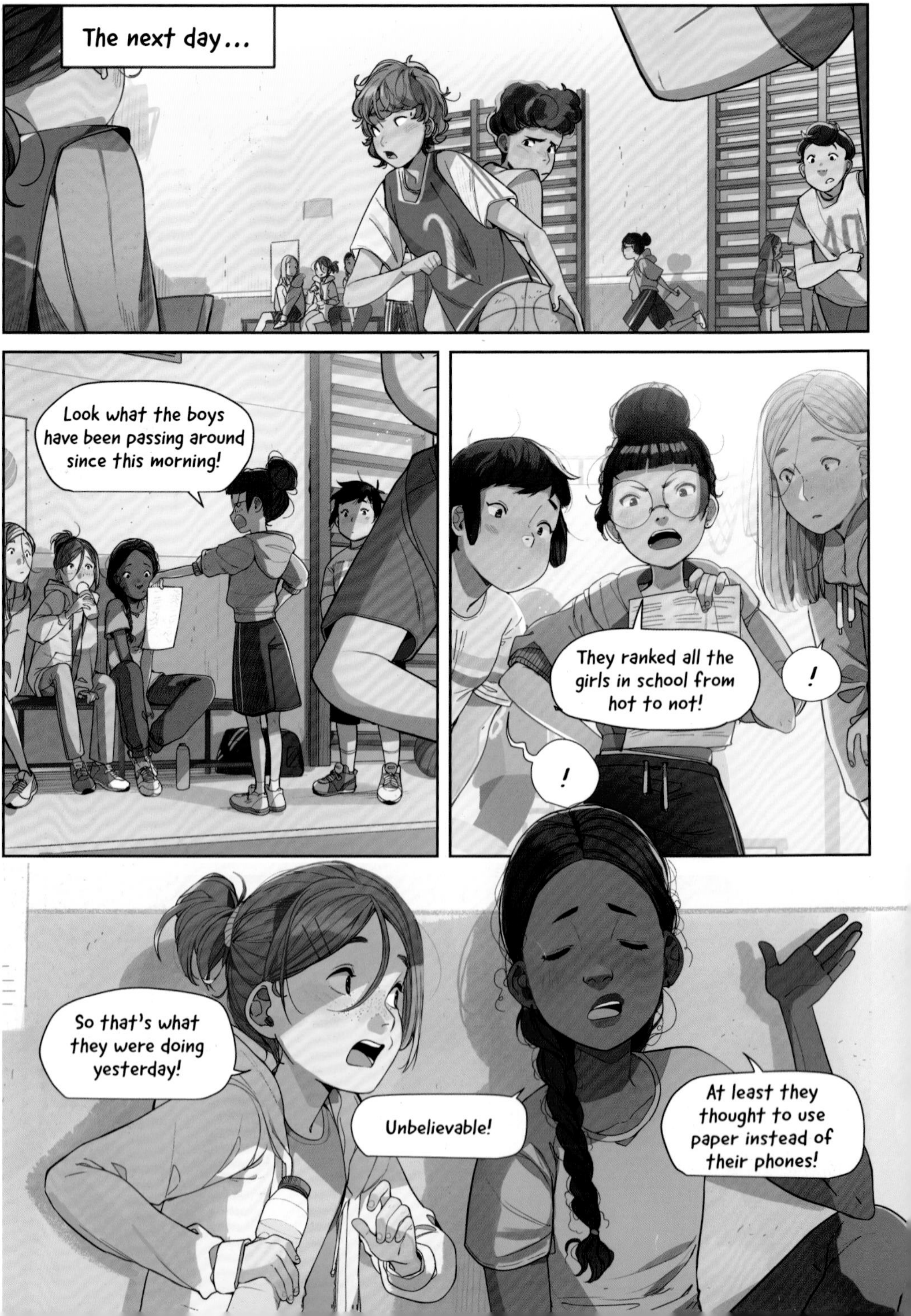

The next day...
Look what the boys have been passing around since this morning!
They ranked all the girls in school from hot to not!
!
!
So that's what they were doing yesterday!
Unbelievable!
At least they thought to use paper instead of their phones!

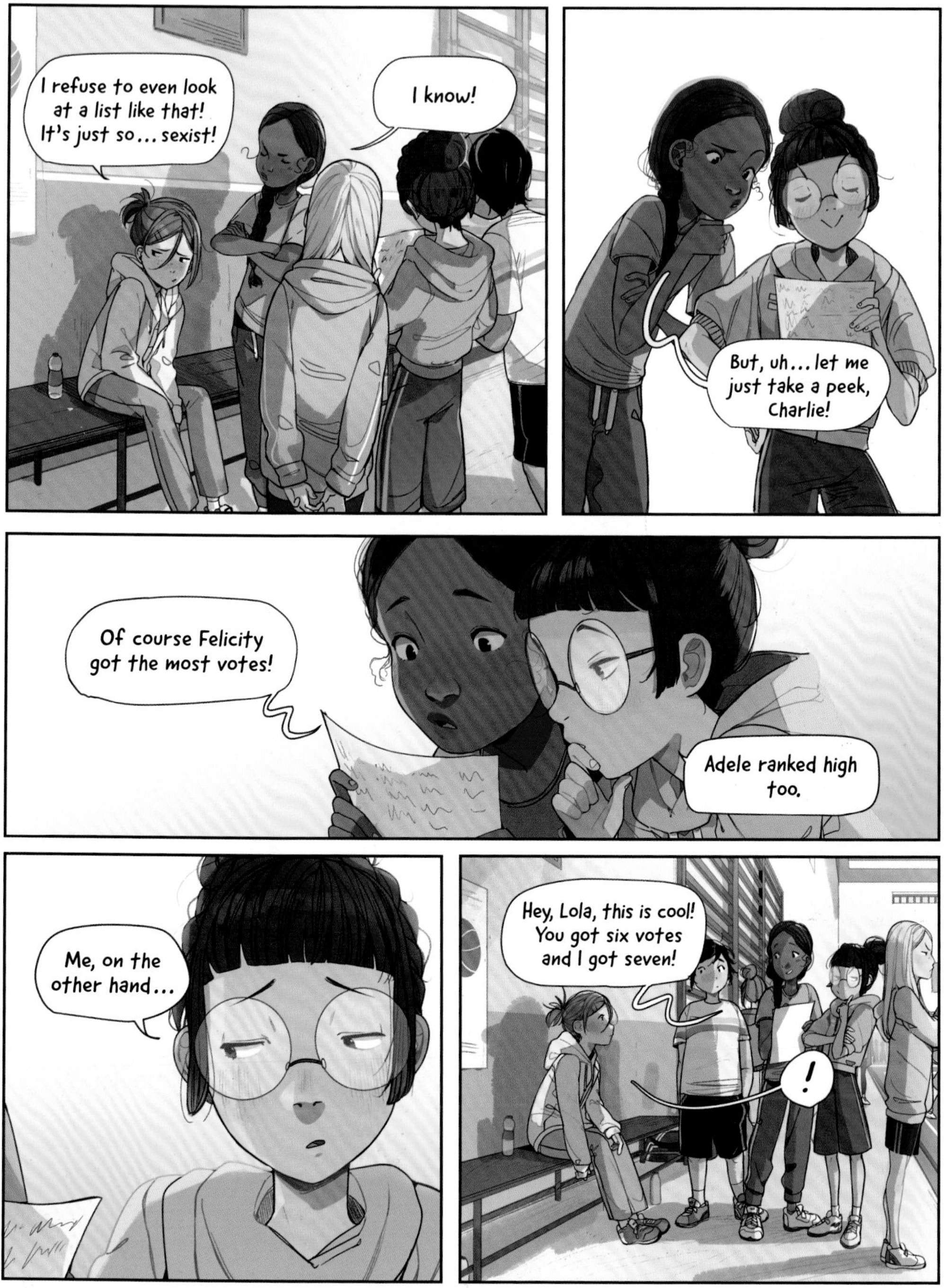
I refuse to even look at a list like that! It's just so... sexist!
I know!
But, uh... let me just take a peek, Charlie!
Of course Felicity got the most votes!
Adele ranked high too.
Me, on the other hand...
Hey, Lola, this is cool! You got six votes and I got seven!
!

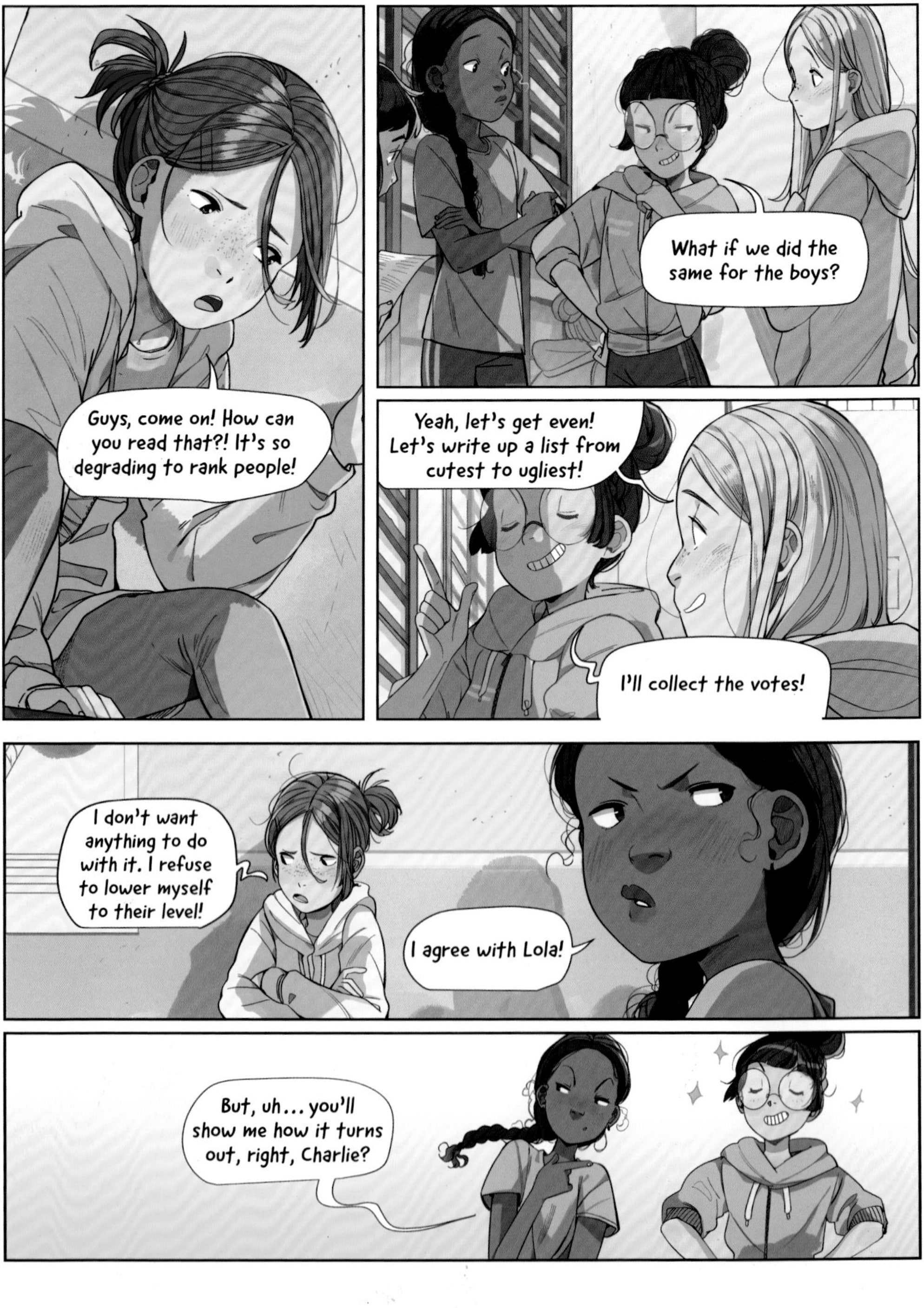
Guys, come on! How can you read that?! It's so degrading to rank people!
What if we did the same for the boys?
Yeah, let's get even! Let's write up a list from cutest to ugliest!
I'll collect the votes!
I don't want anything to do with it. I refuse to lower myself to their level!
I agree with Lola!
But, uh... you'll show me how it turns out, right, Charlie?

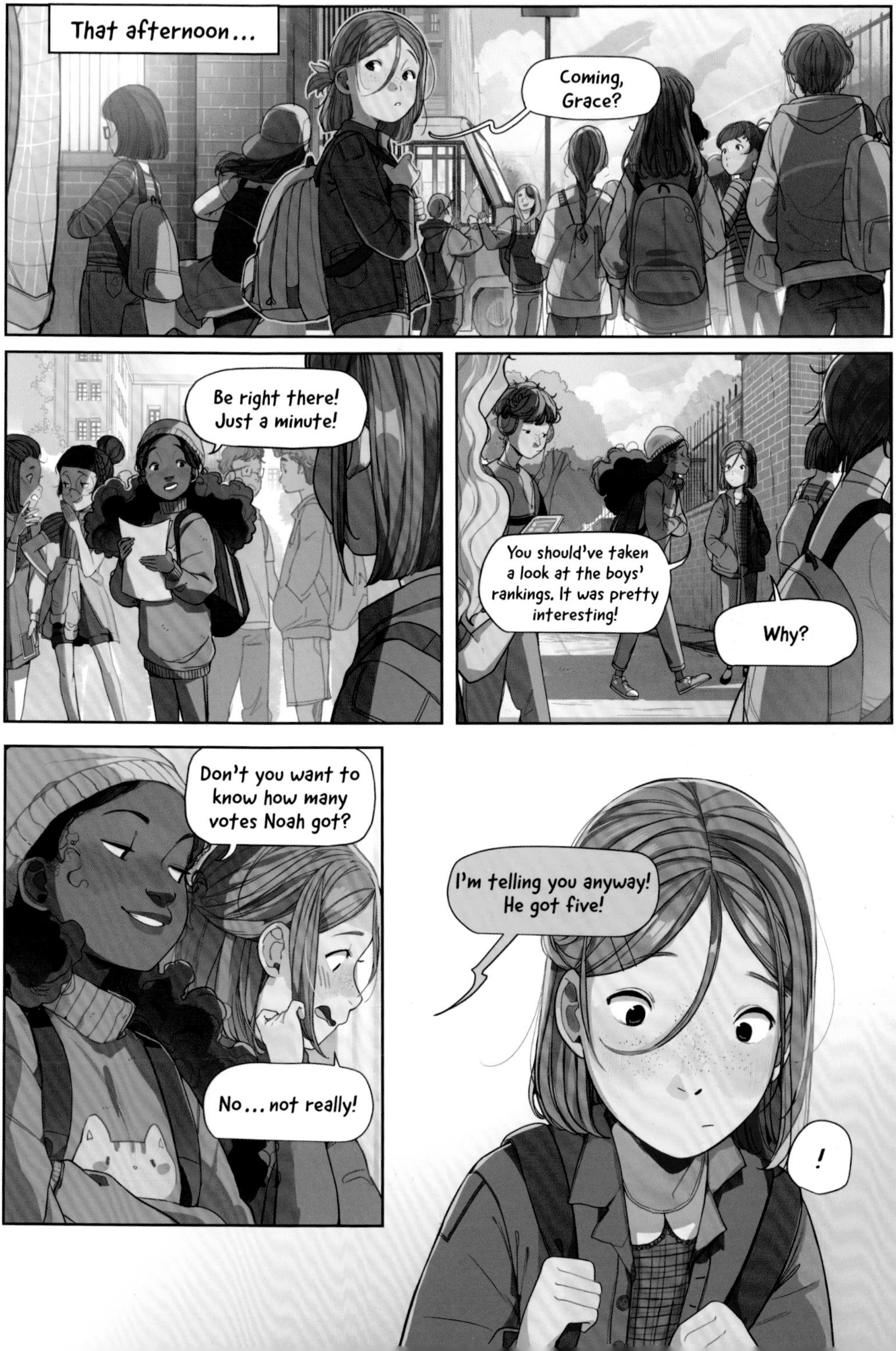
That afternoon...
Coming, Grace?
Be right there! Just a minute!
You should've taken a look at the boys' rankings. It was pretty interesting!
Why?
Don't you want to know how many votes Noah got?
No... not really!
I'm telling you anyway! He got five!
!

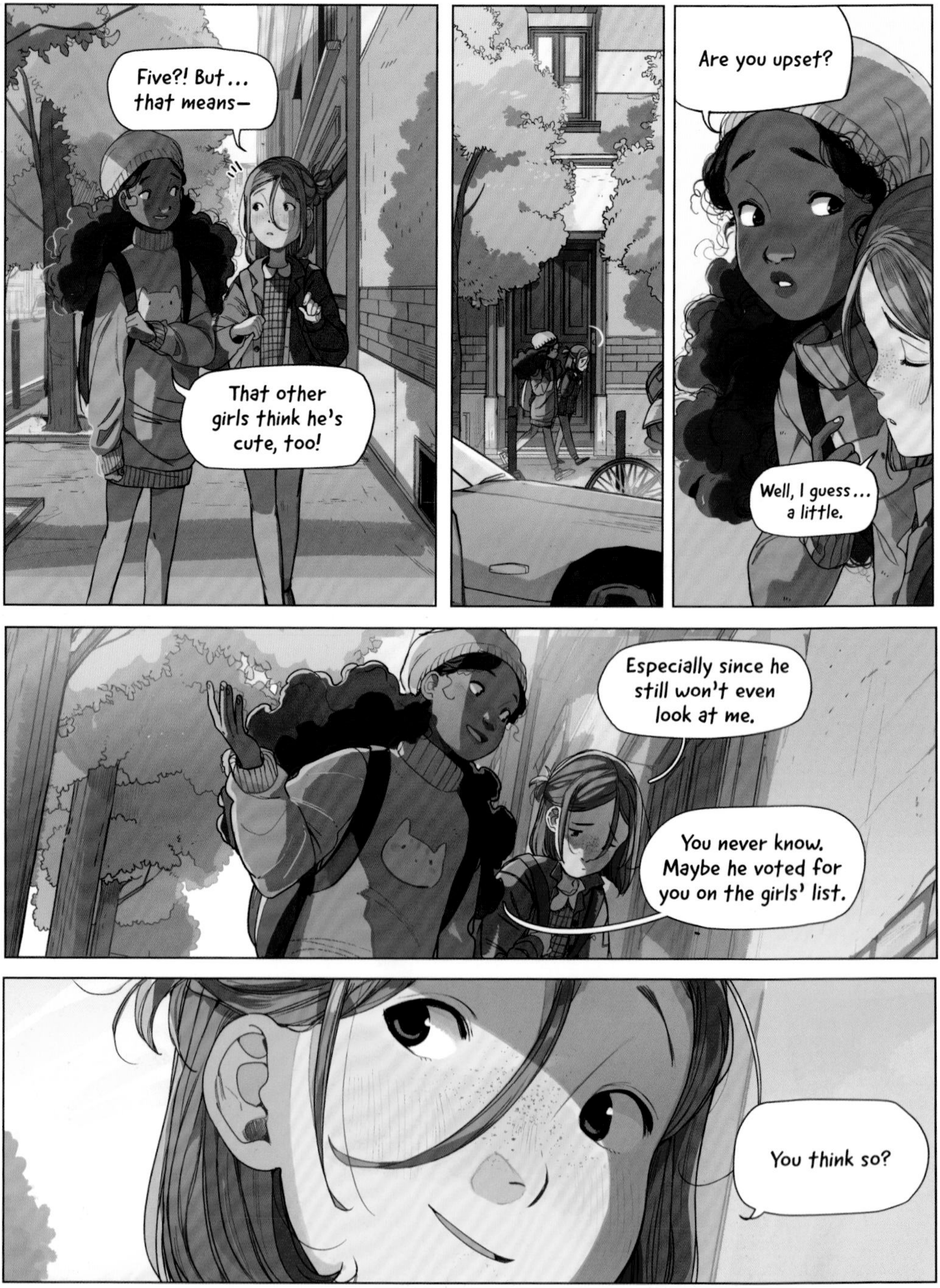
Five?! But...
that means—
That other
girls think he's
cute, too!
Are you upset?
Well, I guess...
a little.
Especially since he
still won't even
look at me.
You never know.
Maybe he voted for
you on the girls' list.
You think so?

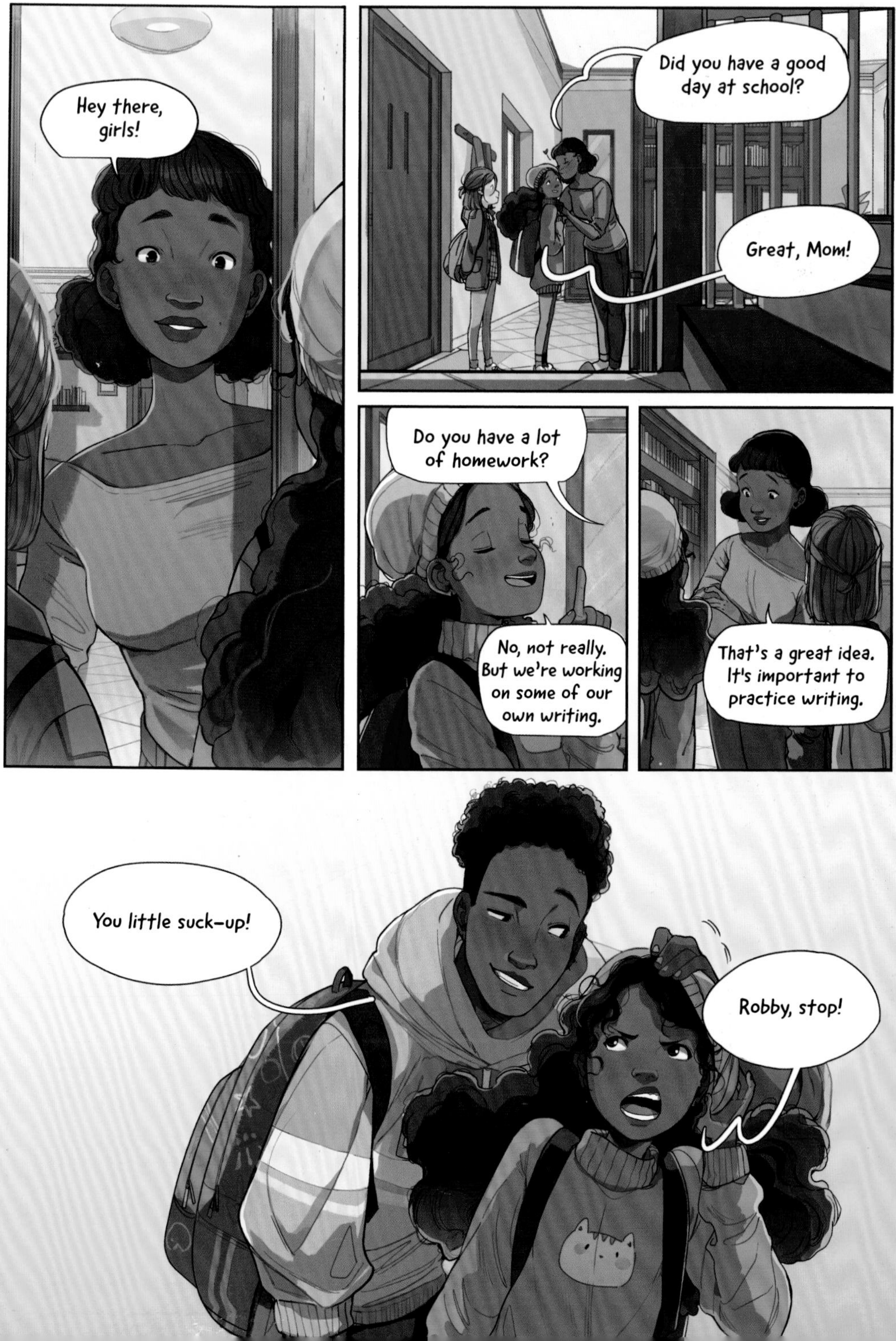
Hey there, girls!
Did you have a good day at school?
Great, Mom!
Do you have a lot of homework?
No, not really. But we're working on some of our own writing.
That's a great idea. It's important to practice writing.
You little suck-up!
Robby, stop!

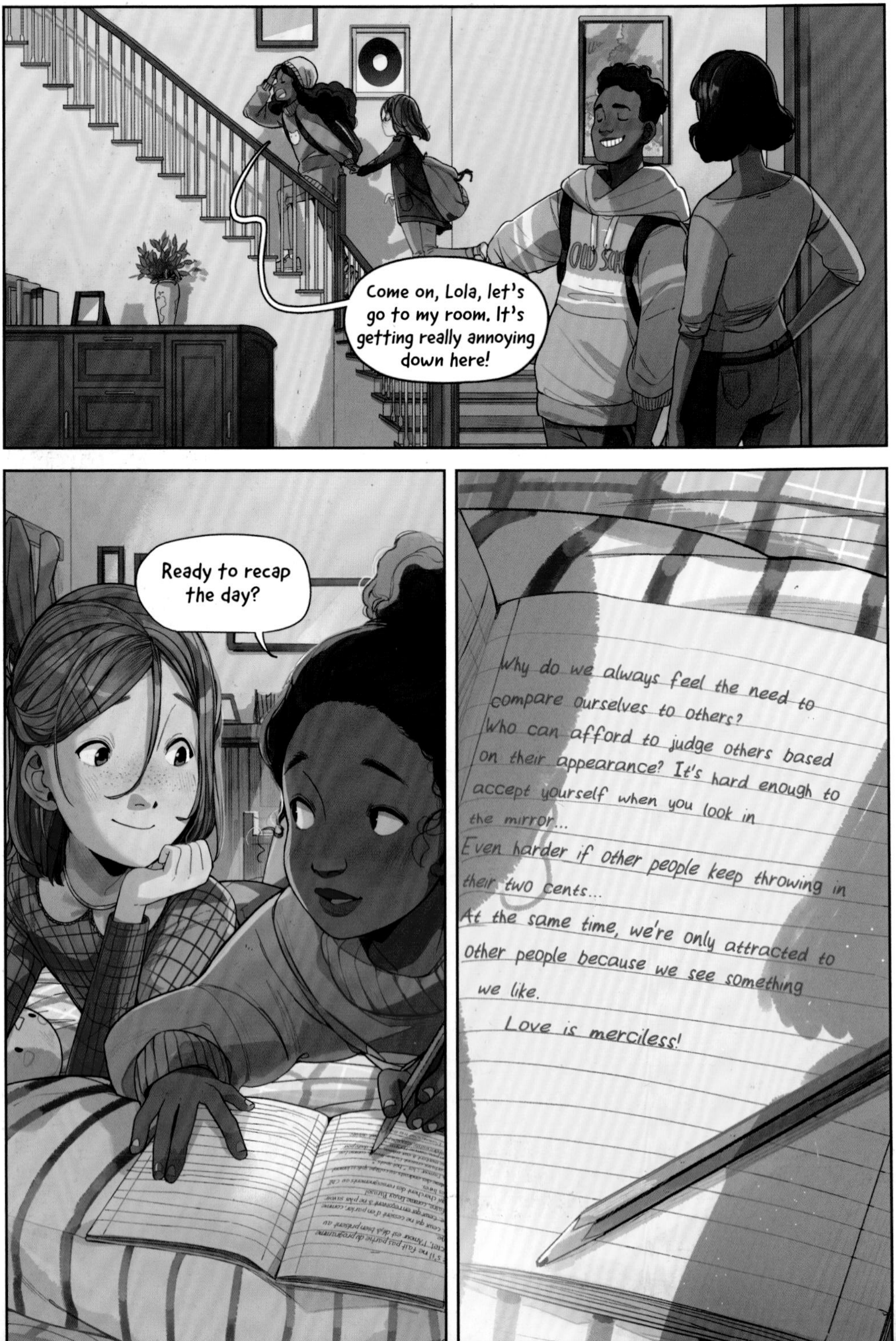
Come on, Lola, let's go to my room. It's getting really annoying down here!
Ready to recap the day?
Why do we always feel the need to compare ourselves to others? Who can afford to judge others based on their appearance? It's hard enough to accept yourself when you look in the mirror...
Even harder if other people keep throwing in their two cents...
At the same time, we're only attracted to other people because we see something we like.
Love is merciless!

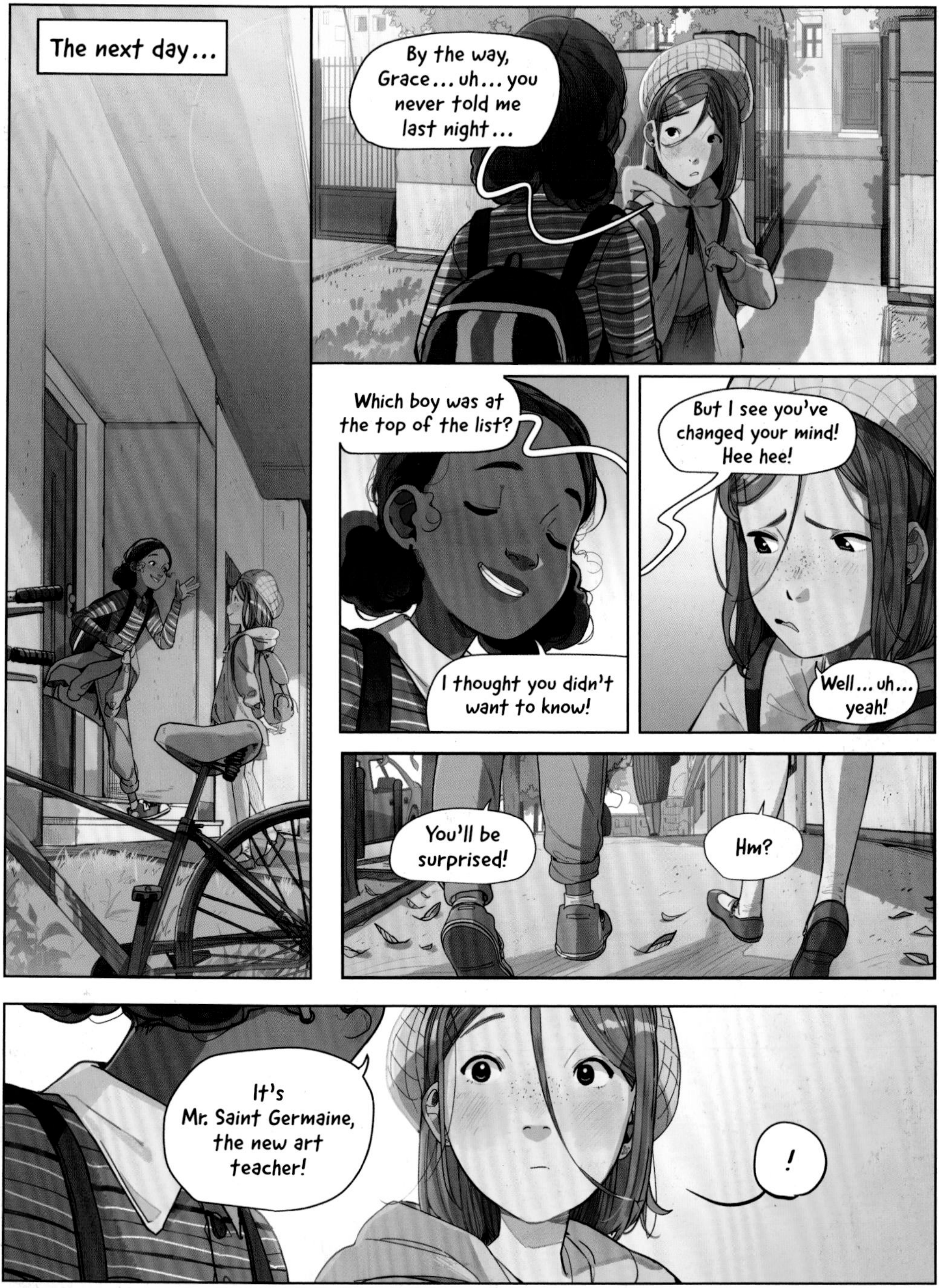
The next day...
By the way, Grace... uh... you never told me last night...
Which boy was at the top of the list?
I thought you didn't want to know!
But I see you've changed your mind! Hee hee!
Well... uh... yeah!
You'll be surprised!
Hm?
It's Mr. Saint Germaine, the new art teacher!
!

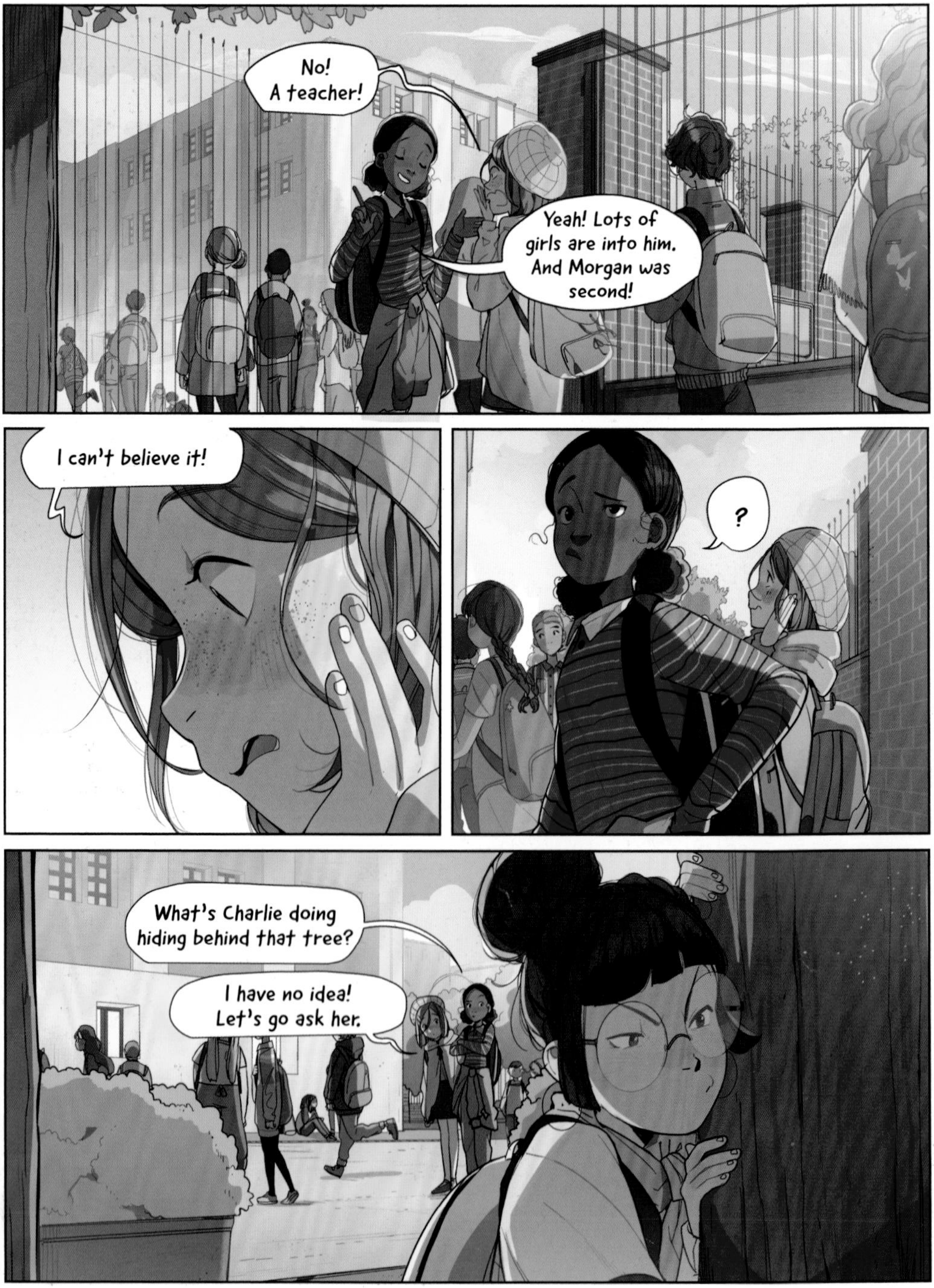
No!
A teacher!
Yeah! Lots of girls are into him. And Morgan was second!
I can't believe it!
?
What's Charlie doing hiding behind that tree?
I have no idea! Let's go ask her.

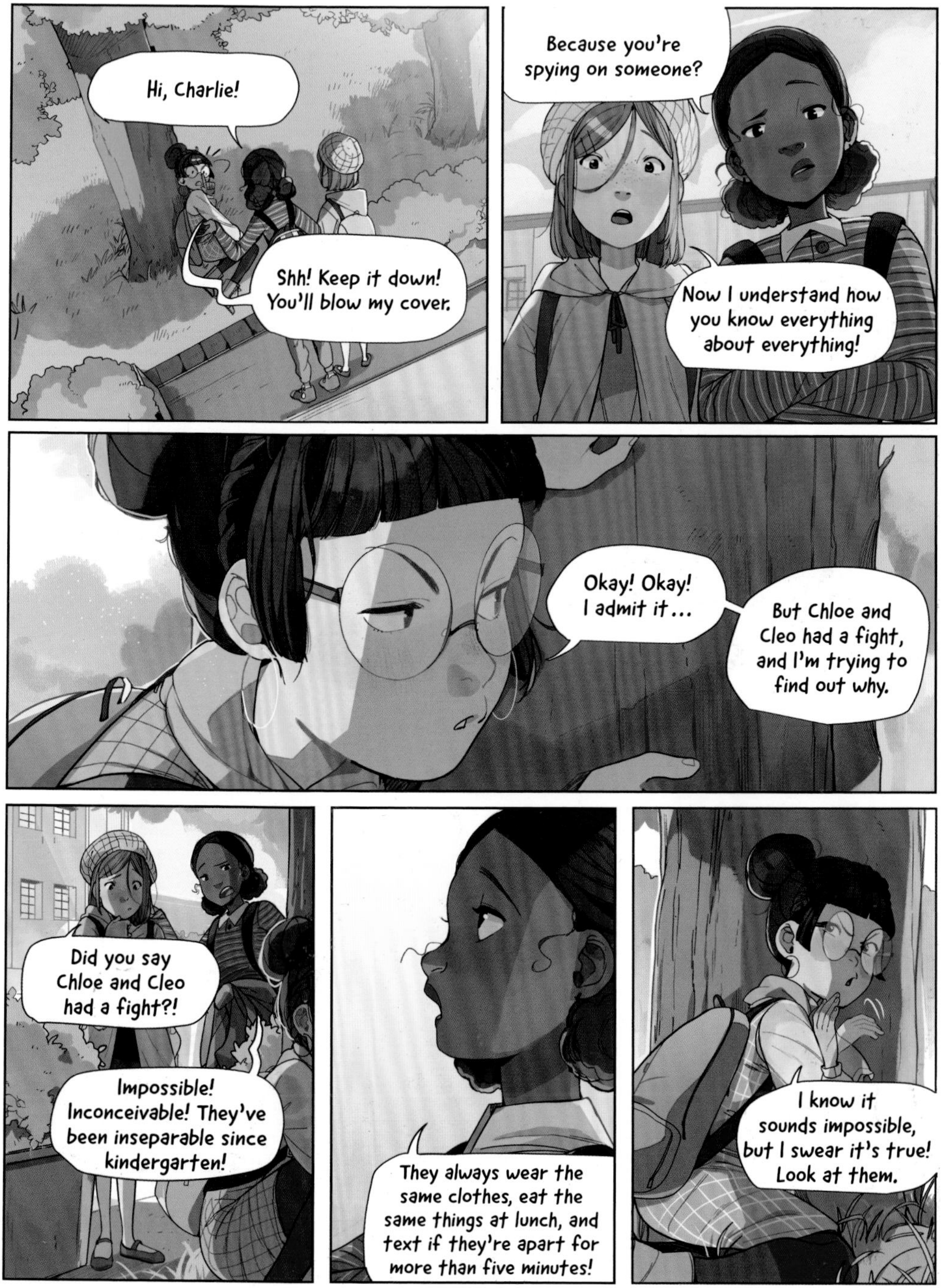
Hi, Charlie!
Shh! Keep it down! You'll blow my cover.
Because you're spying on someone?
Now I understand how you know everything about everything!
Okay! Okay! I admit it...
But Chloe and Cleo had a fight, and I'm trying to find out why.
Did you say Chloe and Cleo had a fight?!
Impossible! Inconceivable! They've been inseparable since kindergarten!
They always wear the same clothes, eat the same things at lunch, and text if they're apart for more than five minutes!
I know it sounds impossible, but I swear it's true! Look at them.

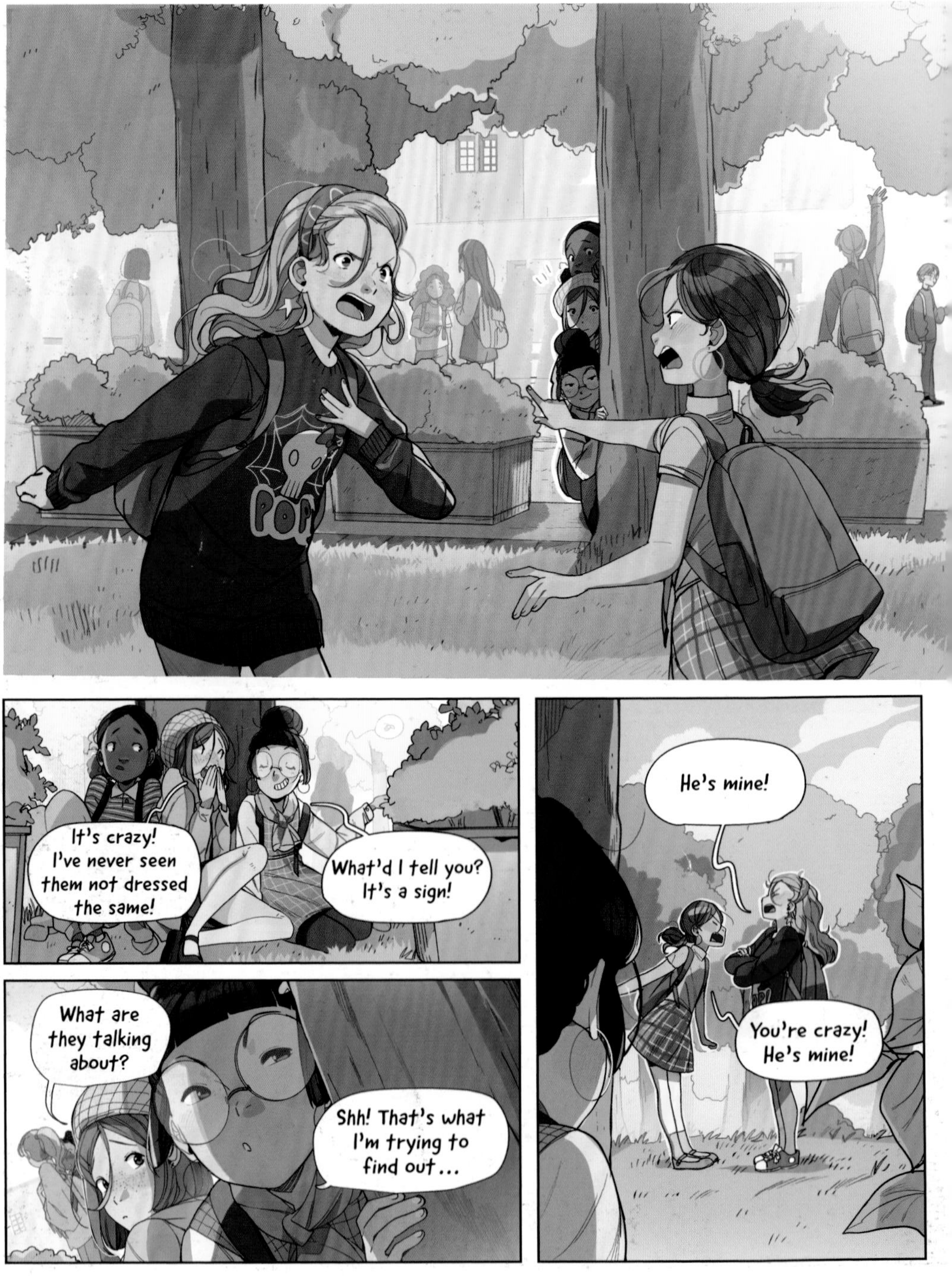

It's crazy! I've never seen them not dressed the same!
What'd I tell you? It's a sign!
What are they talking about?
Shh! That's what I'm trying to find out...
He's mine!
You're crazy! He's mine!

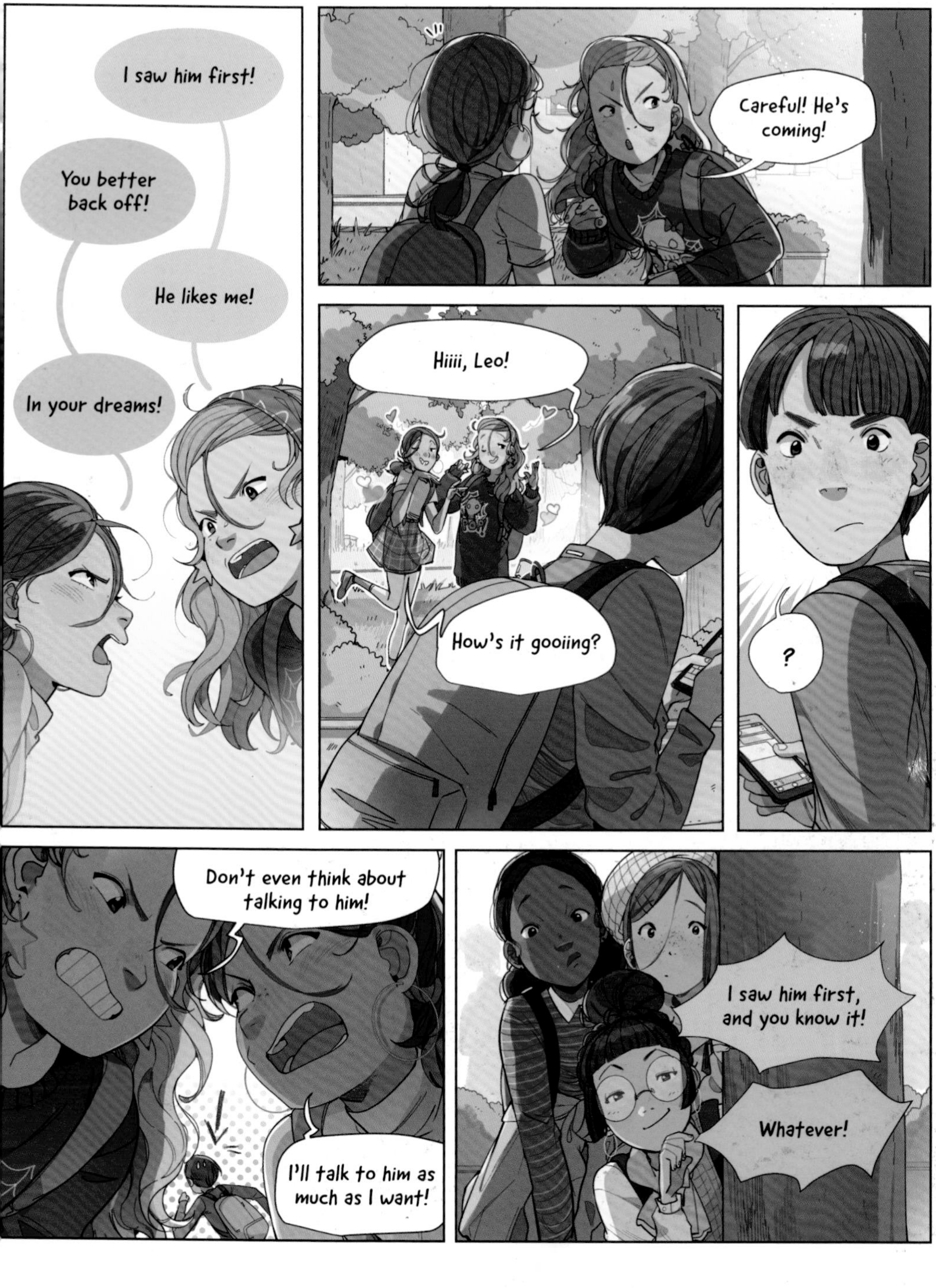
I saw him first!
You better back off!
He likes me!
In your dreams!
Careful! He's coming!
Hiiii, Leo!
How's it gooiing?
?
Don't even think about talking to him!
I'll talk to him as much as I want!
I saw him first, and you know it!
Whatever!

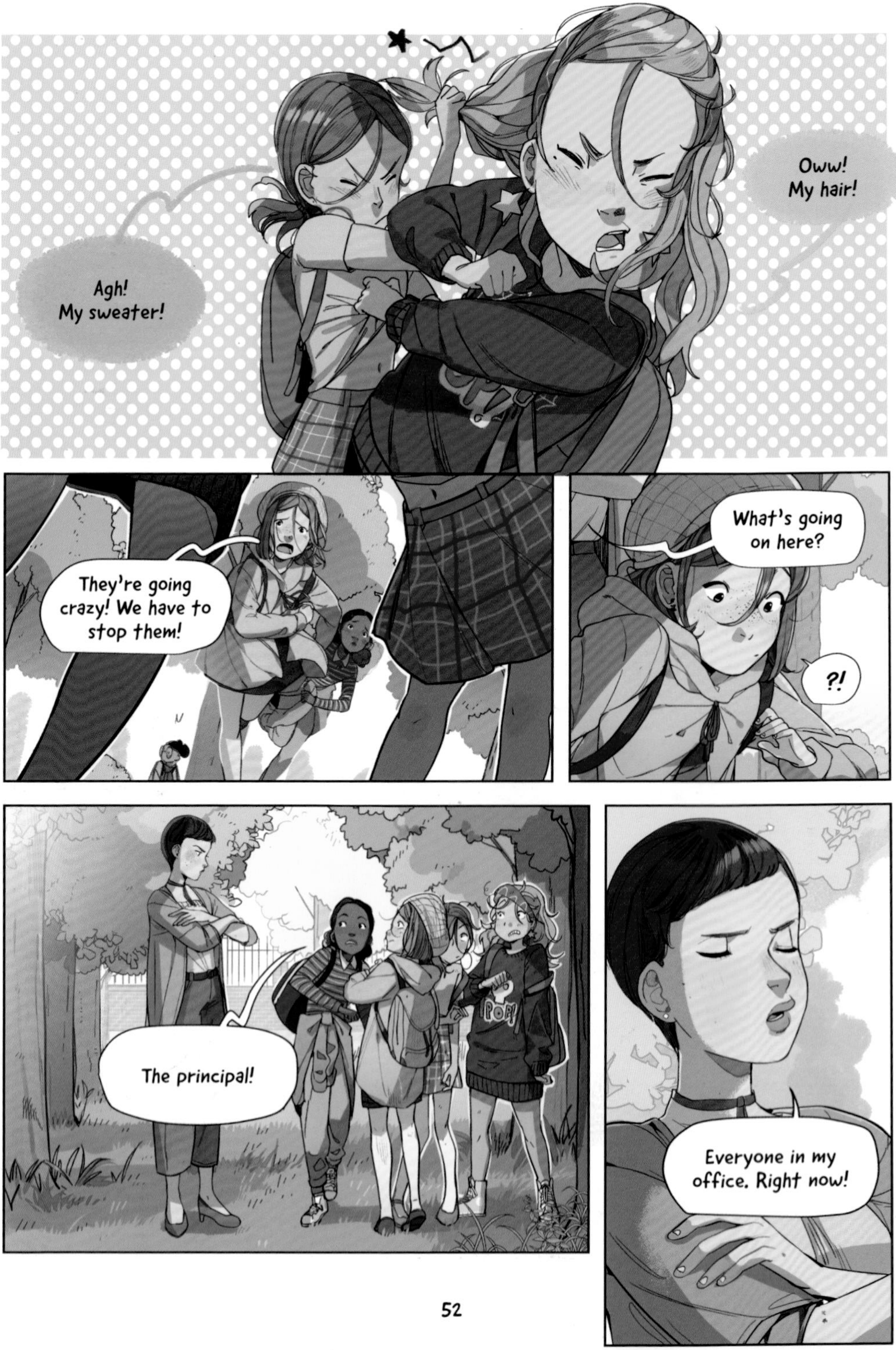
Oww! My hair!
Agh! My sweater!
They're going crazy! We have to stop them!
What's going on here?
?!
The principal!
Everyone in my office. Right now!

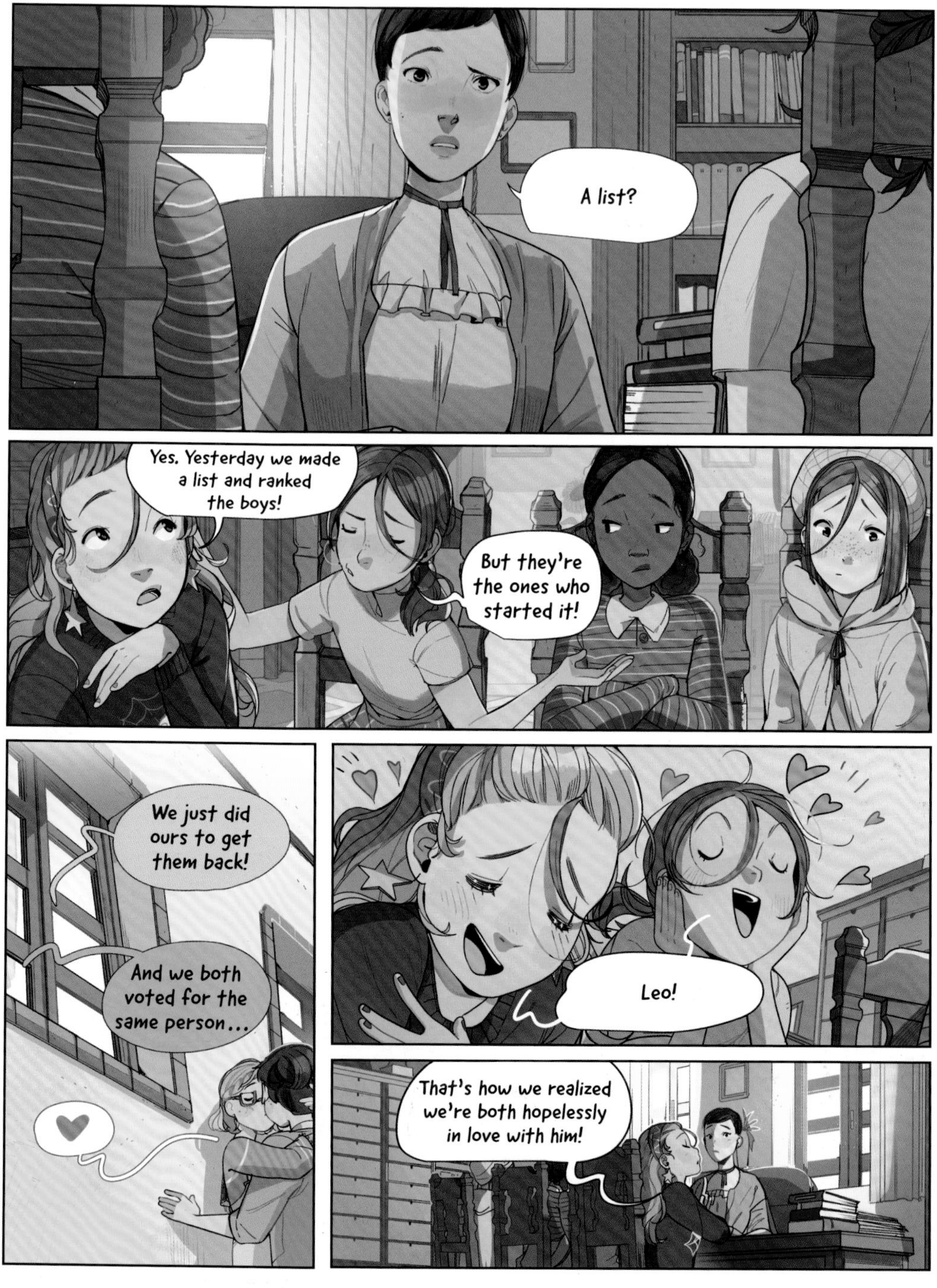
A list?
Yes. Yesterday we made a list and ranked the boys!
But they're the ones who started it!
We just did ours to get them back!
And we both voted for the same person...
Leo!
That's how we realized we're both hopelessly in love with him!

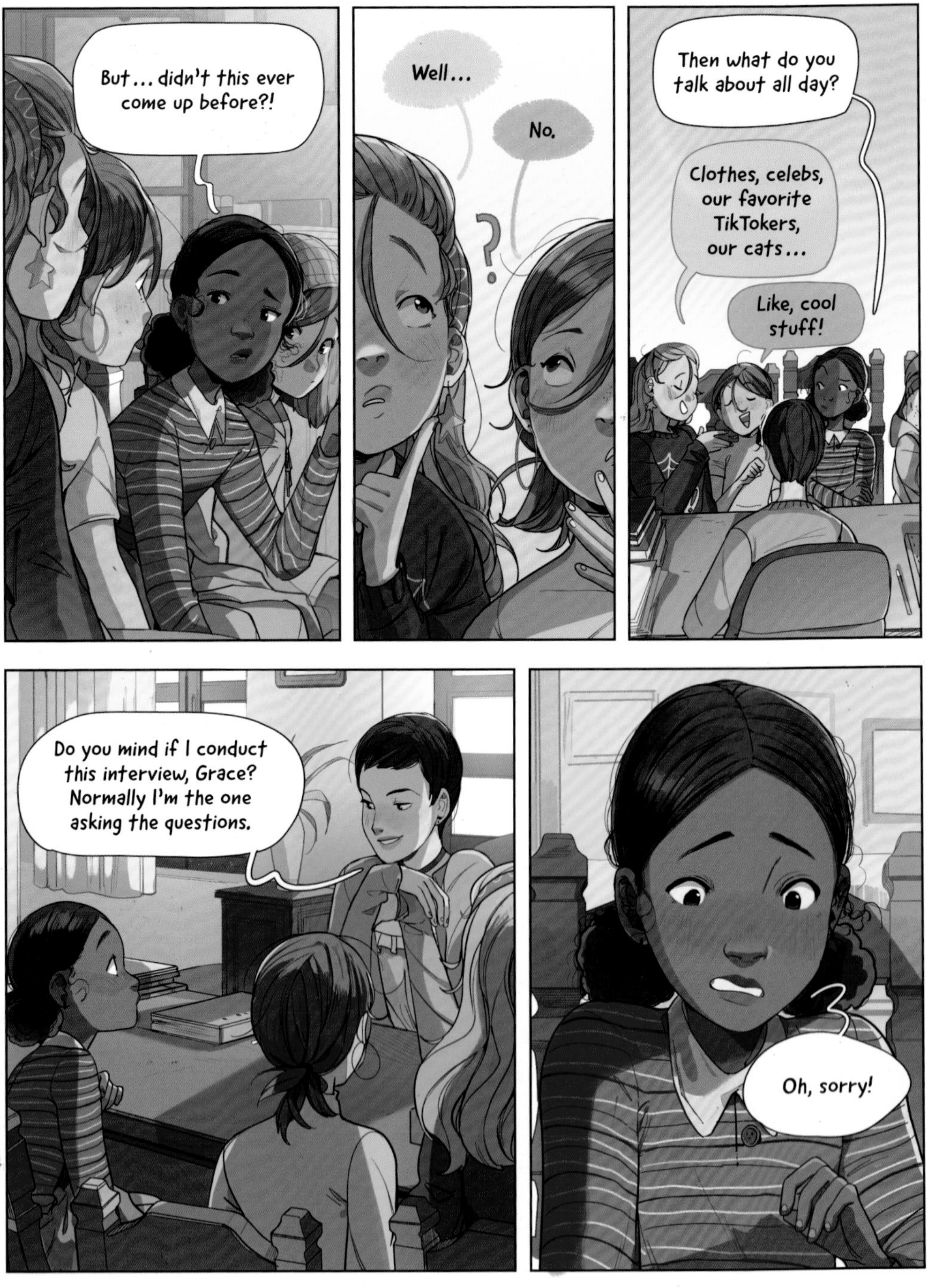
But... didn't this ever come up before?!
Well...
No.
?
Then what do you talk about all day?
Clothes, celebs, our favorite TikTokers, our cats...
Like, cool stuff!
Do you mind if I conduct this interview, Grace? Normally I'm the one asking the questions.
Oh, sorry!

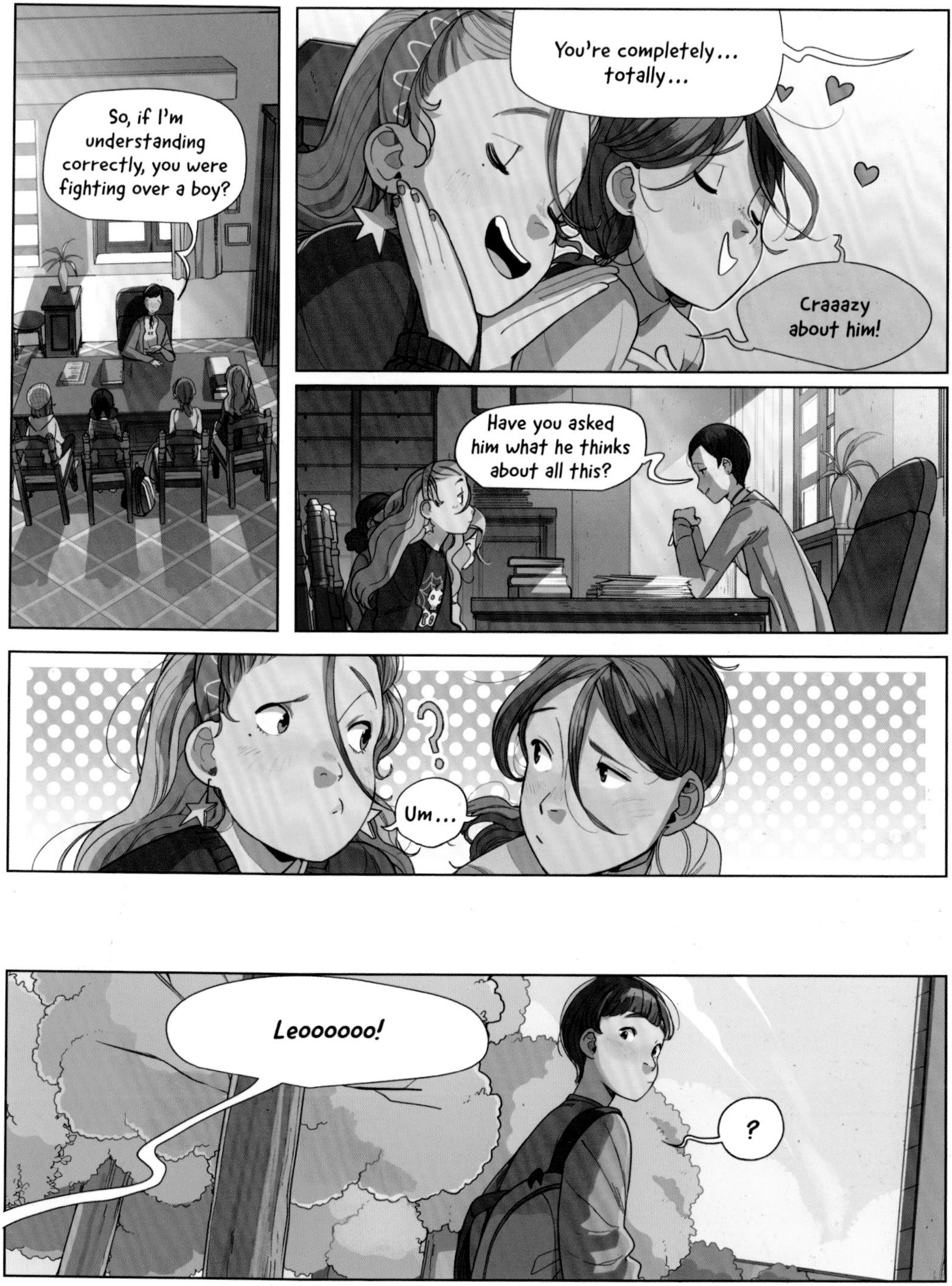
So, if I'm understanding correctly, you were fighting over a boy?
You're completely... totally...
Craaazy about him!
Have you asked him what he thinks about all this?
?
Um...
Leoooooo!
?

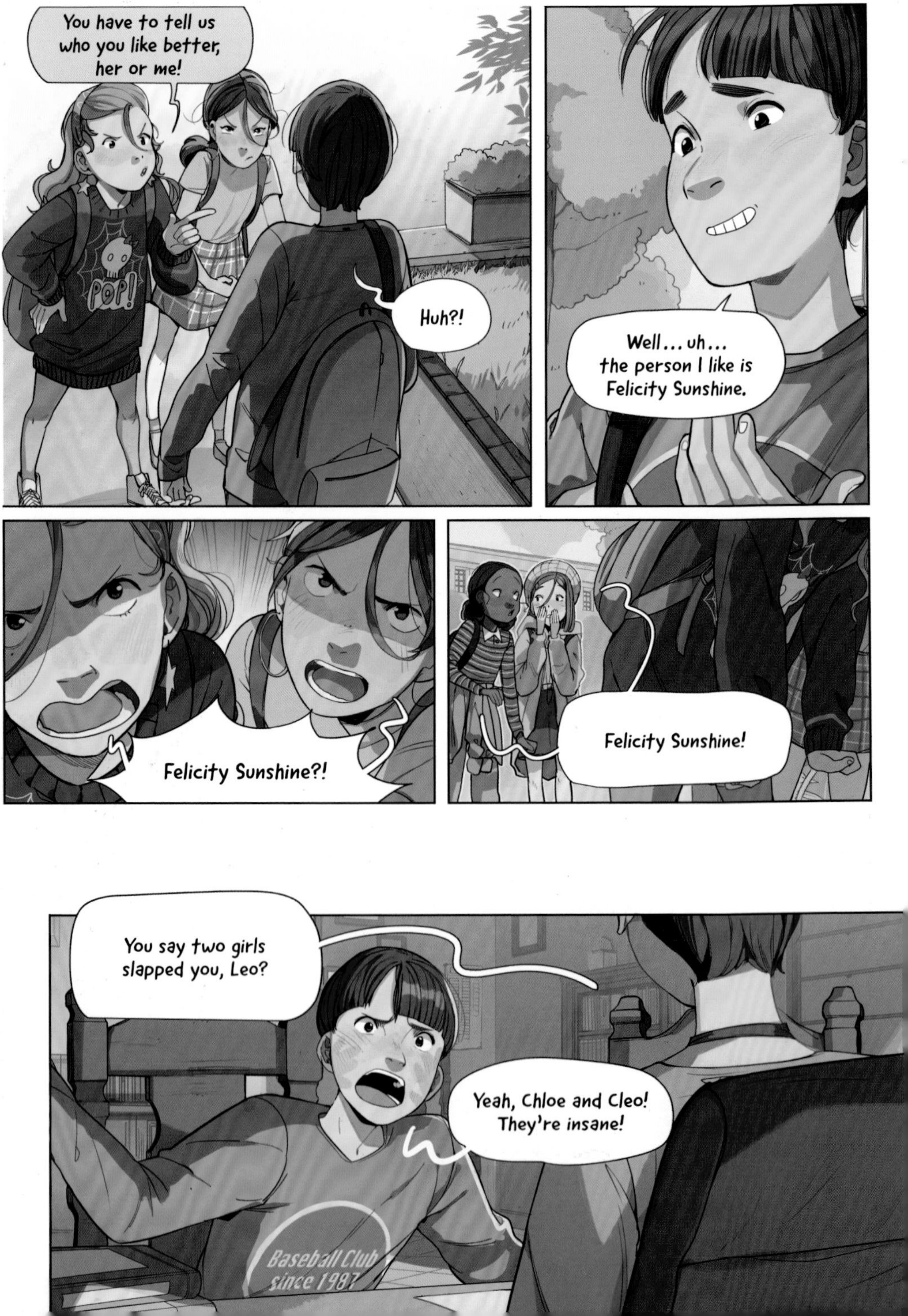
You have to tell us who you like better, her or me!
Huh?!
Well... uh... the person I like is Felicity Sunshine.
Felicity Sunshine?!
Felicity Sunshine!
You say two girls slapped you, Leo?
Yeah, Chloe and Cleo! They're insane!
Baseball Club since 1987

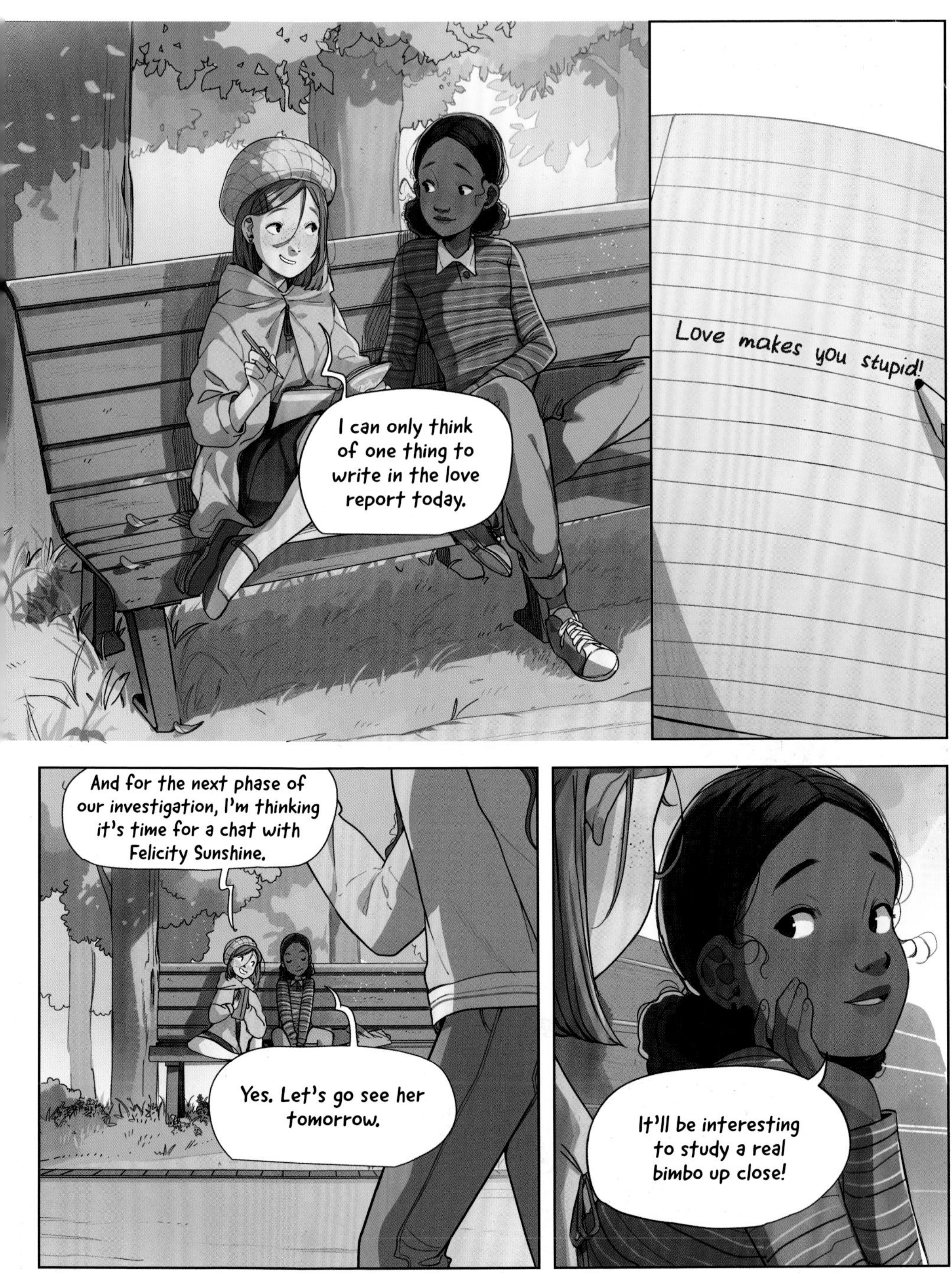
I can only think of one thing to write in the love report today.
Love makes you stupid!
And for the next phase of our investigation, I'm thinking it's time for a chat with Felicity Sunshine.
Yes. Let's go see her tomorrow.
It'll be interesting to study a real bimbo up close!

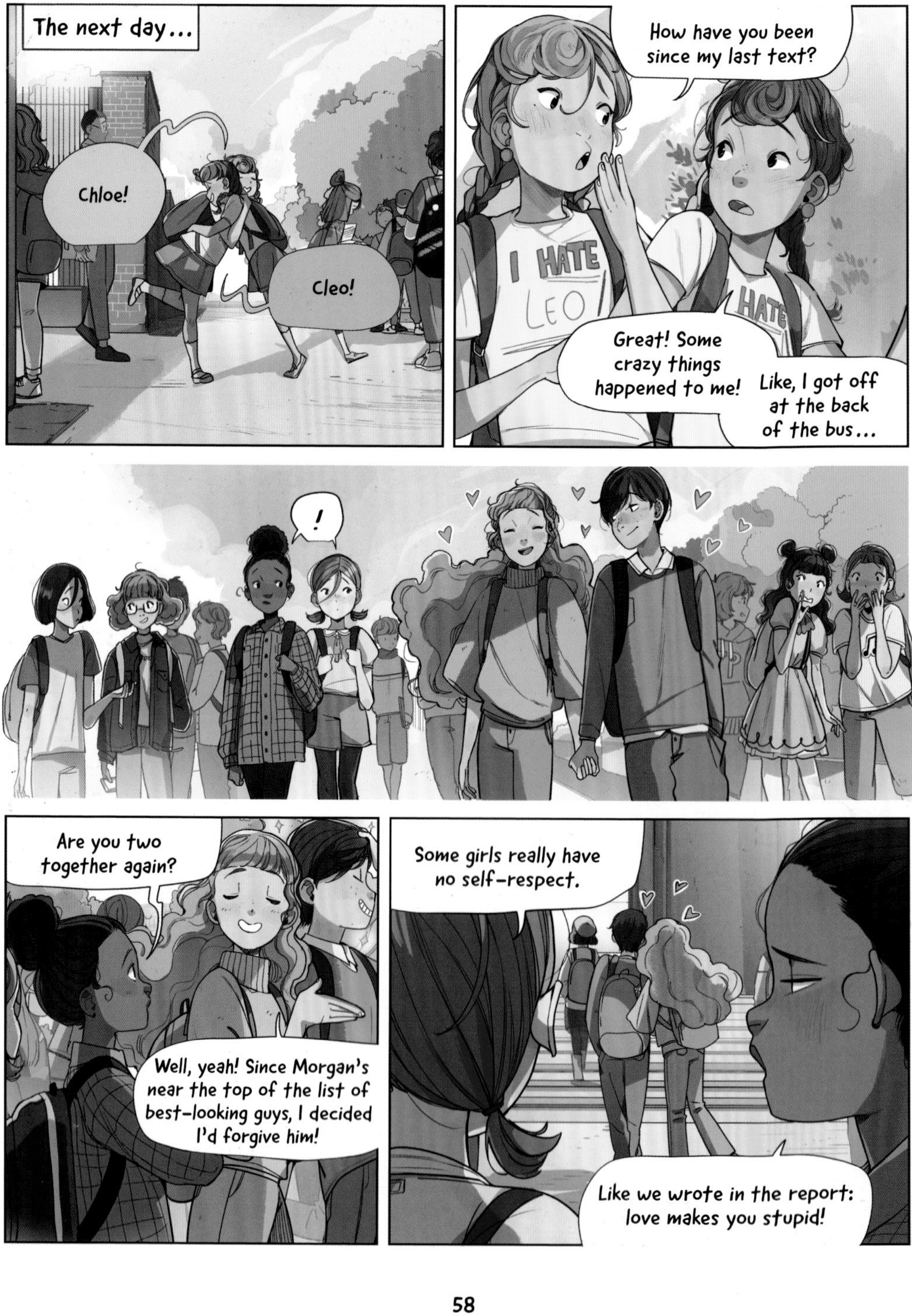
The next day...
Chloe!
Cleo!
How have you been since my last text?
I HATE LEO
I HATE
Great! Some crazy things happened to me!
Like, I got off at the back of the bus...
!
Are you two together again?
Well, yeah! Since Morgan's near the top of the list of best-looking guys, I decided I'd forgive him!
Some girls really have no self-respect.
Like we wrote in the report: love makes you stupid!

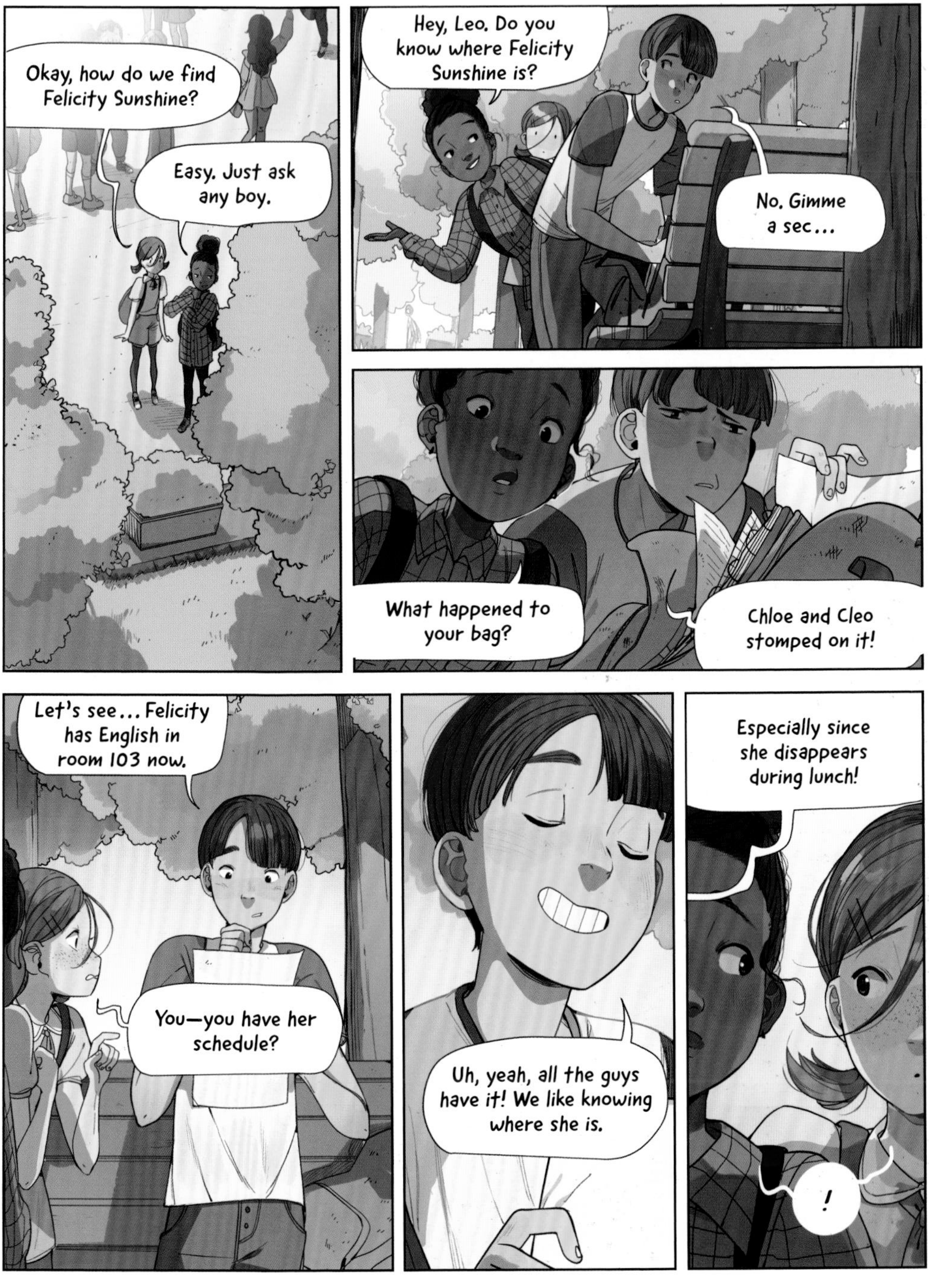
Okay, how do we find Felicity Sunshine?
Easy. Just ask any boy.
Hey, Leo. Do you know where Felicity Sunshine is?
No. Gimme a sec...
What happened to your bag?
Chloe and Cleo stomped on it!
Let's see... Felicity has English in room 103 now.
You—you have her schedule?
Uh, yeah, all the guys have it! We like knowing where she is.
Especially since she disappears during lunch!
!

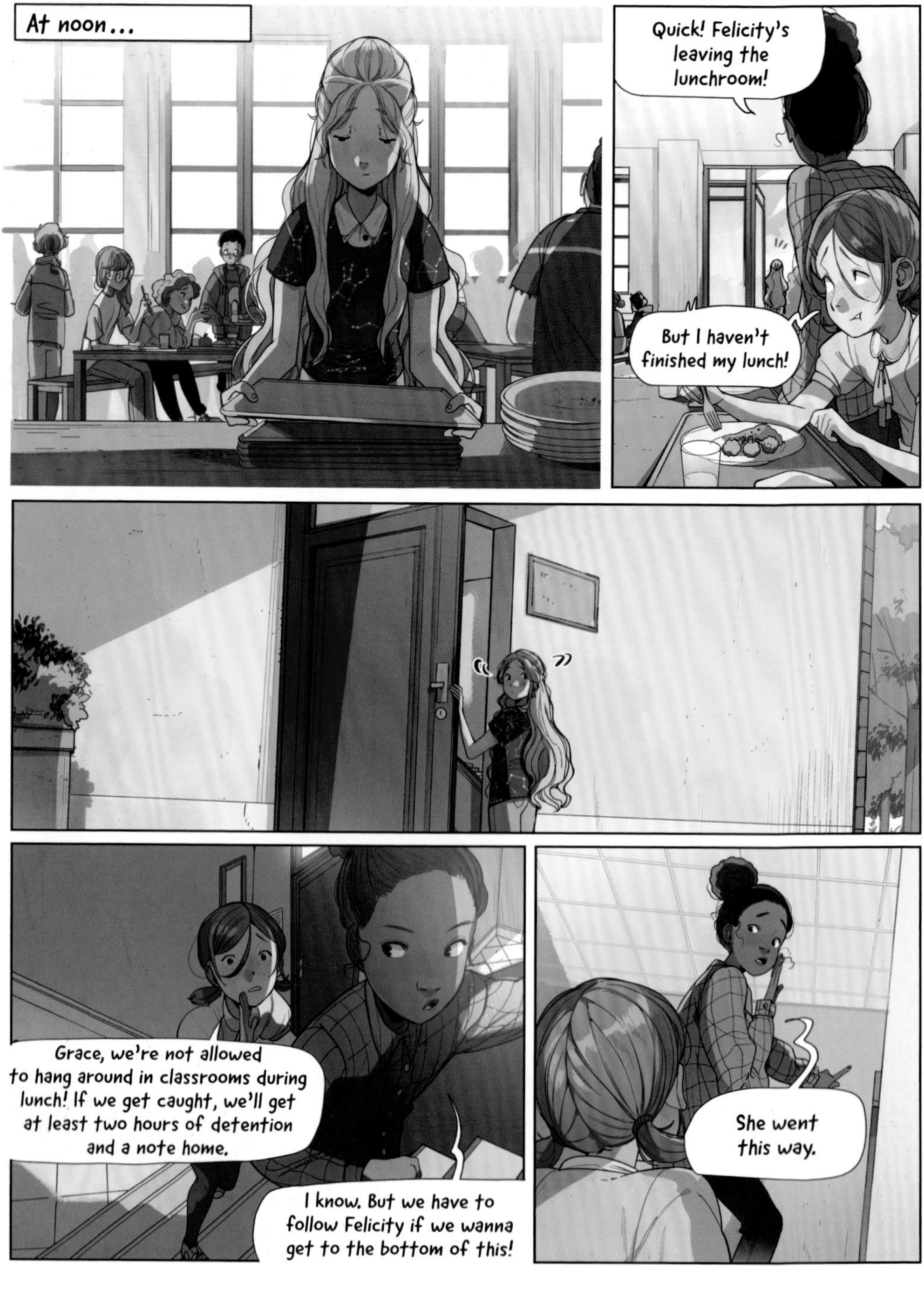
At noon...
Quick! Felicity's leaving the lunchroom!
But I haven't finished my lunch!
Grace, we're not allowed to hang around in classrooms during lunch! If we get caught, we'll get at least two hours of detention and a note home.
I know. But we have to follow Felicity if we wanna get to the bottom of this!
She went this way.

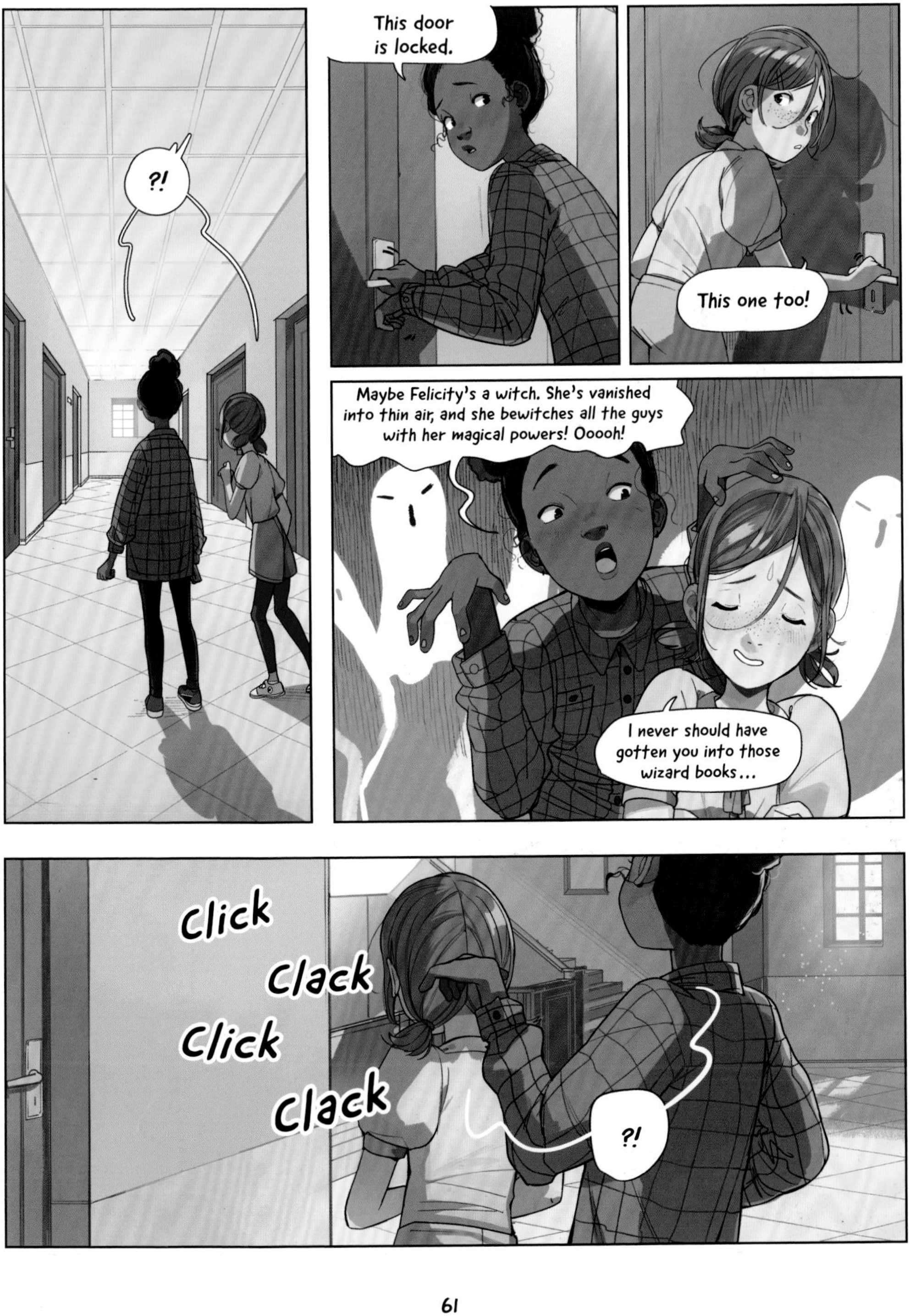
?!
This door is locked.
This one too!
Maybe Felicity's a witch. She's vanished into thin air, and she bewitches all the guys with her magical powers! Ooooh!
I never should have gotten you into those wizard books...
Click
Clack
Click
Clack
?!

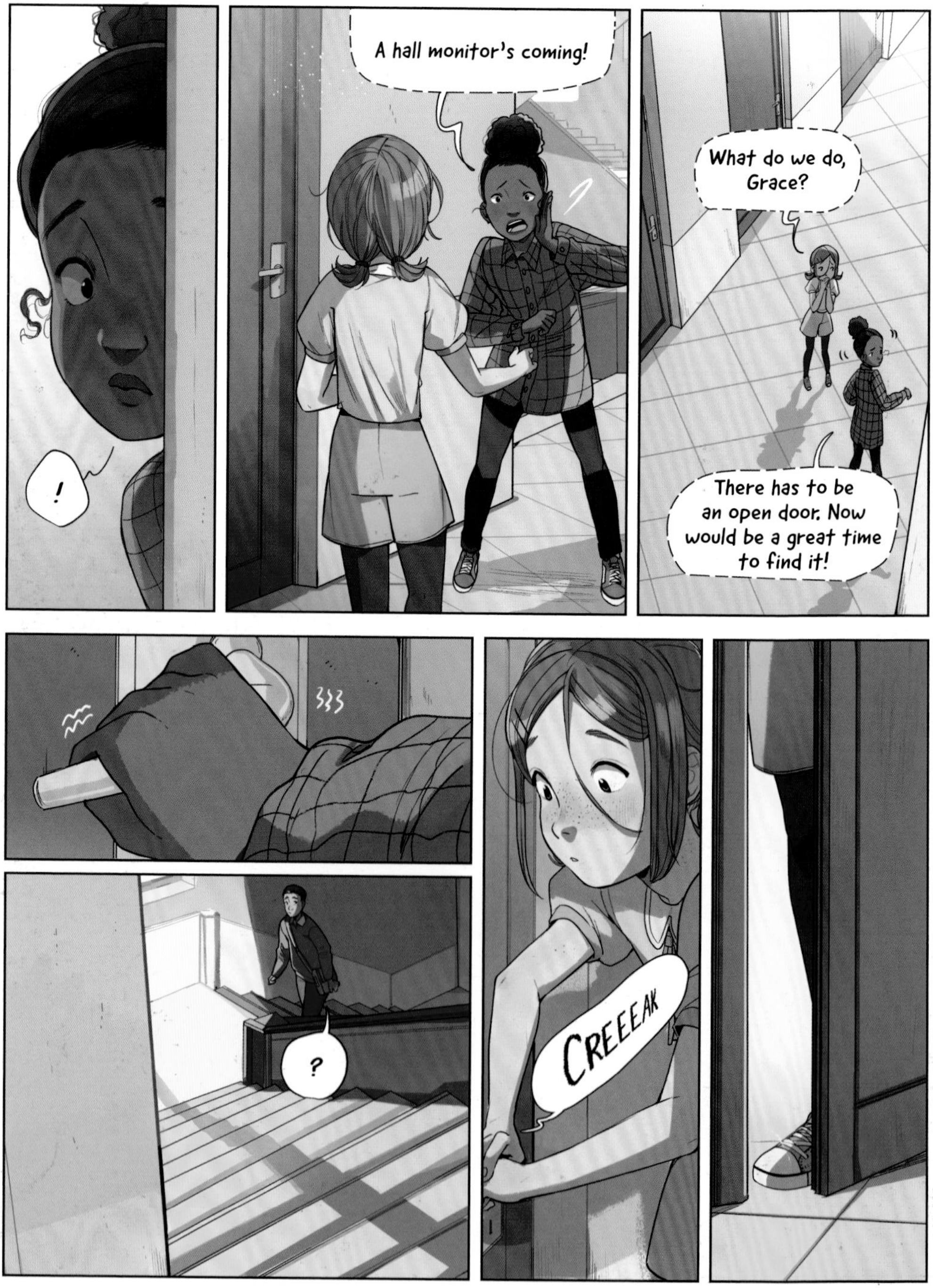
!
A hall monitor's coming!
What do we do, Grace?
There has to be an open door. Now would be a great time to find it!
?
CREEEAK

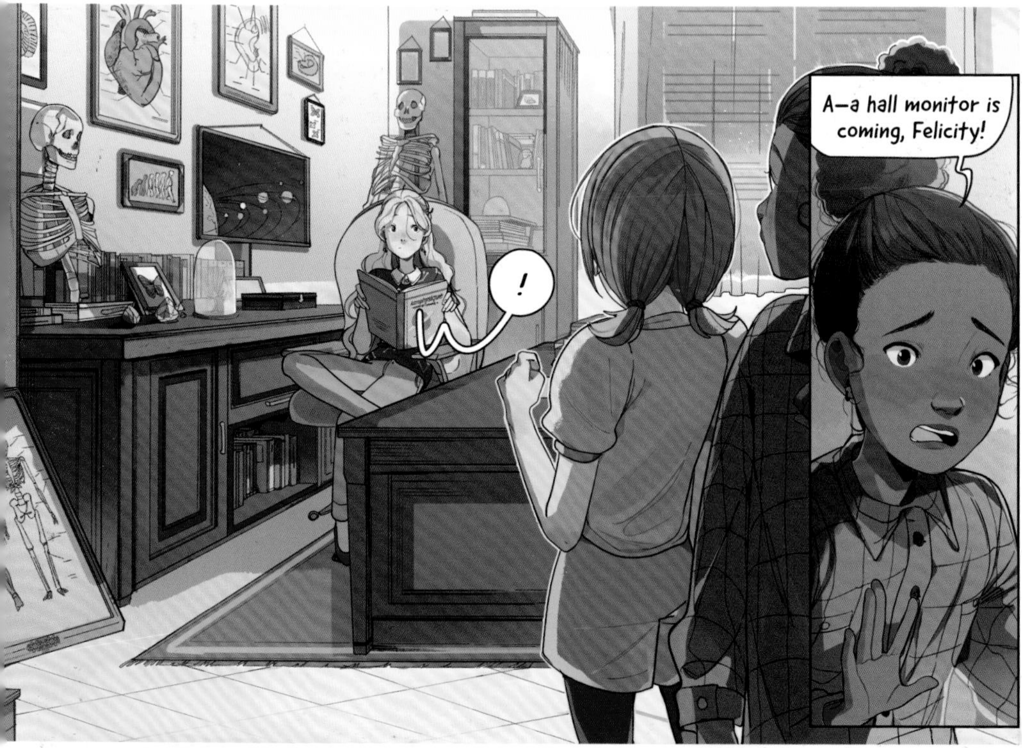
!
A—a hall monitor is coming, Felicity!

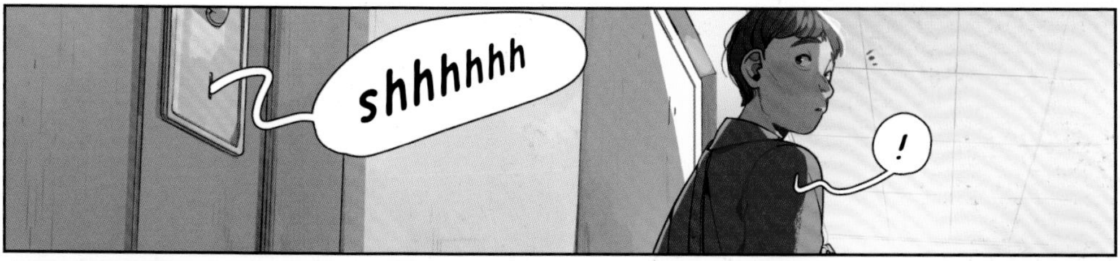
shhhhhh
!

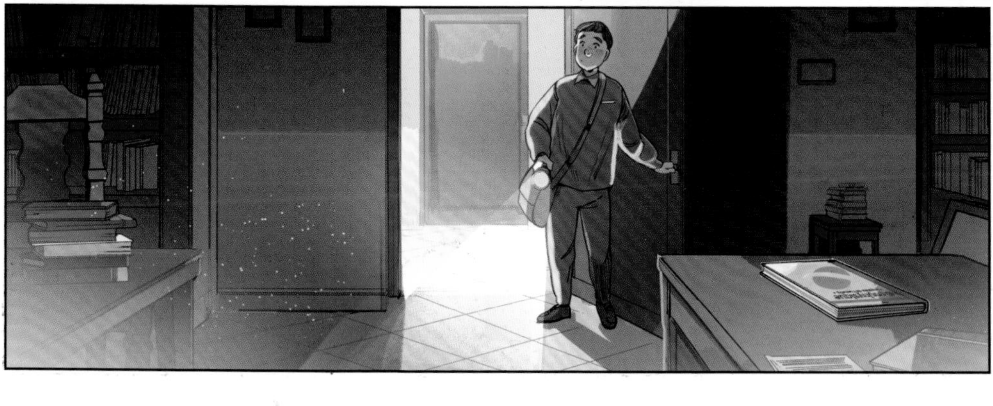

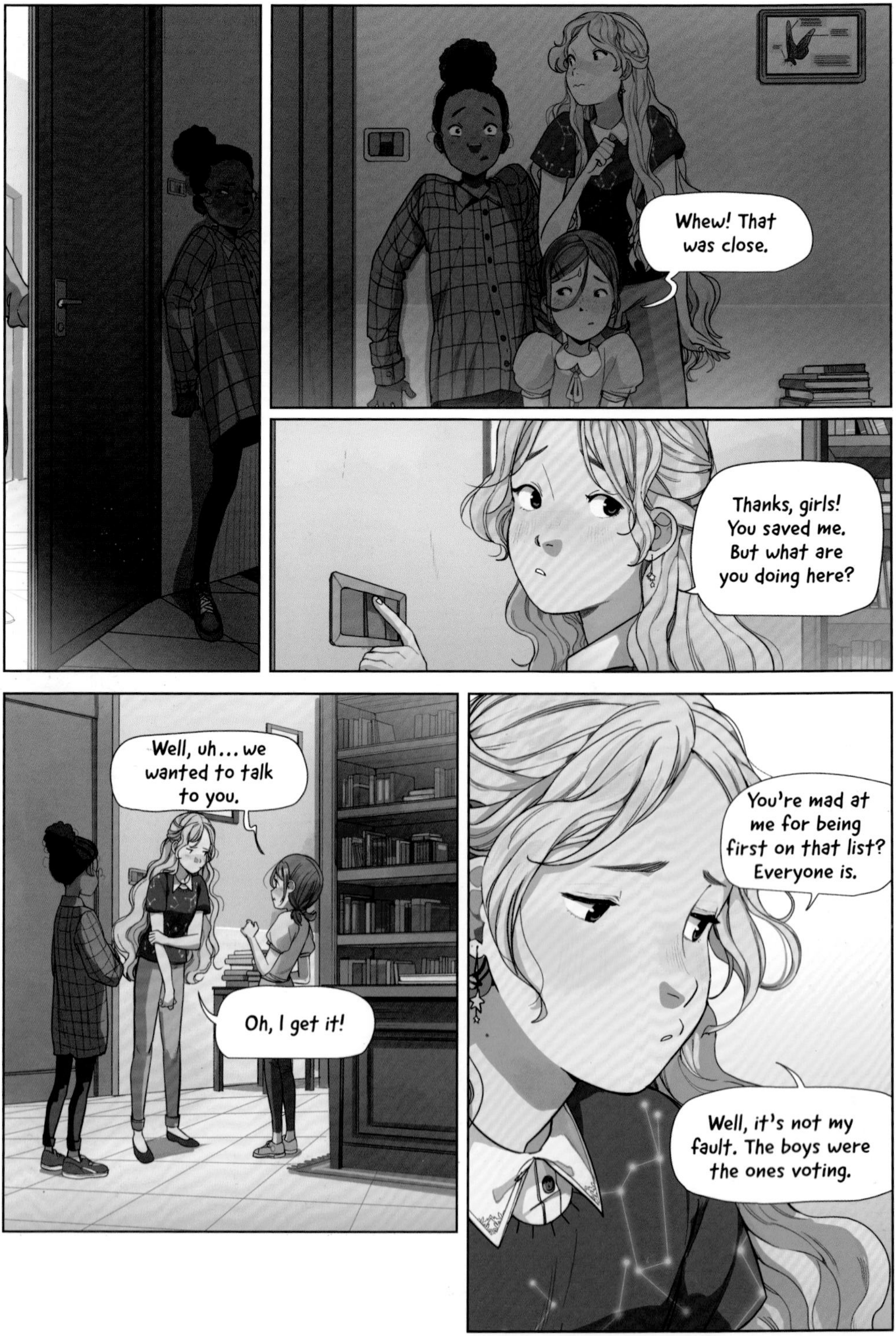
Whew! That was close.
Thanks, girls! You saved me. But what are you doing here?
Well, uh... we wanted to talk to you.
Oh, I get it!
You're mad at me for being first on that list? Everyone is.
Well, it's not my fault. The boys were the ones voting.

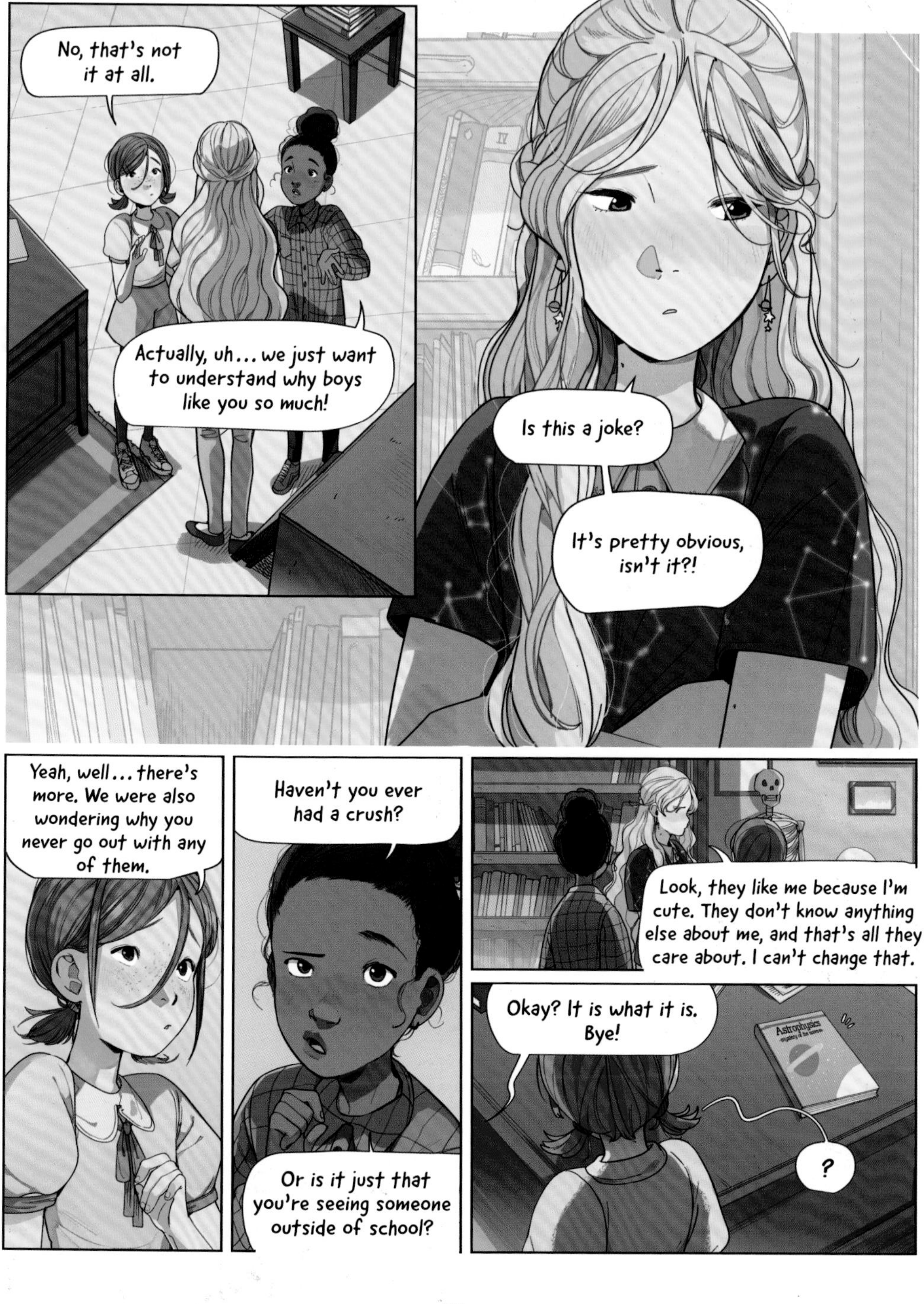
No, that's not it at all.
Actually, uh... we just want to understand why boys like you so much!
Is this a joke?
It's pretty obvious, isn't it?!
Yeah, well... there's more. We were also wondering why you never go out with any of them.
Haven't you ever had a crush?
Or is it just that you're seeing someone outside of school?
Look, they like me because I'm cute. They don't know anything else about me, and that's all they care about. I can't change that.
Okay? It is what it is. Bye!
Astrophysics
?

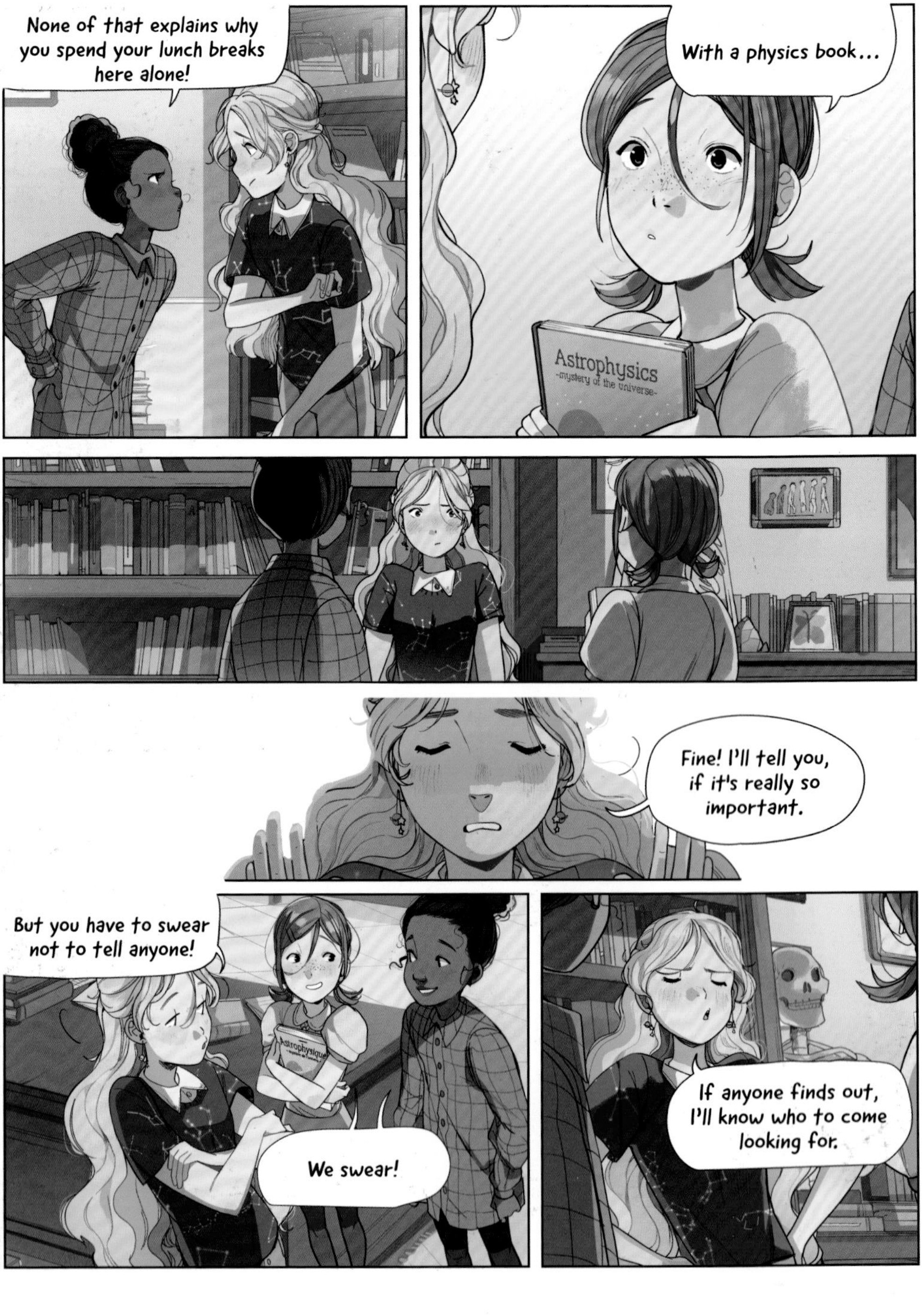
None of that explains why you spend your lunch breaks here alone!
With a physics book...
Astrophysics
-mystery of the universe-
Fine! I'll tell you, if it's really so important.
But you have to swear not to tell anyone!
Astrophysique
We swear!
If anyone finds out, I'll know who to come looking for.

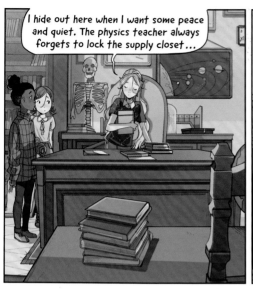

I hide out here when I want some peace and quiet. The physics teacher always forgets to lock the supply closet...

The thing is, I'm obsessed with space. My big dream is to become an astrophysicist!

Astro— what?

Astrophysicist. It's what they call scientists who study the planets and the cosmos.

And you haven't told anyone?

No. I don't want people laughing at me or saying it's impossible. I want to keep my dream alive, my own private universe.

Is that why you don't want a boyfriend?

Yes. I'd much rather spend time doing what I love.

Besides, I've never met a guy I could share that with...

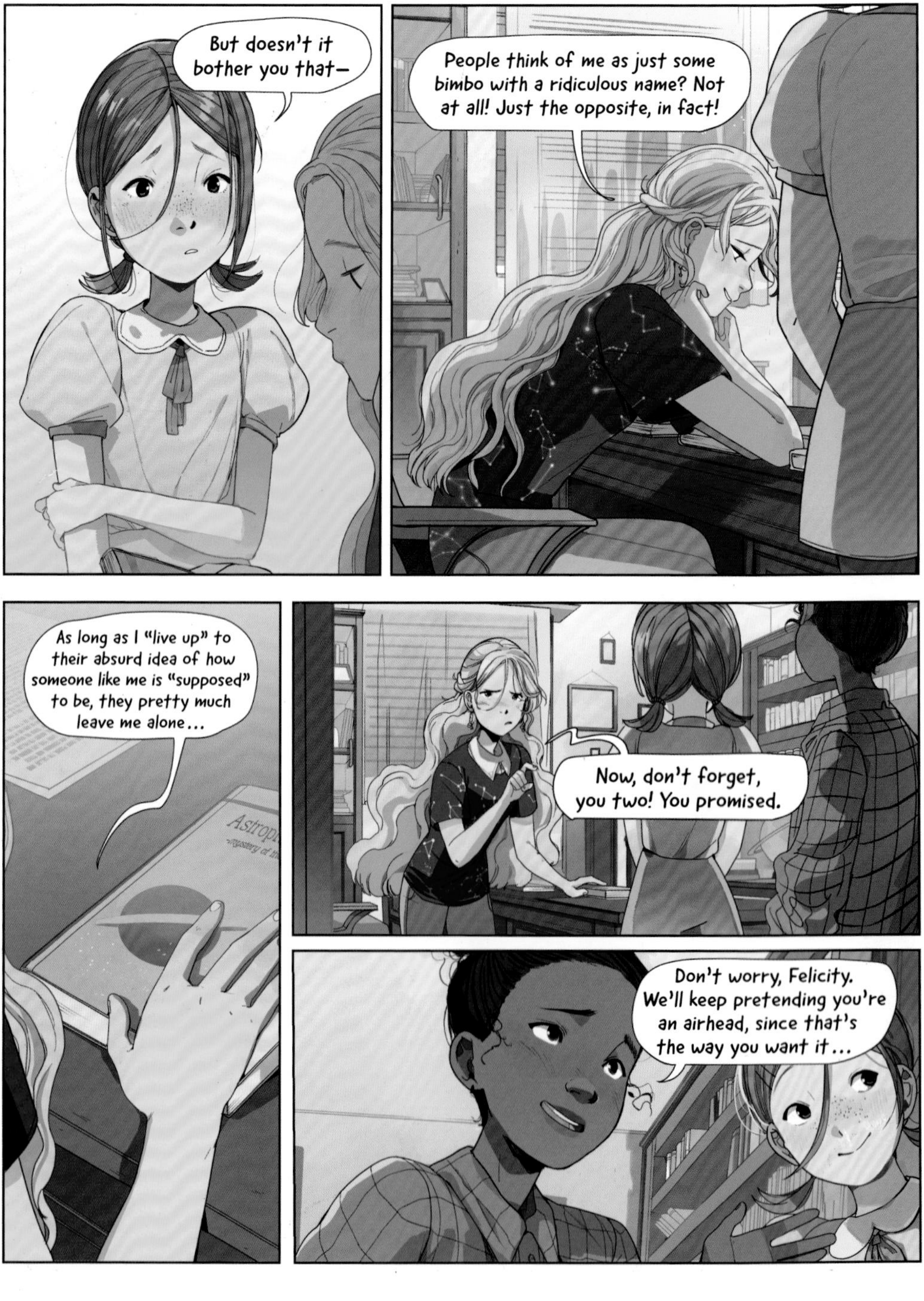
But doesn't it bother you that—
People think of me as just some bimbo with a ridiculous name? Not at all! Just the opposite, in fact!
As long as I "live up" to their absurd idea of how someone like me is "supposed" to be, they pretty much leave me alone...
Now, don't forget, you two! You promised.
Don't worry, Felicity. We'll keep pretending you're an airhead, since that's the way you want it...

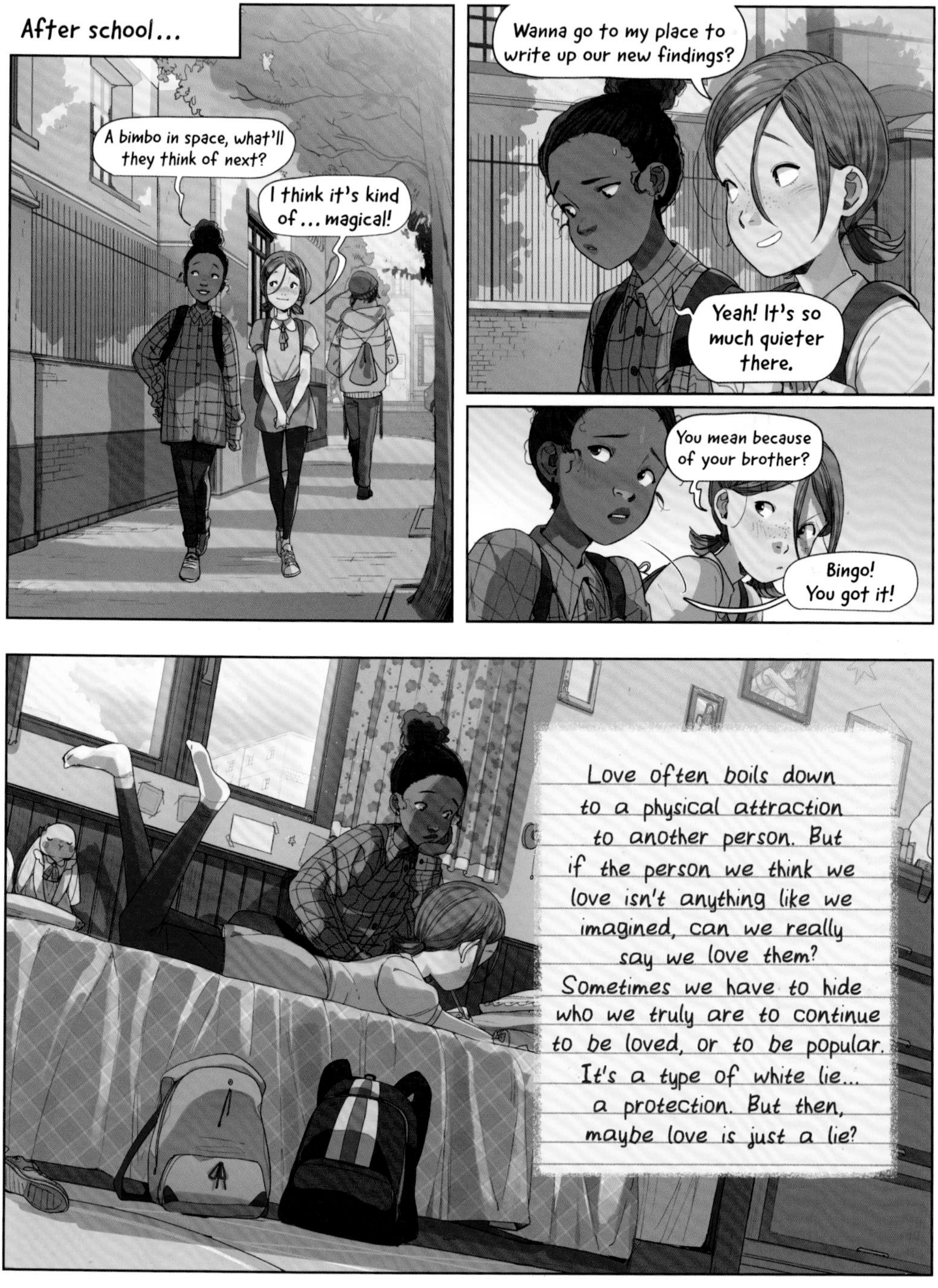
After school...
A bimbo in space, what'll they think of next?
I think it's kind of... magical!
Wanna go to my place to write up our new findings?
Yeah! It's so much quieter there.
You mean because of your brother?
Bingo! You got it!
Love often boils down to a physical attraction to another person. But if the person we think we love isn't anything like we imagined, can we really say we love them? Sometimes we have to hide who we truly are to continue to be loved, or to be popular. It's a type of white lie... a protection. But then, maybe love is just a lie?

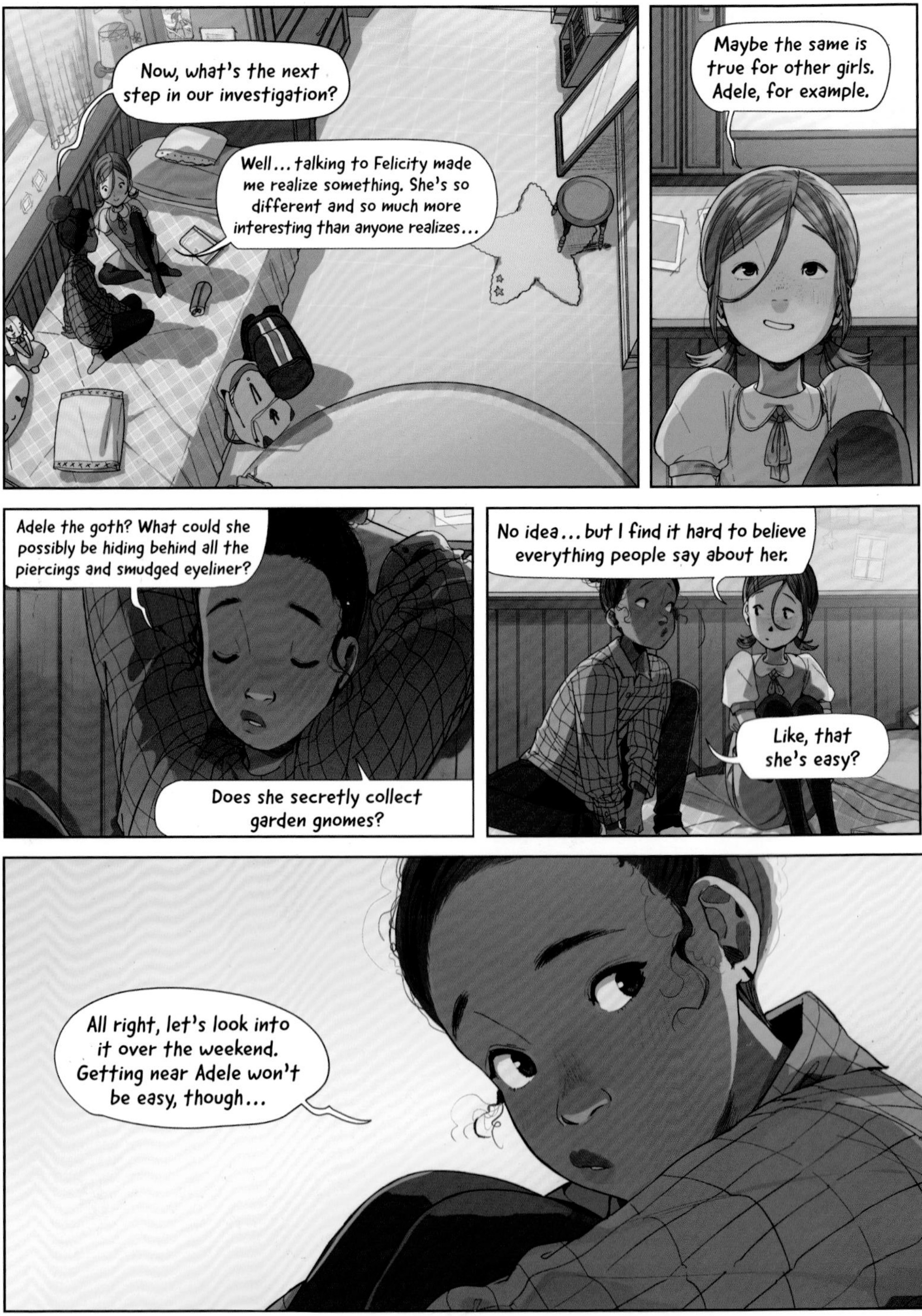
Now, what's the next step in our investigation?
Well... talking to Felicity made me realize something. She's so different and so much more interesting than anyone realizes...
Maybe the same is true for other girls. Adele, for example.
Adele the goth? What could she possibly be hiding behind all the piercings and smudged eyeliner?
Does she secretly collect garden gnomes?
No idea... but I find it hard to believe everything people say about her.
Like, that she's easy?
All right, let's look into it over the weekend. Getting near Adele won't be easy, though...

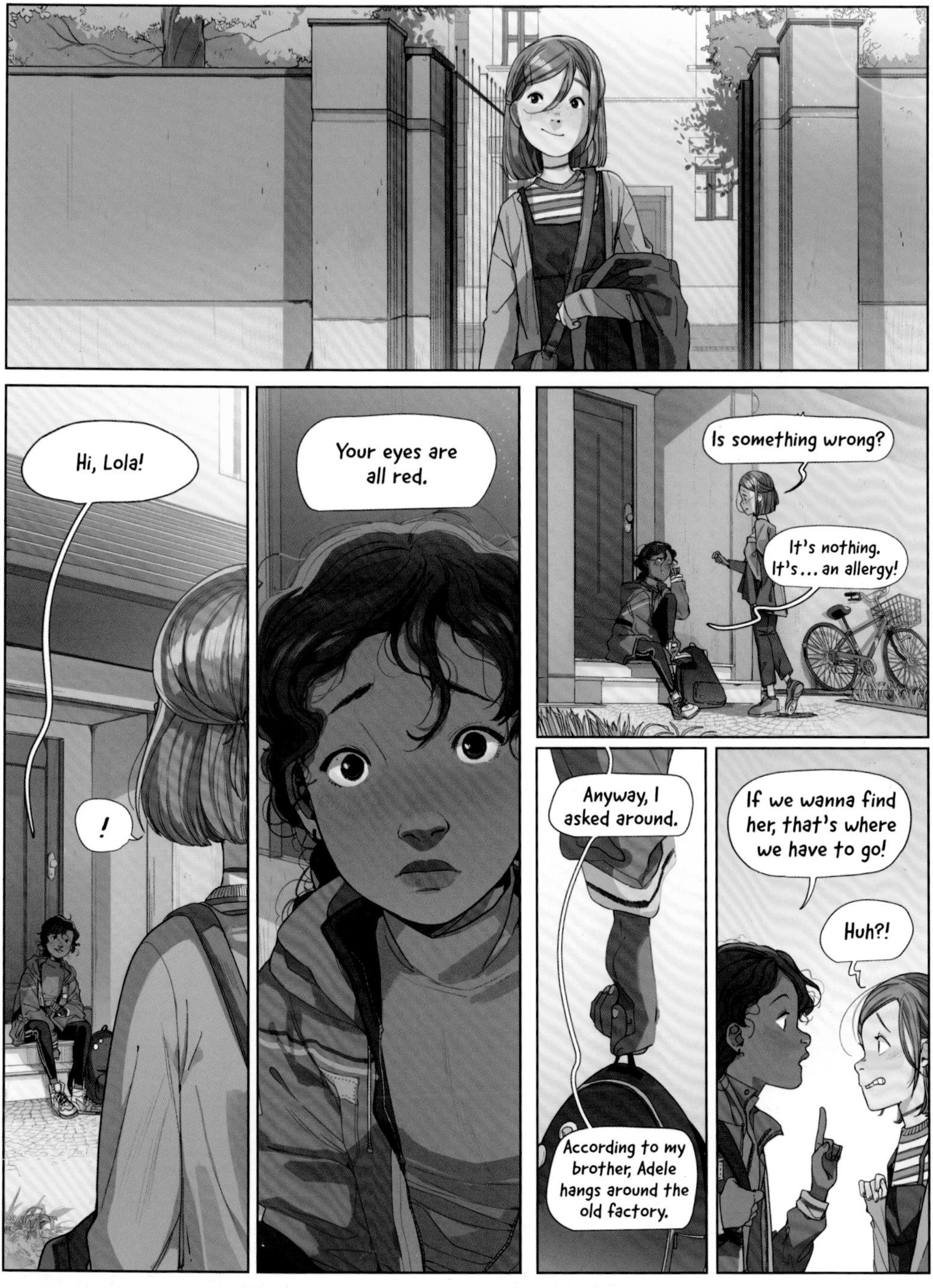
Hi, Lola!
!
Your eyes are all red.
Is something wrong?
It's nothing. It's... an allergy!
Anyway, I asked around.
According to my brother, Adele hangs around the old factory.
If we wanna find her, that's where we have to go!
Huh?!

Grace, I—I feel kinda nervous!

Just admit you're scared, Lola.

I won't lie, me too!

But if we want to talk to Adele, we have no choice...

You picked the wrong place to take a walk, girls!

?

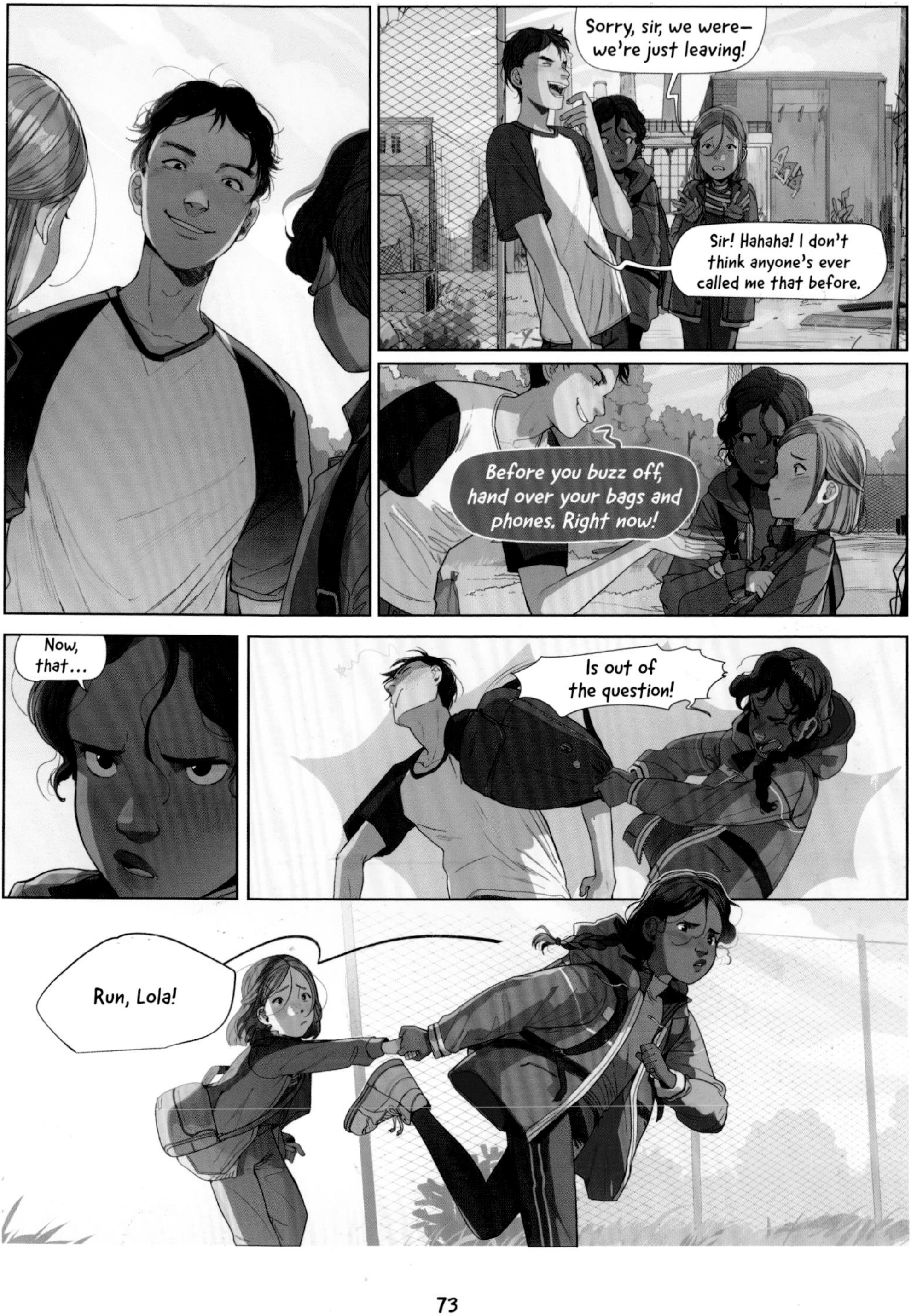
Sorry, sir, we were— we're just leaving!
Sir! Hahaha! I don't think anyone's ever called me that before.
Before you buzz off, hand over your bags and phones. Right now!
Now, that...
Is out of the question!
Run, Lola!

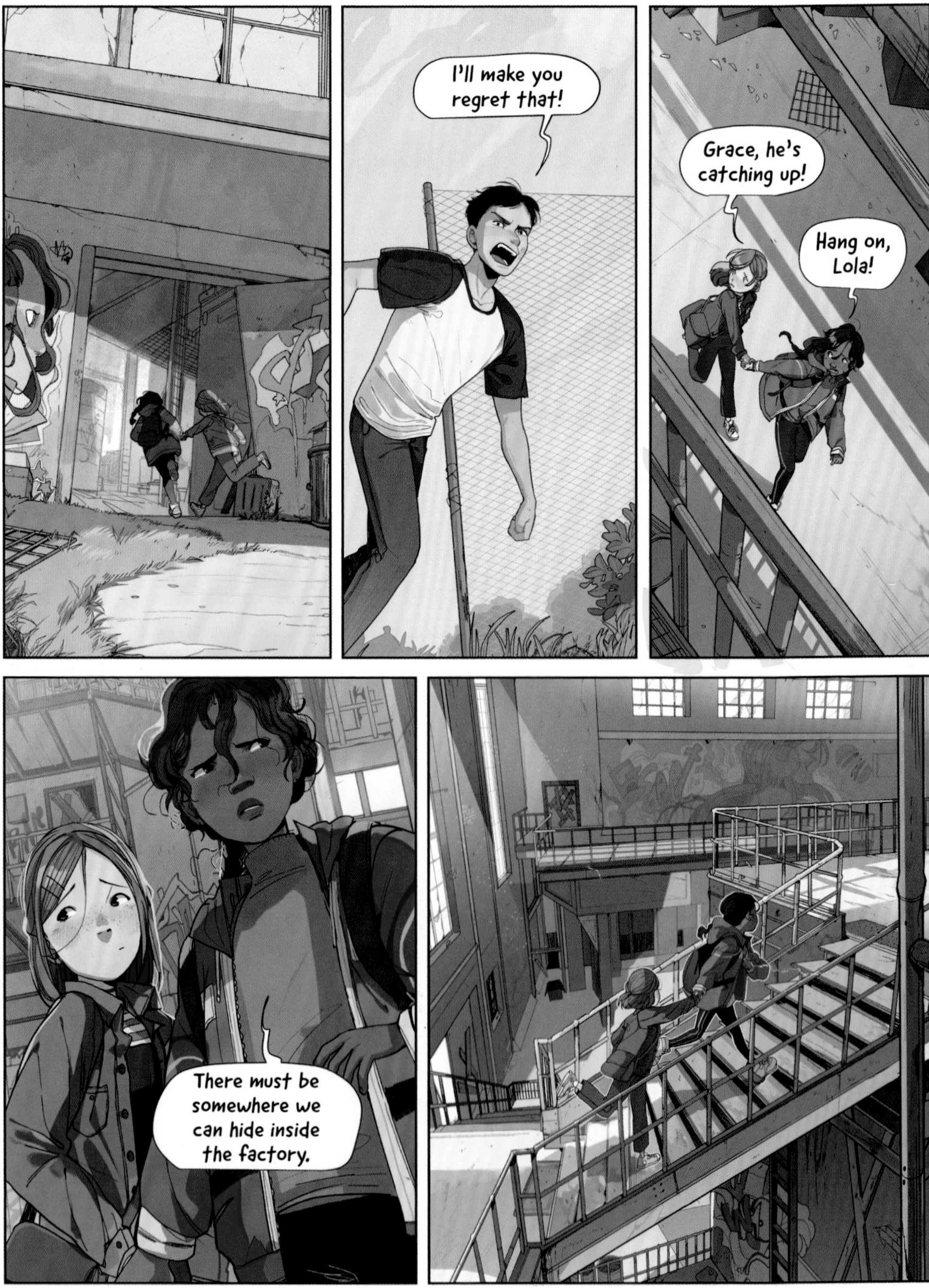
I'll make you regret that!
Grace, he's catching up!
Hang on, Lola!
There must be somewhere we can hide inside the factory.

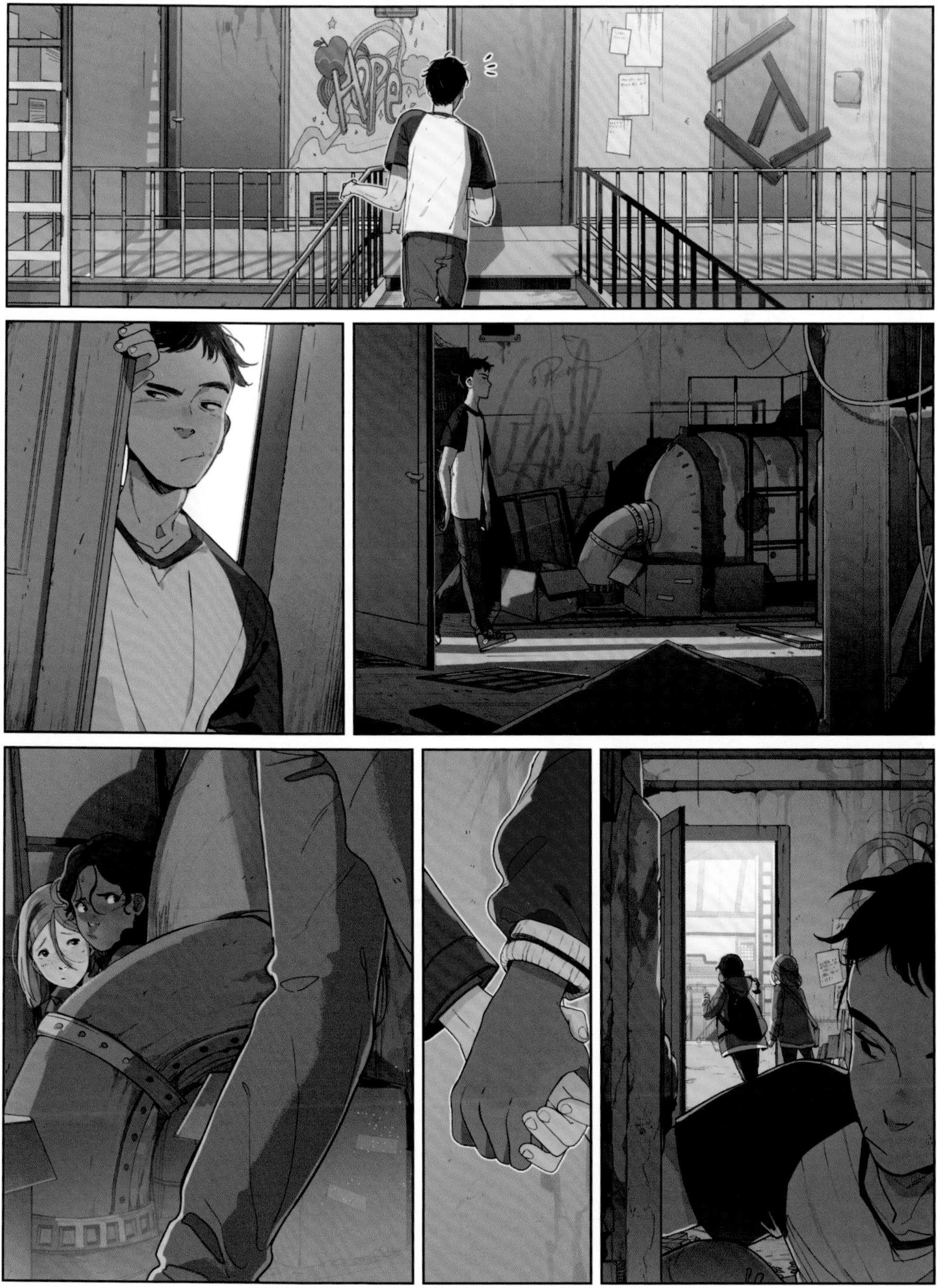
Hope

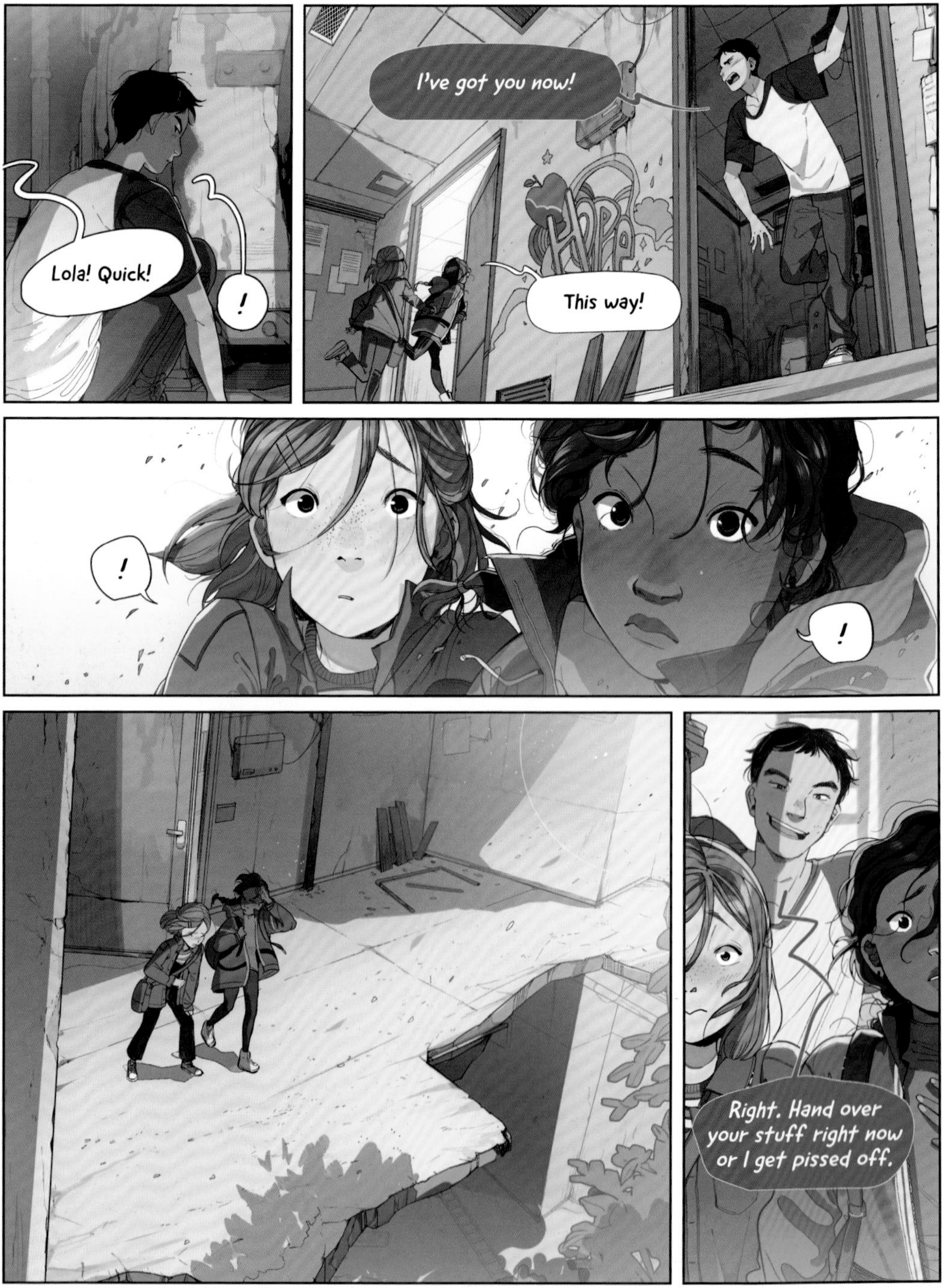

Lola! Quick!
!
I've got you now!
This way!
!
!
Right. Hand over your stuff right now or I get pissed off.

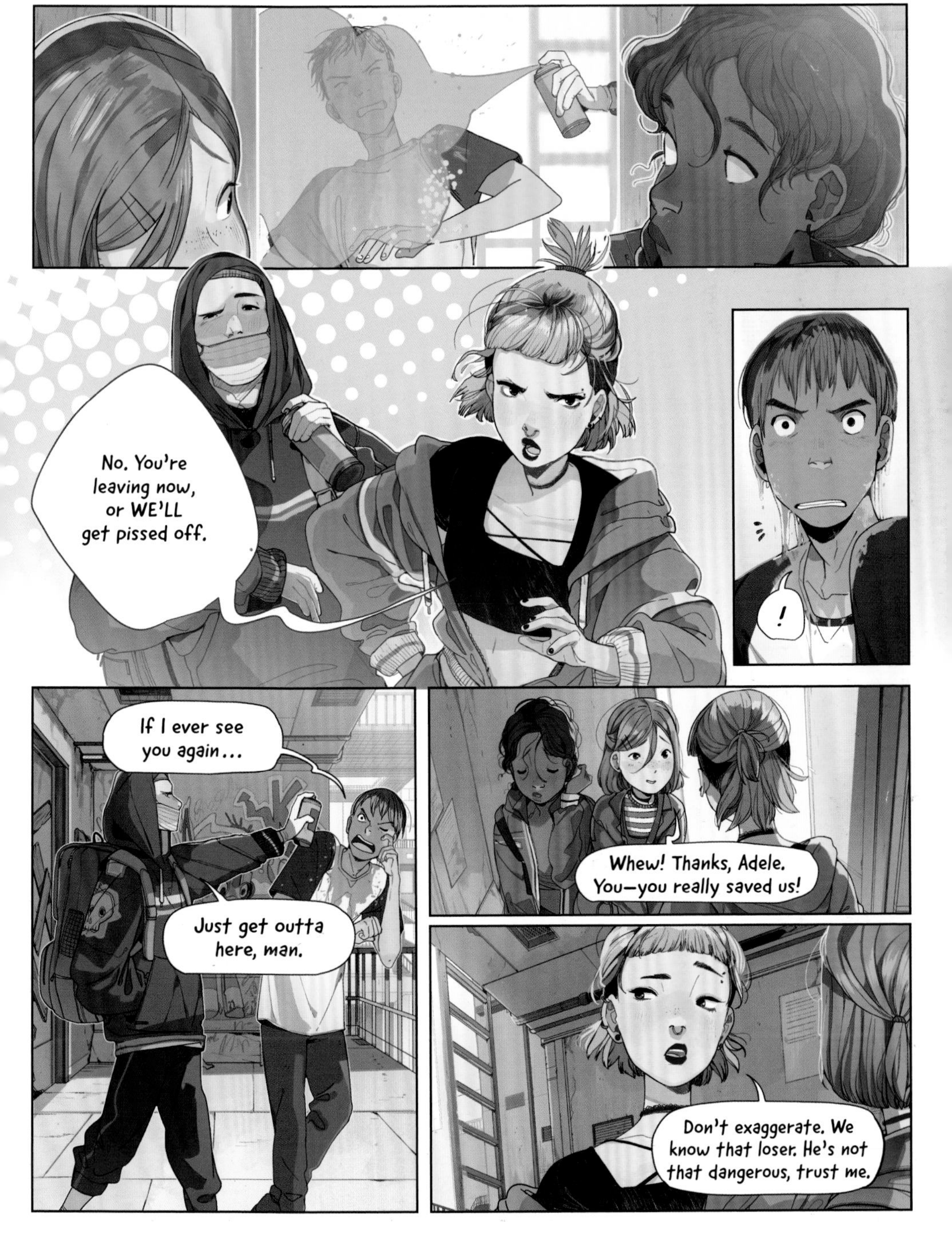
No. You're leaving now, or WE'LL get pissed off.
!
If I ever see you again...
Just get outta here, man.
Whew! Thanks, Adele. You—you really saved us!
Don't exaggerate. We know that loser. He's not that dangerous, trust me.

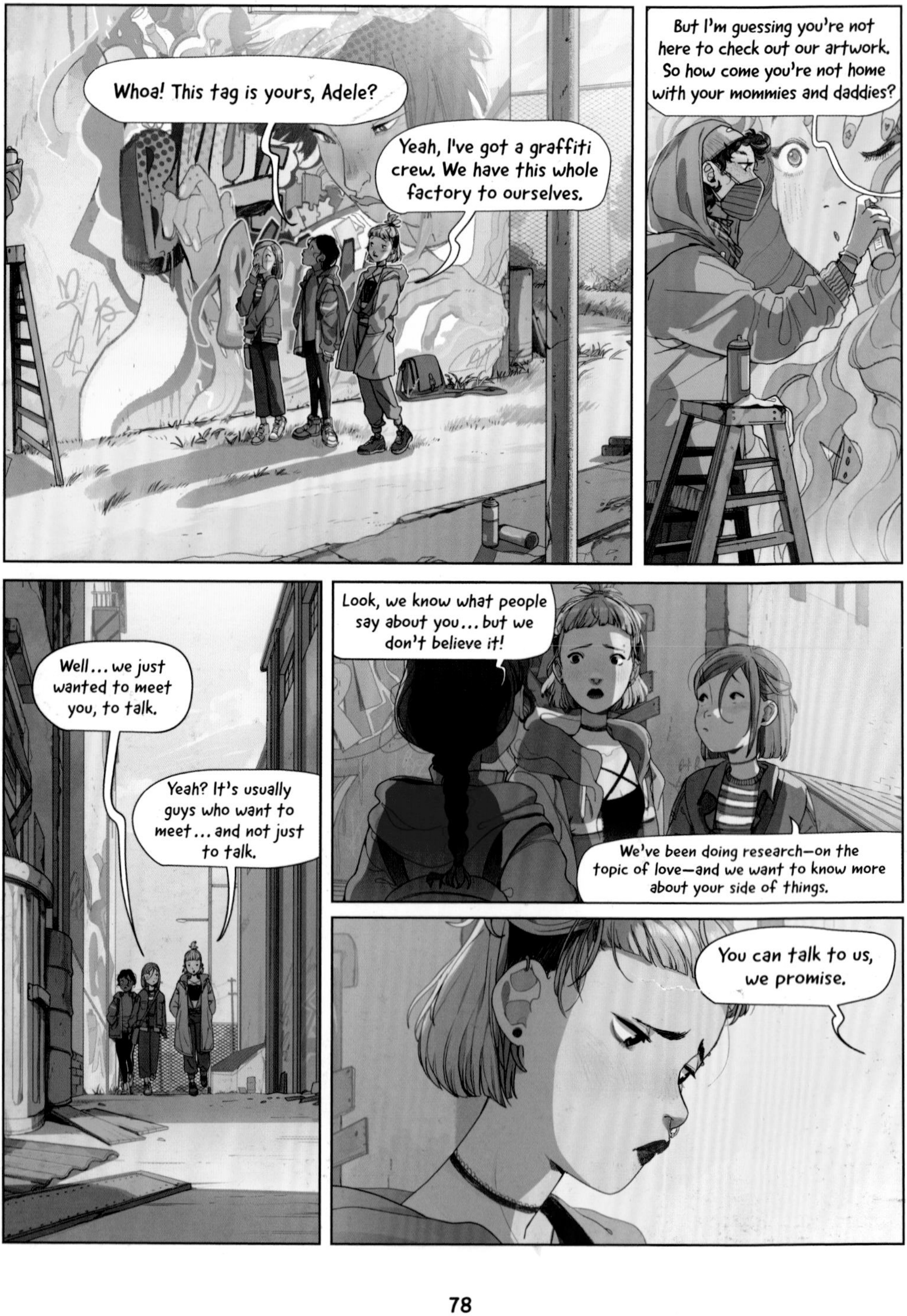
Whoa! This tag is yours, Adele?
Yeah, I've got a graffiti crew. We have this whole factory to ourselves.
But I'm guessing you're not here to check out our artwork. So how come you're not home with your mommies and daddies?
Well... we just wanted to meet you, to talk.
Yeah? It's usually guys who want to meet... and not just to talk.
Look, we know what people say about you... but we don't believe it!
We've been doing research—on the topic of love—and we want to know more about your side of things.
You can talk to us, we promise.

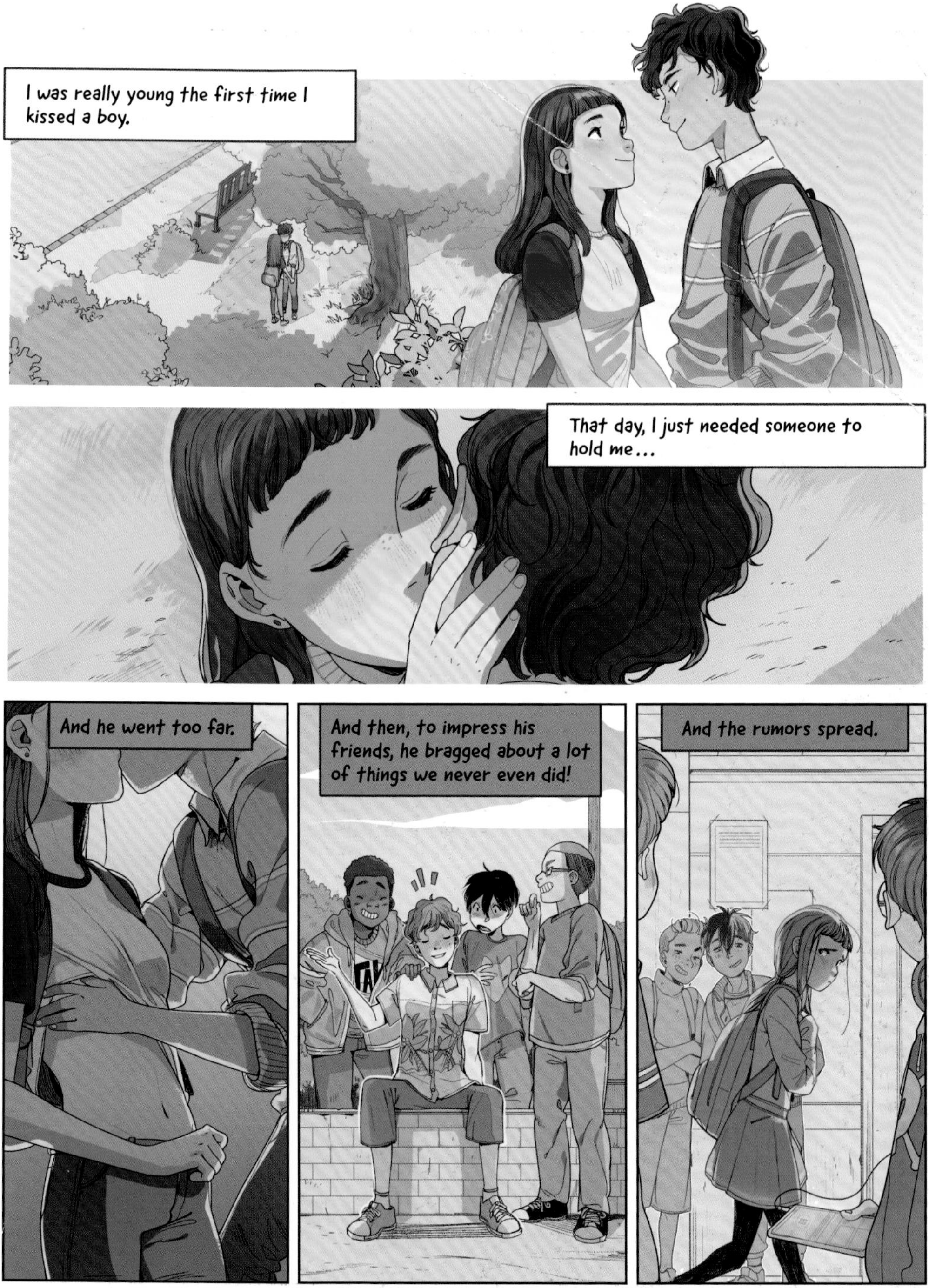
I was really young the first time I kissed a boy.
That day, I just needed someone to hold me...
And he went too far.
And then, to impress his friends, he bragged about a lot of things we never even did!
And the rumors spread.

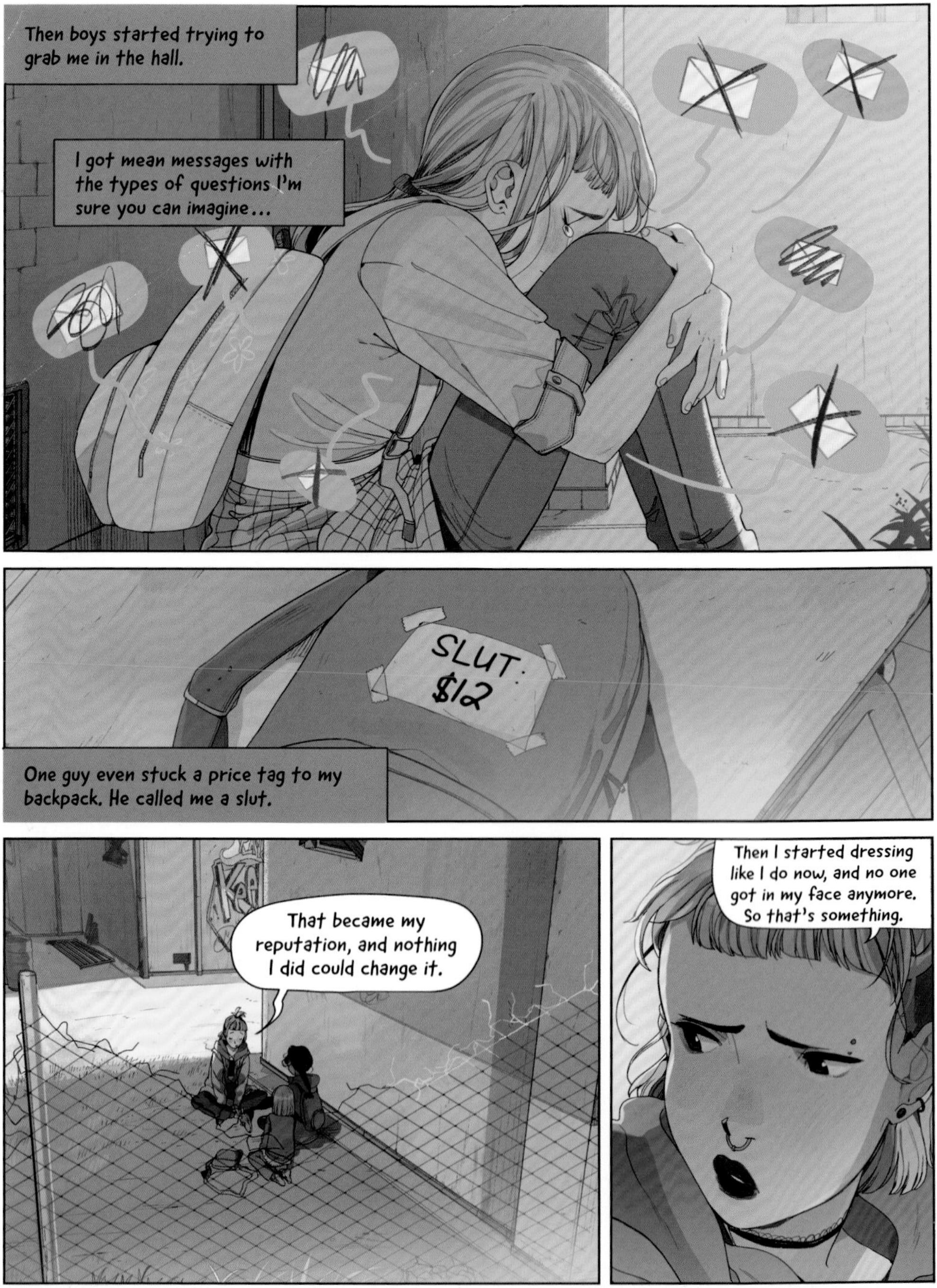
Then boys started trying to grab me in the hall.
I got mean messages with the types of questions I'm sure you can imagine...
SLUT: $12
One guy even stuck a price tag to my backpack. He called me a slut.
That became my reputation, and nothing I did could change it.
Then I started dressing like I do now, and no one got in my face anymore. So that's something.

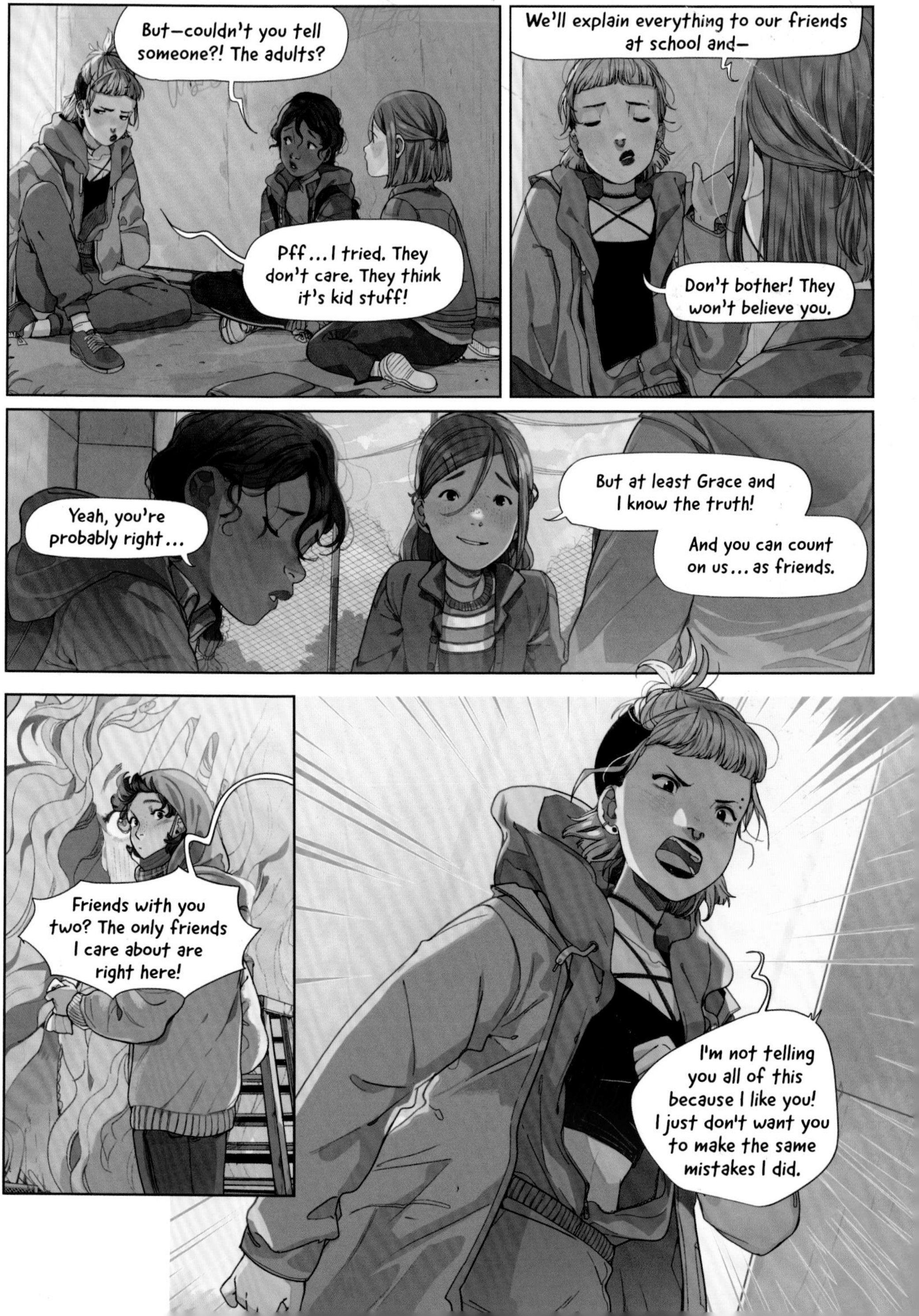
But—couldn't you tell someone?! The adults?
Pff... I tried. They don't care. They think it's kid stuff!
We'll explain everything to our friends at school and—
Don't bother! They won't believe you.
Yeah, you're probably right...
But at least Grace and I know the truth!
And you can count on us... as friends.
Friends with you two? The only friends I care about are right here!
I'm not telling you all of this because I like you! I just don't want you to make the same mistakes I did.

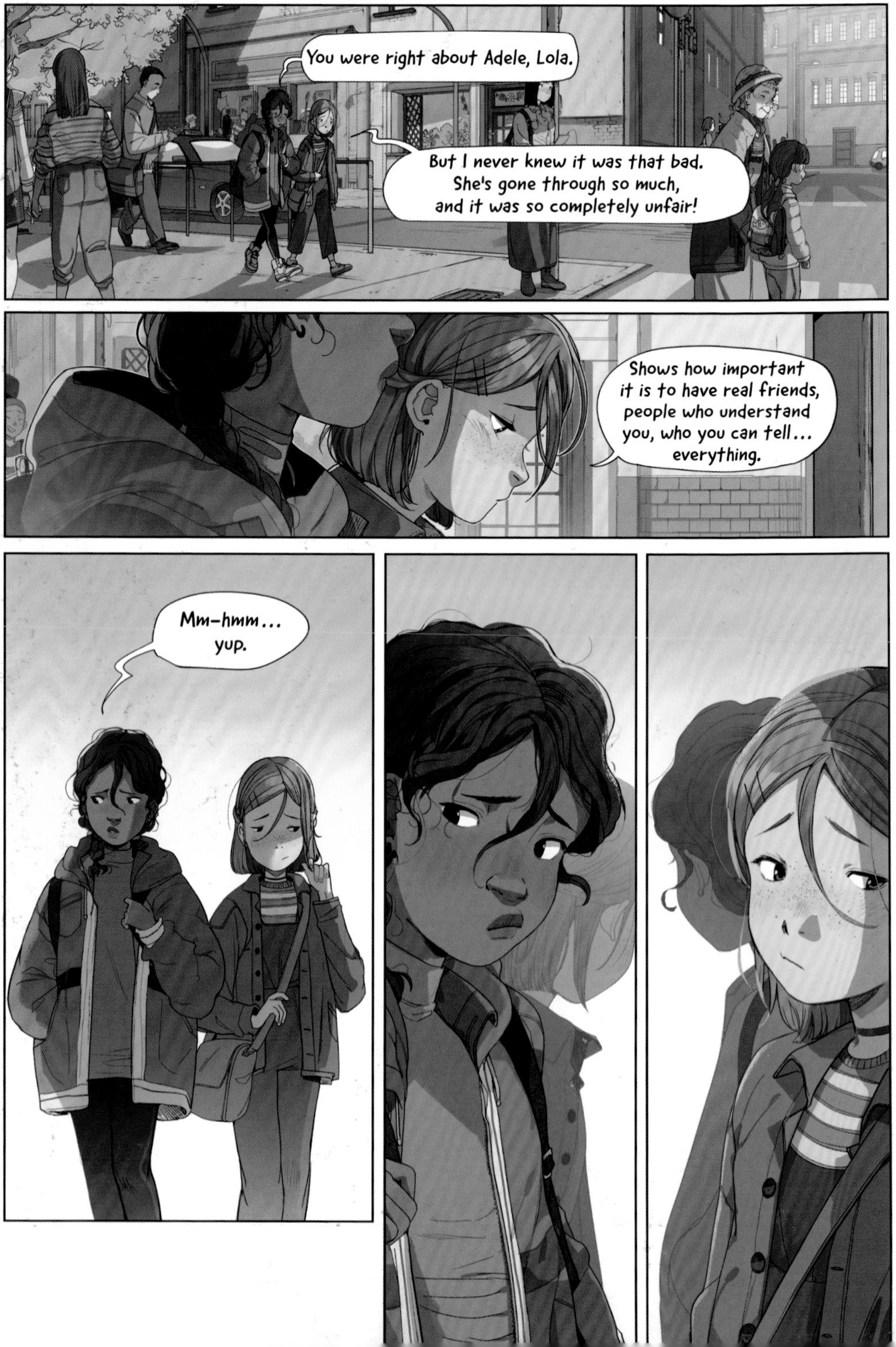
You were right about Adele, Lola.
But I never knew it was that bad. She's gone through so much, and it was so completely unfair!
Shows how important it is to have real friends, people who understand you, who you can tell... everything.
Mm-hmm... yup.

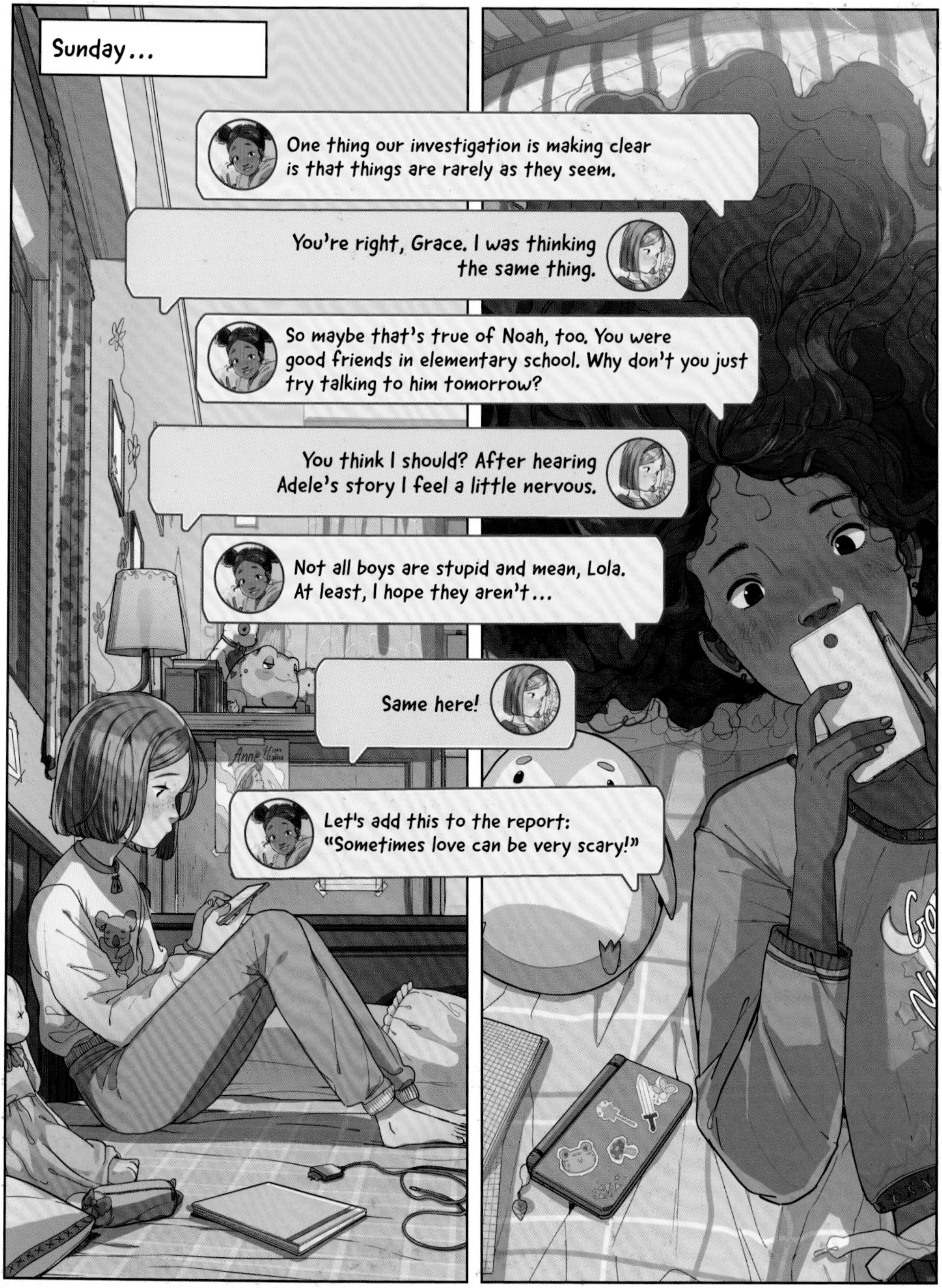
Sunday...
One thing our investigation is making clear is that things are rarely as they seem.
You're right, Grace. I was thinking the same thing.
So maybe that's true of Noah, too. You were good friends in elementary school. Why don't you just try talking to him tomorrow?
You think I should? After hearing Adele's story I feel a little nervous.
Not all boys are stupid and mean, Lola. At least, I hope they aren't...
Same here!
Let's add this to the report: "Sometimes love can be very scary!"

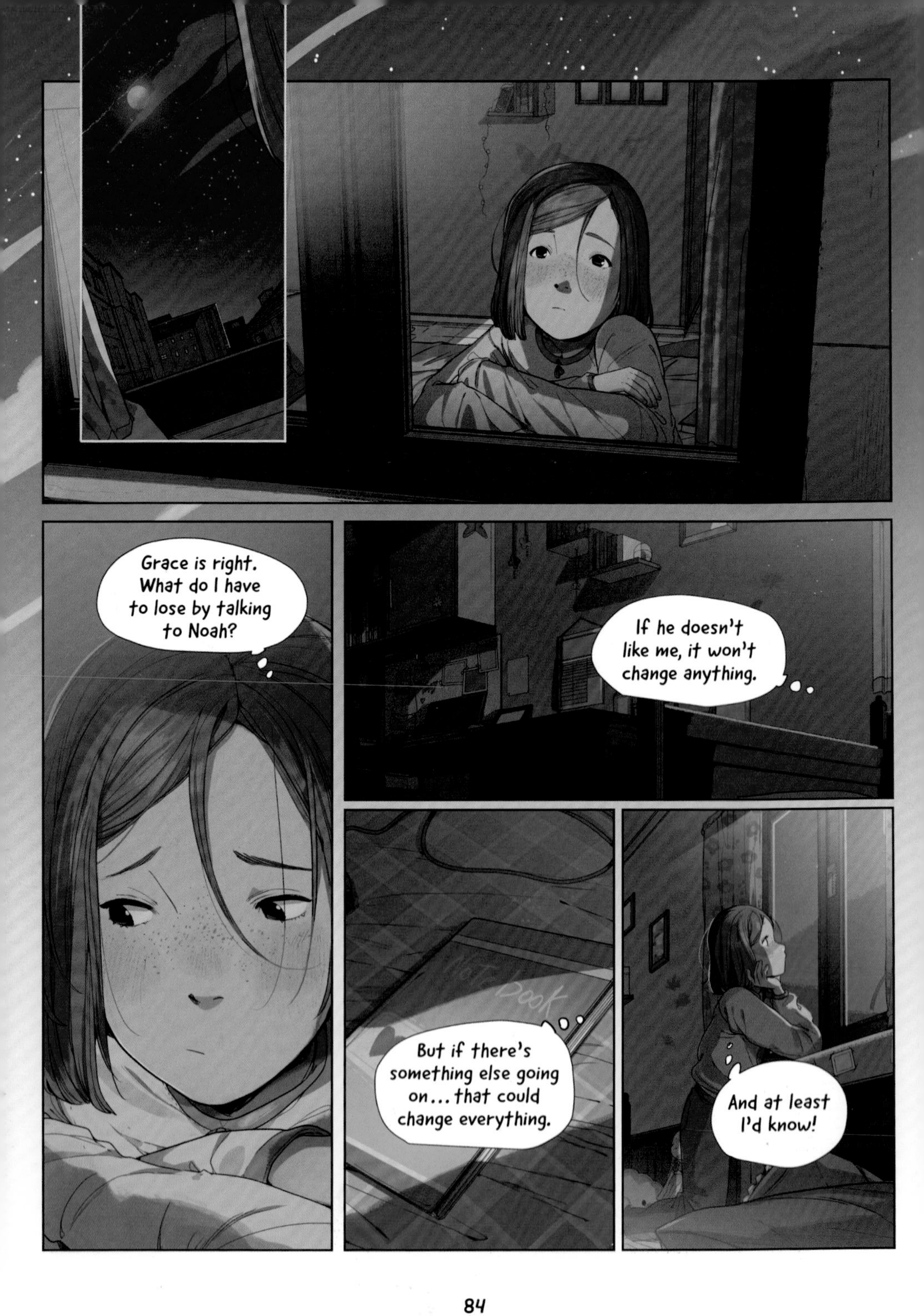
Grace is right. What do I have to lose by talking to Noah?
If he doesn't like me, it won't change anything.
But if there's something else going on... that could change everything.
And at least I'd know!

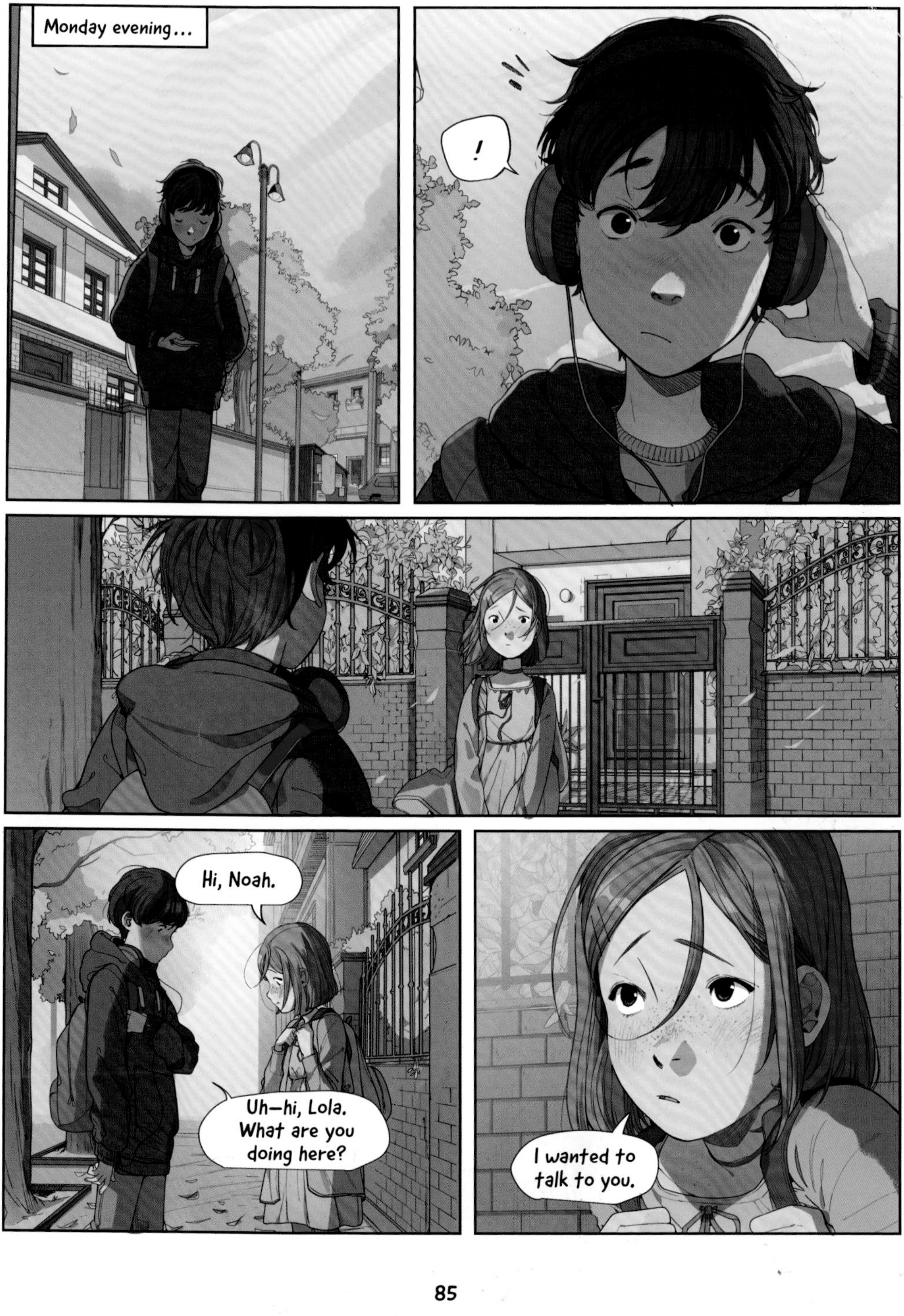
Monday evening...
!
Hi, Noah.
Uh—hi, Lola.
What are you
doing here?
I wanted to
talk to you.

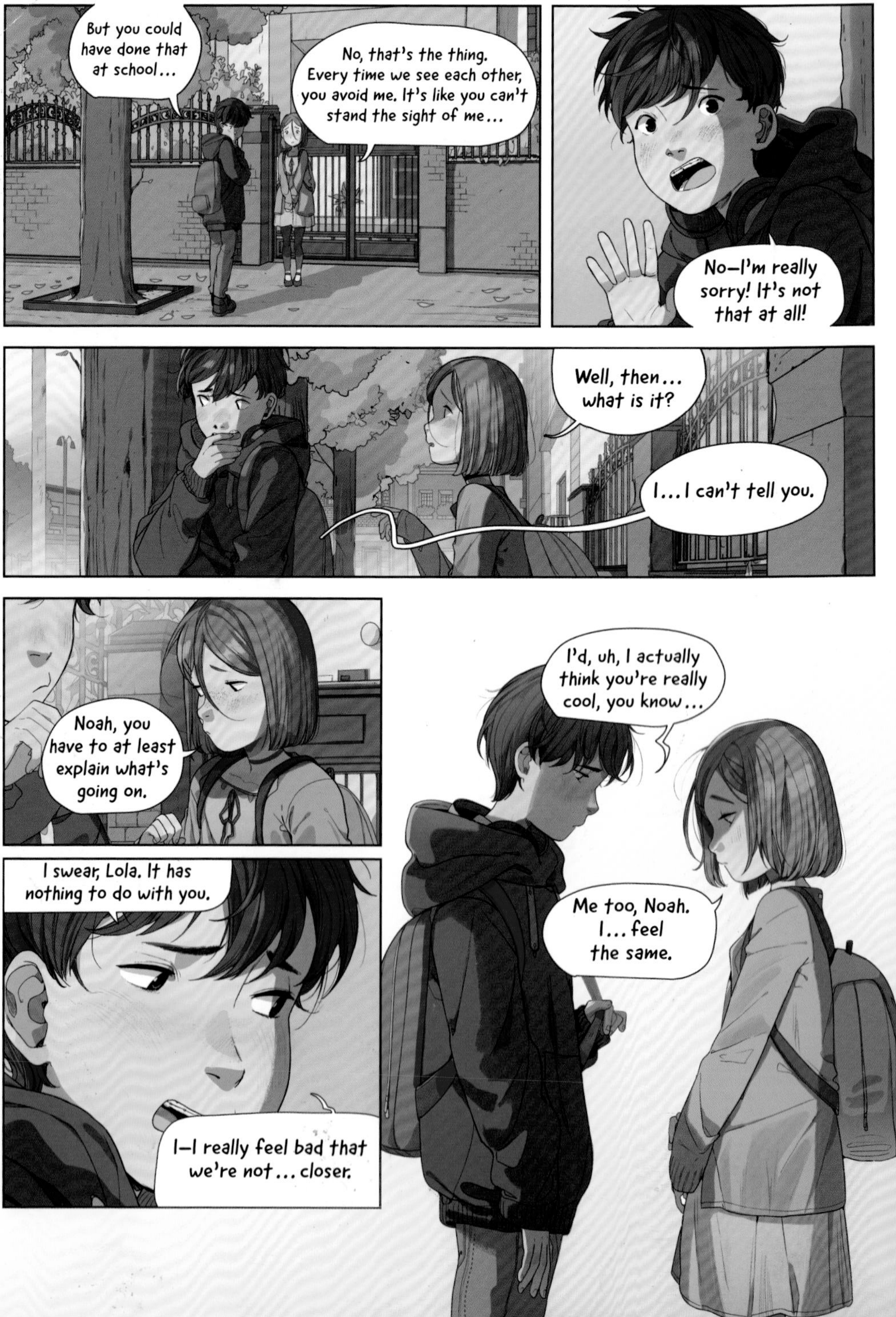
But you could have done that at school...
No, that's the thing. Every time we see each other, you avoid me. It's like you can't stand the sight of me...
No—I'm really sorry! It's not that at all!
Well, then... what is it?
I... I can't tell you.
Noah, you have to at least explain what's going on.
I swear, Lola. It has nothing to do with you.
I—I really feel bad that we're not... closer.
I'd, uh, I actually think you're really cool, you know...
Me too, Noah. I... feel the same.

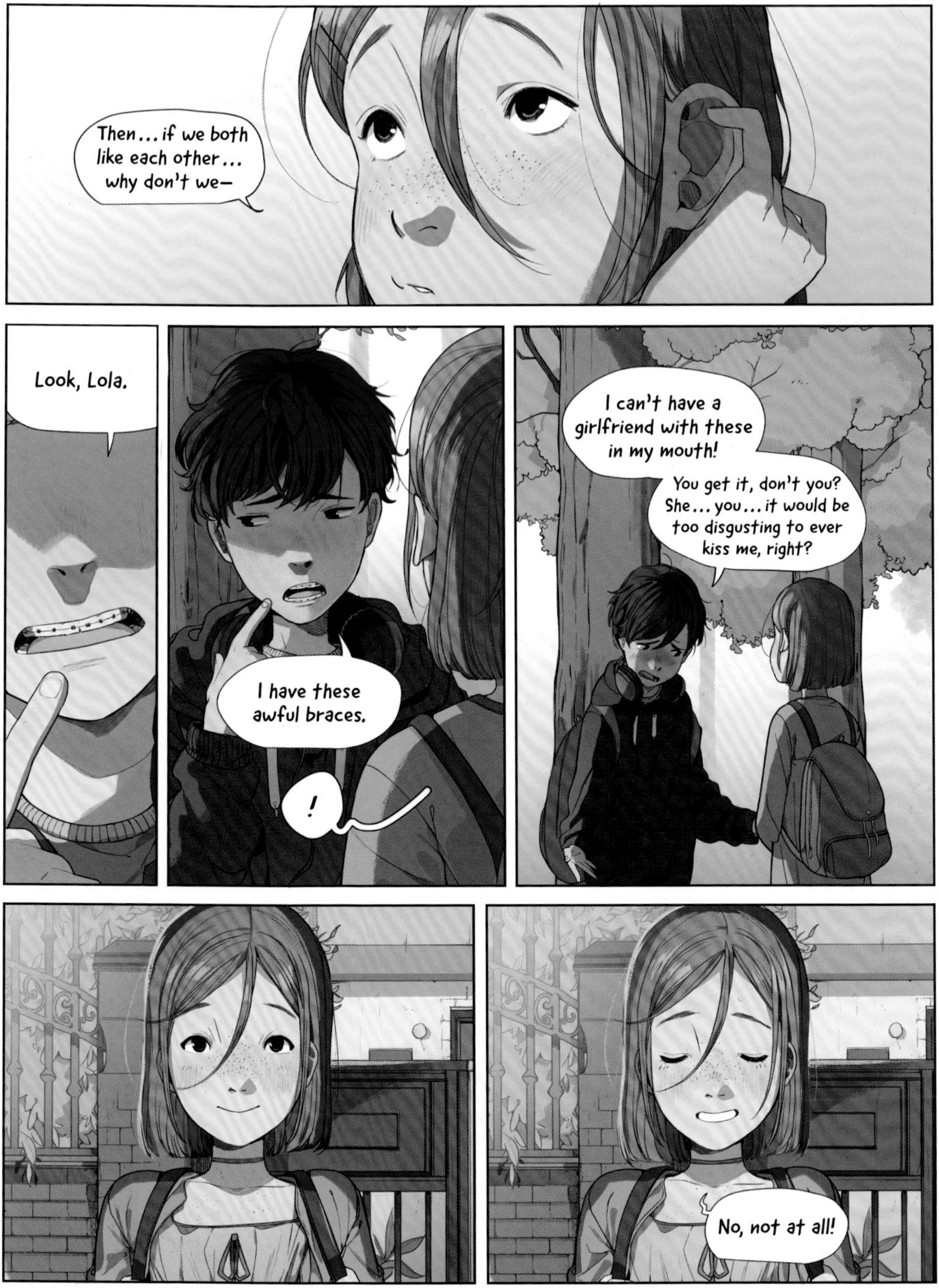

Then... if we both like each other... why don't we—
Look, Lola.
I have these awful braces.
!
I can't have a girlfriend with these in my mouth!
You get it, don't you? She... you... it would be too disgusting to ever kiss me, right?
No, not at all!

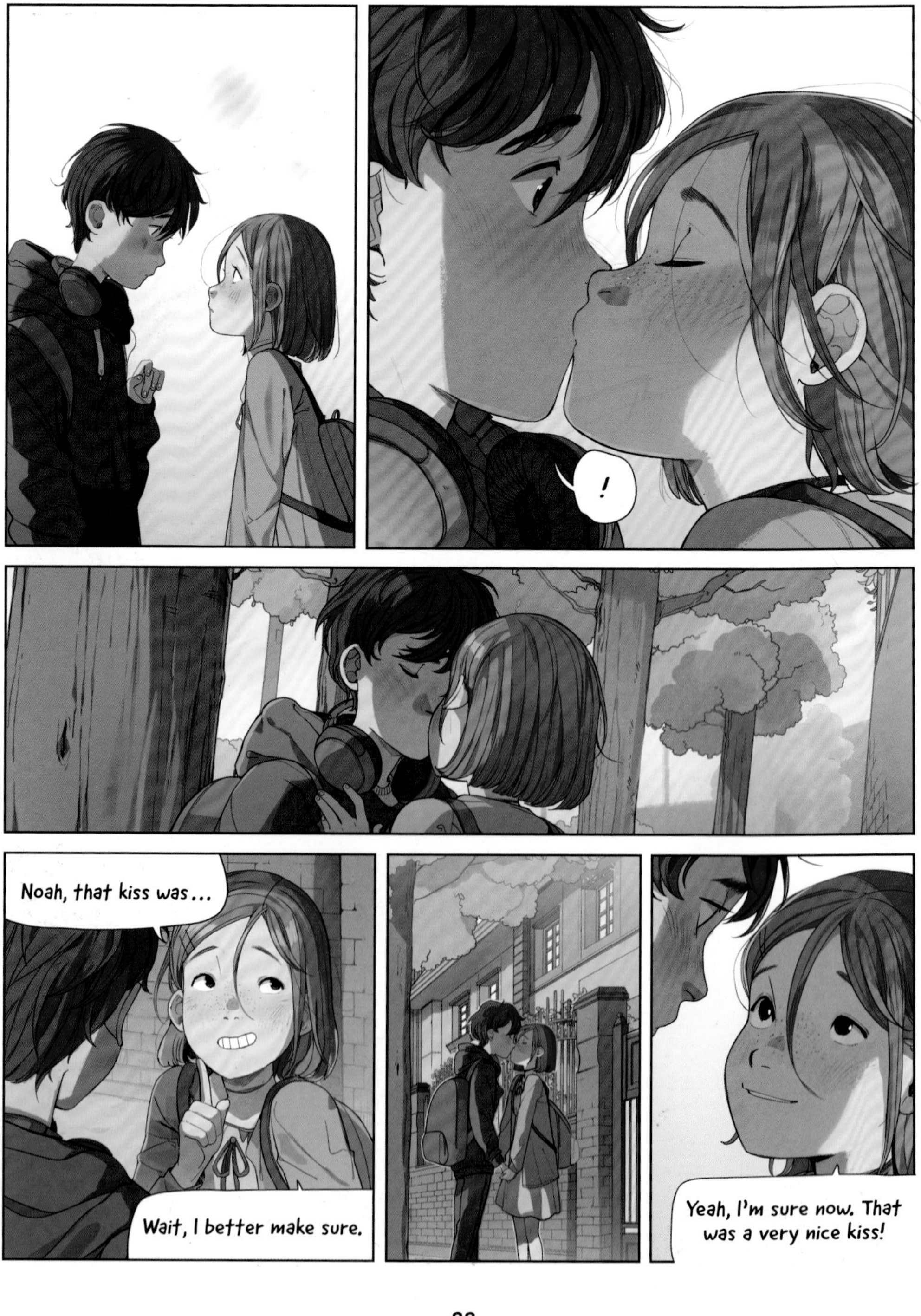
!
Noah, that kiss was...
Wait, I better make sure.
Yeah, I'm sure now. That was a very nice kiss!

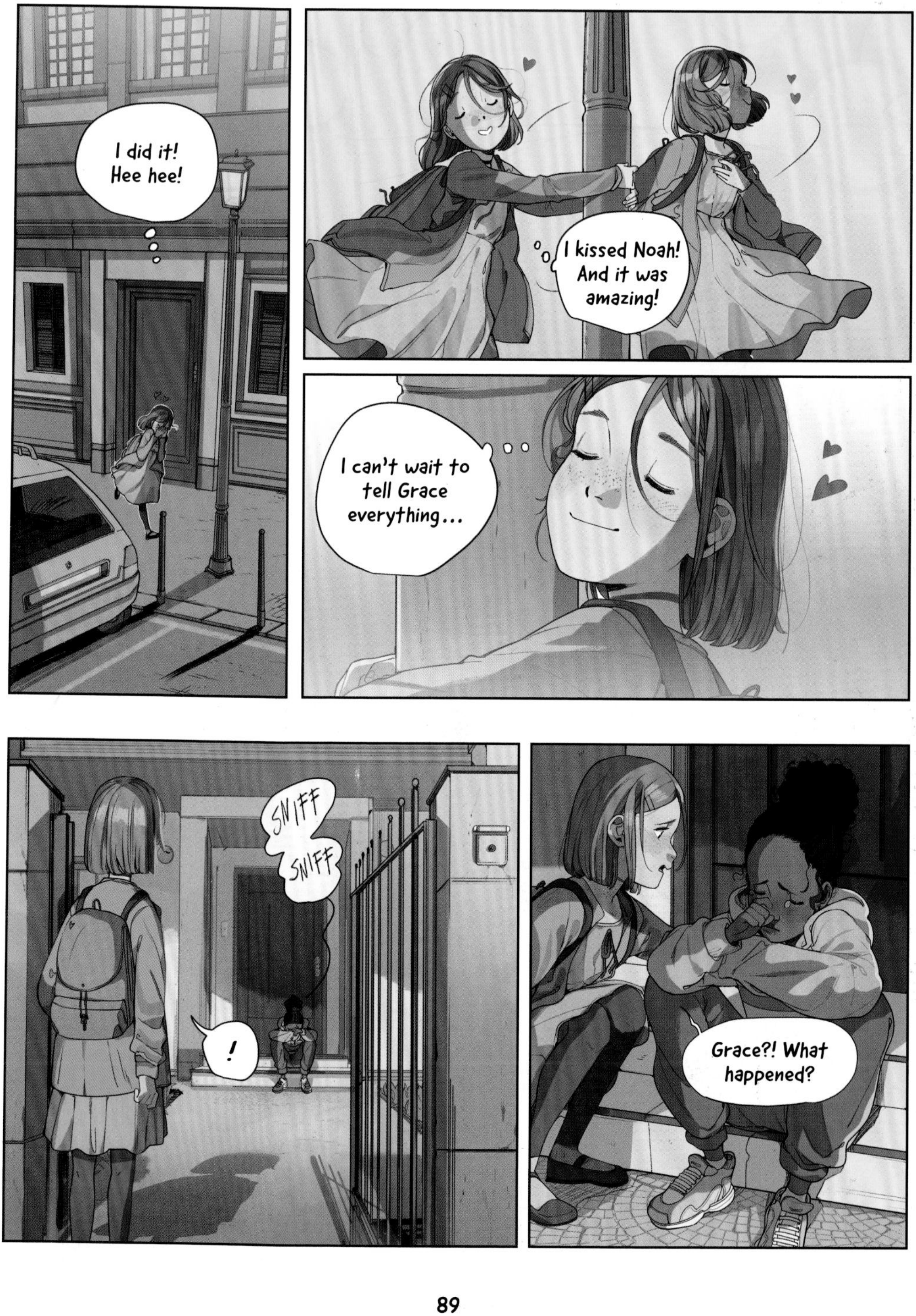
I did it! Hee hee!
I kissed Noah! And it was amazing!
I can't wait to tell Grace everything...
SNIFF
SNIFF
!
Grace?! What happened?

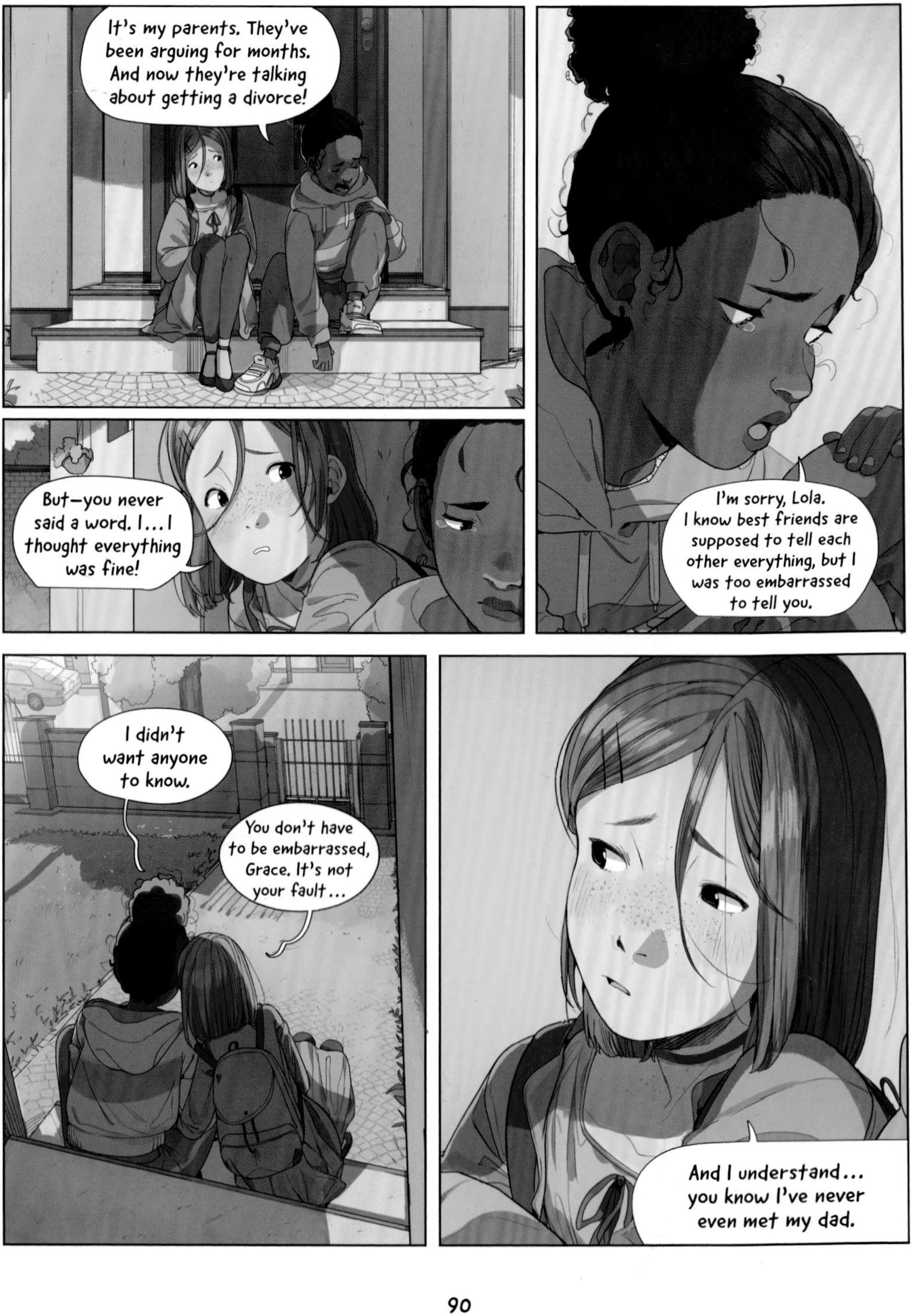
It's my parents. They've been arguing for months. And now they're talking about getting a divorce!
I'm sorry, Lola. I know best friends are supposed to tell each other everything, but I was too embarrassed to tell you.
But—you never said a word. I...I thought everything was fine!
I didn't want anyone to know.
You don't have to be embarrassed, Grace. It's not your fault...
And I understand... you know I've never even met my dad.

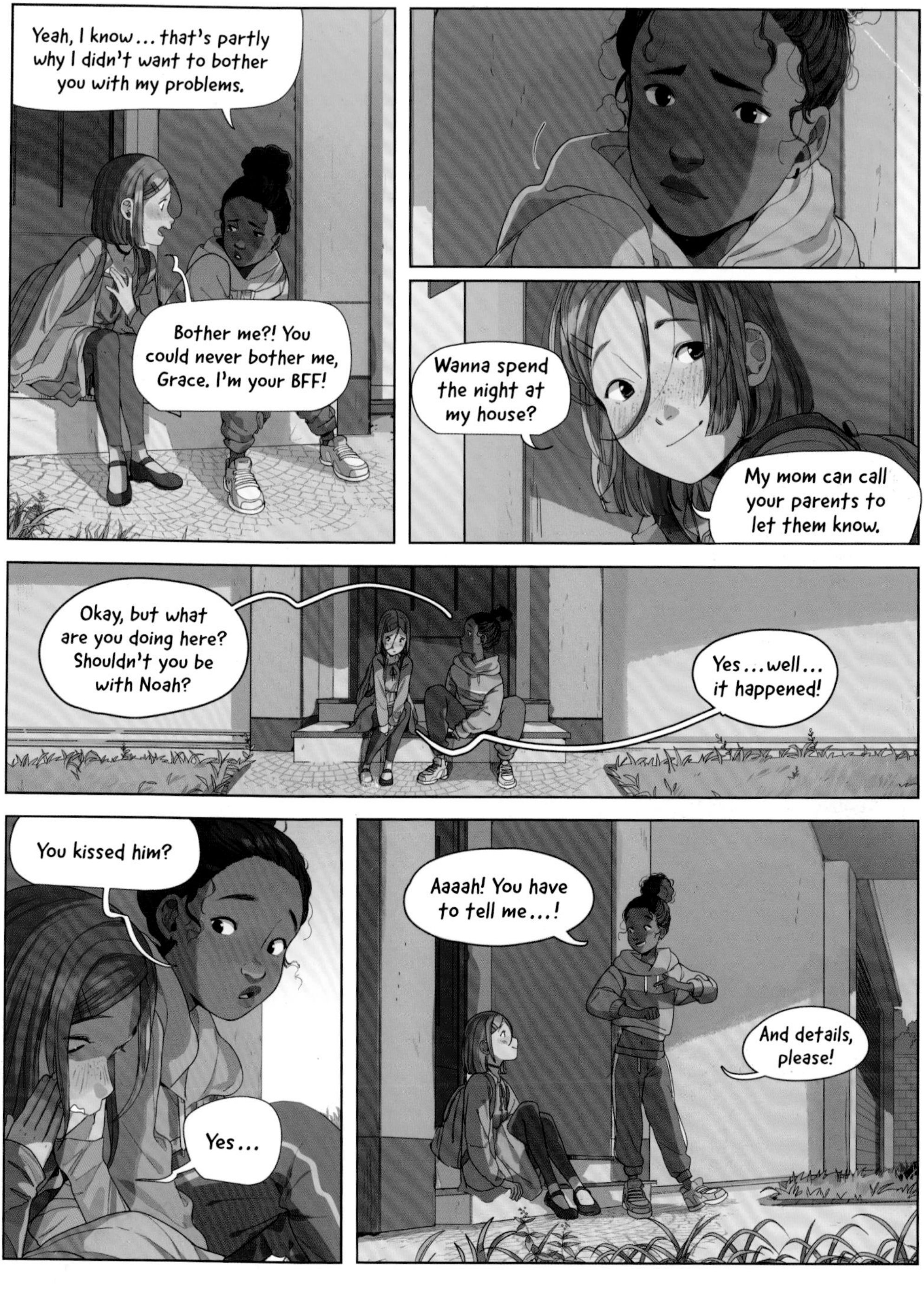
Yeah, I know... that's partly why I didn't want to bother you with my problems.
Bother me?! You could never bother me, Grace. I'm your BFF!
Wanna spend the night at my house?
My mom can call your parents to let them know.
Okay, but what are you doing here? Shouldn't you be with Noah?
Yes...well... it happened!
You kissed him?
Yes...
Aaaah! You have to tell me...!
And details, please!

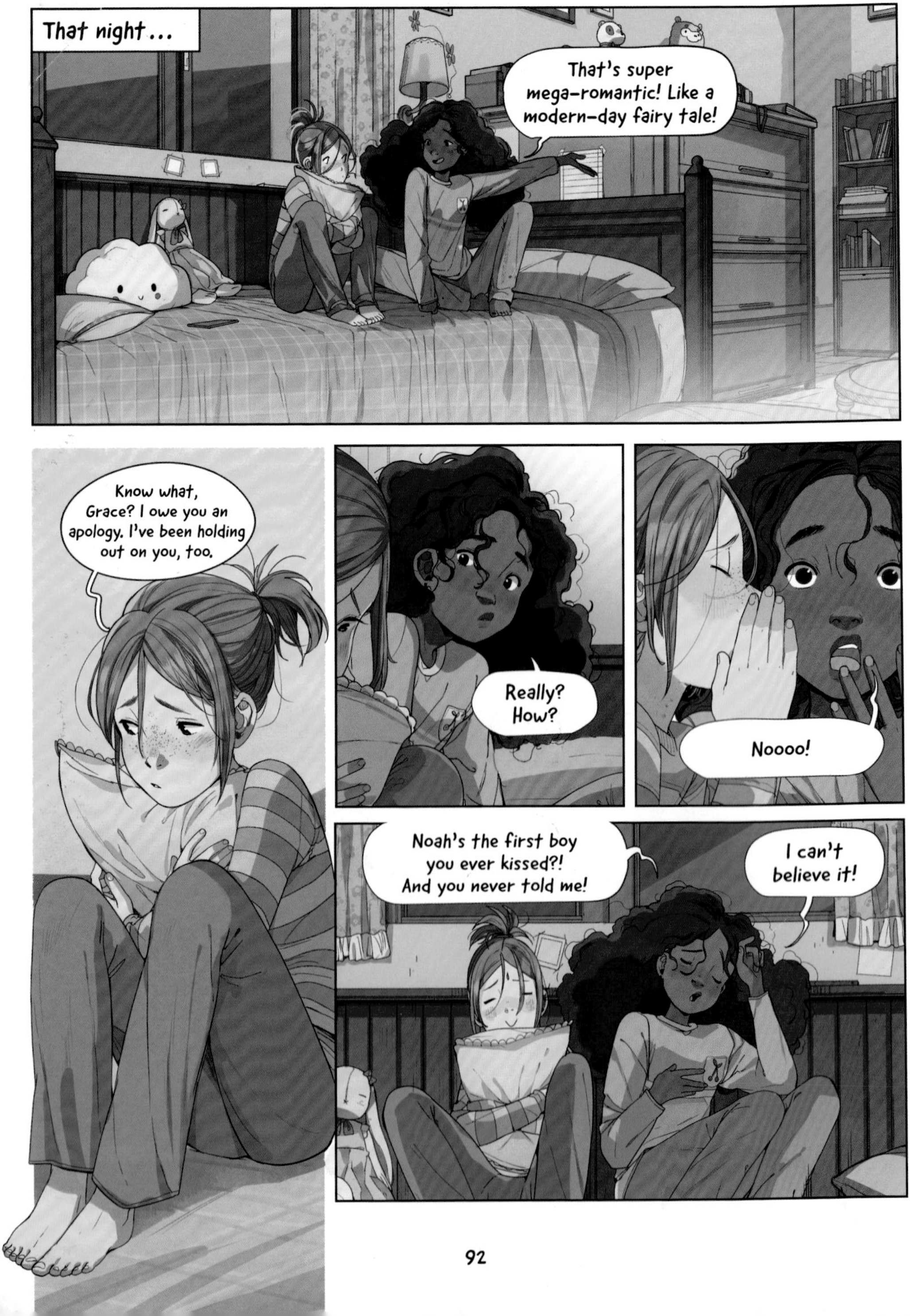

That night...
That's super mega-romantic! Like a modern-day fairy tale!
Know what, Grace? I owe you an apology. I've been holding out on you, too.
Really? How?
Noooo!
Noah's the first boy you ever kissed?! And you never told me!
I can't believe it!

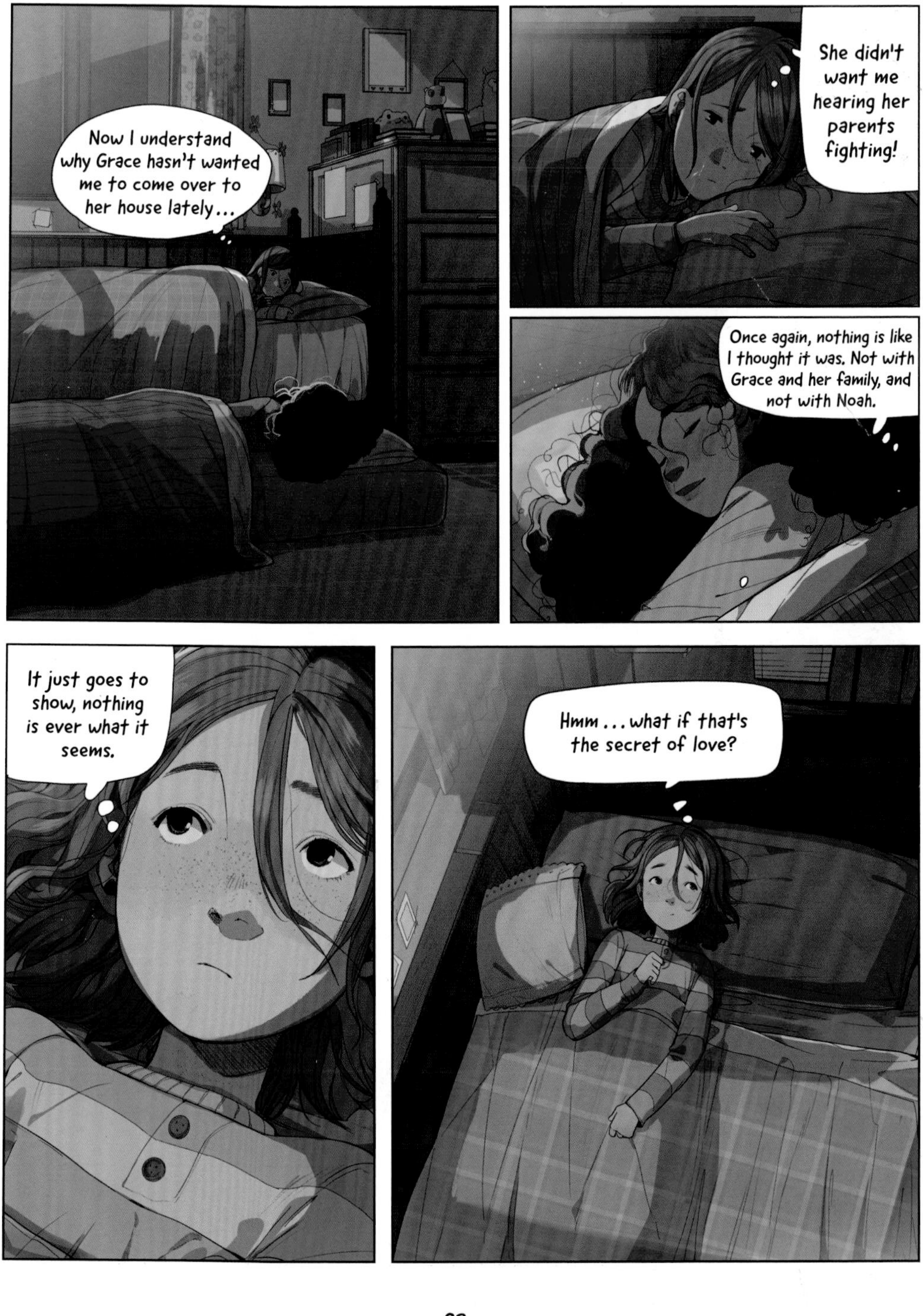

Now I understand why Grace hasn't wanted me to come over to her house lately...
She didn't want me hearing her parents fighting!
Once again, nothing is like I thought it was. Not with Grace and her family, and not with Noah.
It just goes to show, nothing is ever what it seems.
Hmm... what if that's the secret of love?

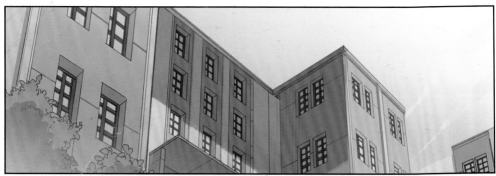

Now that I'm going out with Noah, I want to write up our latest findings about love for the report.

What do you think, Grace?

Okay, but with everything going on at home with my parents... it's hard for me to believe in it!

Okay, then how about we take turns—one sentence each to describe our different points of view.

Okay!

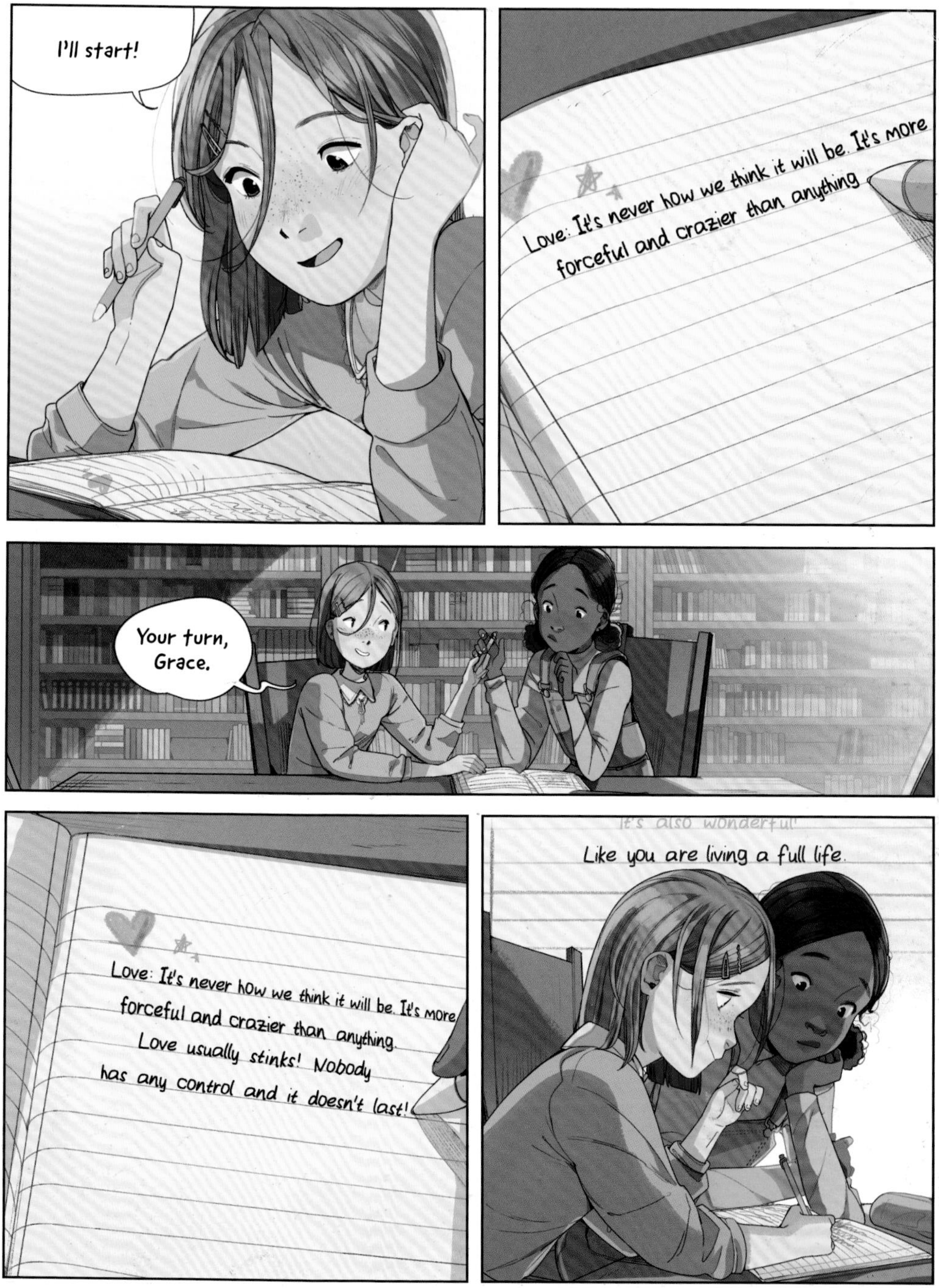

I'll start!
Love: It's never how we think it will be. It's more forceful and crazier than anything
Your turn, Grace.
Love: It's never how we think it will be. It's more forceful and crazier than anything.
Love usually stinks! Nobody has any control and it doesn't last!
It's also wonderful!
Like you are living a full life.

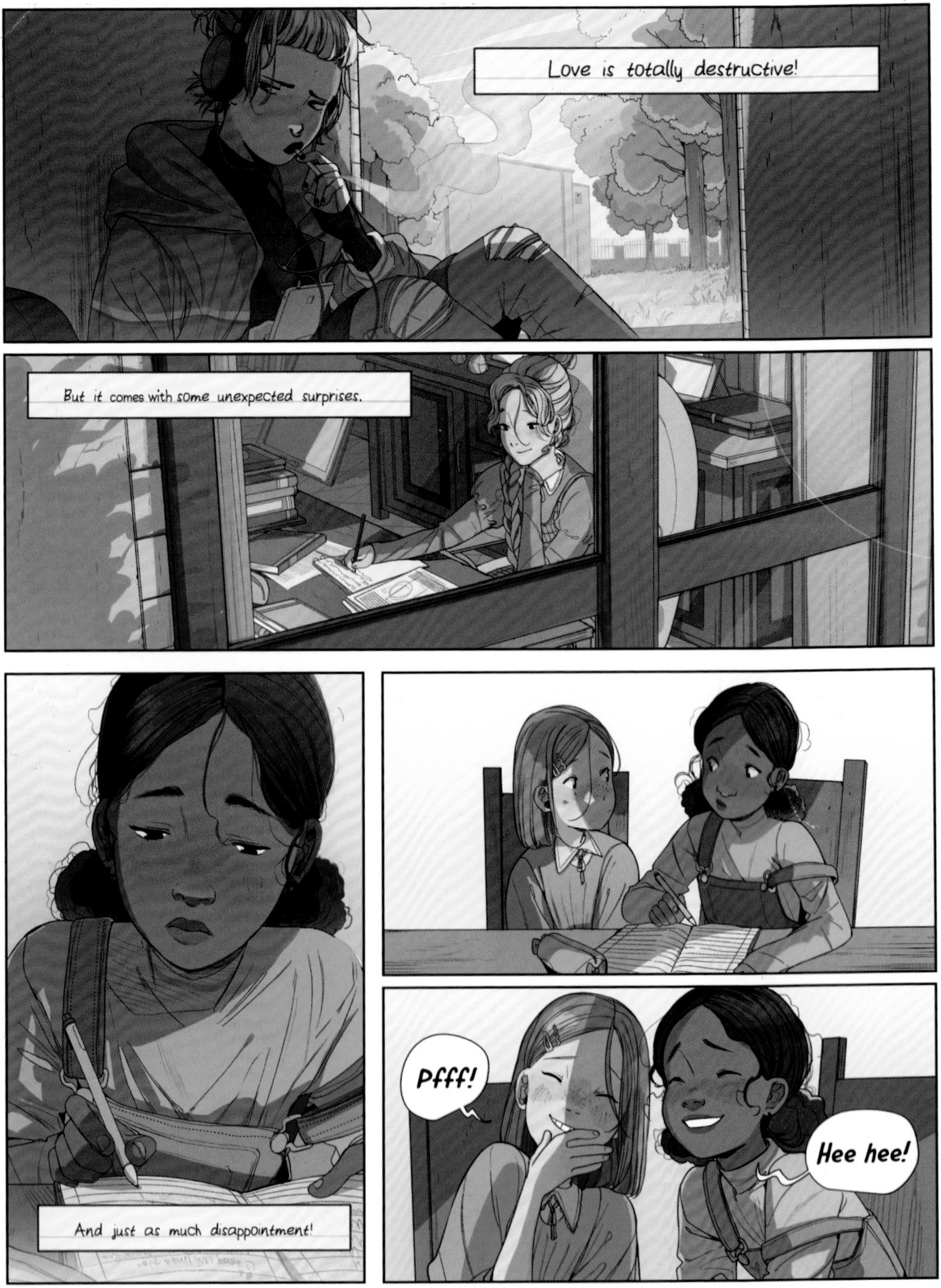
Love is totally destructive!
But it comes with some unexpected surprises.
And just as much disappointment!
Pfff!
Hee hee!

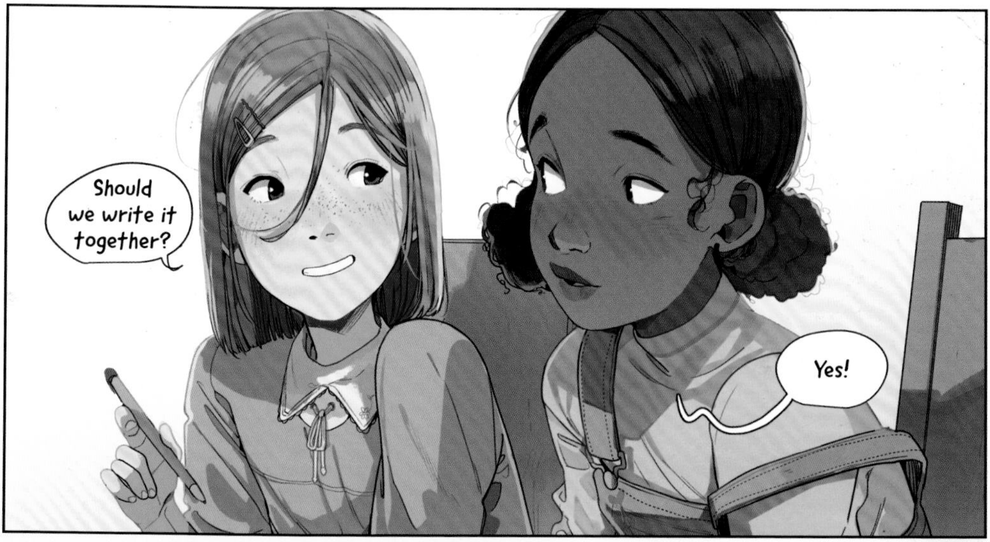
Should we write it together?
Yes!

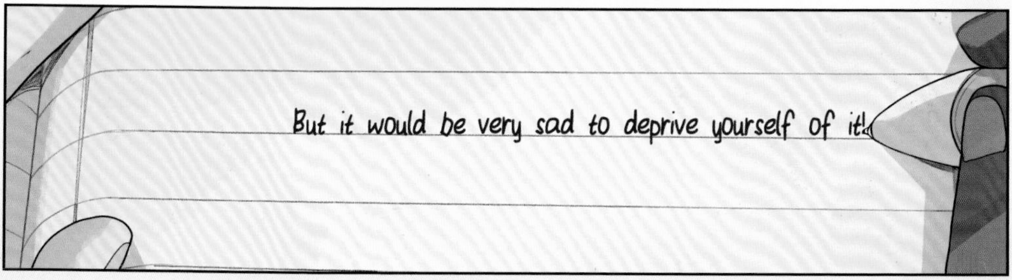
But it would be very sad to deprive yourself of it!

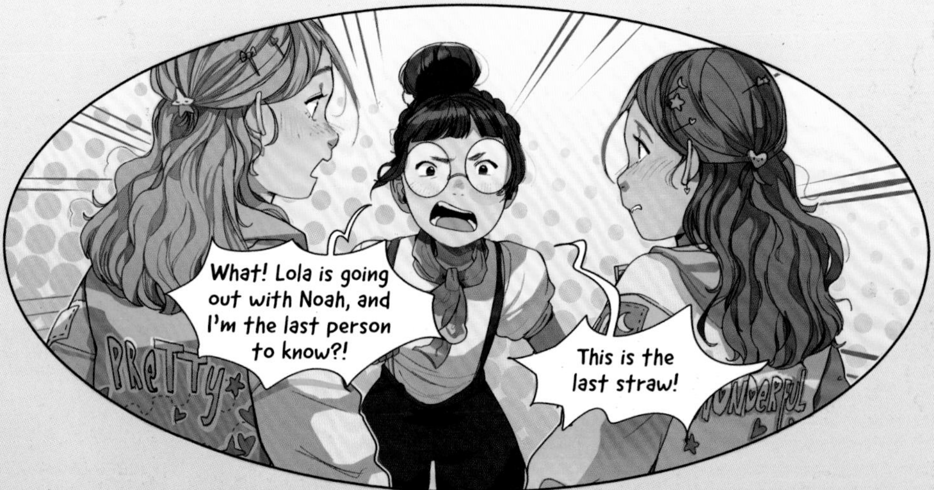
What! Lola is going out with Noah, and I'm the last person to know?!
This is the last straw!
PRETTY
WONDERFUL

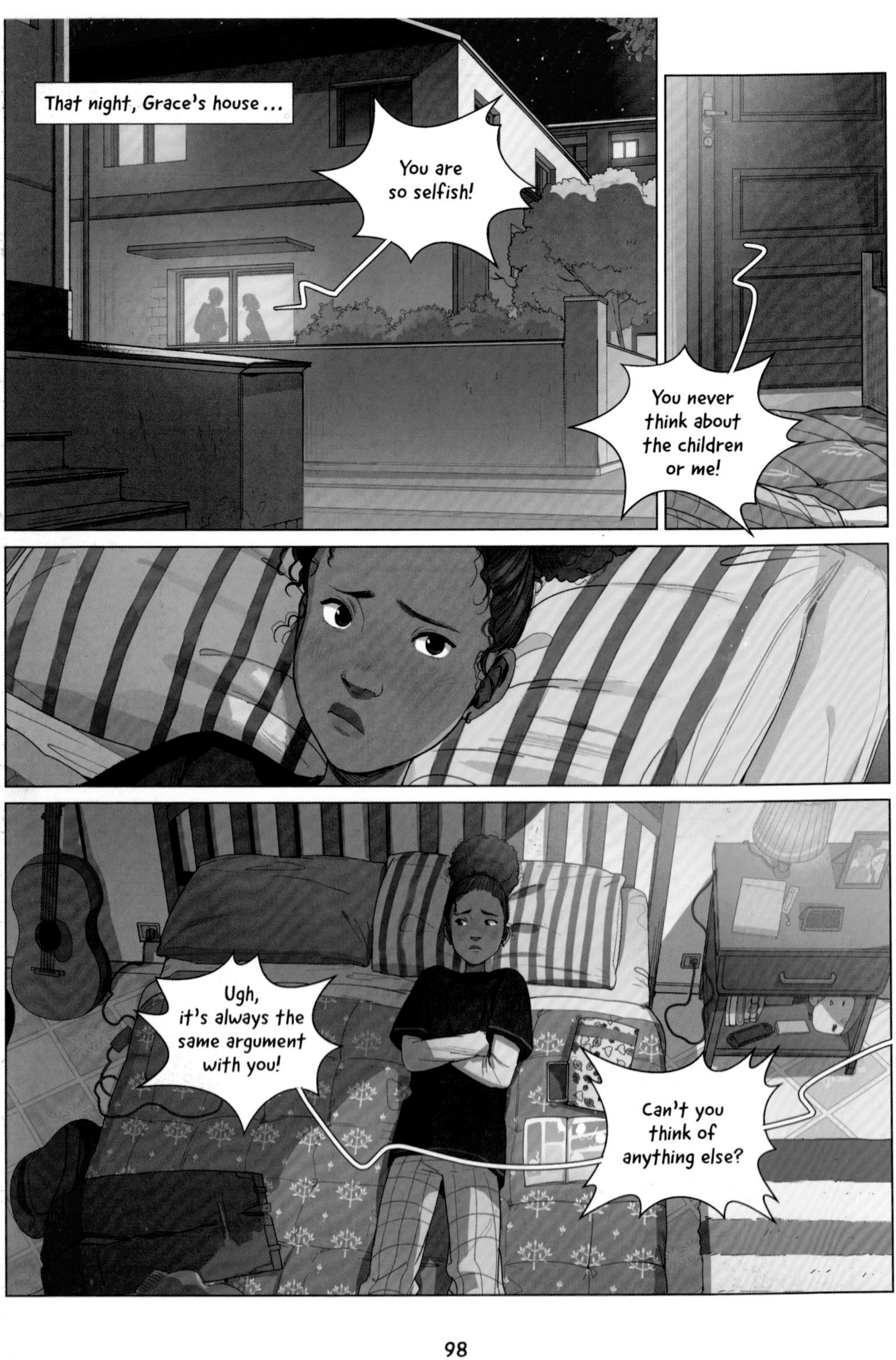
That night, Grace's house...
You are so selfish!
You never think about the children or me!
Ugh, it's always the same argument with you!
Can't you think of anything else?

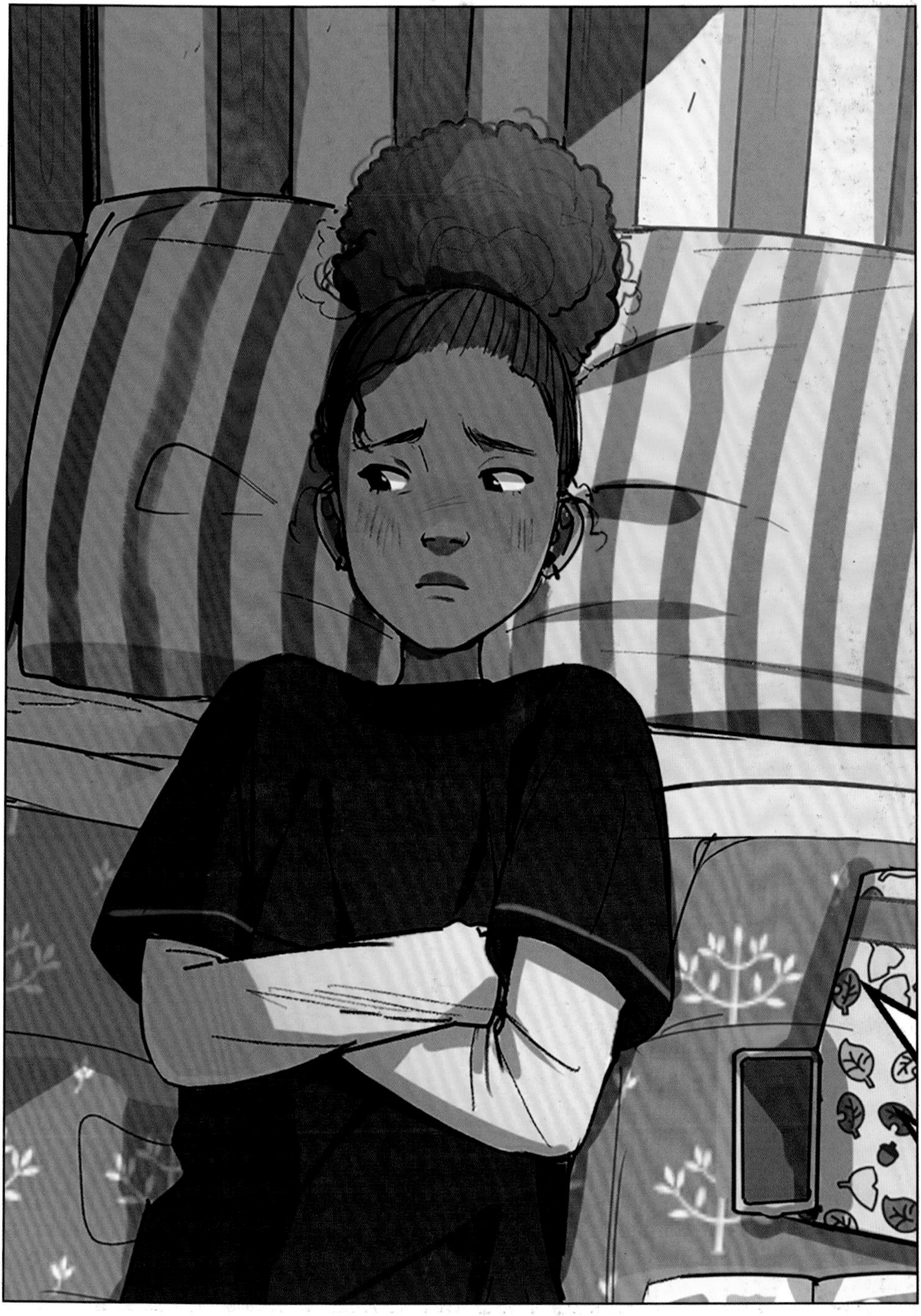

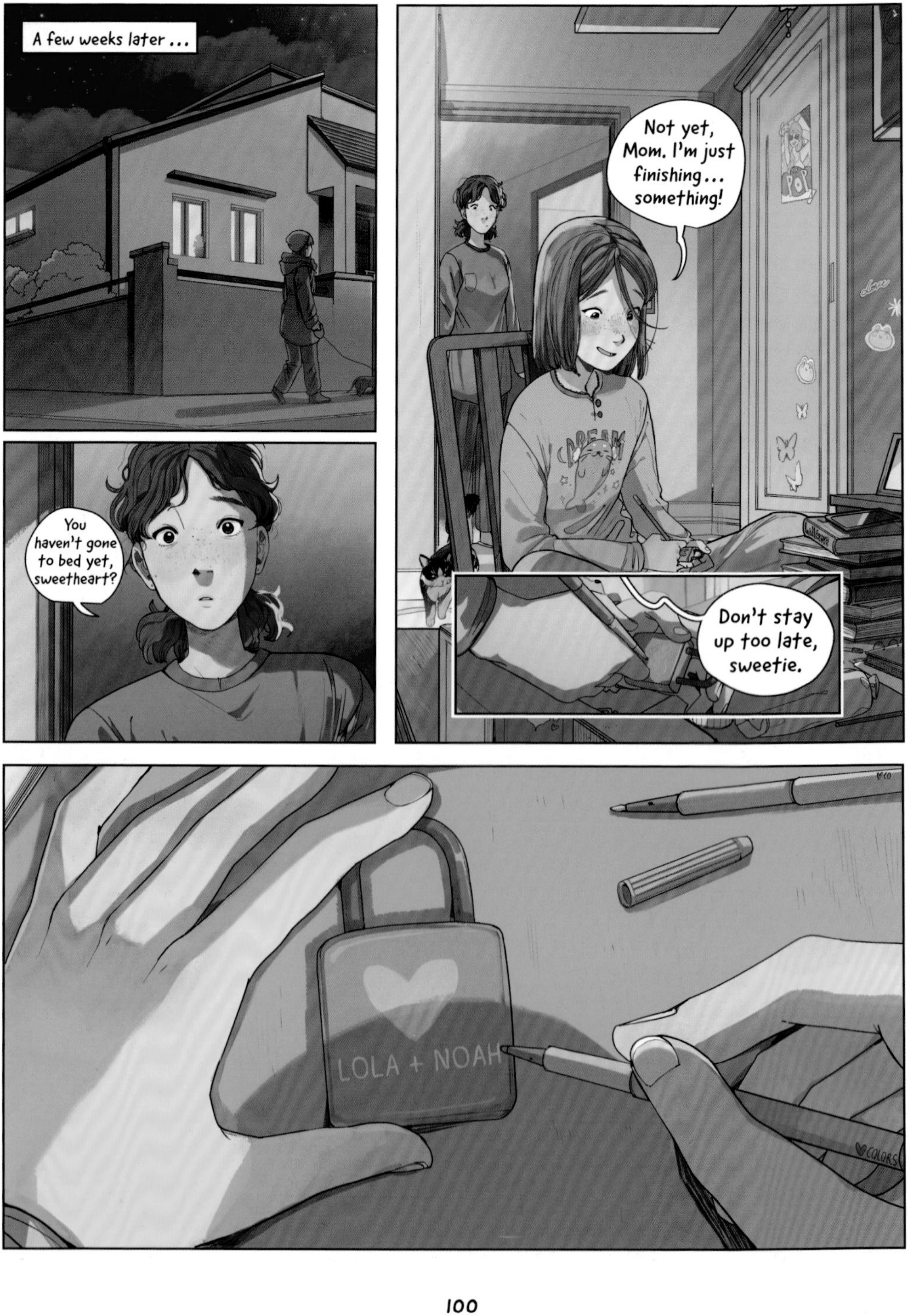
A few weeks later...
You haven't gone to bed yet, sweetheart?
Not yet, Mom. I'm just finishing... something!
Don't stay up too late, sweetie.
LOLA + NOAH

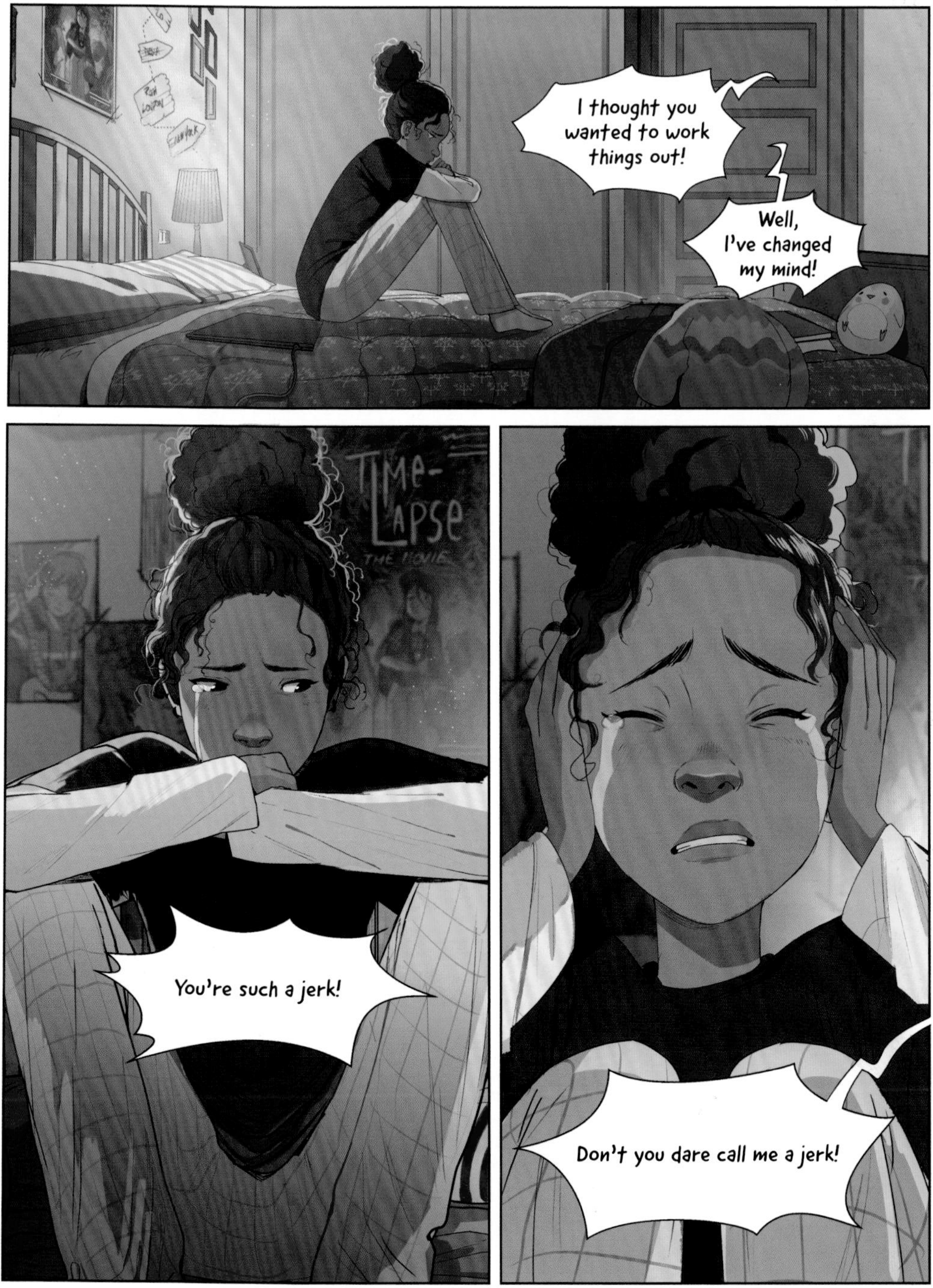
I thought you wanted to work things out!
Well, I've changed my mind!
TIME-LAPSE
THE MOVIE
You're such a jerk!
Don't you dare call me a jerk!

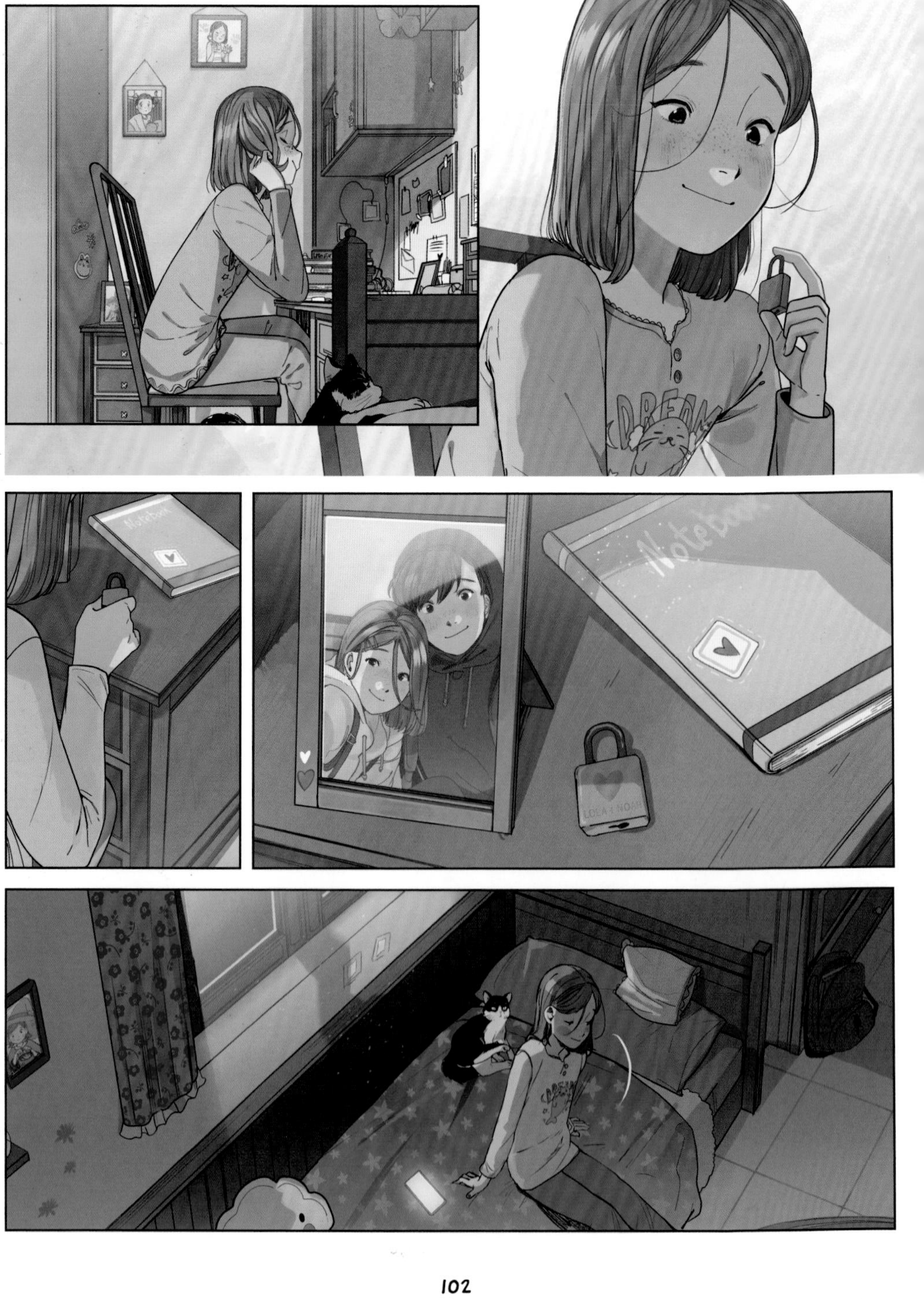
Notebook

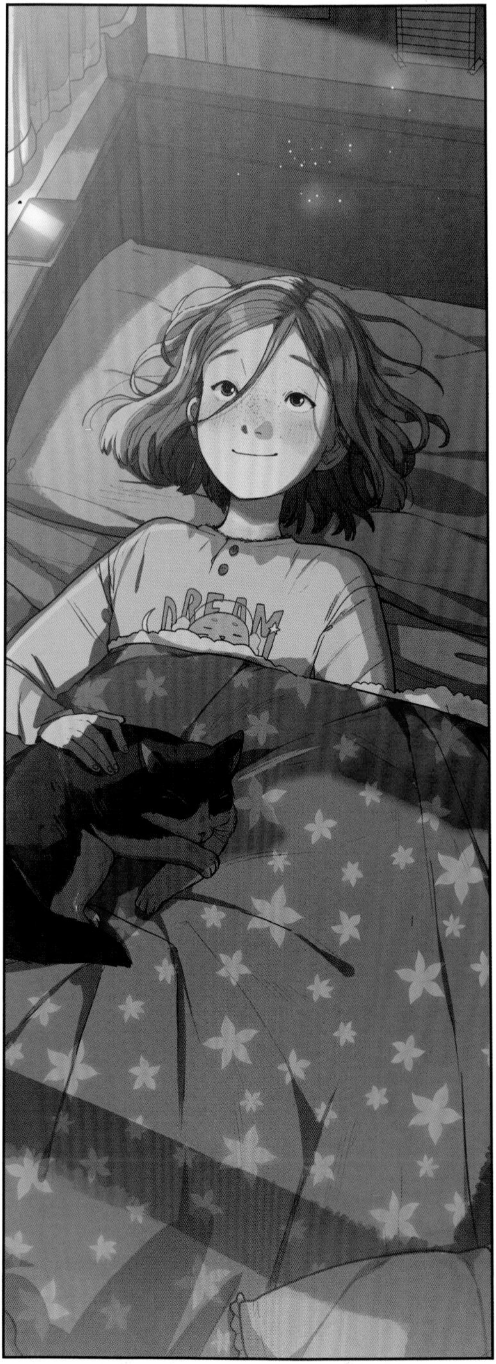

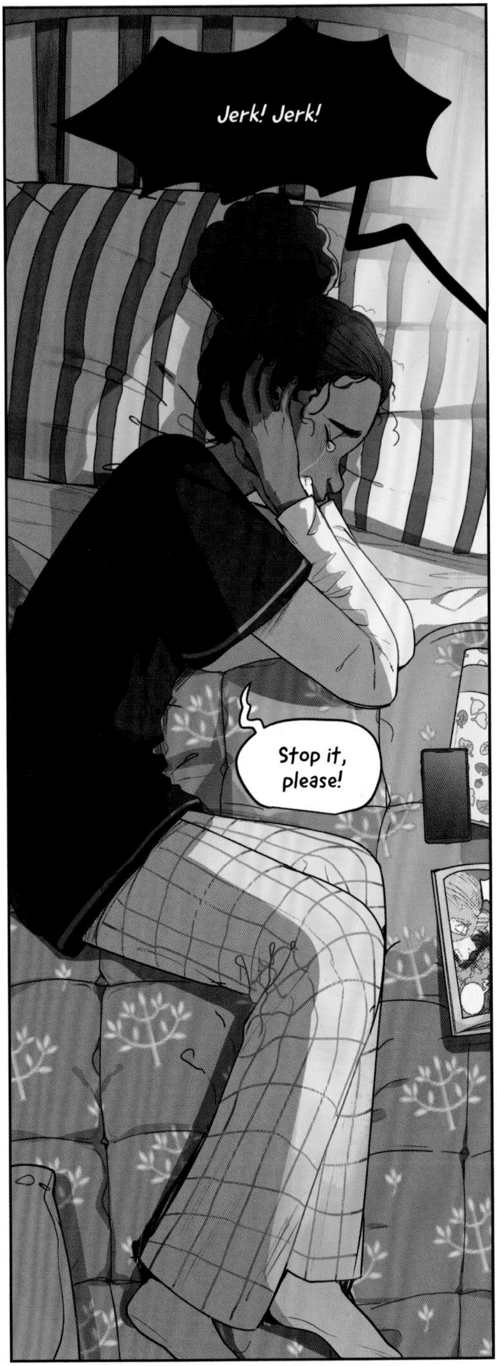
Jerk! Jerk!
Stop it, please!

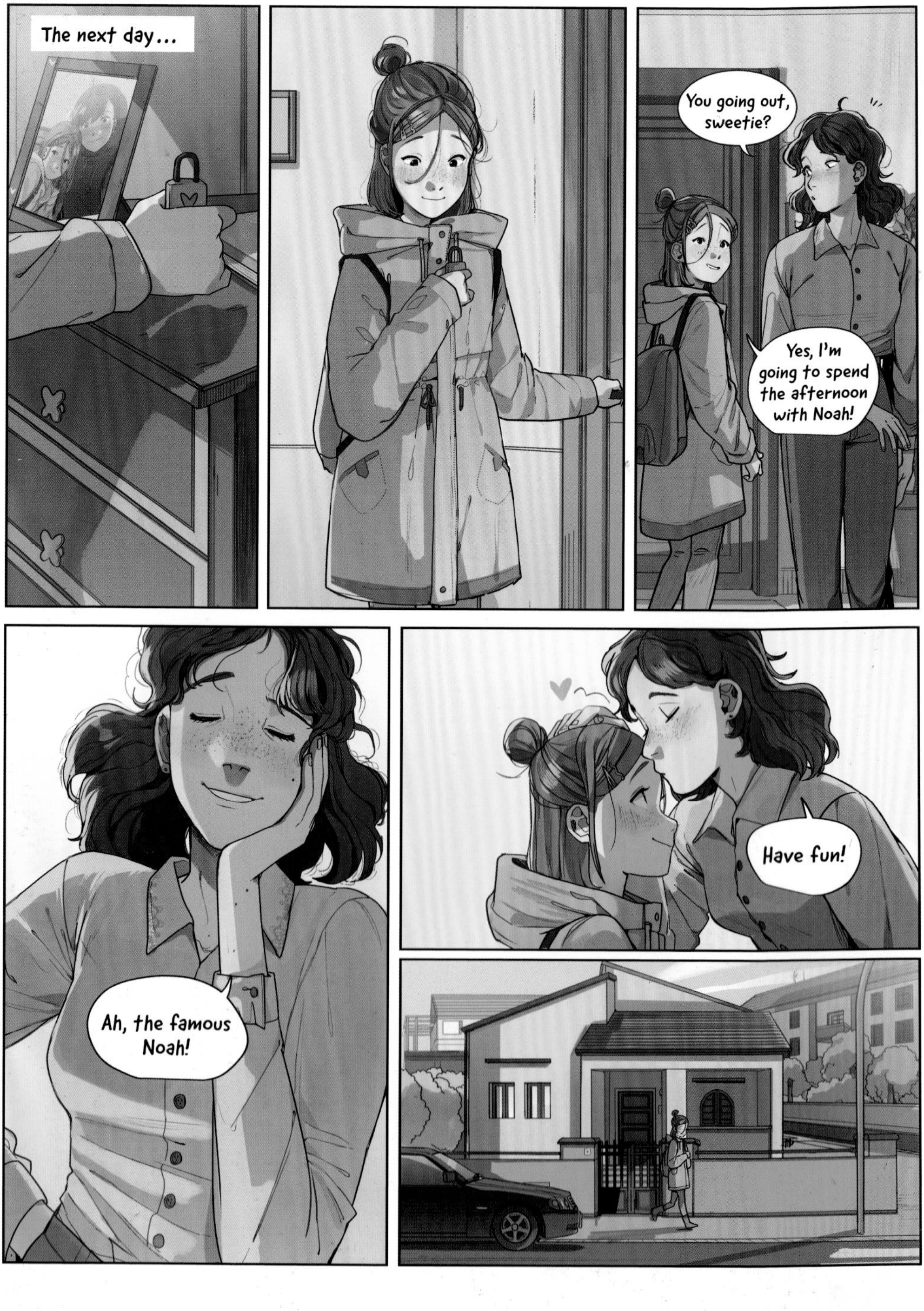
The next day...
You going out, sweetie?
Yes, I'm going to spend the afternoon with Noah!
Ah, the famous Noah!
Have fun!

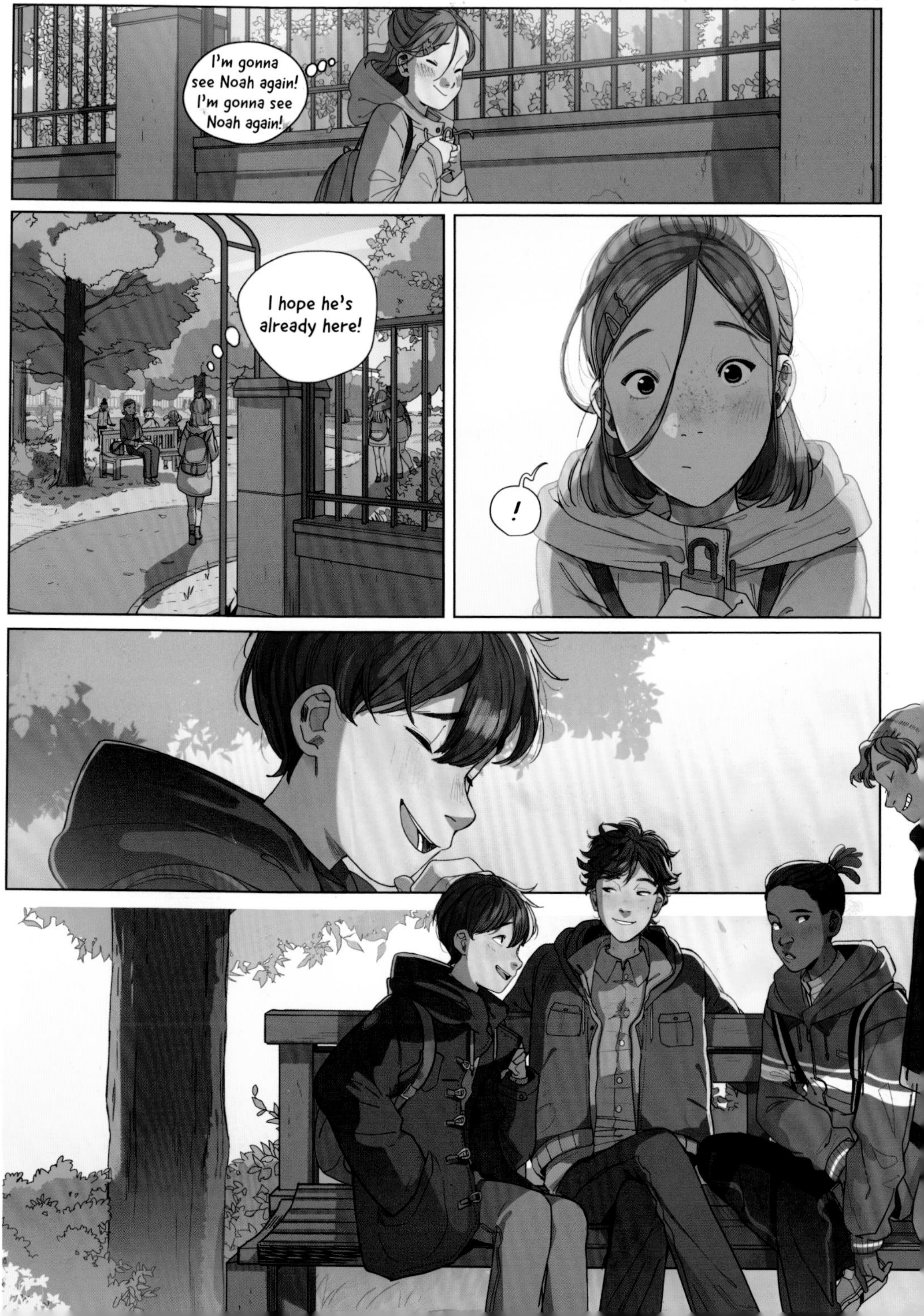

I'm gonna see Noah again! I'm gonna see Noah again!
I hope he's already here!
!

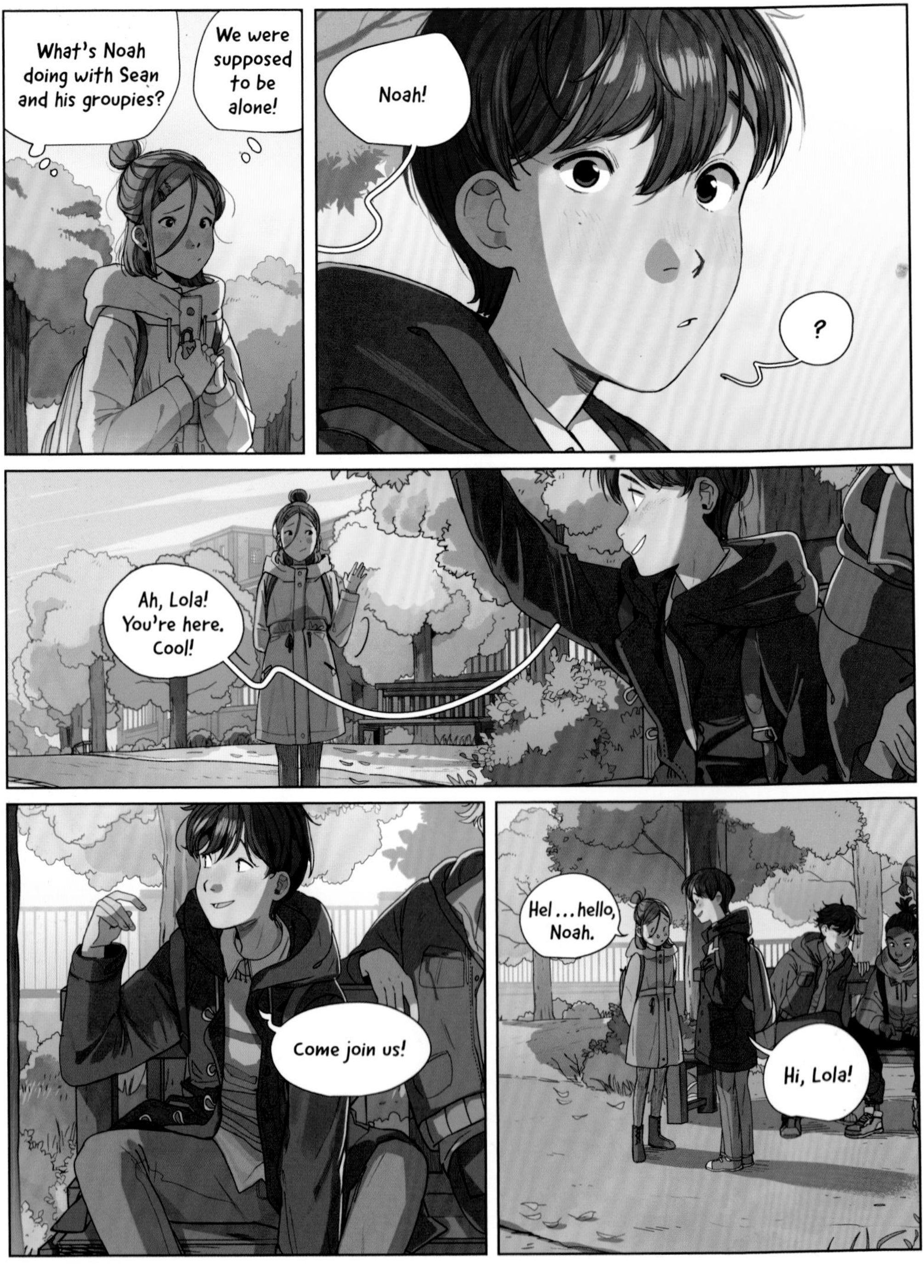
What's Noah doing with Sean and his groupies?
We were supposed to be alone!
Noah!
?
Ah, Lola! You're here. Cool!
Come join us!
Hel...hello, Noah.
Hi, Lola!

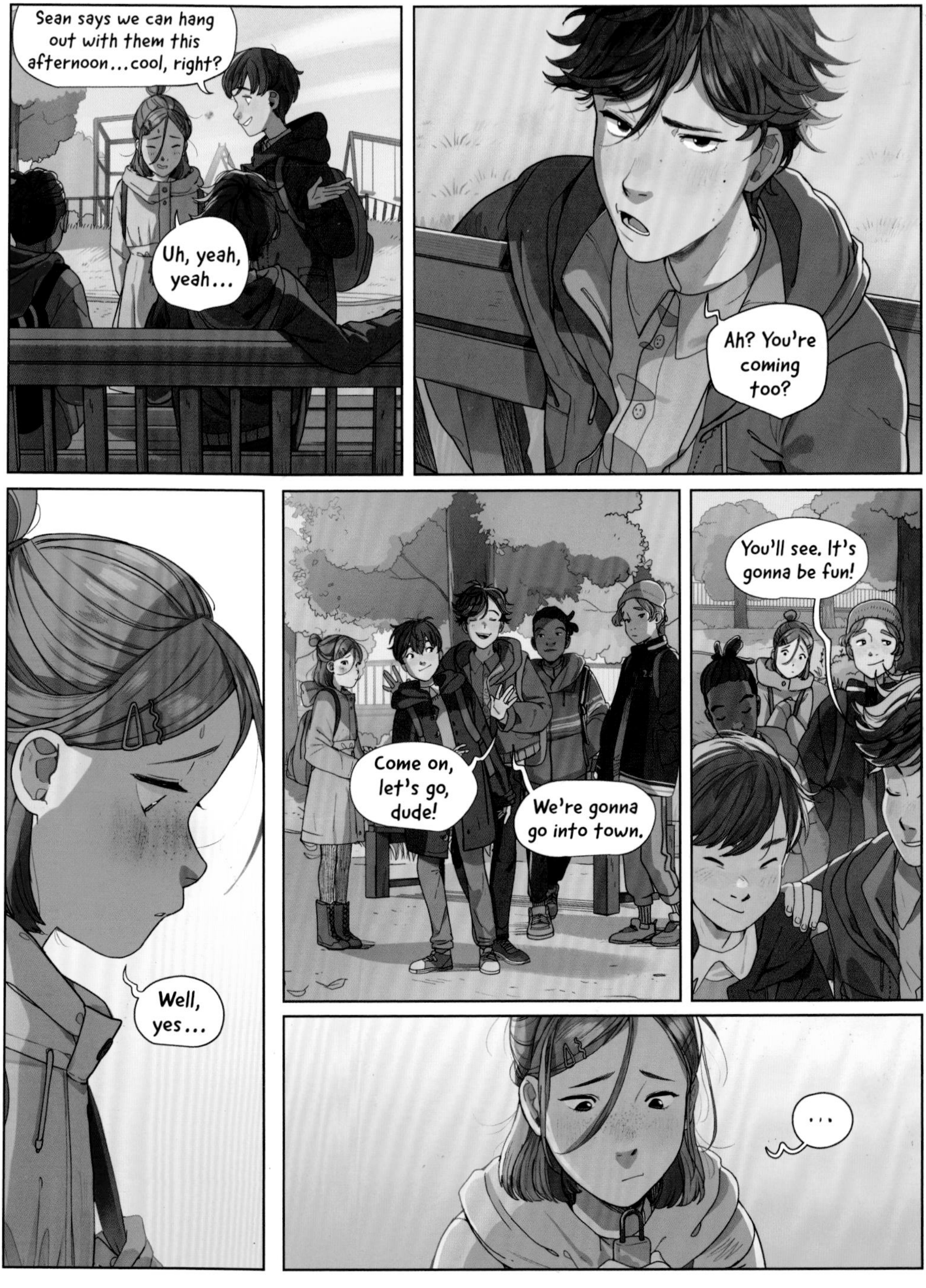

Sean says we can hang out with them this afternoon...cool, right?
Uh, yeah, yeah...
Ah? You're coming too?
Well, yes...
Come on, let's go, dude!
We're gonna go into town.
You'll see. It's gonna be fun!
...

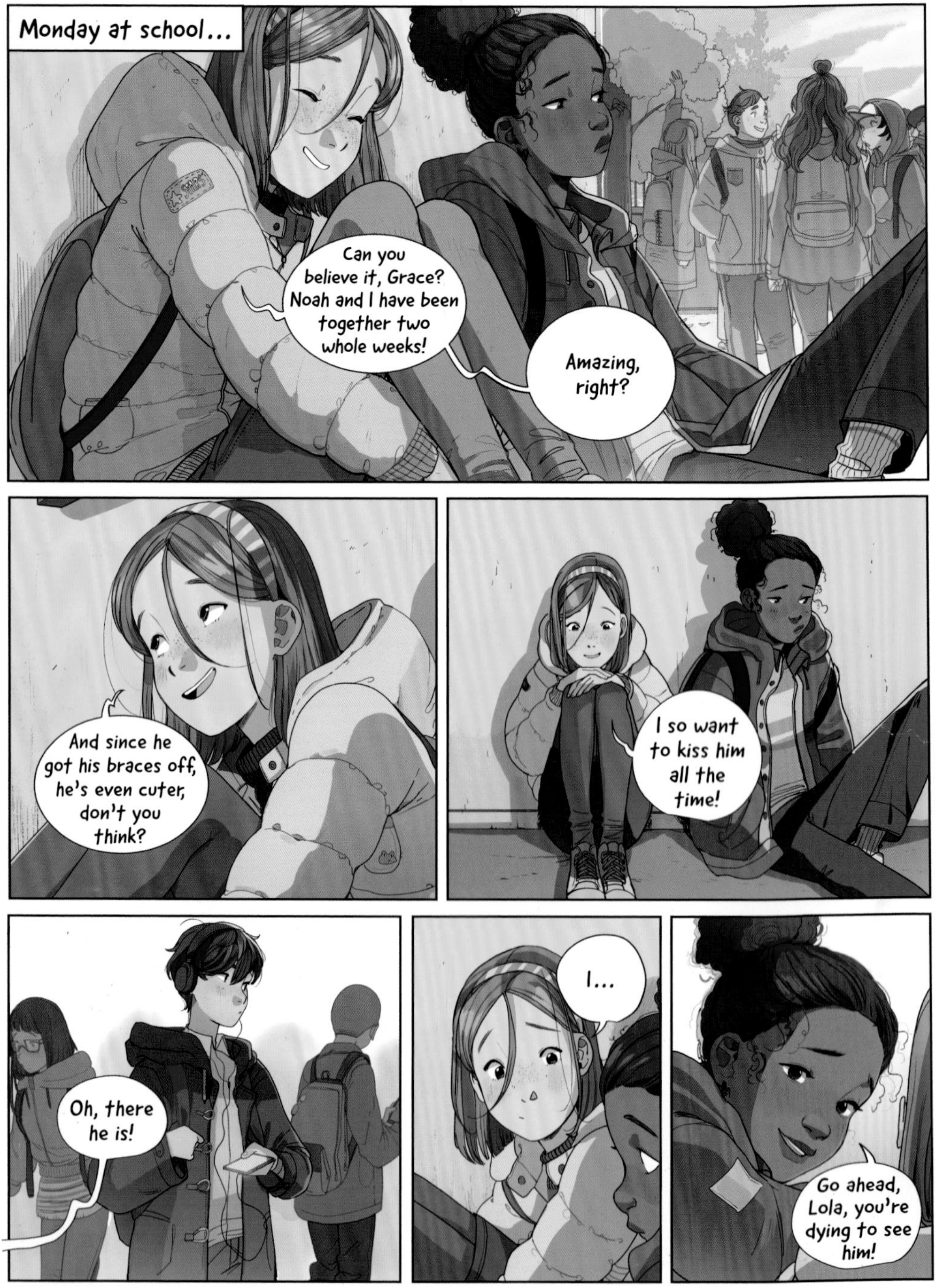
Monday at school...
Can you believe it, Grace? Noah and I have been together two whole weeks!
Amazing, right?
And since he got his braces off, he's even cuter, don't you think?
I so want to kiss him all the time!
Oh, there he is!
I...
Go ahead, Lola, you're dying to see him!

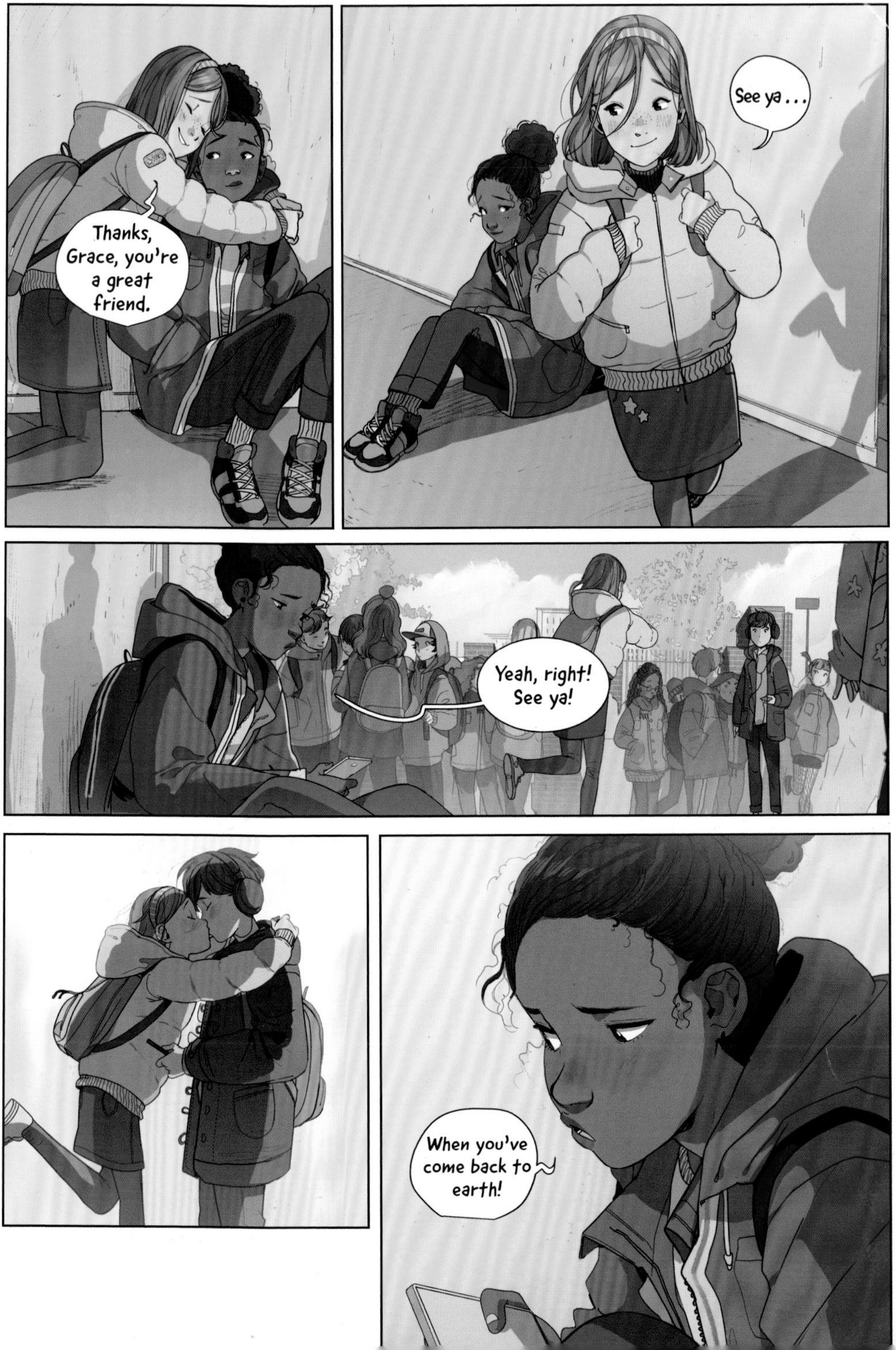
Thanks, Grace, you're a great friend.
See ya . . .
Yeah, right! See ya!
When you've come back to earth!

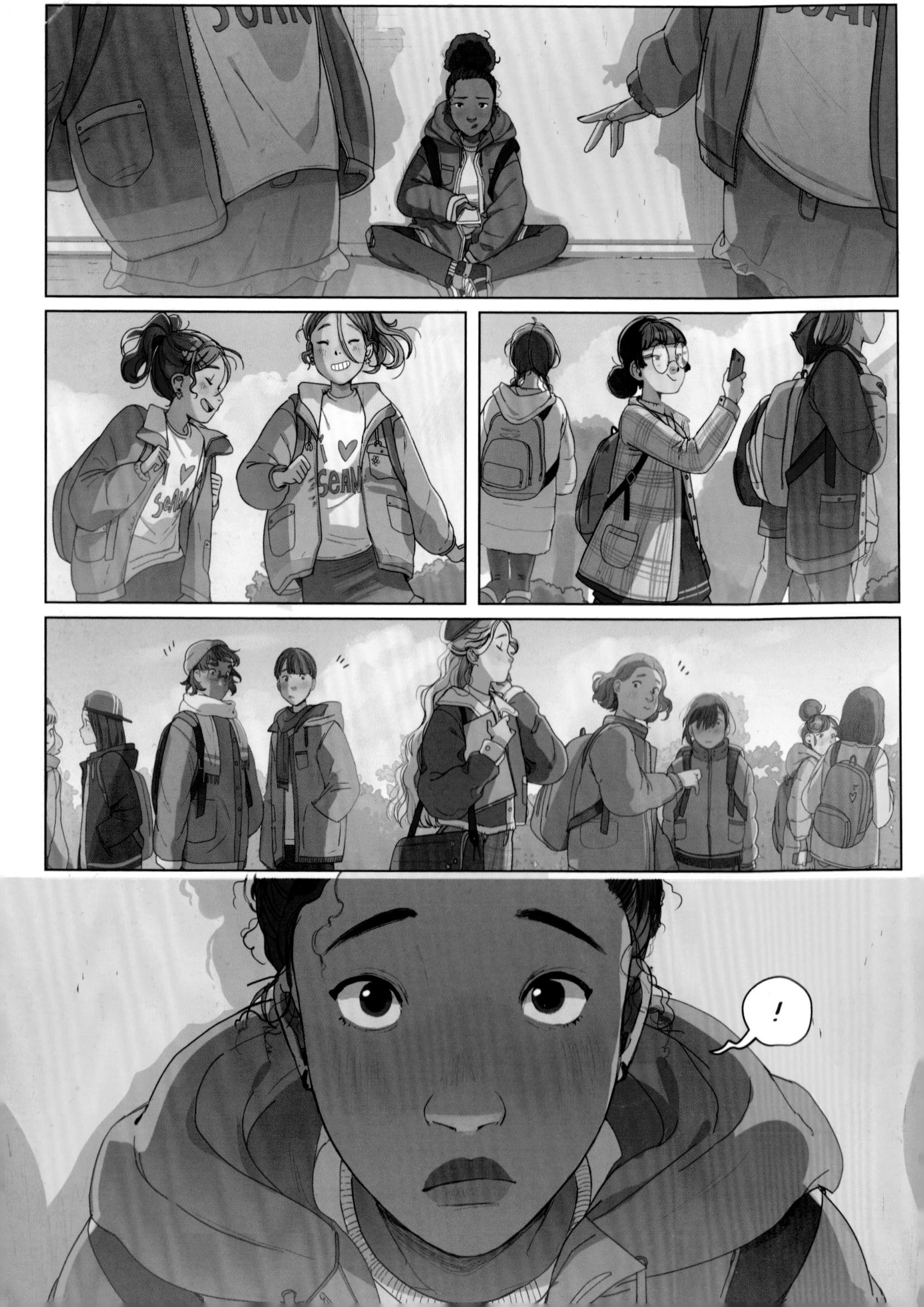
!

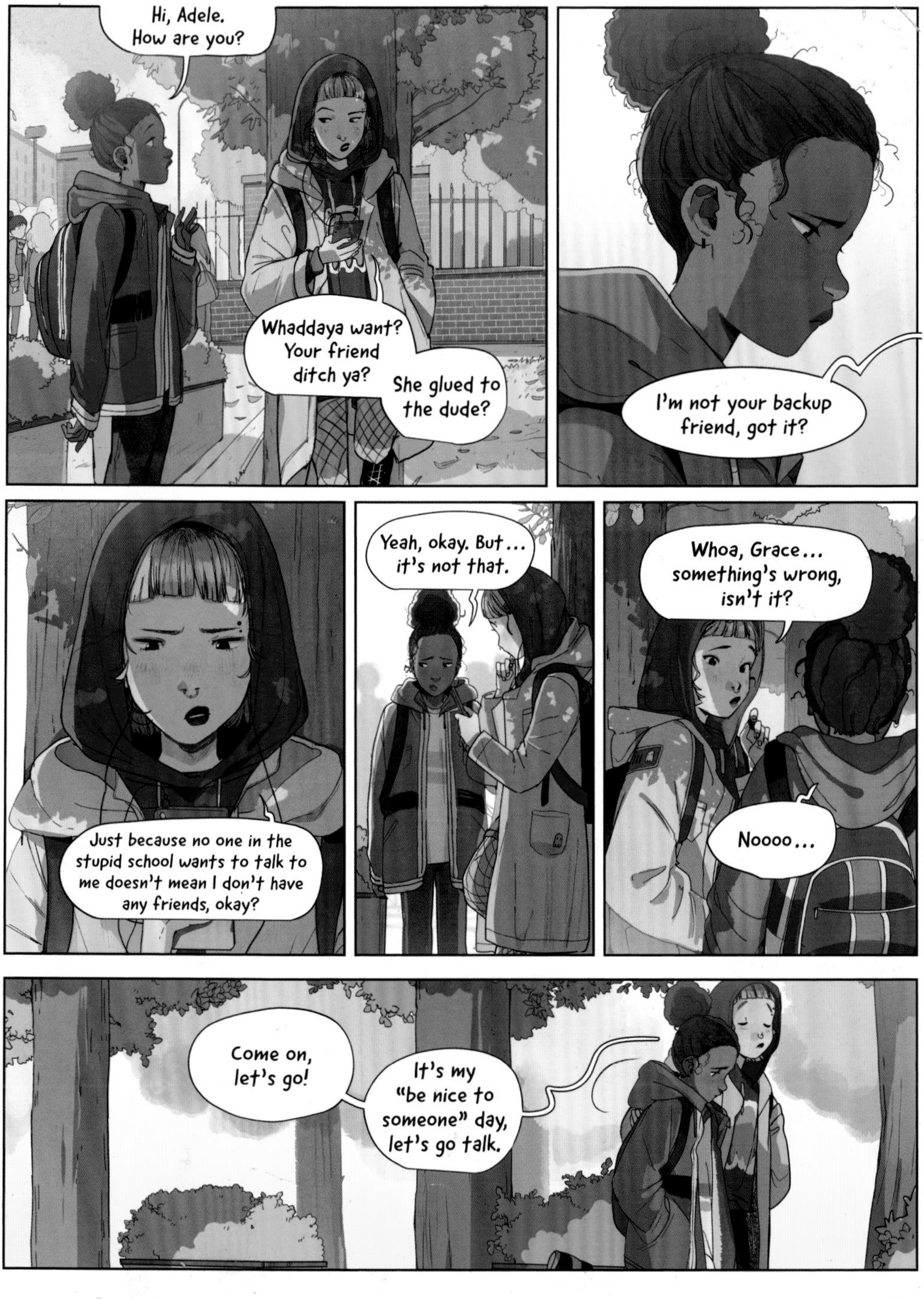
Hi, Adele.
How are you?
Whaddaya want? Your friend ditch ya?
She glued to the dude?
I'm not your backup friend, got it?
Just because no one in the stupid school wants to talk to me doesn't mean I don't have any friends, okay?
Yeah, okay. But... it's not that.
Whoa, Grace... something's wrong, isn't it?
Noooo...
Come on, let's go!
It's my "be nice to someone" day, let's go talk.

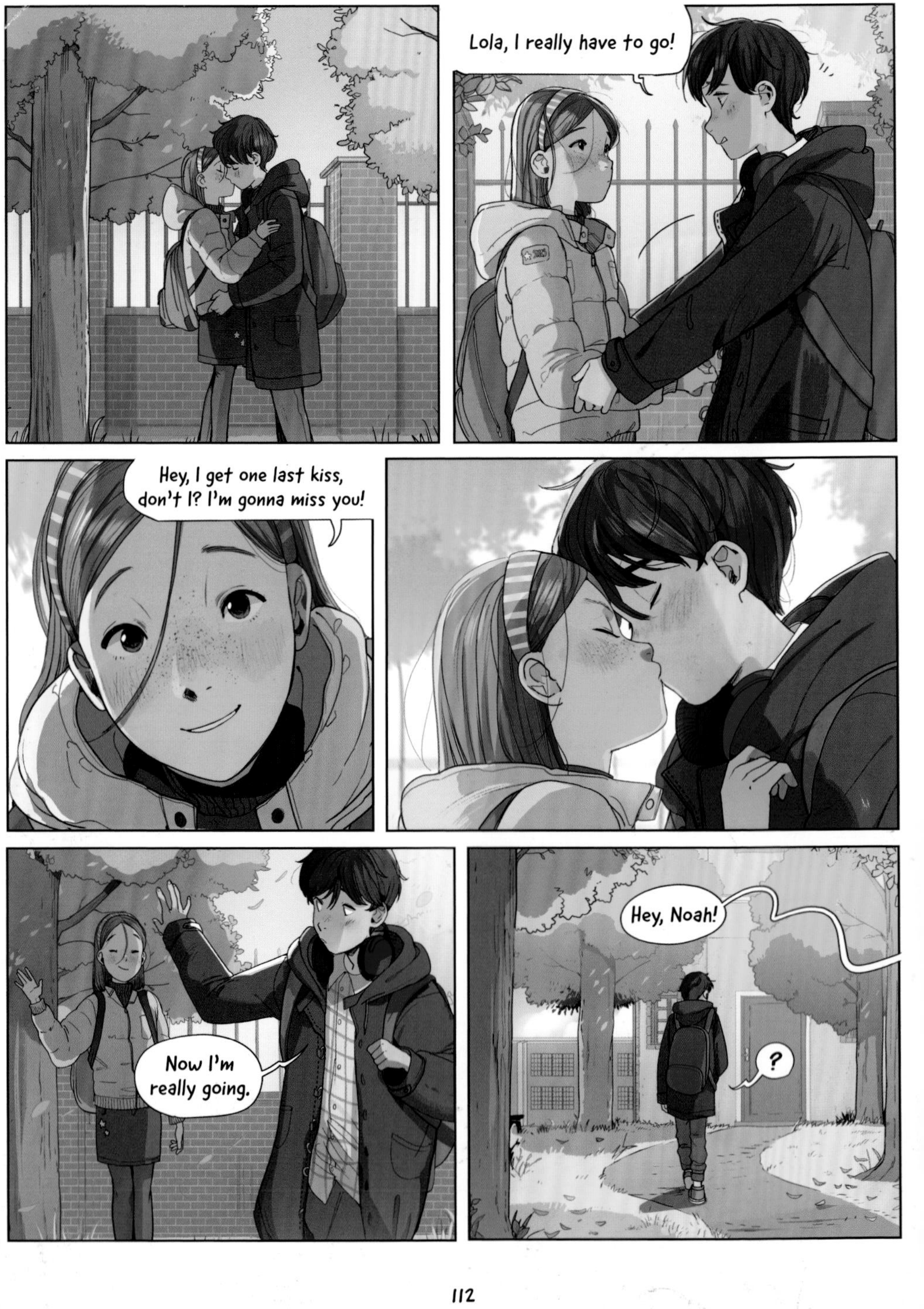
Lola, I really have to go!
Hey, I get one last kiss, don't I? I'm gonna miss you!
Now I'm really going.
Hey, Noah!
?

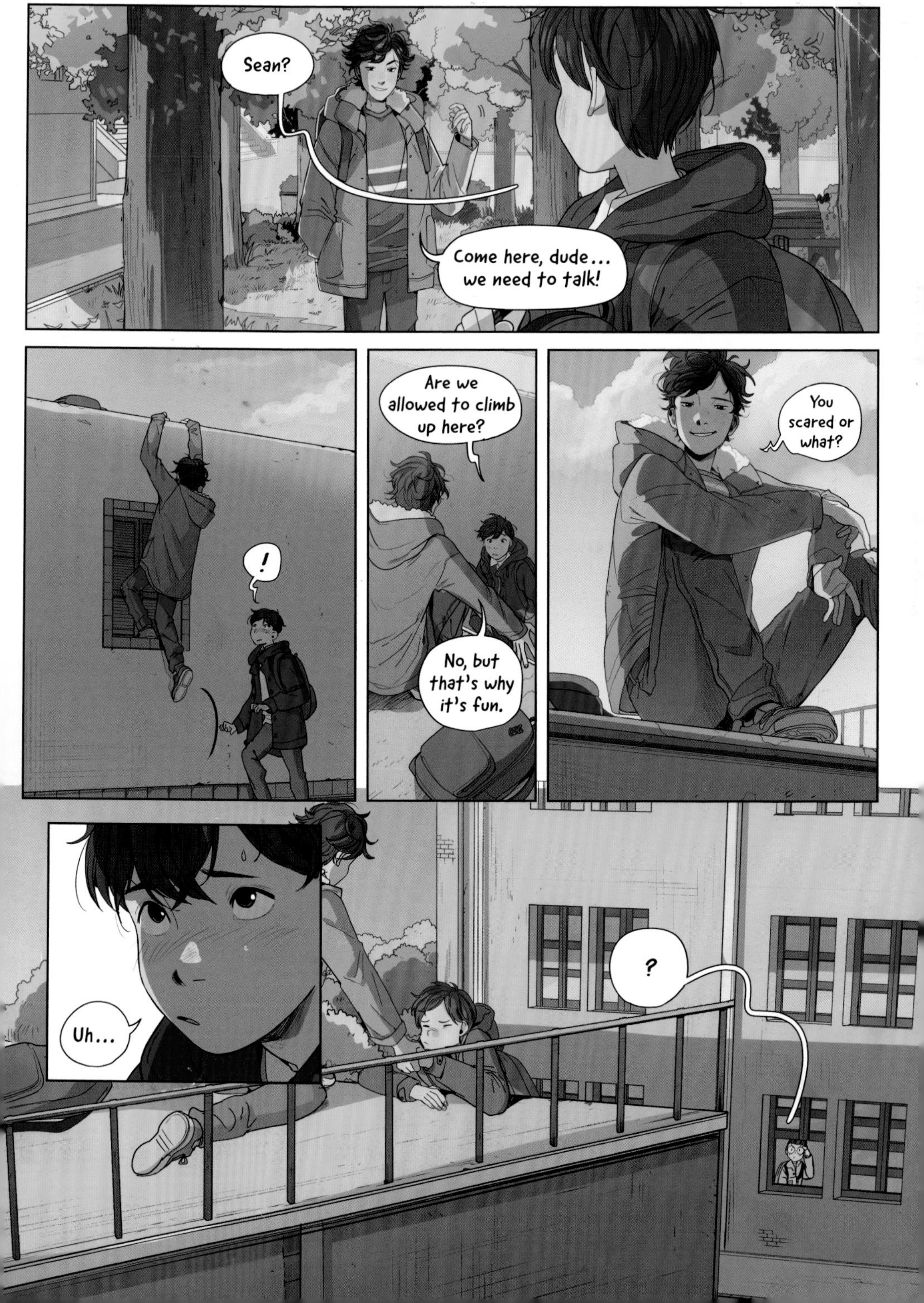
Sean?
Come here, dude... we need to talk!
!
Are we allowed to climb up here?
No, but that's why it's fun.
You scared or what?
Uh...
?

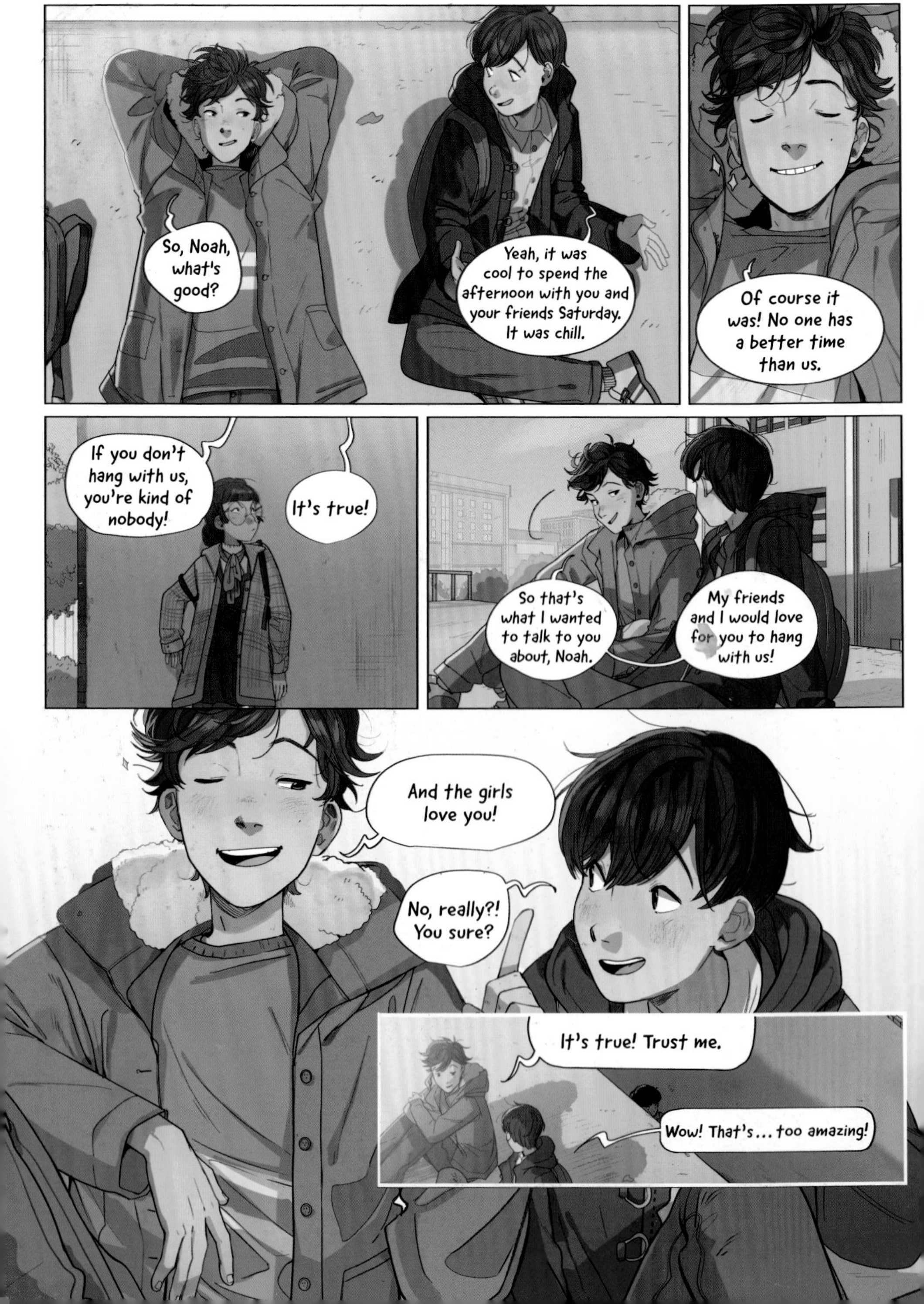
So, Noah, what's good?
Yeah, it was cool to spend the afternoon with you and your friends Saturday. It was chill.
Of course it was! No one has a better time than us.
If you don't hang with us, you're kind of nobody!
It's true!
So that's what I wanted to talk to you about, Noah.
My friends and I would love for you to hang with us!
And the girls love you!
No, really?! You sure?
It's true! Trust me.
Wow! That's... too amazing!

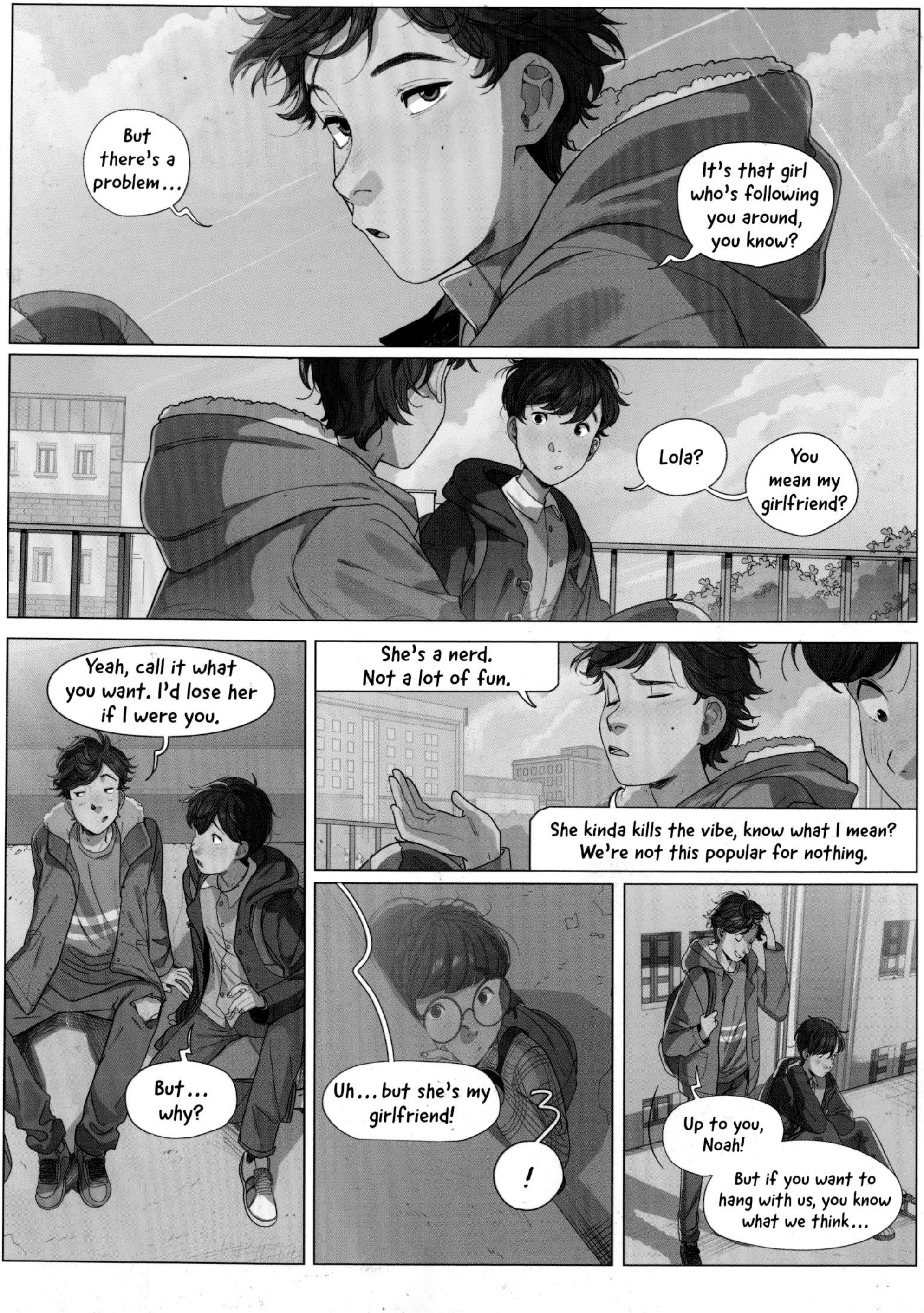

But there's a problem...
It's that girl who's following you around, you know?
Lola?
You mean my girlfriend?
Yeah, call it what you want. I'd lose her if I were you.
She's a nerd. Not a lot of fun.
She kinda kills the vibe, know what I mean? We're not this popular for nothing.
But... why?
Uh... but she's my girlfriend!
!
Up to you, Noah!
But if you want to hang with us, you know what we think...

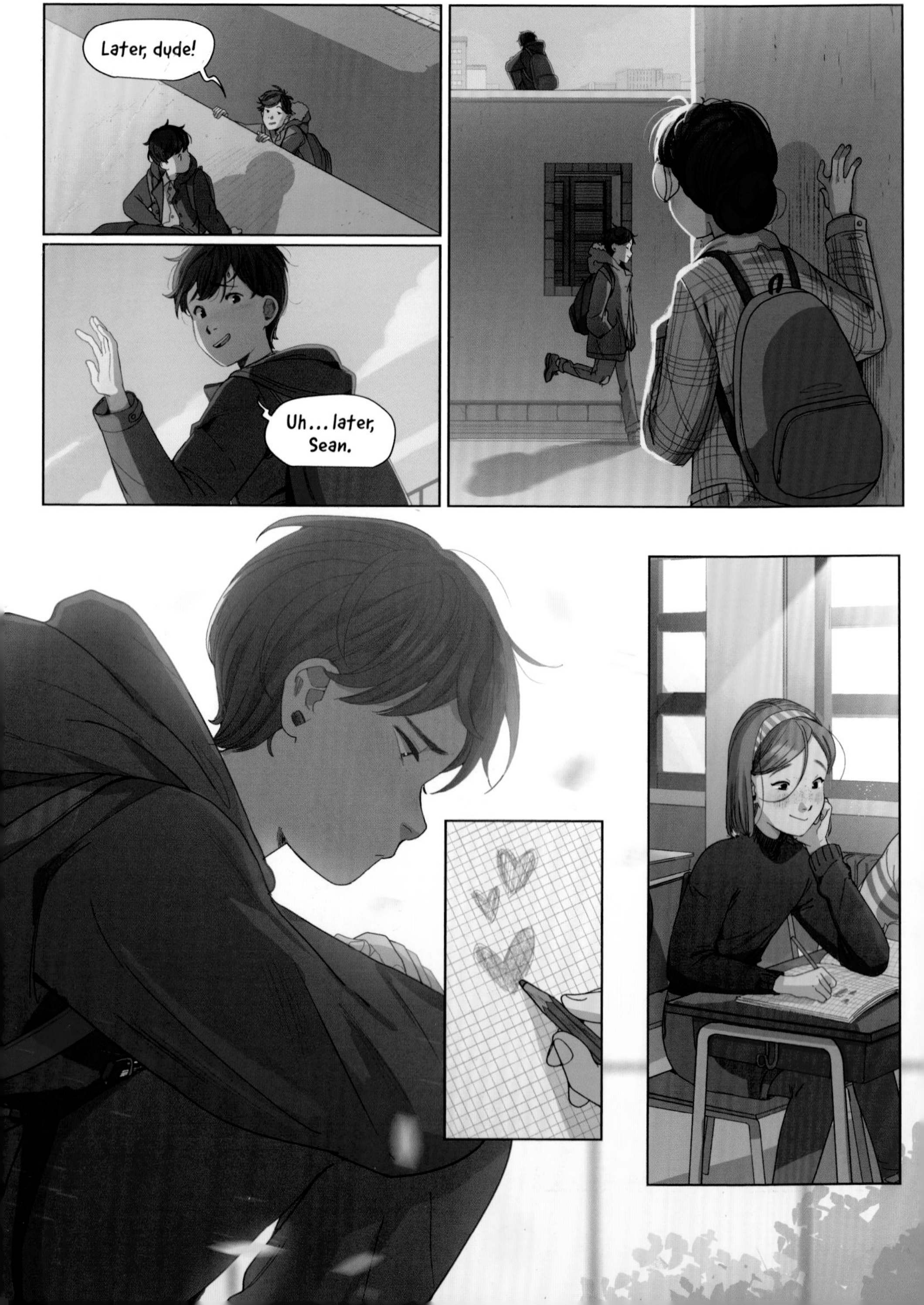
Later, dude!
Uh... later, Sean.

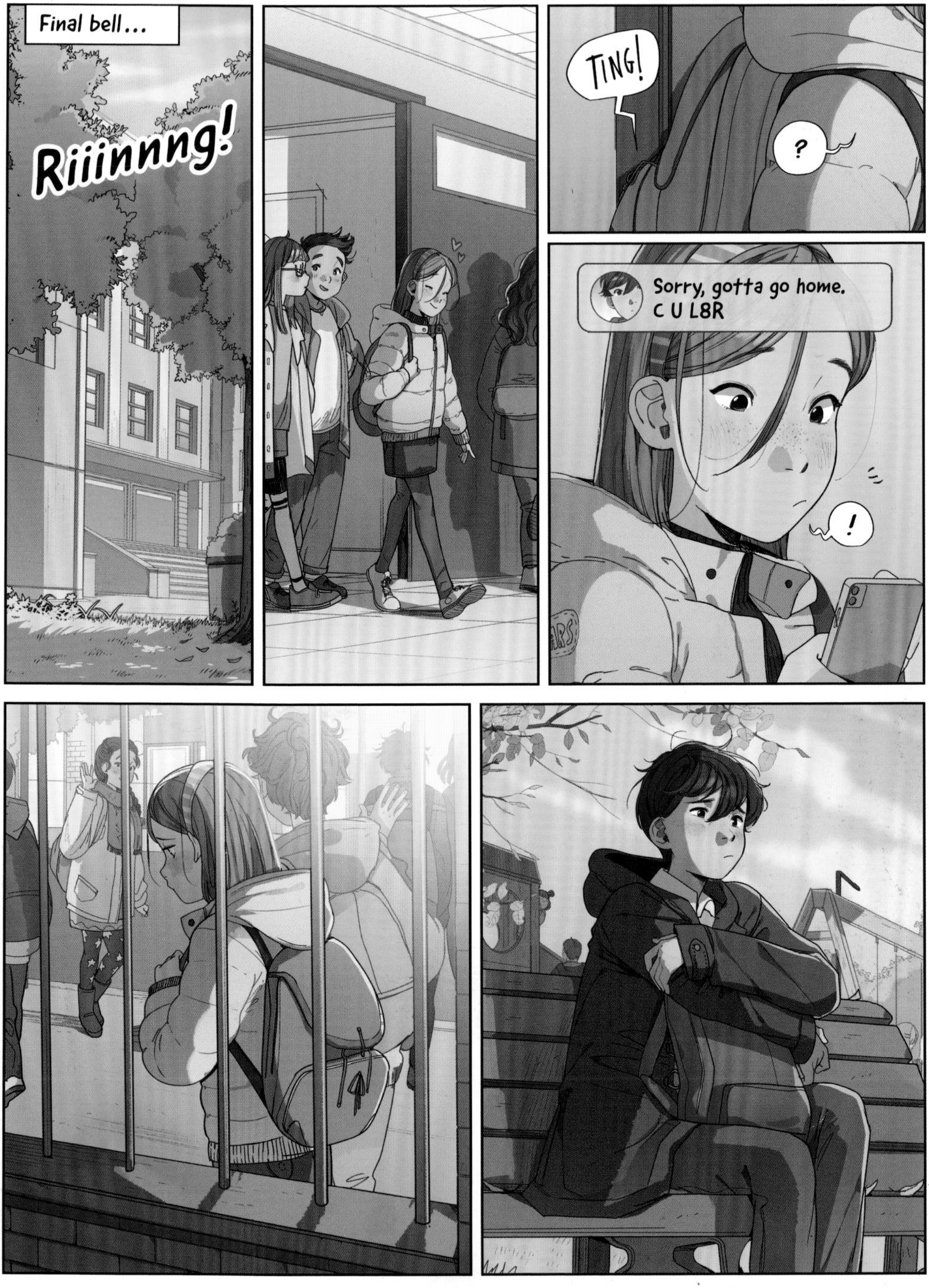
Final bell...
Riiinnng!
TING!
?
Sorry, gotta go home.
C U L8R
!

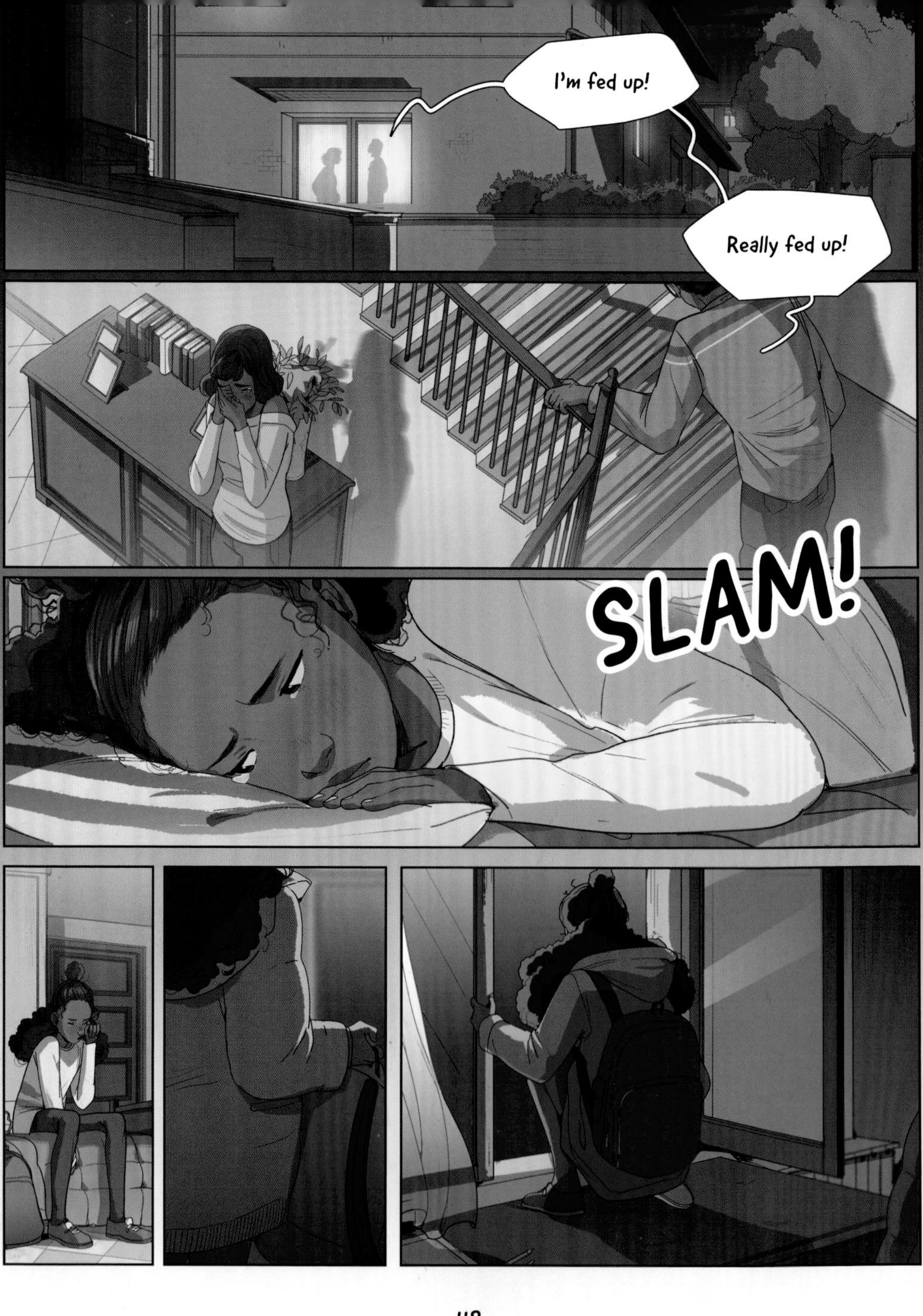
I'm fed up!
Really fed up!
SLAM!

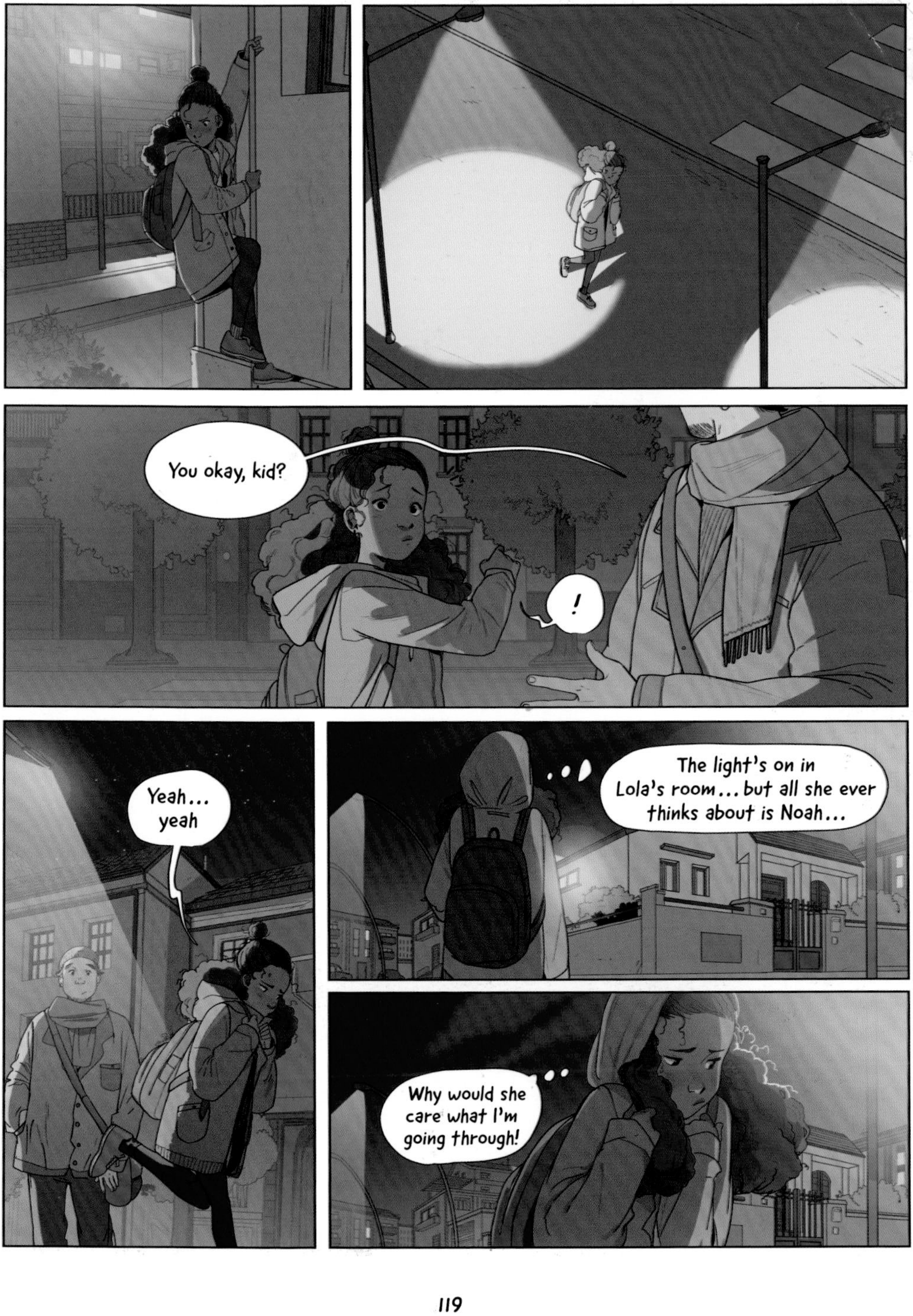
You okay, kid?
!
Yeah... yeah
The light's on in Lola's room... but all she ever thinks about is Noah...
Why would she care what I'm going through!

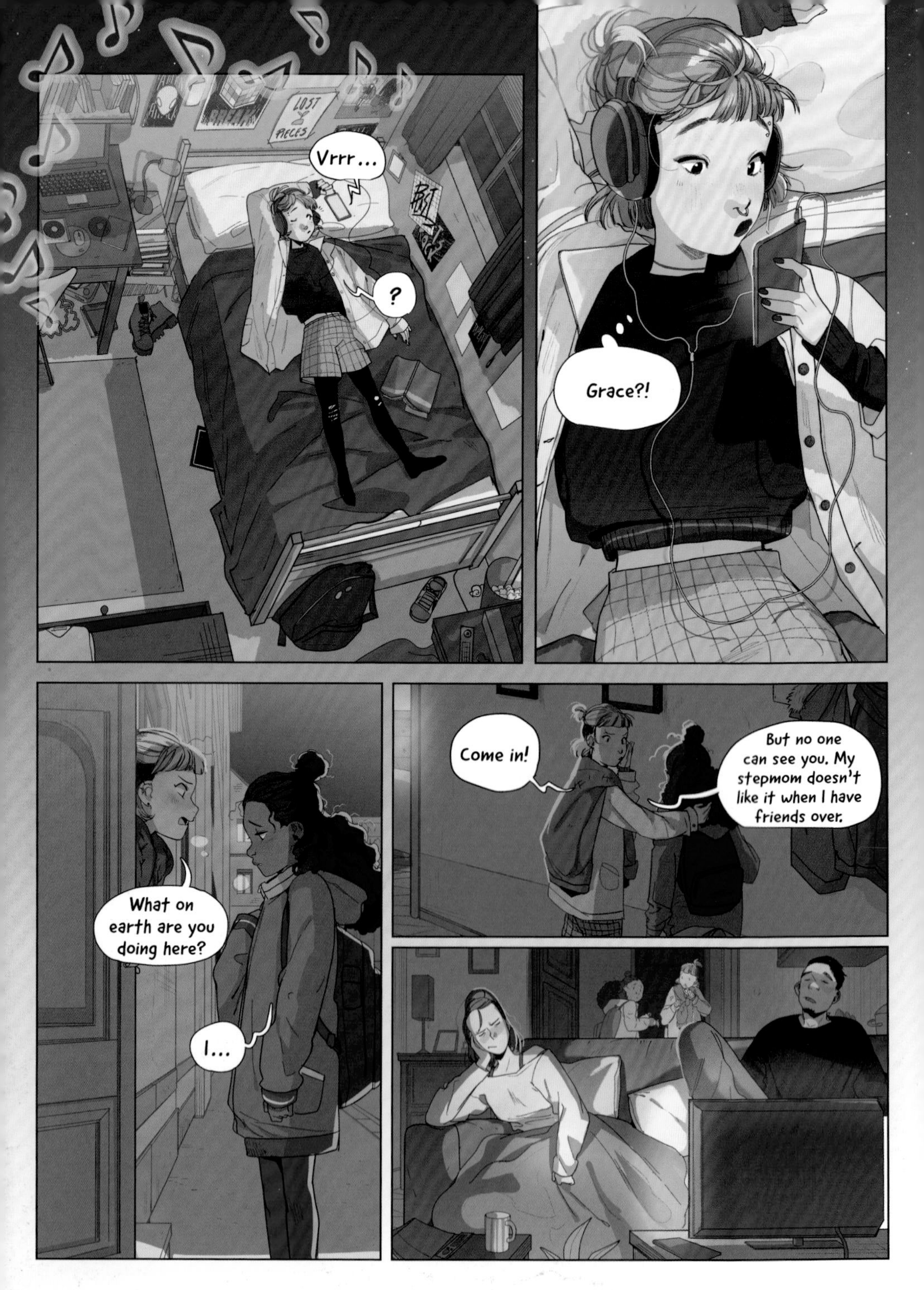
Vrrr...
?
Grace?!
What on earth are you doing here?
I...
Come in!
But no one can see you. My stepmom doesn't like it when I have friends over.

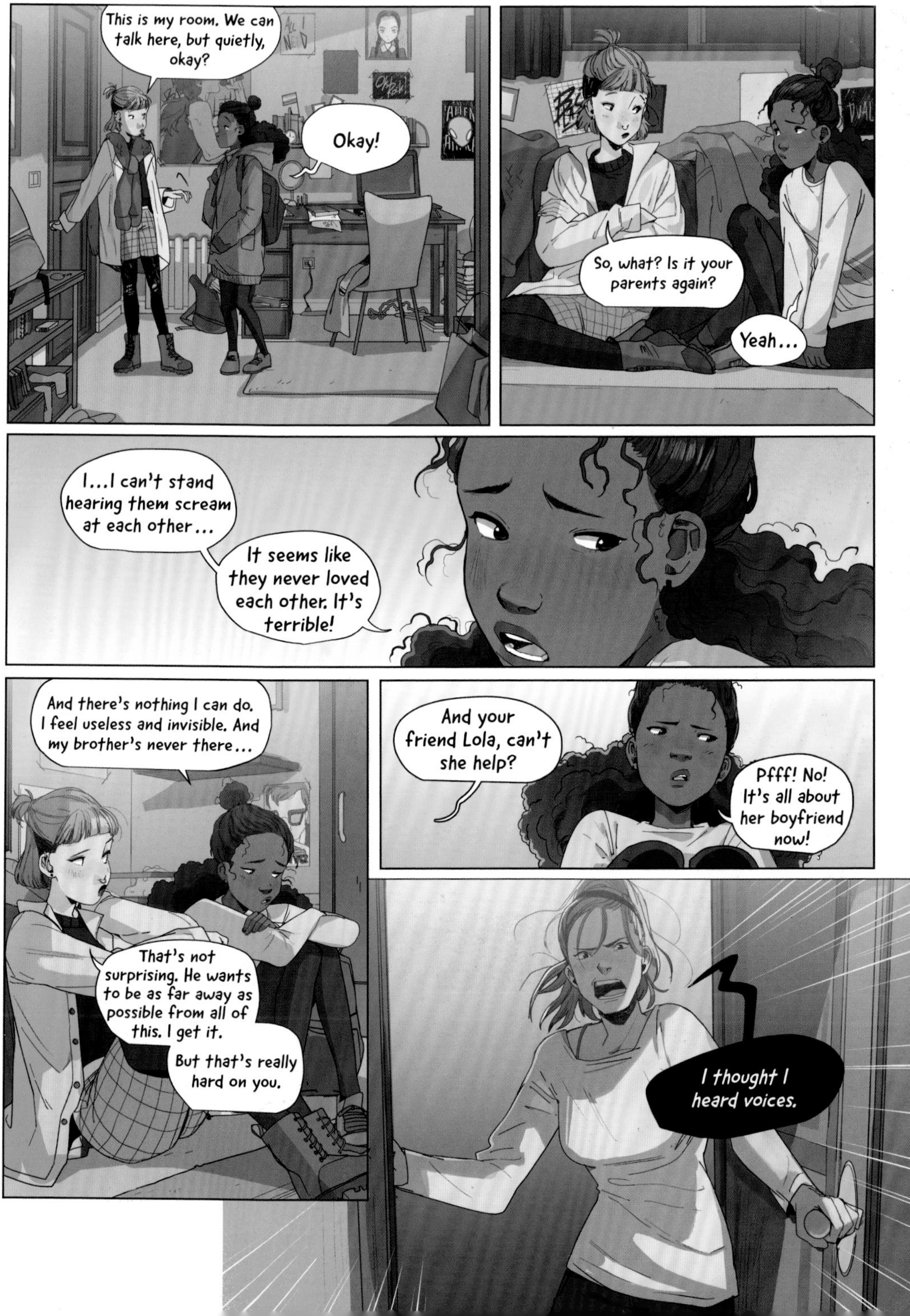

This is my room. We can talk here, but quietly, okay?
Okay!
So, what? Is it your parents again?
Yeah...
I...I can't stand hearing them scream at each other...
It seems like they never loved each other. It's terrible!
And there's nothing I can do. I feel useless and invisible. And my brother's never there...
That's not surprising. He wants to be as far away as possible from all of this. I get it.
But that's really hard on you.
And your friend Lola, can't she help?
Pfff! No! It's all about her boyfriend now!
I thought I heard voices.

You, get out!

Adele knows she's not allowed to let just anybody in my house!

This is not your house! It's my father's!

You still don't get it, do you? Your father wishes you weren't here at all!

Both of us would be happier without you around! So don't bring her back here or I'll kick you out!

I'm sure your mother would love to have you back, don't you think?

Witch!

Come on, Grace, let's get out of here!

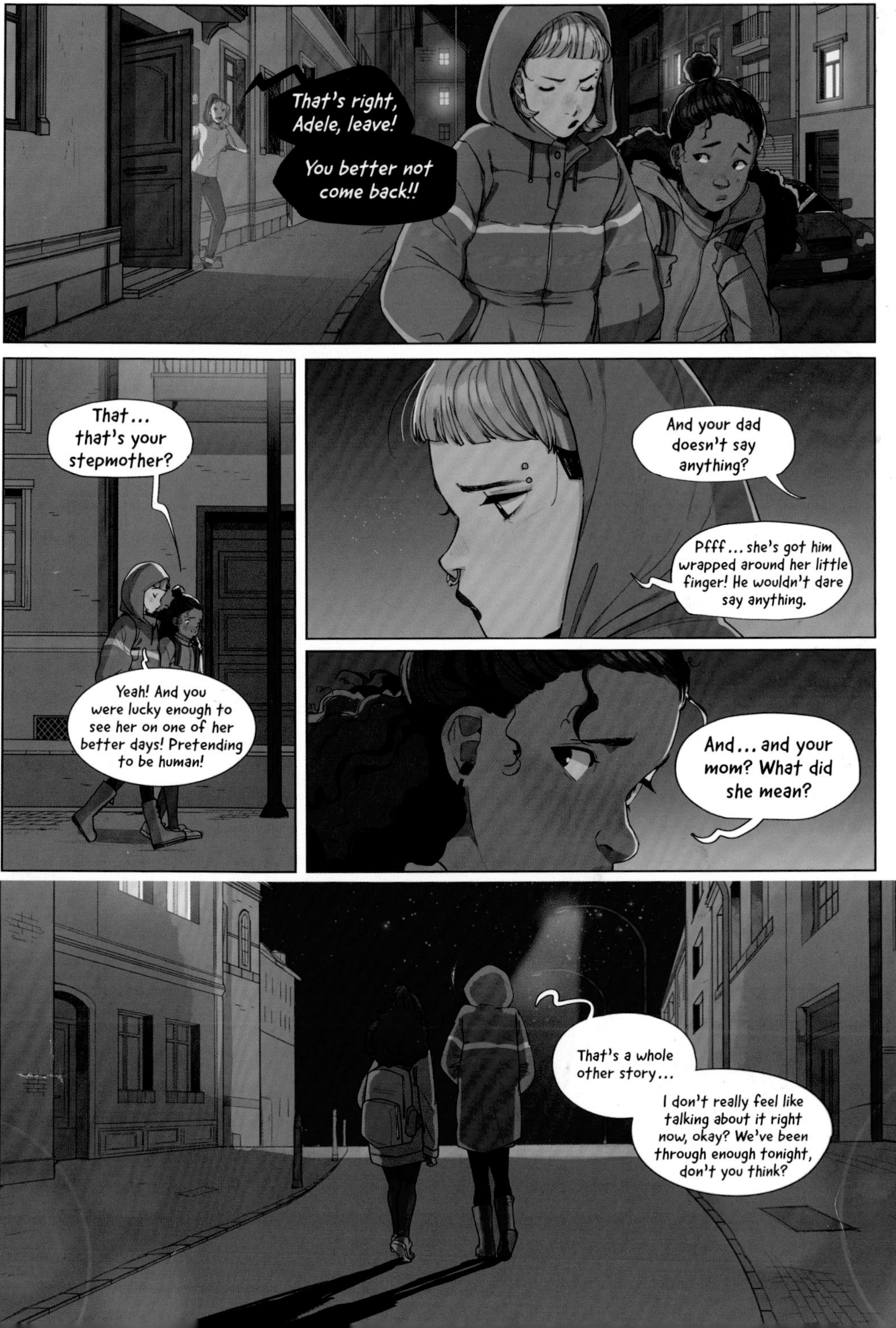
That's right, Adele, leave!
You better not come back!!
That... that's your stepmother?
Yeah! And you were lucky enough to see her on one of her better days! Pretending to be human!
And your dad doesn't say anything?
Pfff... she's got him wrapped around her little finger! He wouldn't dare say anything.
And... and your mom? What did she mean?
That's a whole other story...
I don't really feel like talking about it right now, okay? We've been through enough tonight, don't you think?

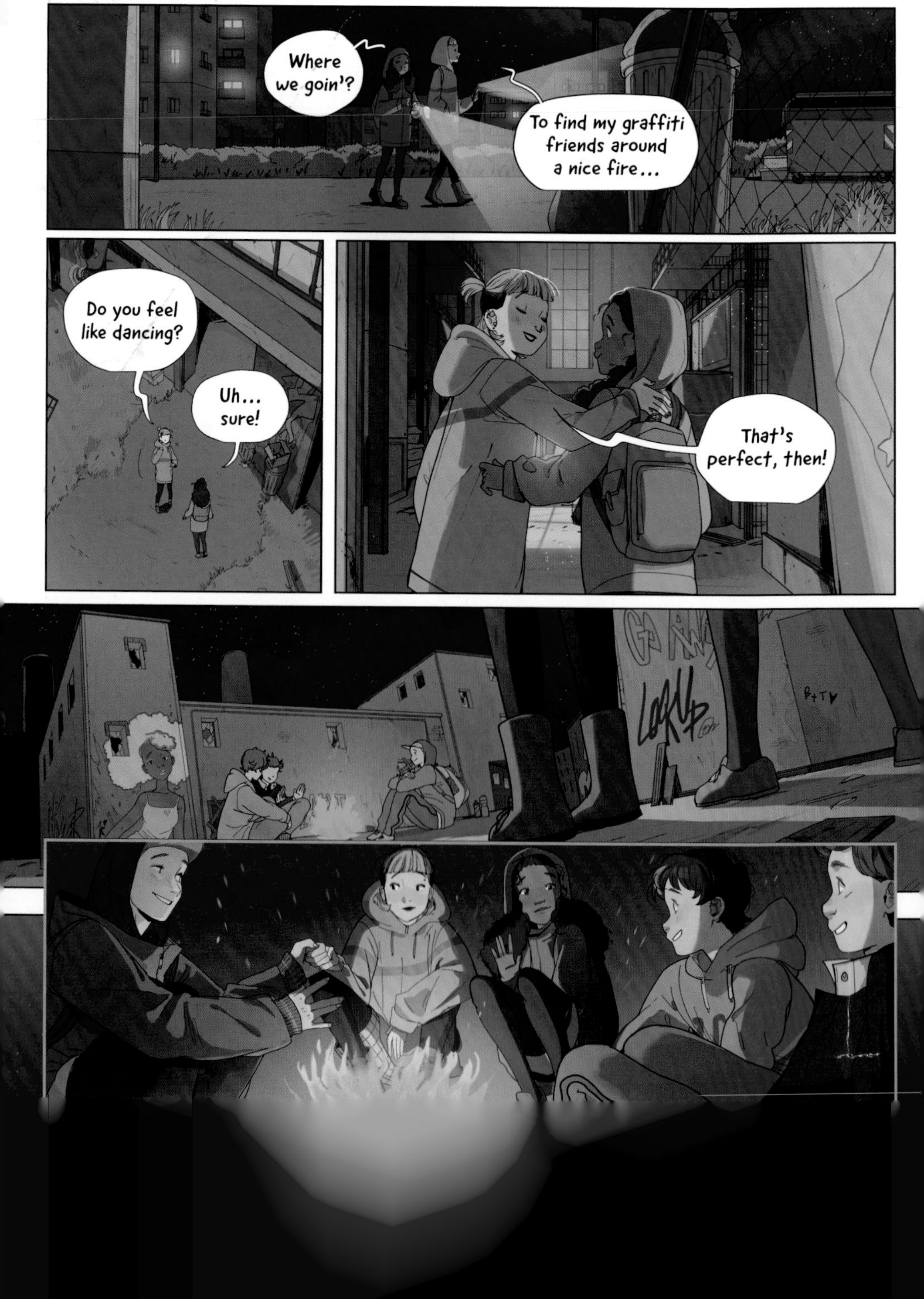
Where we goin'?
To find my graffiti friends around a nice fire...
Do you feel like dancing?
Uh... sure!
That's perfect, then!

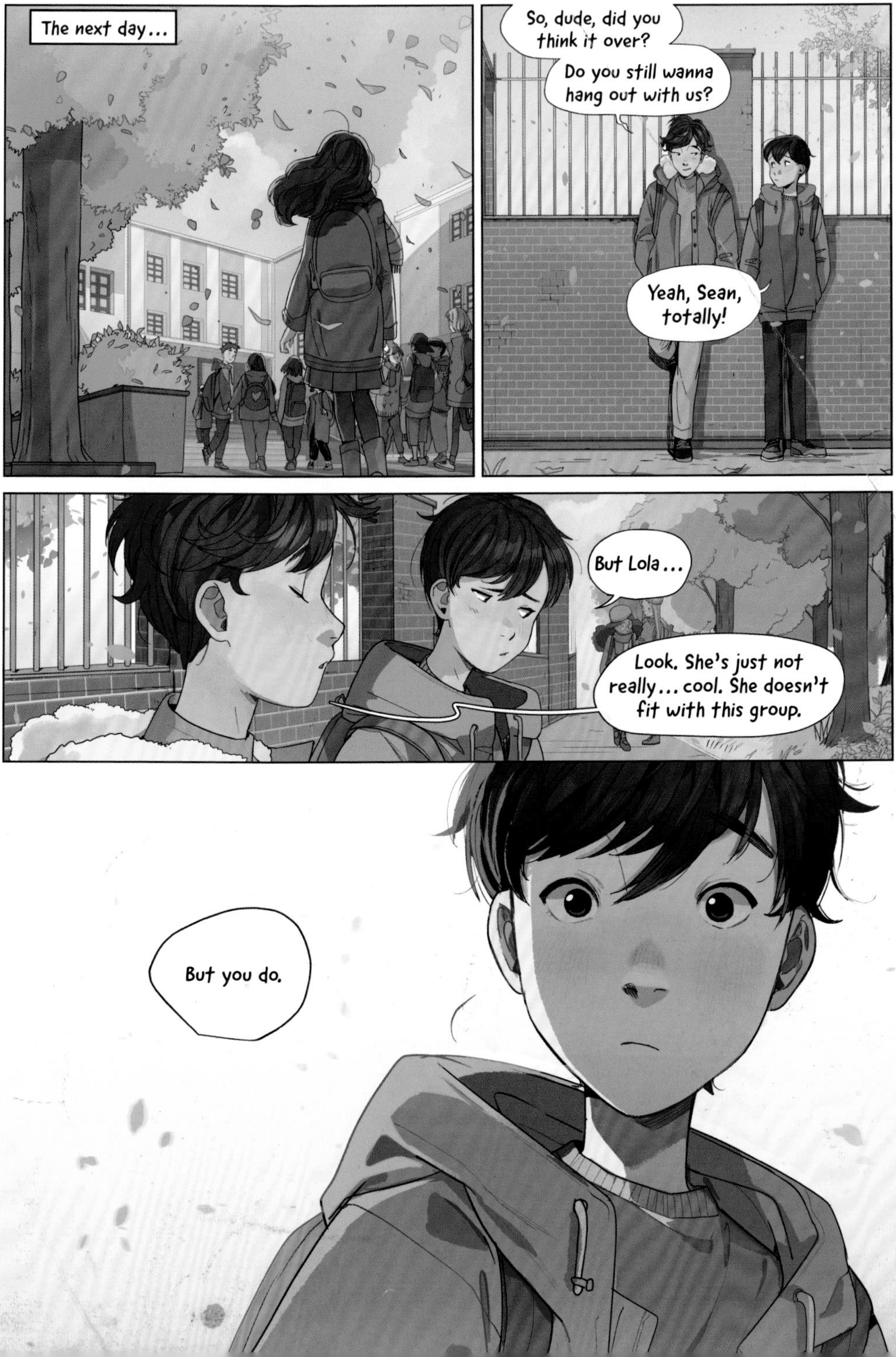
The next day...
So, dude, did you think it over?
Do you still wanna hang out with us?
Yeah, Sean, totally!
But Lola...
Look. She's just not really... cool. She doesn't fit with this group.
But you do.

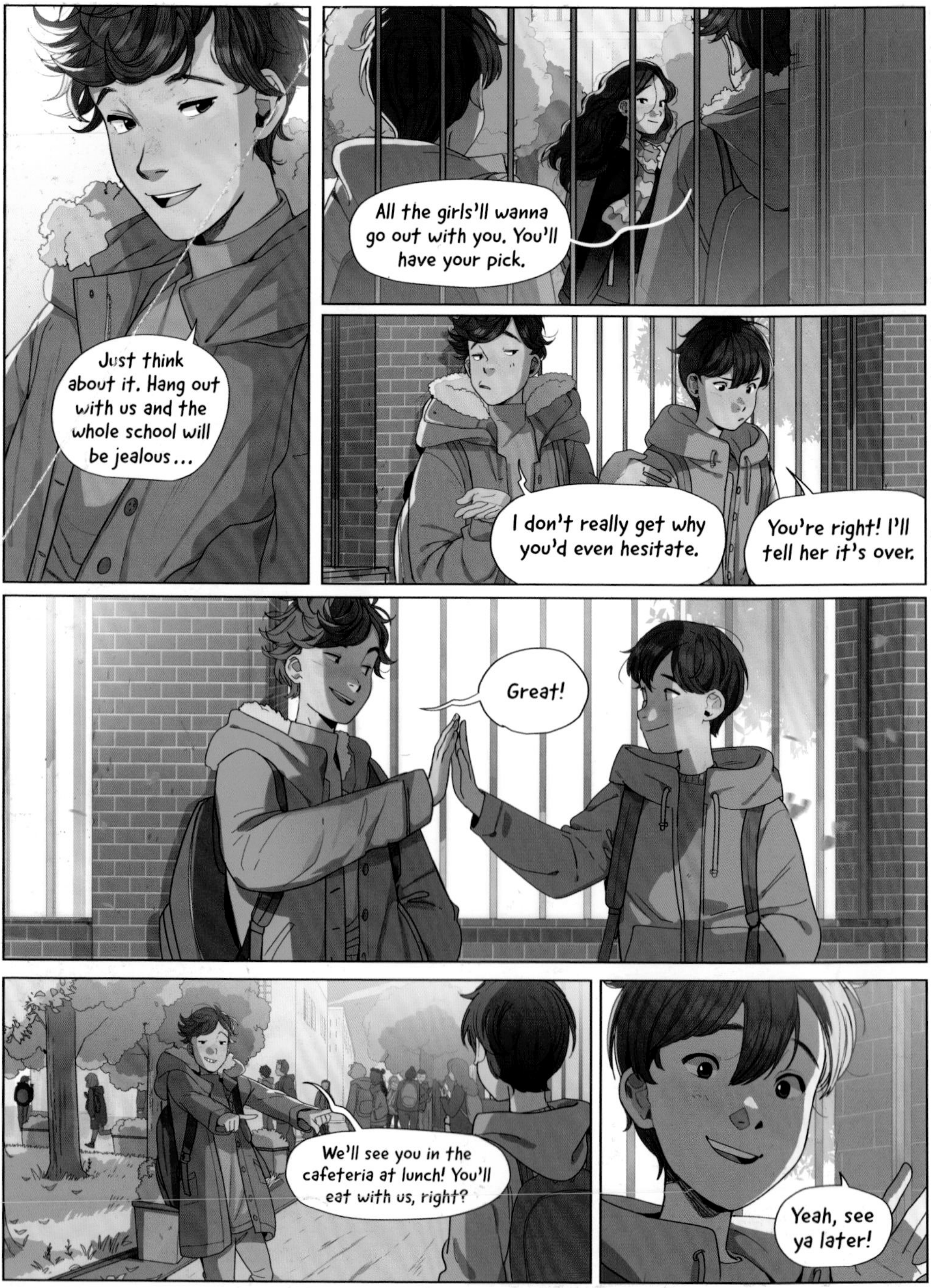
All the girls'll wanna go out with you. You'll have your pick.
Just think about it. Hang out with us and the whole school will be jealous...
I don't really get why you'd even hesitate.
You're right! I'll tell her it's over.
Great!
We'll see you in the cafeteria at lunch! You'll eat with us, right?
Yeah, see ya later!

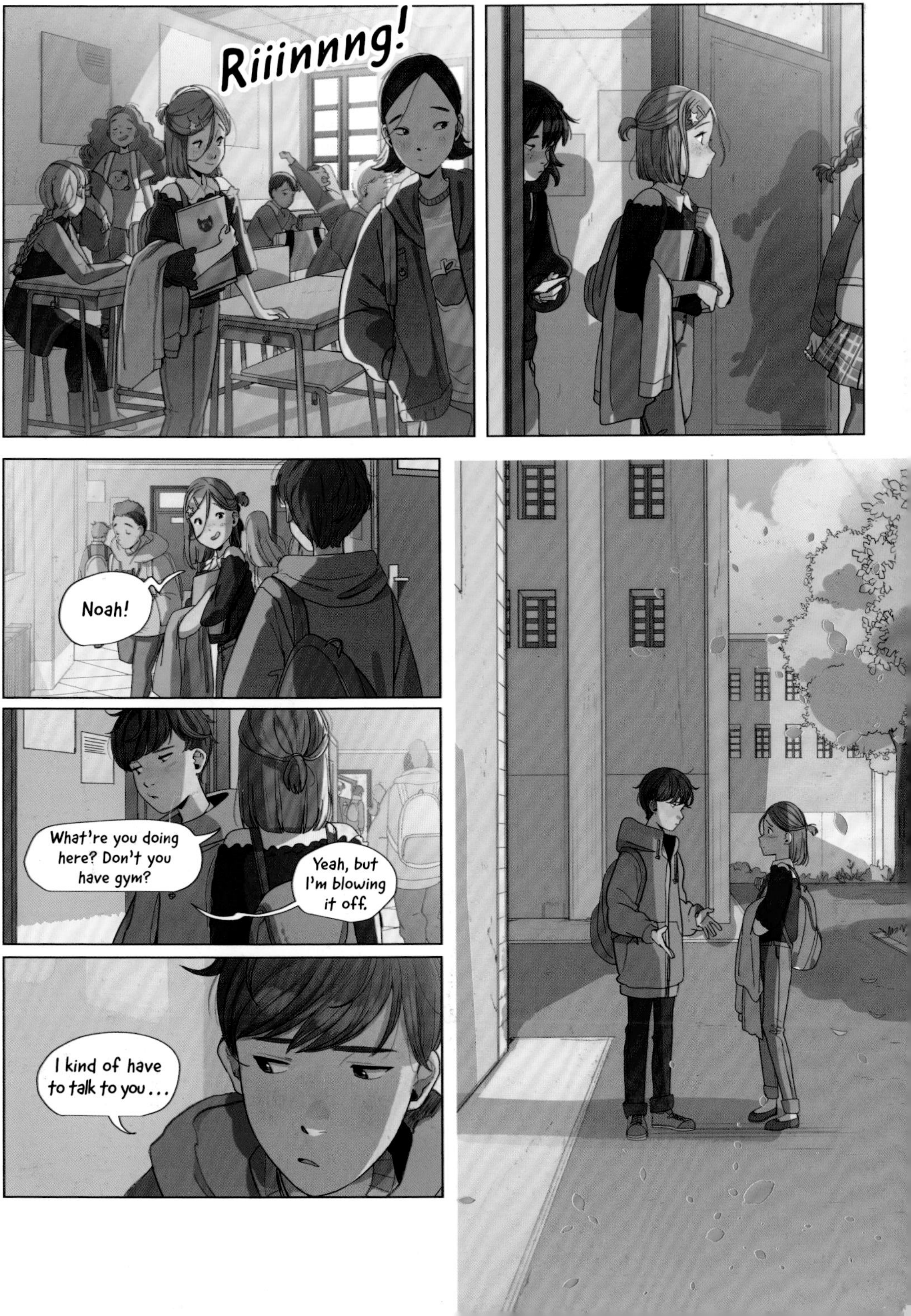
Riiinnng!
Noah!
What're you doing here? Don't you have gym?
Yeah, but I'm blowing it off.
I kind of have to talk to you . . .

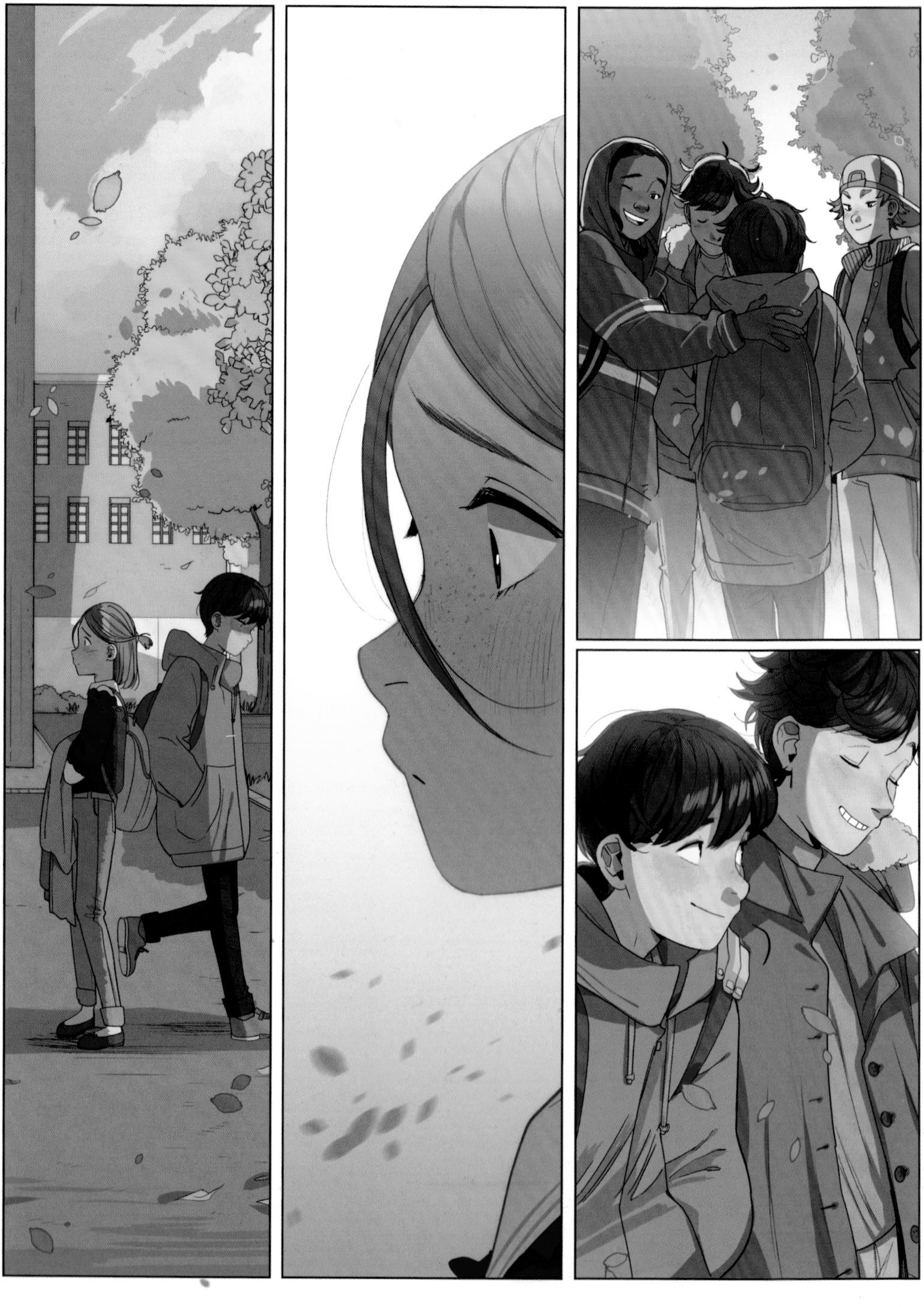

SPLOOSH!

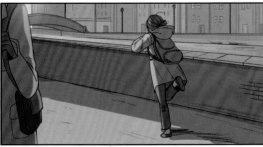

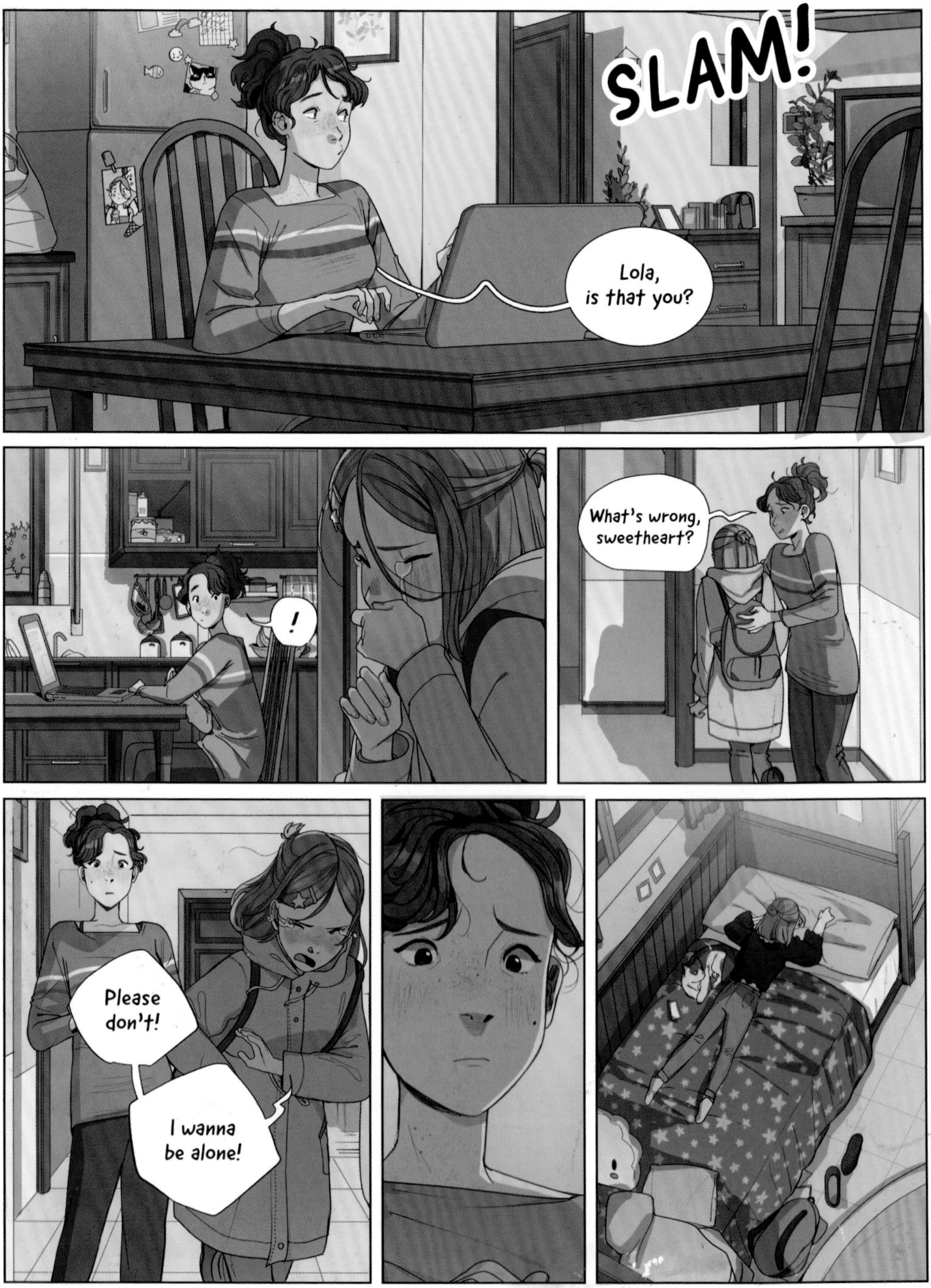
SLAM!
Lola, is that you?
!
What's wrong, sweetheart?
Please don't!
I wanna be alone!

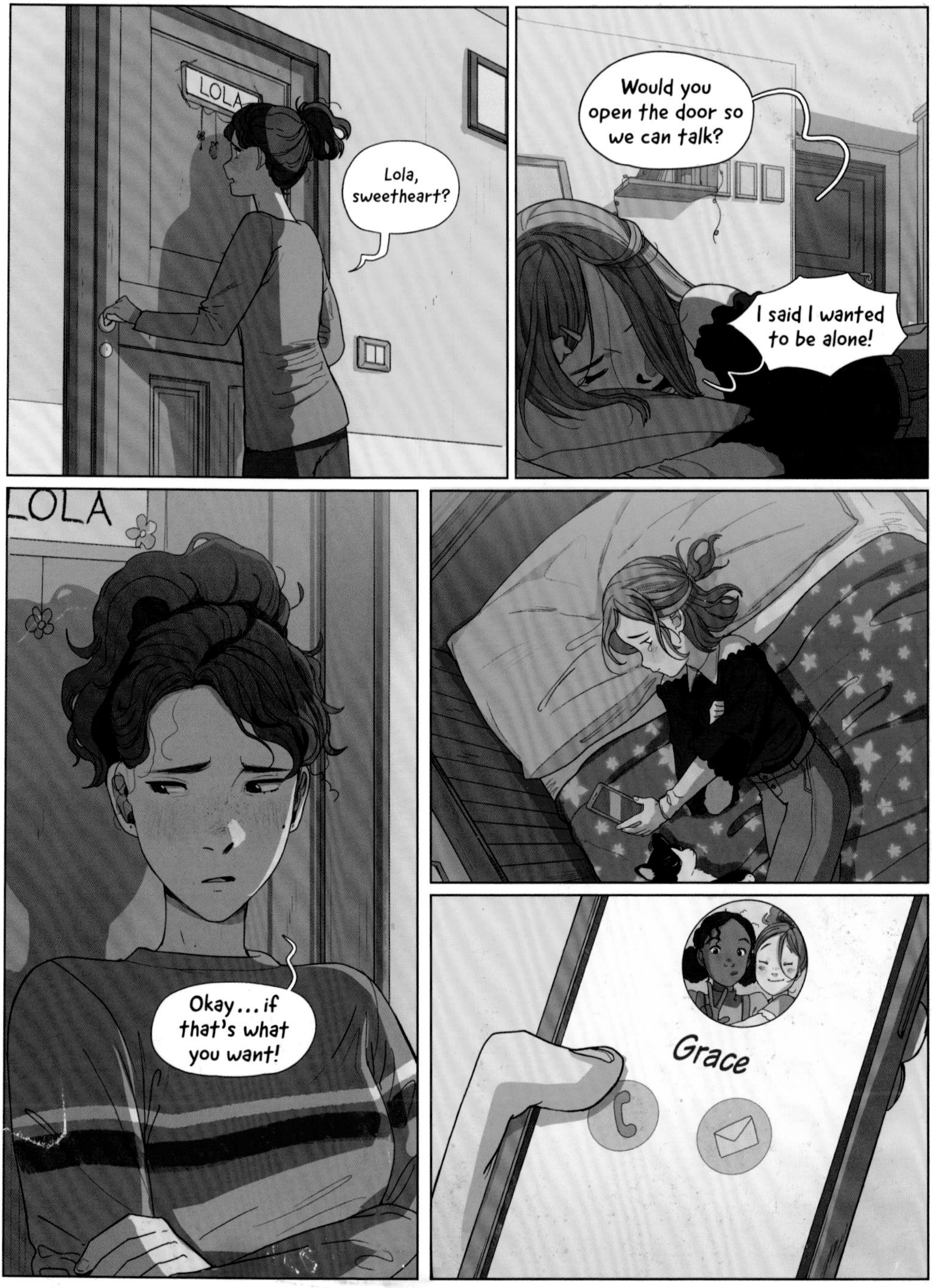
LOLA
Lola, sweetheart?
Would you open the door so we can talk?
I said I wanted to be alone!
LOLA
Okay... if that's what you want!
Grace

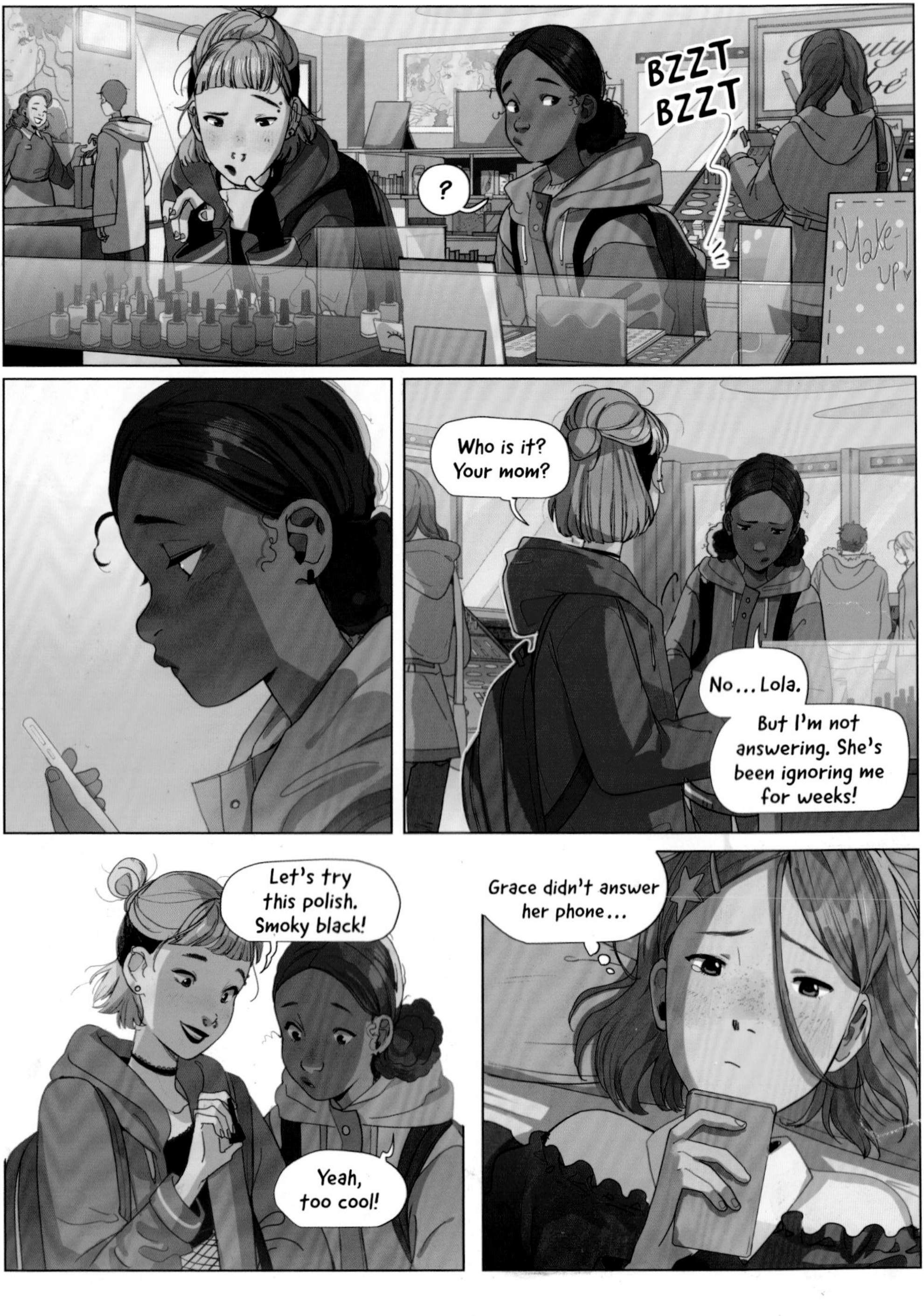
BZZT
BZZT
?
Who is it? Your mom?
No... Lola.
But I'm not answering. She's been ignoring me for weeks!
Let's try this polish. Smoky black!
Yeah, too cool!
Grace didn't answer her phone...

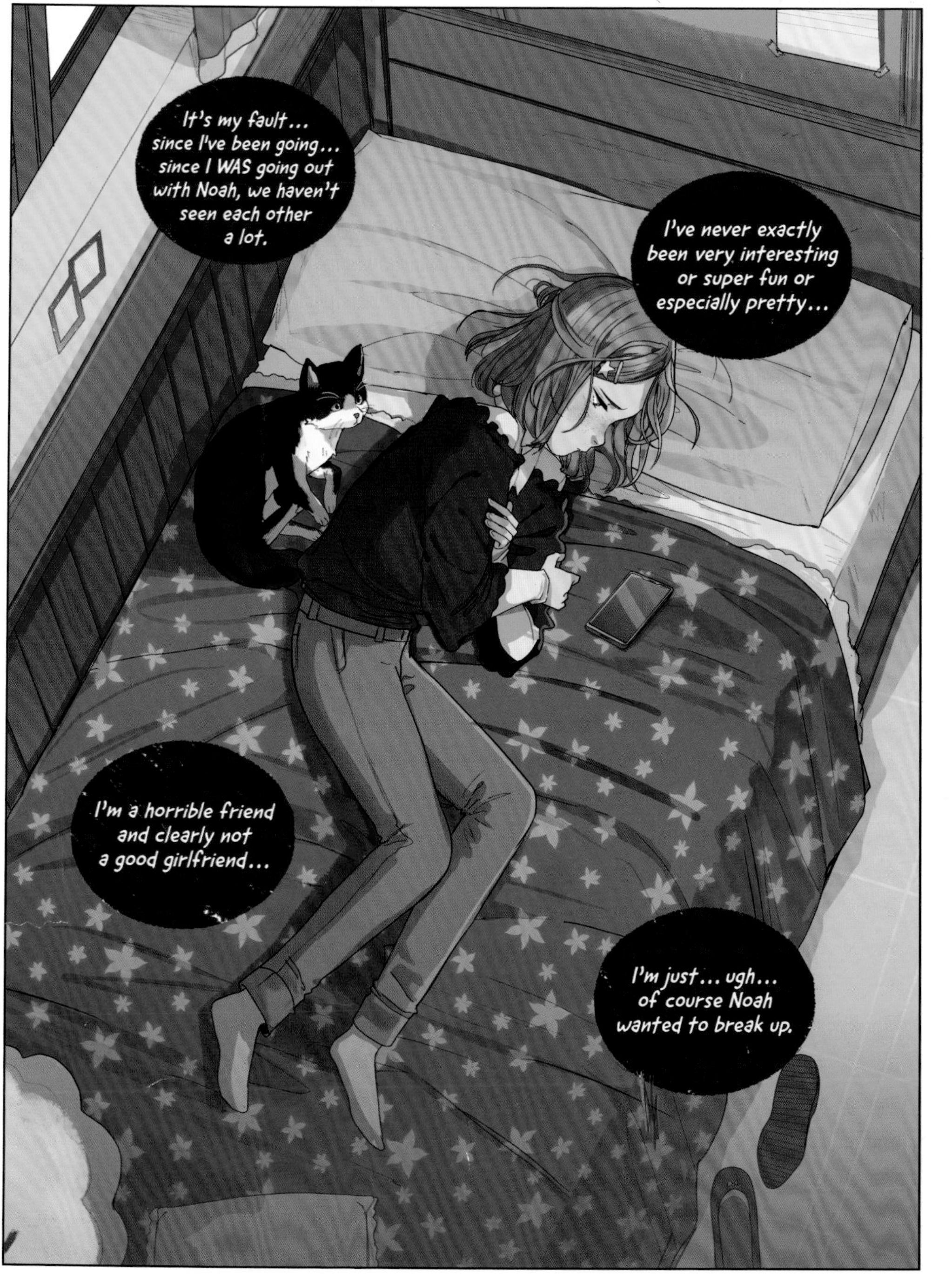
It's my fault... since I've been going... since I WAS going out with Noah, we haven't seen each other a lot.
I've never exactly been very interesting or super fun or especially pretty...
I'm a horrible friend and clearly not a good girlfriend...
I'm just... ugh... of course Noah wanted to break up.

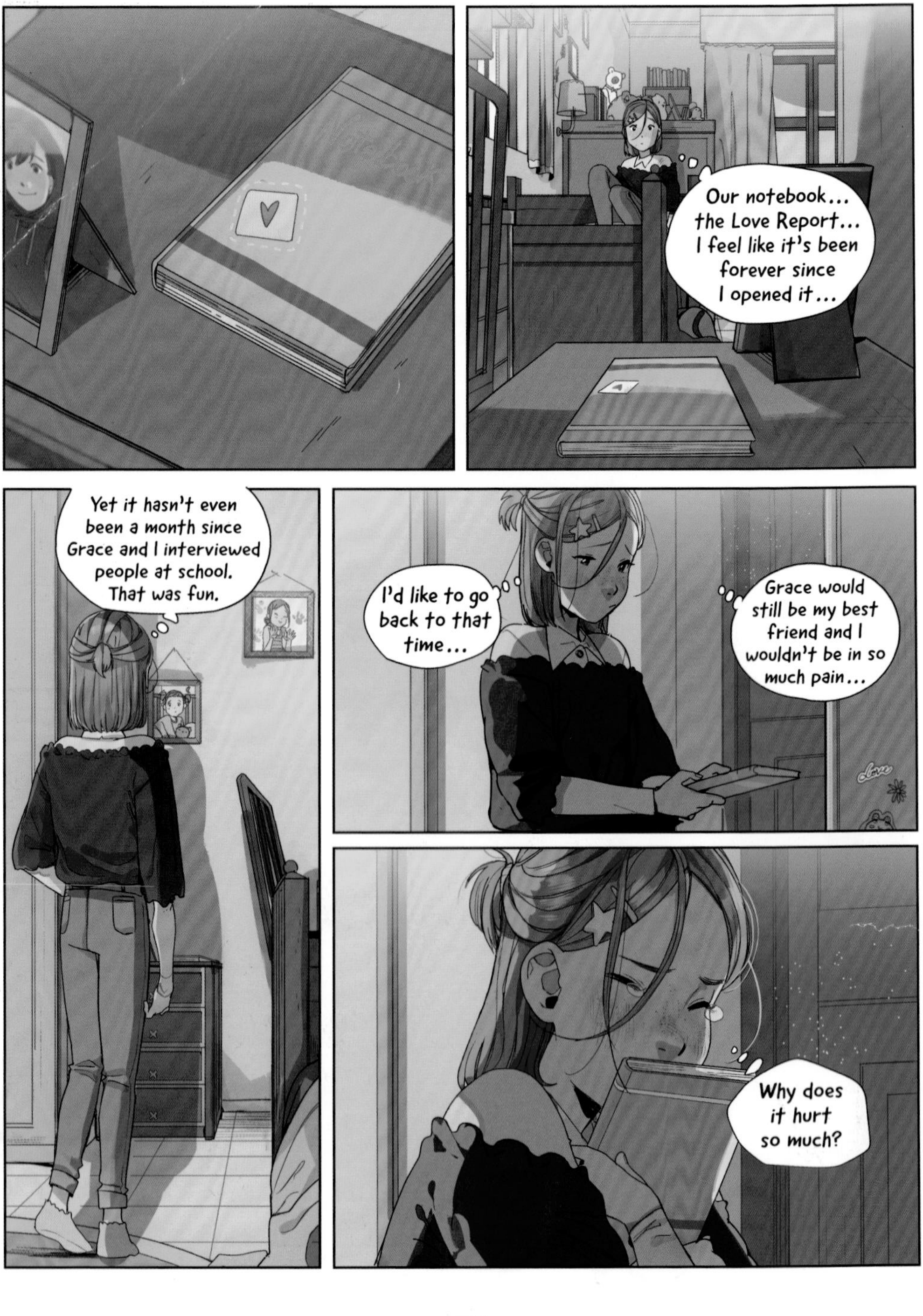
Our notebook... the Love Report... I feel like it's been forever since I opened it...
Yet it hasn't even been a month since Grace and I interviewed people at school. That was fun.
I'd like to go back to that time...
Grace would still be my best friend and I wouldn't be in so much pain...
Why does it hurt so much?

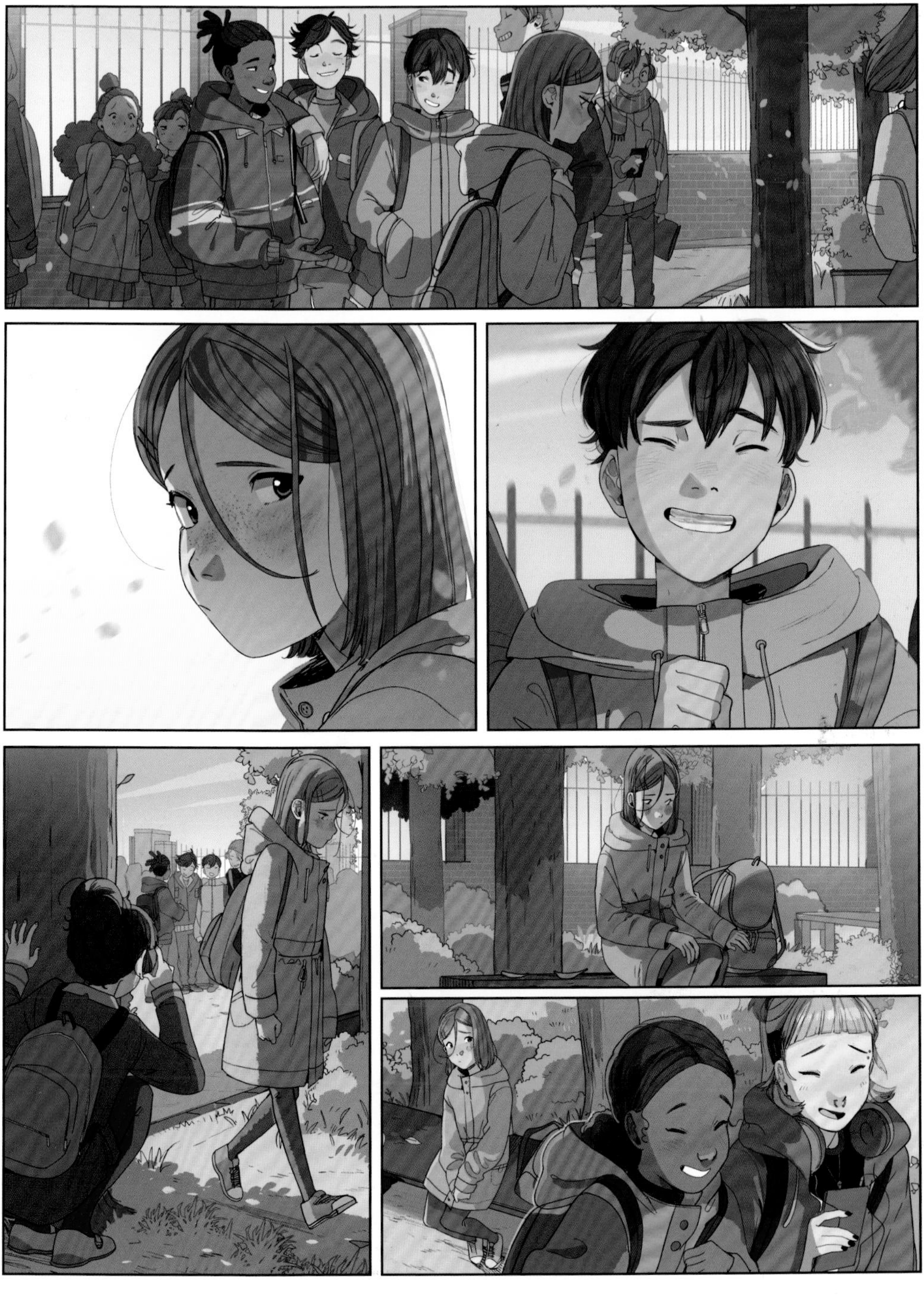

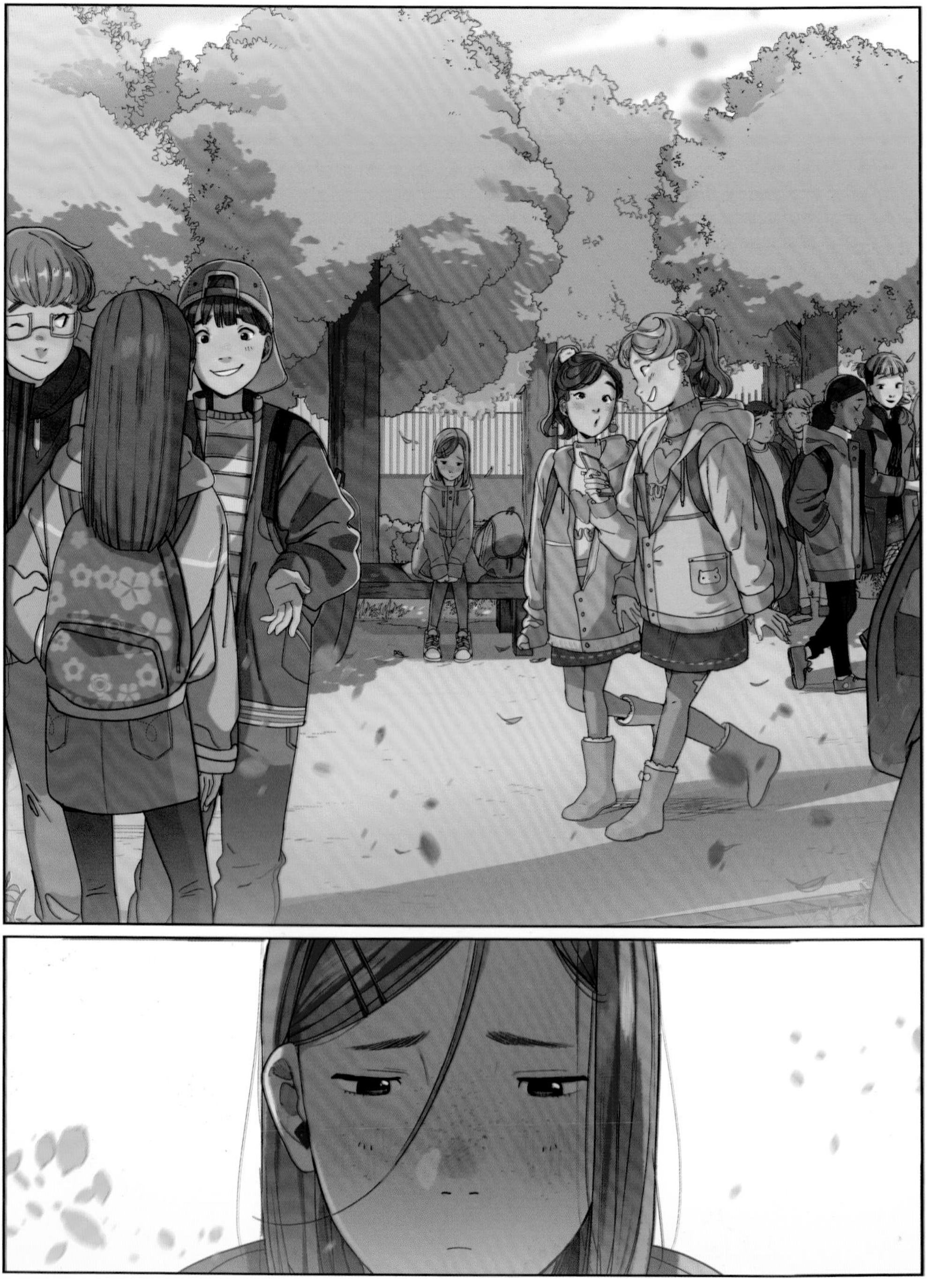

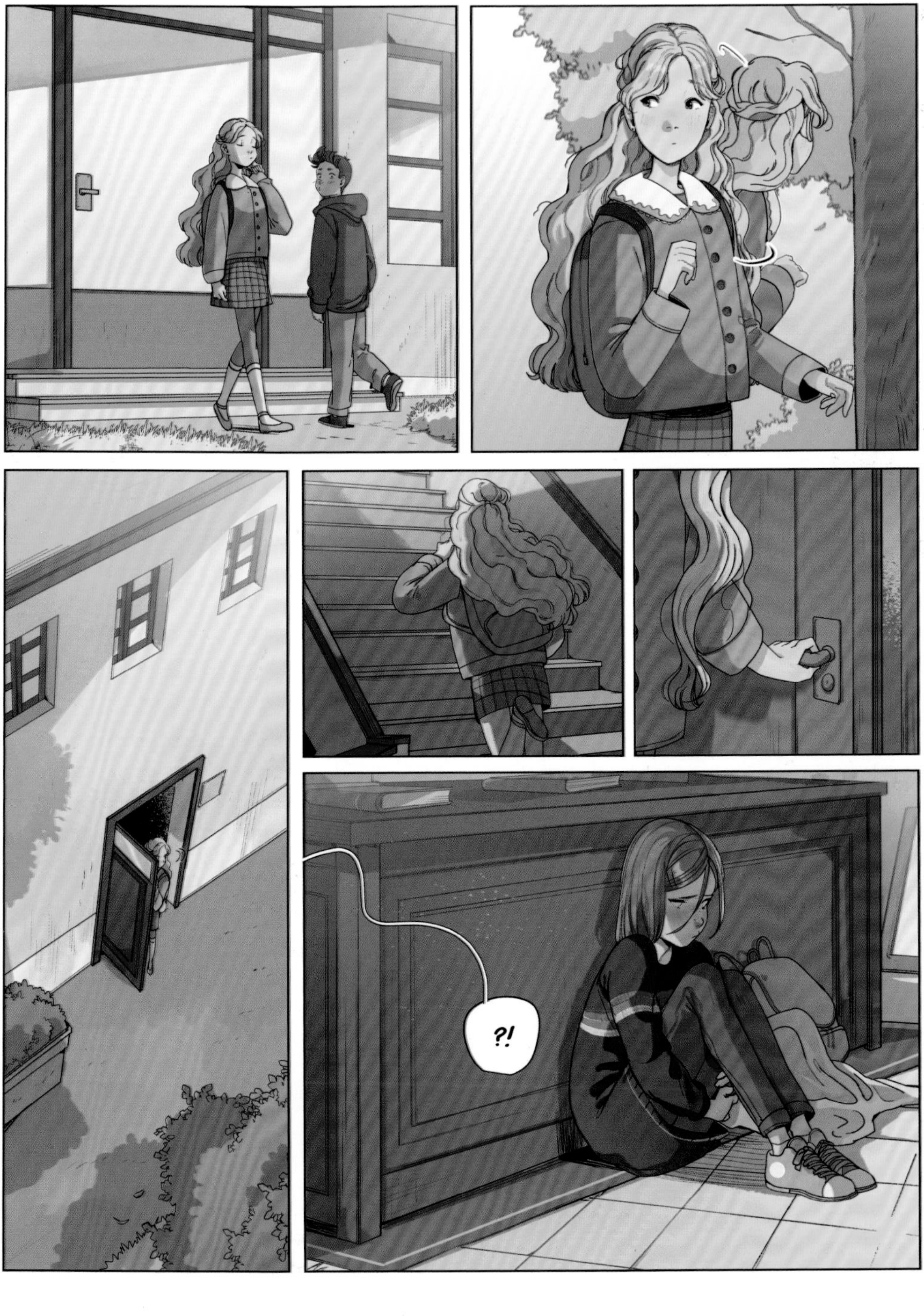
?!

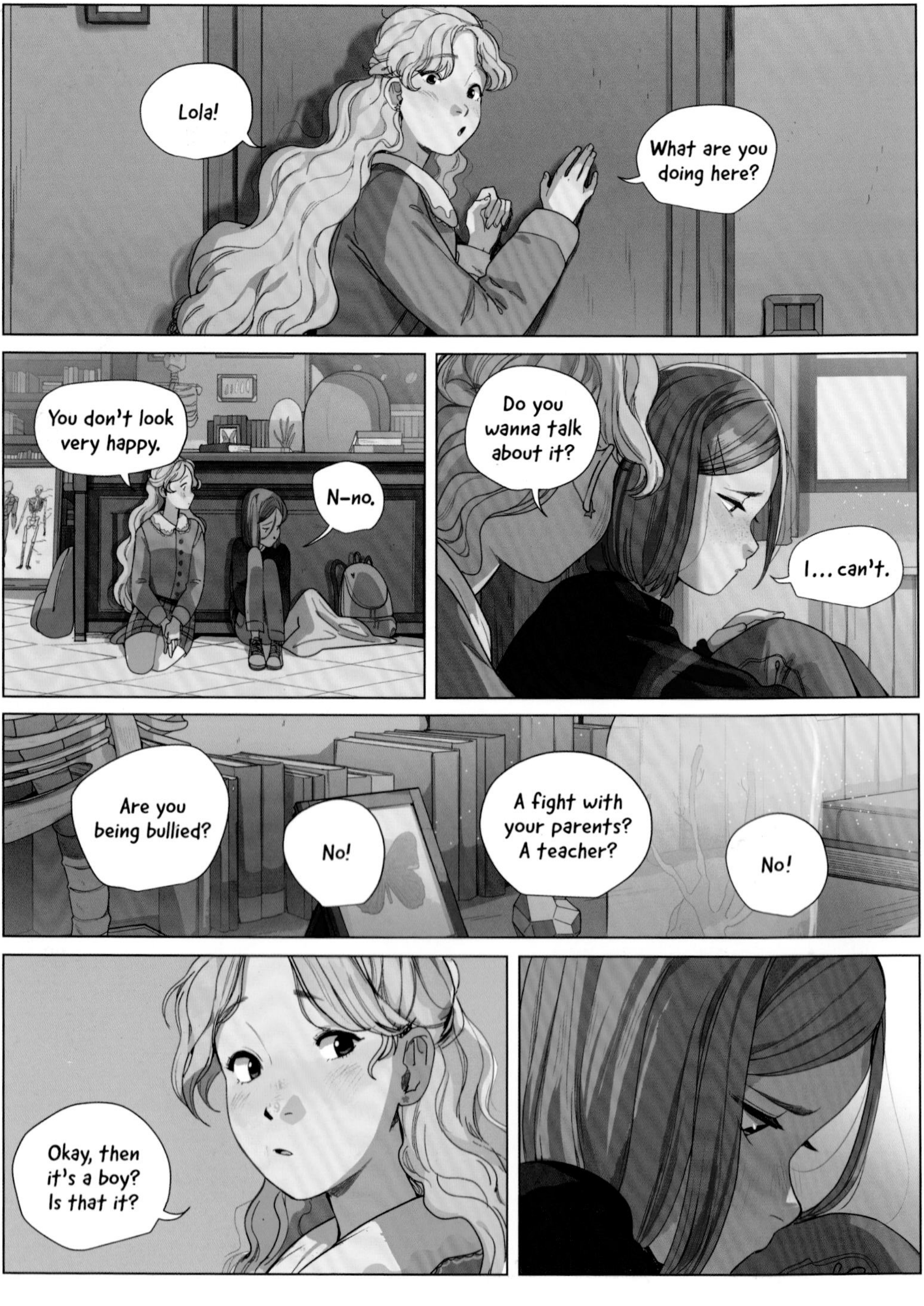
Lola!
What are you doing here?
You don't look very happy.
N-no.
Do you wanna talk about it?
I... can't.
Are you being bullied?
No!
A fight with your parents? A teacher?
No!
Okay, then it's a boy? Is that it?

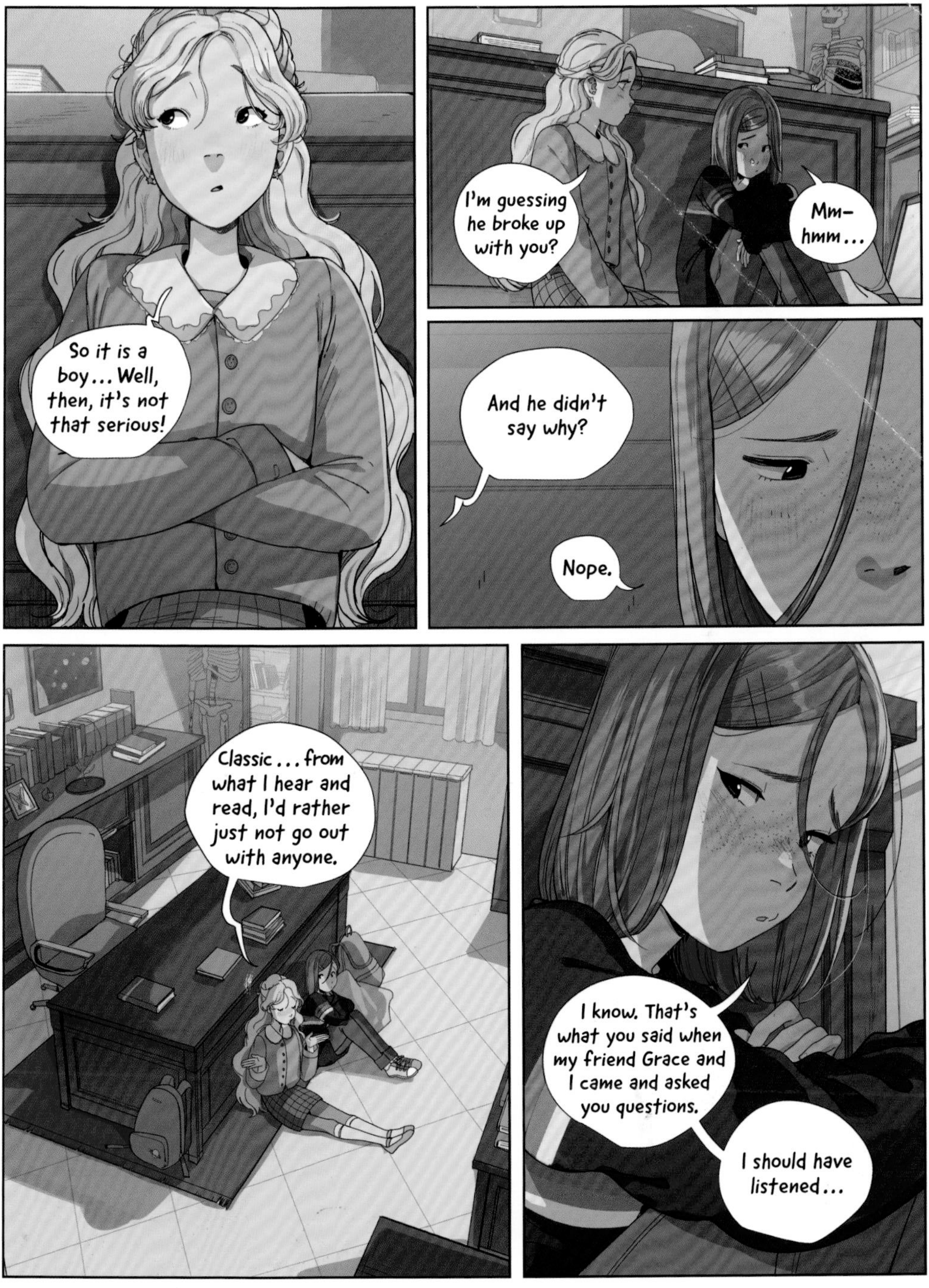
So it is a boy... Well, then, it's not that serious!
I'm guessing he broke up with you?
Mm-hmm...
And he didn't say why?
Nope.
Classic... from what I hear and read, I'd rather just not go out with anyone.
I know. That's what you said when my friend Grace and I came and asked you questions.
I should have listened...

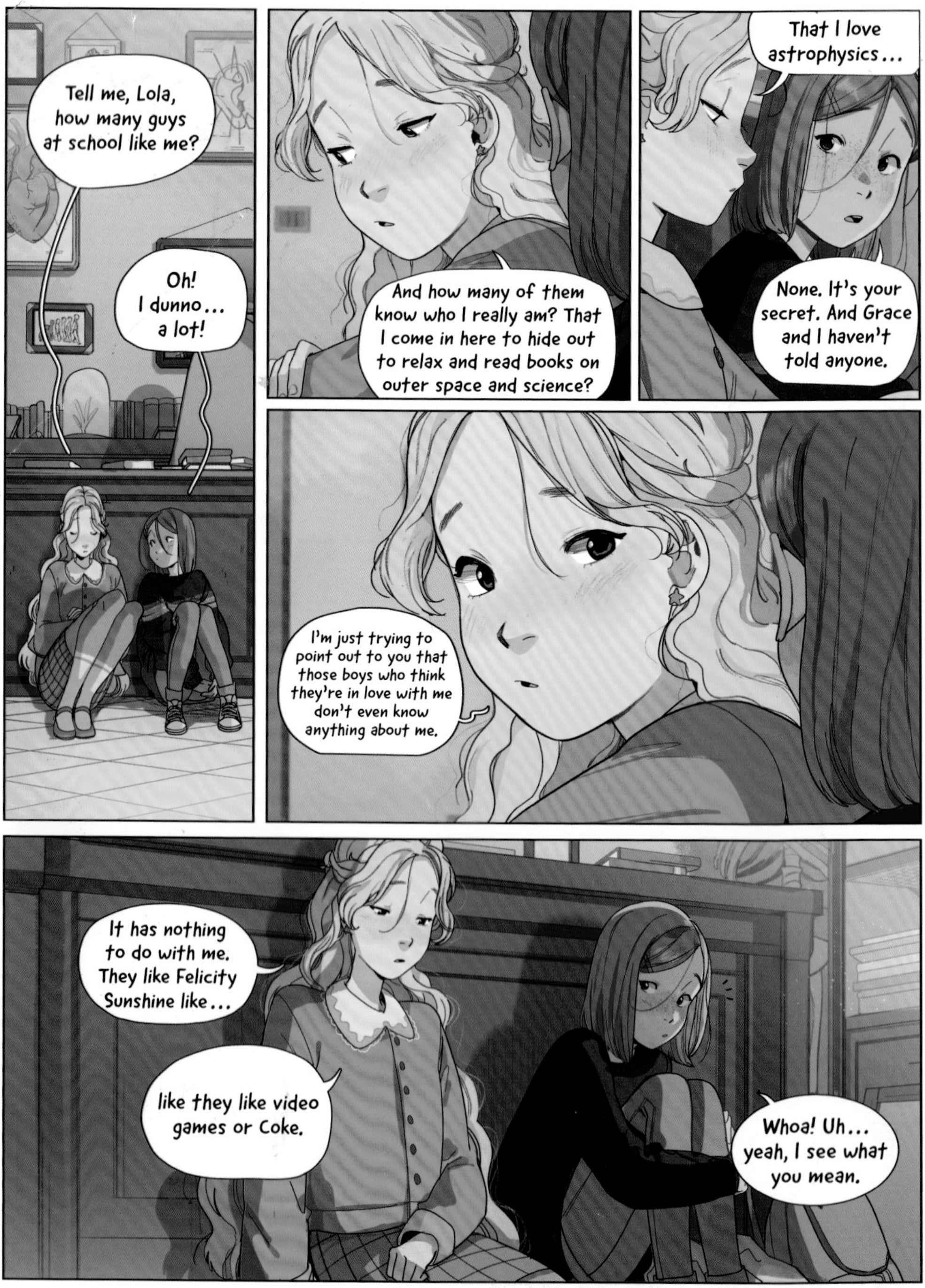
Tell me, Lola, how many guys at school like me?
Oh! I dunno... a lot!
And how many of them know who I really am? That I come in here to hide out to relax and read books on outer space and science?
That I love astrophysics...
None. It's your secret. And Grace and I haven't told anyone.
I'm just trying to point out to you that those boys who think they're in love with me don't even know anything about me.
It has nothing to do with me. They like Felicity Sunshine like...
like they like video games or Coke.
Whoa! Uh... yeah, I see what you mean.

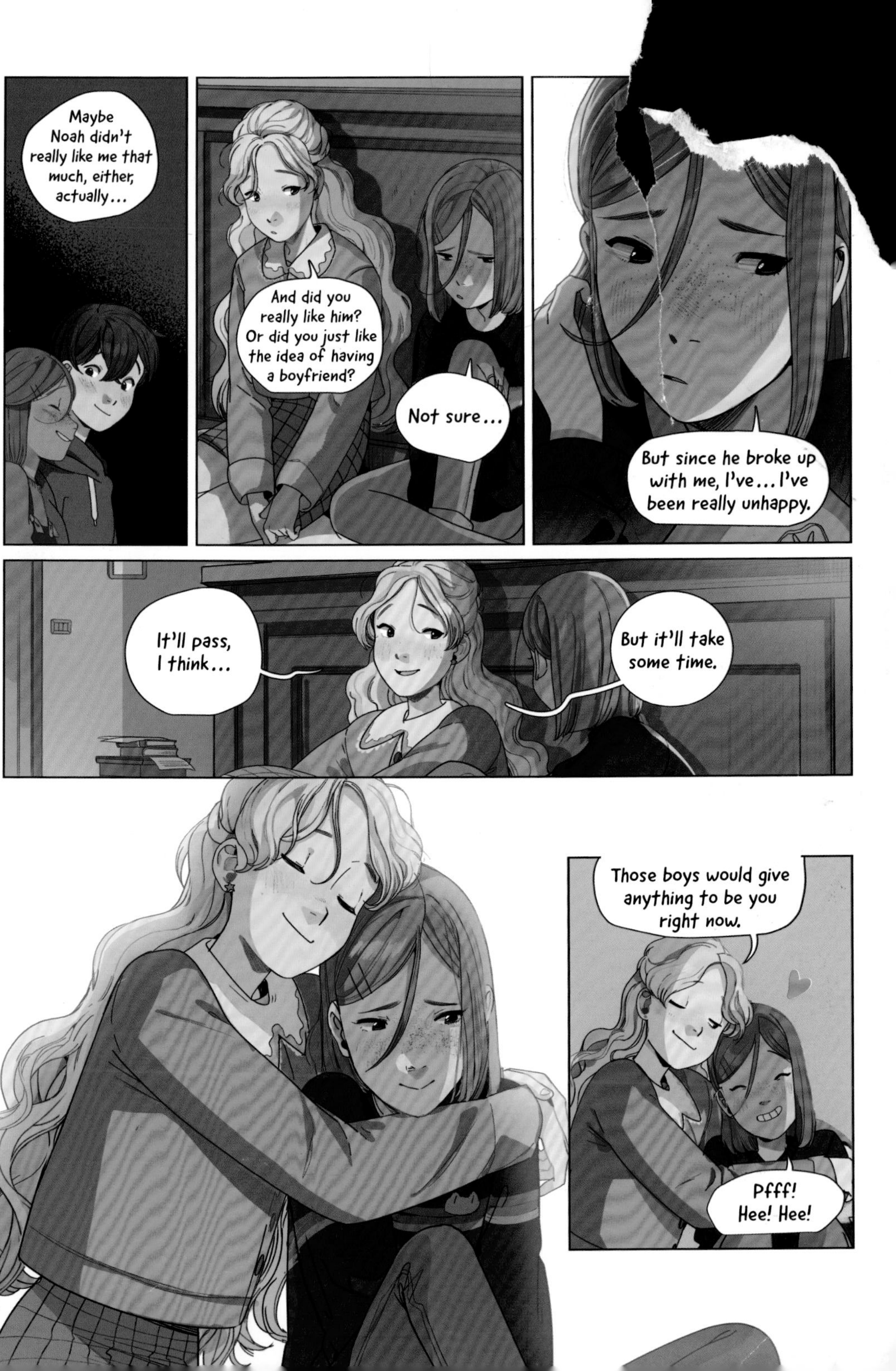
Maybe Noah didn't really like me that much, either, actually...
And did you really like him? Or did you just like the idea of having a boyfriend?
Not sure...
But since he broke up with me, I've... I've been really unhappy.
It'll pass, I think...
But it'll take some time.
Those boys would give anything to be you right now.
Pfff! Hee! Hee!

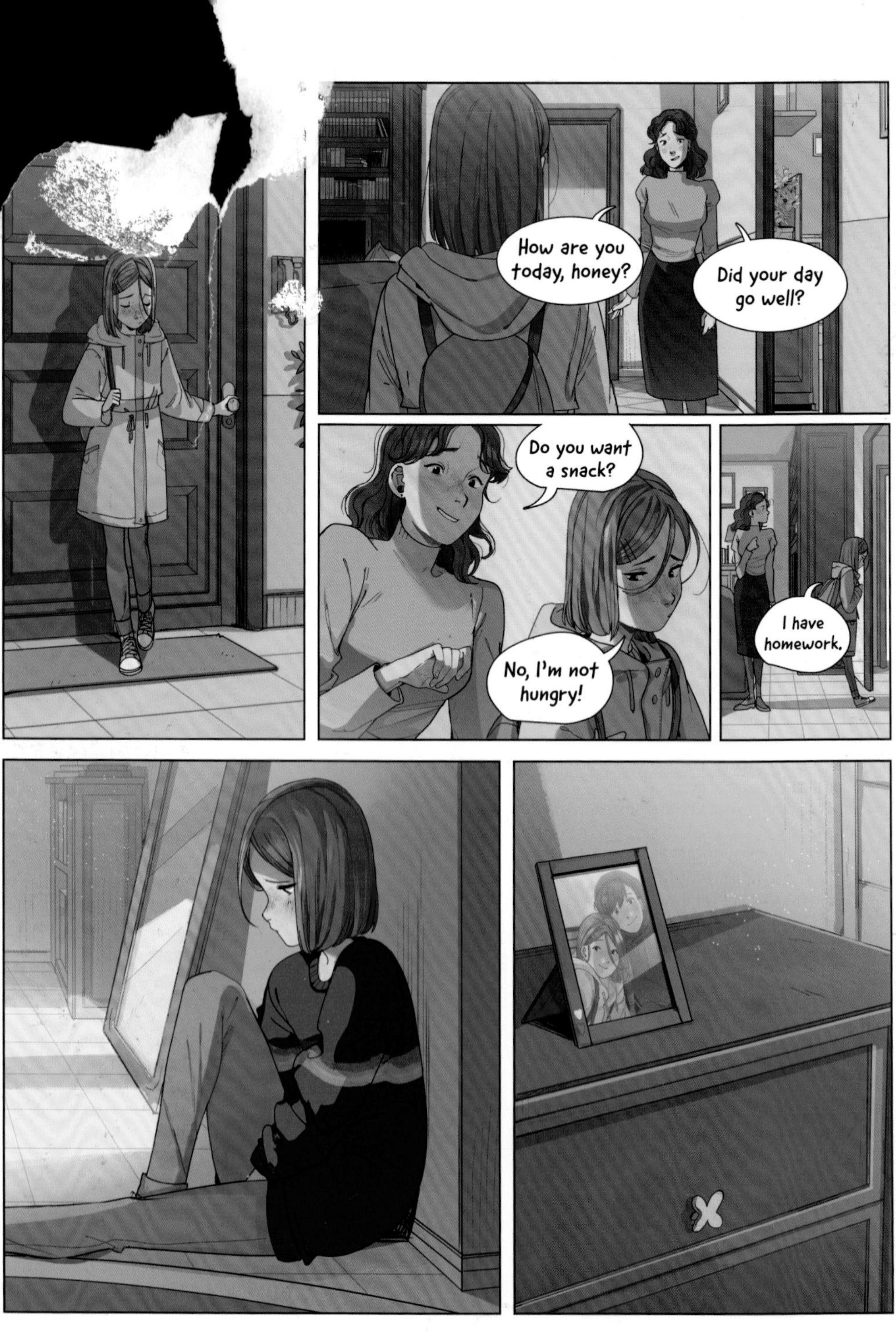
How are you today, honey?
Did your day go well?
Do you want a snack?
No, I'm not hungry!
I have homework.

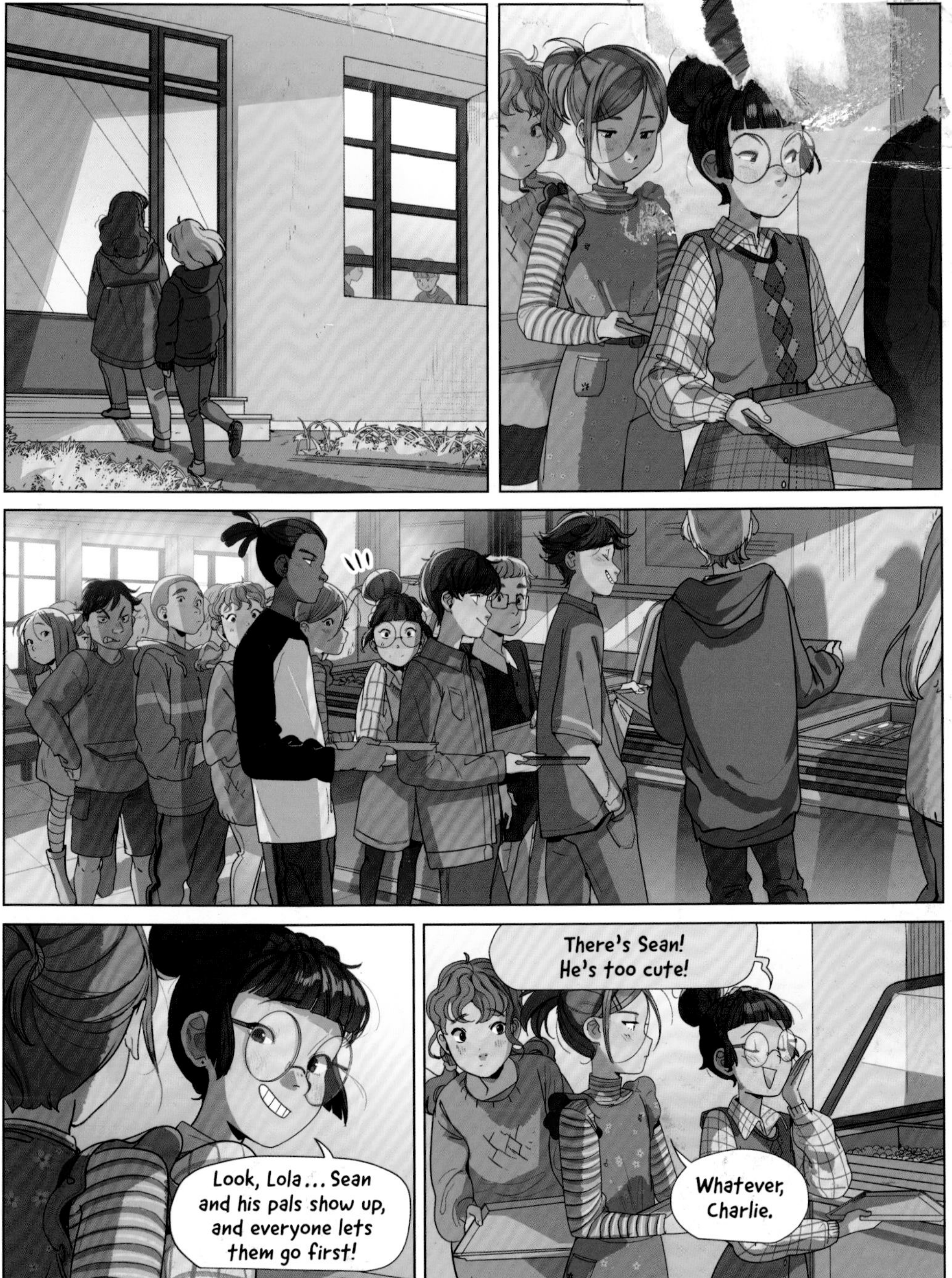

Look, Lola... Sean and his pals show up, and everyone lets them go first!
There's Sean! He's too cute!
Whatever, Charlie.

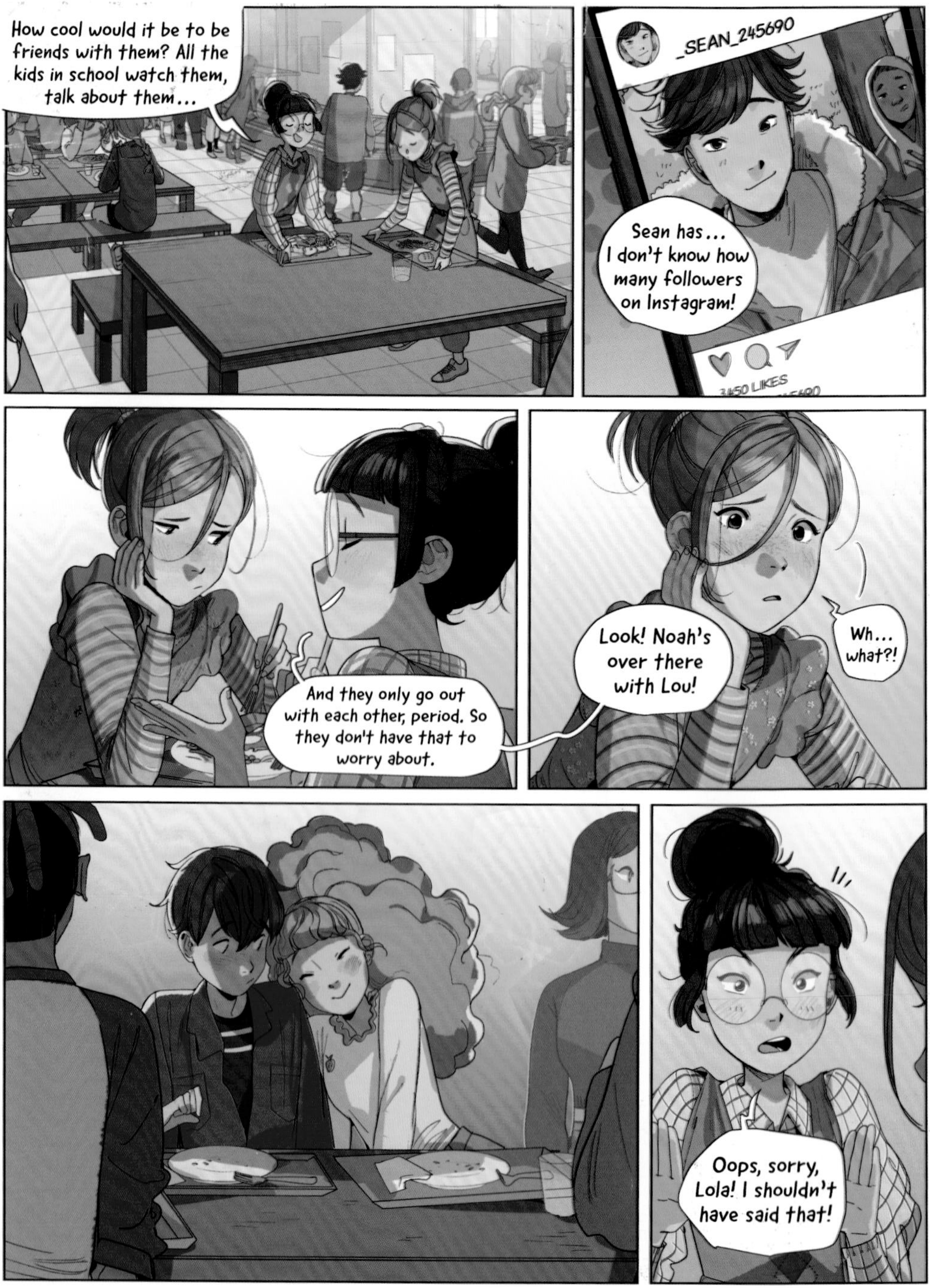
How cool would it be to be friends with them? All the kids in school watch them, talk about them...
_SEAN_245690
Sean has... I don't know how many followers on Instagram!
3450 LIKES
And they only go out with each other, period. So they don't have that to worry about.
Look! Noah's over there with Lou!
Wh... what?!
Oops, sorry, Lola! I shouldn't have said that!

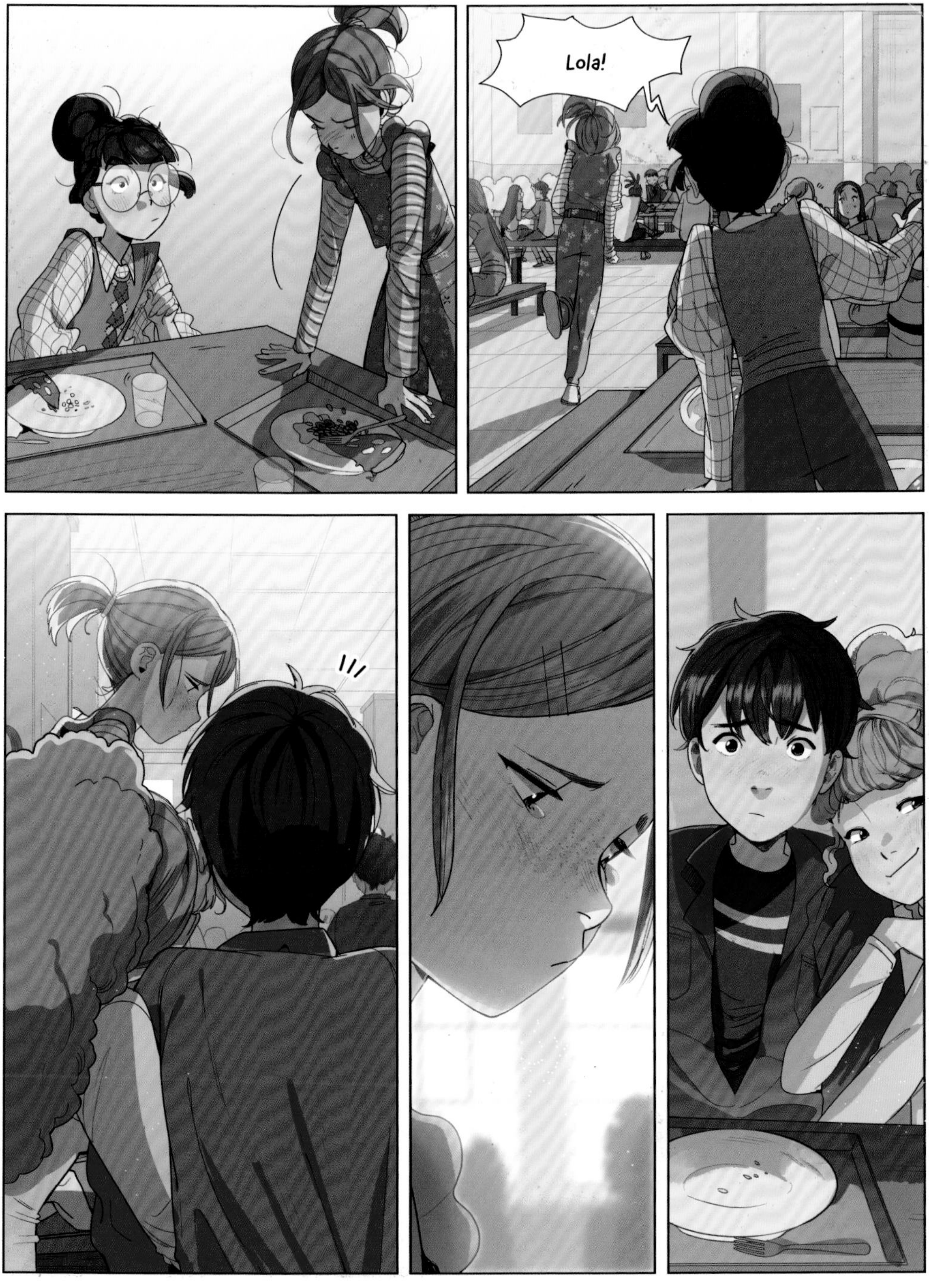
Lola!

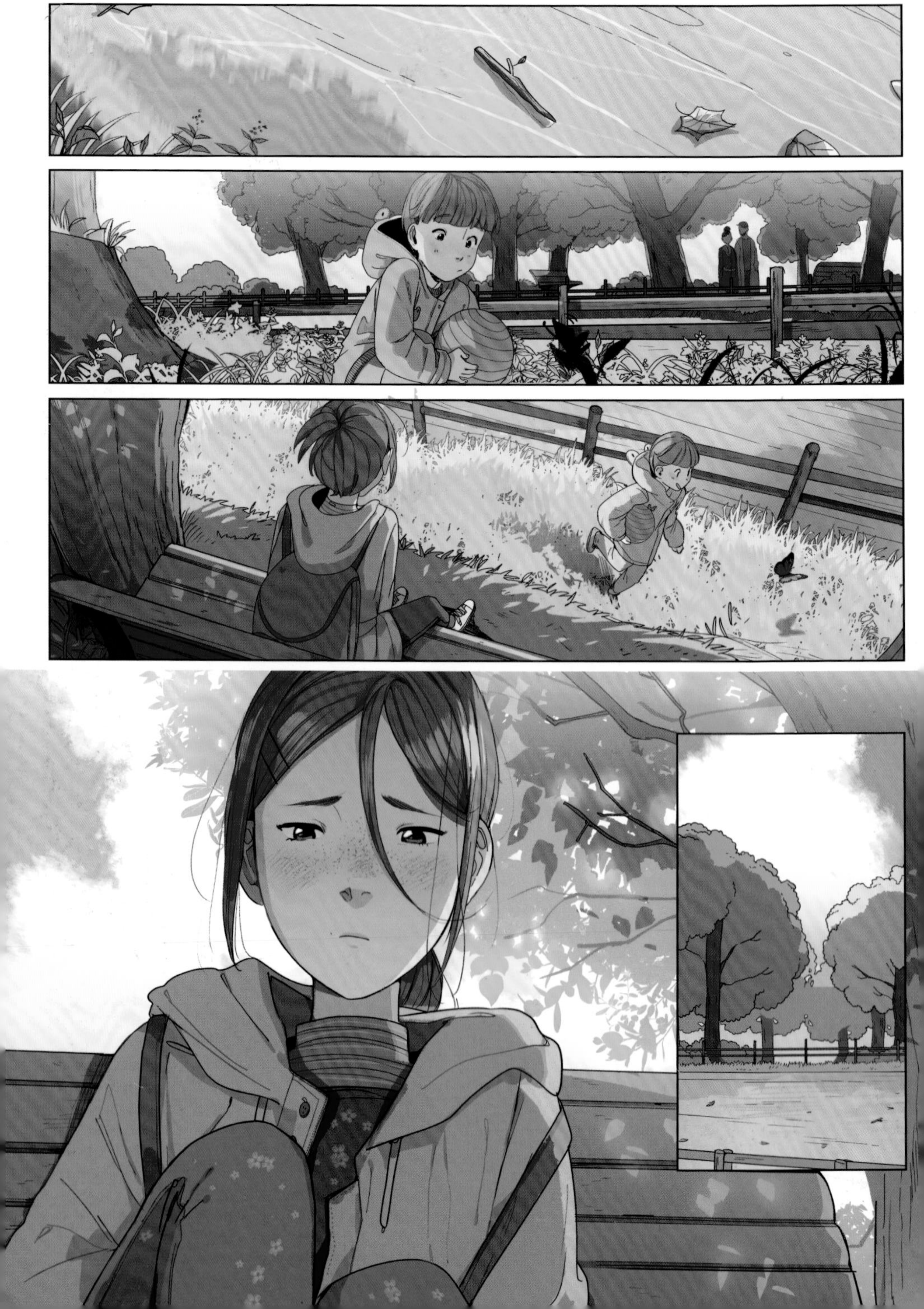

No lights on at Grace's house...

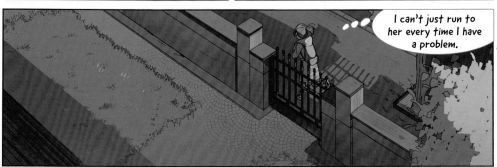

I can't just run to her every time I have a problem.

Mom's home... but I don't feel like going in.

She'll just want to have a talk.

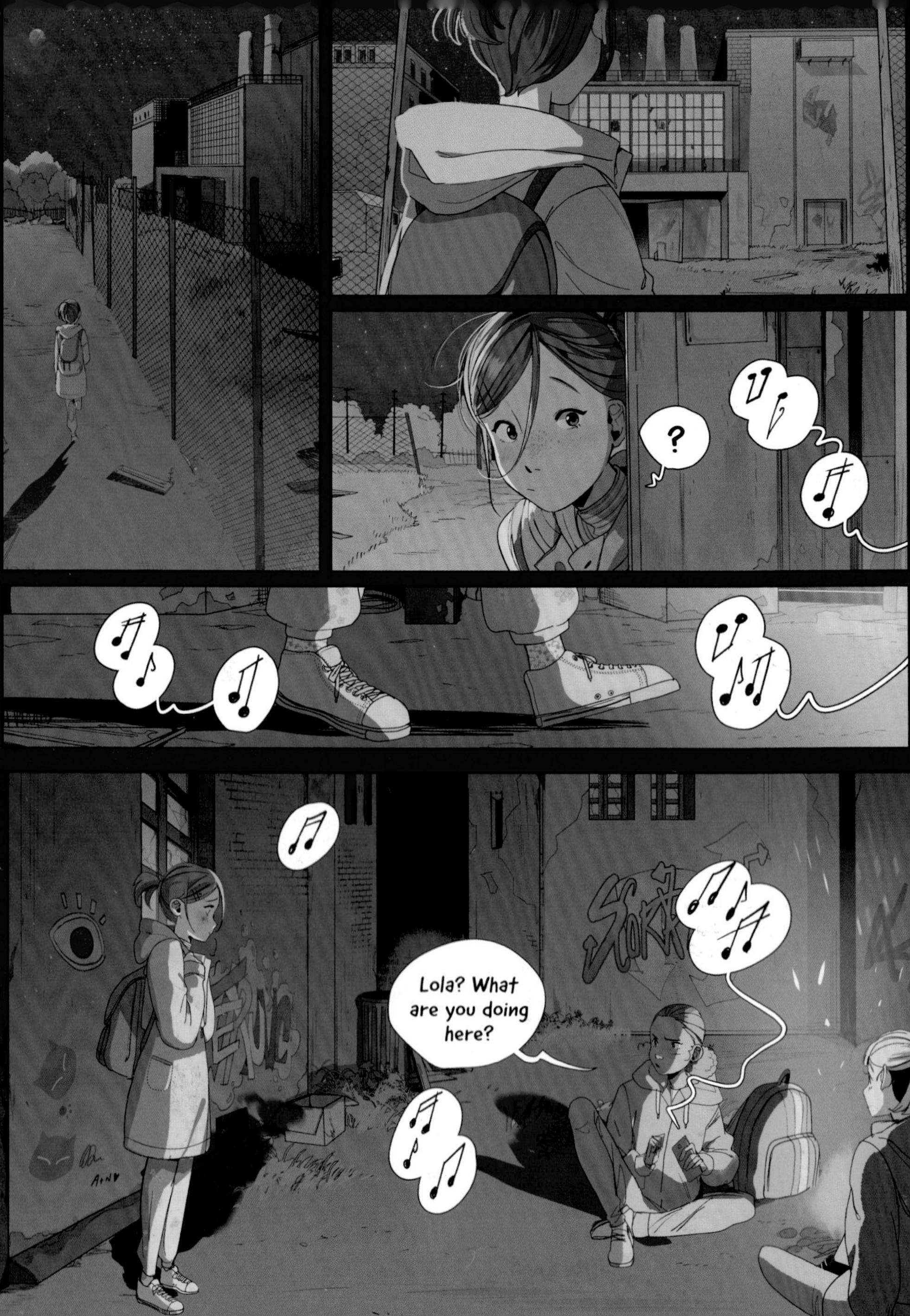
?
Lola? What are you doing here?

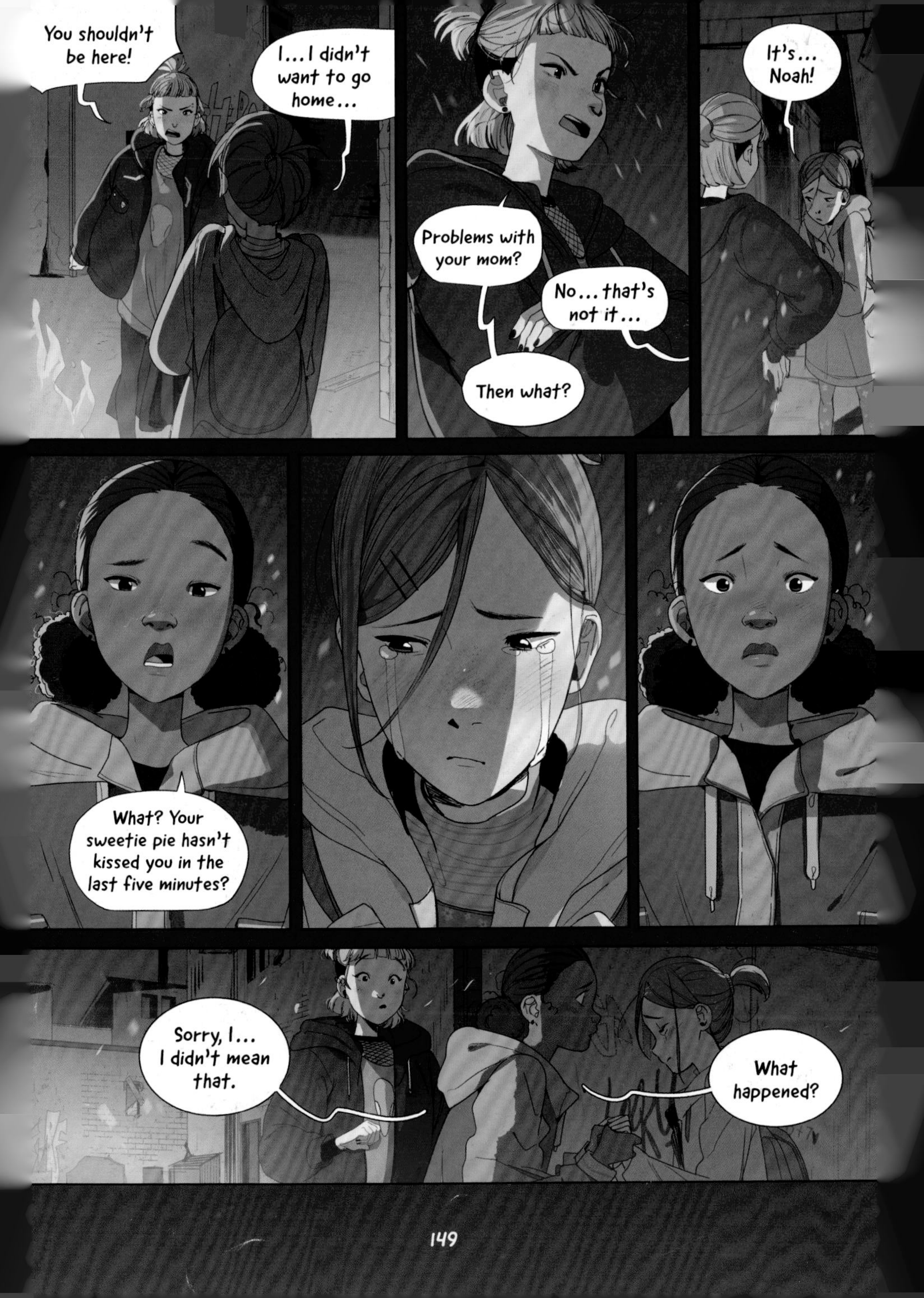
You shouldn't be here!
I... I didn't want to go home...
Problems with your mom?
No... that's not it...
Then what?
It's... Noah!
What? Your sweetie pie hasn't kissed you in the last five minutes?
Sorry, I... I didn't mean that.
What happened?

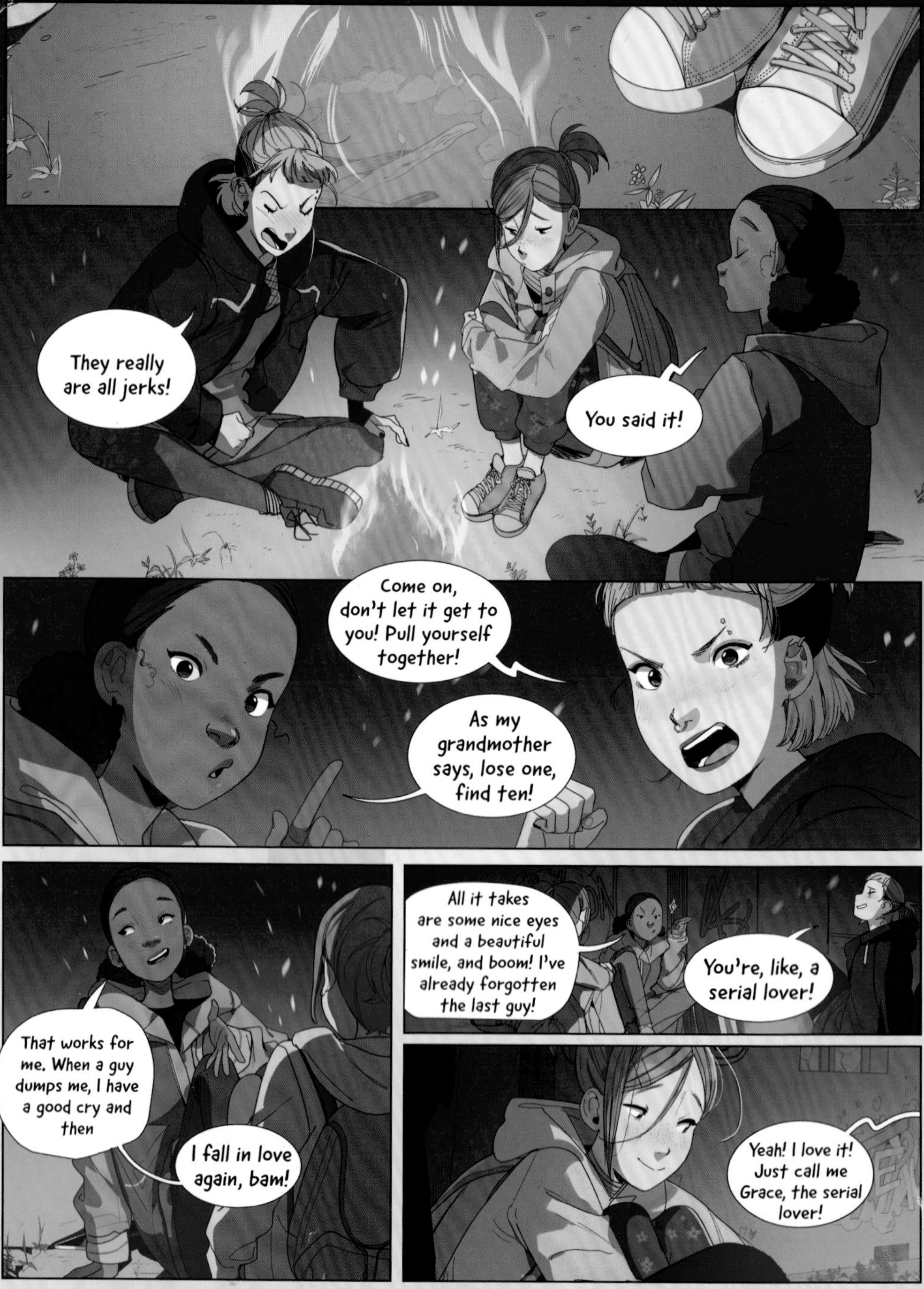
They really are all jerks!
You said it!
Come on, don't let it get to you! Pull yourself together!
As my grandmother says, lose one, find ten!
That works for me. When a guy dumps me, I have a good cry and then
I fall in love again, bam!
All it takes are some nice eyes and a beautiful smile, and boom! I've already forgotten the last guy!
You're, like, a serial lover!
Yeah! I love it! Just call me Grace, the serial lover!

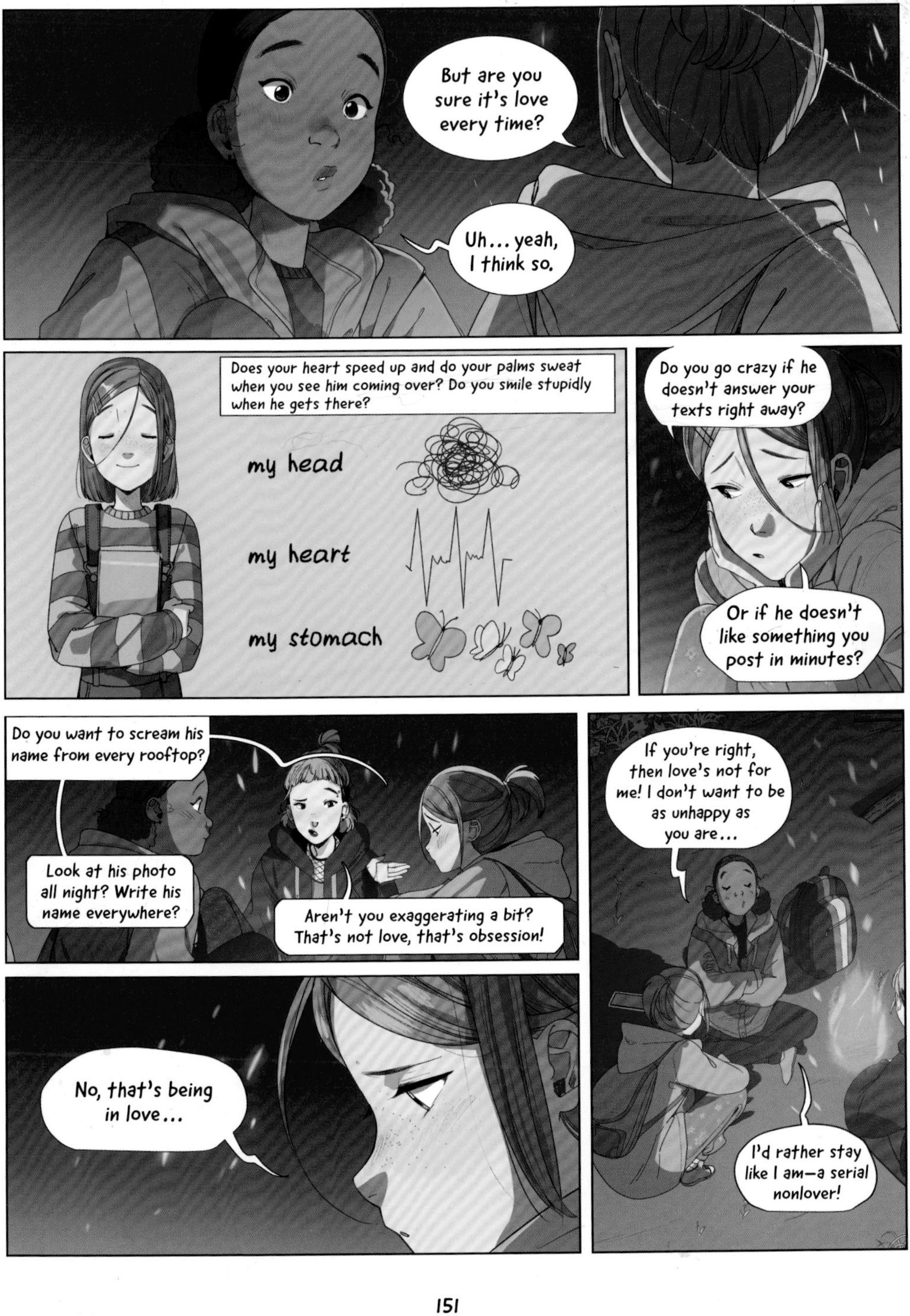
But are you sure it's love every time?
Uh... yeah, I think so.
Does your heart speed up and do your palms sweat when you see him coming over? Do you smile stupidly when he gets there?
my head
my heart
my stomach
Do you go crazy if he doesn't answer your texts right away?
Or if he doesn't like something you post in minutes?
Do you want to scream his name from every rooftop?
Look at his photo all night? Write his name everywhere?
Aren't you exaggerating a bit? That's not love, that's obsession!
If you're right, then love's not for me! I don't want to be as unhappy as you are...
I'd rather stay like I am—a serial nonlover!
No, that's being in love...

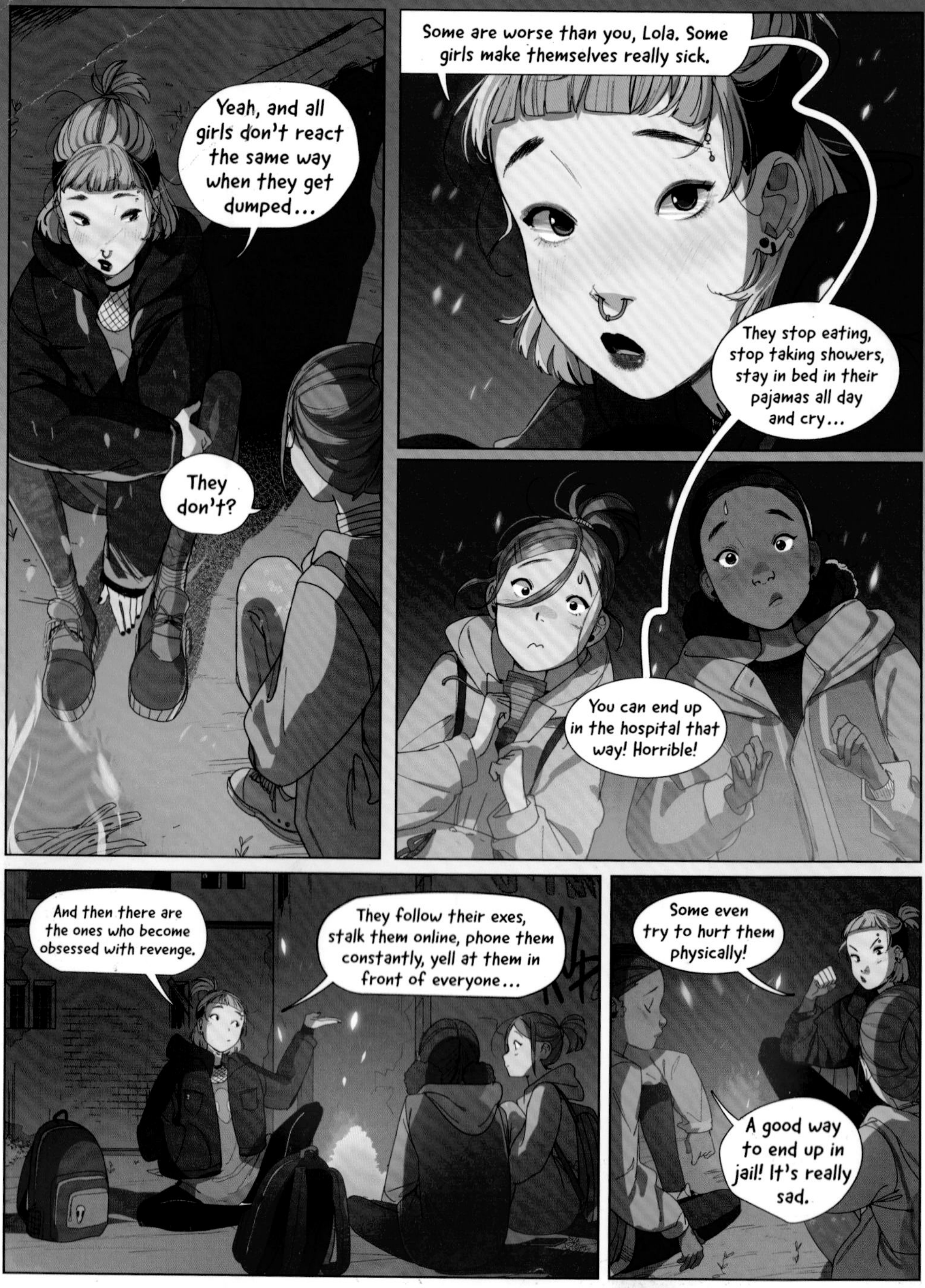
Yeah, and all girls don't react the same way when they get dumped...
They don't?
Some are worse than you, Lola. Some girls make themselves really sick.
They stop eating, stop taking showers, stay in bed in their pajamas all day and cry...
You can end up in the hospital that way! Horrible!
And then there are the ones who become obsessed with revenge.
They follow their exes, stalk them online, phone them constantly, yell at them in front of everyone...
Some even try to hurt them physically!
A good way to end up in jail! It's really sad.

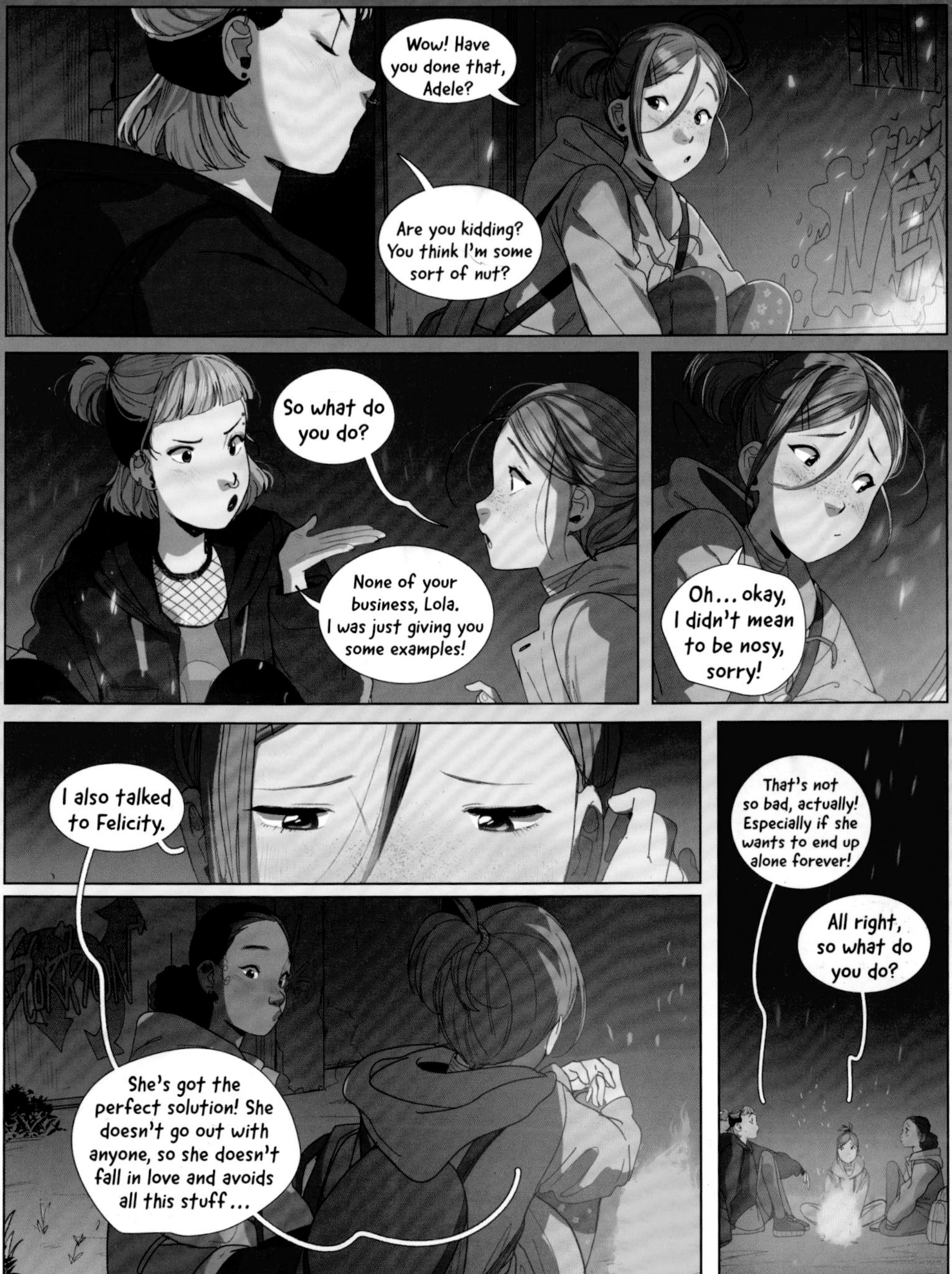
Wow! Have you done that, Adele?
Are you kidding? You think I'm some sort of nut?
So what do you do?
None of your business, Lola. I was just giving you some examples!
Oh... okay, I didn't mean to be nosy, sorry!
I also talked to Felicity.
She's got the perfect solution! She doesn't go out with anyone, so she doesn't fall in love and avoids all this stuff...
That's not so bad, actually! Especially if she wants to end up alone forever!
All right, so what do you do?

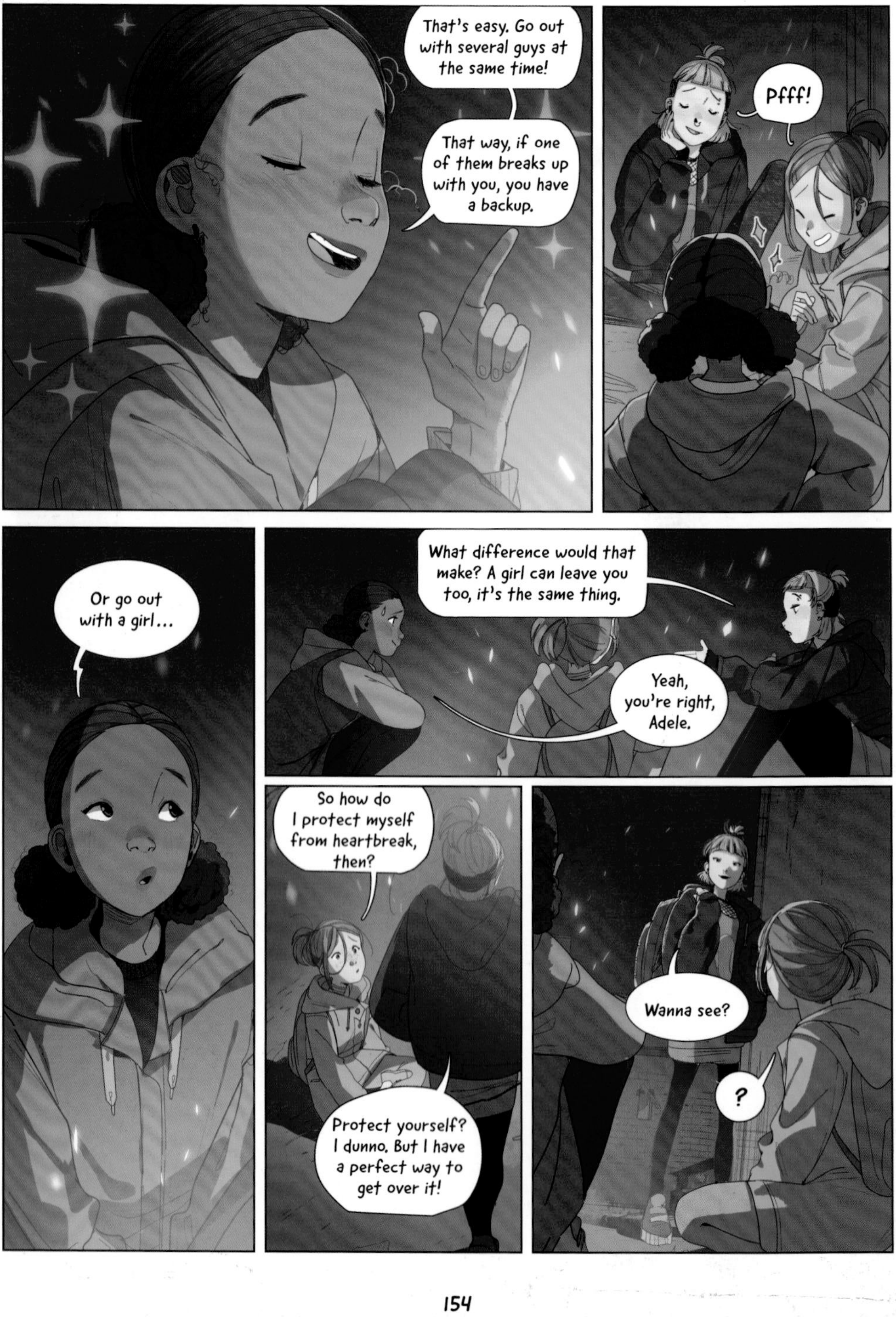
That's easy. Go out with several guys at the same time!
That way, if one of them breaks up with you, you have a backup.
Pfff!
Or go out with a girl...
What difference would that make? A girl can leave you too, it's the same thing.
Yeah, you're right, Adele.
So how do I protect myself from heartbreak, then?
Protect yourself? I dunno. But I have a perfect way to get over it!
Wanna see?
?

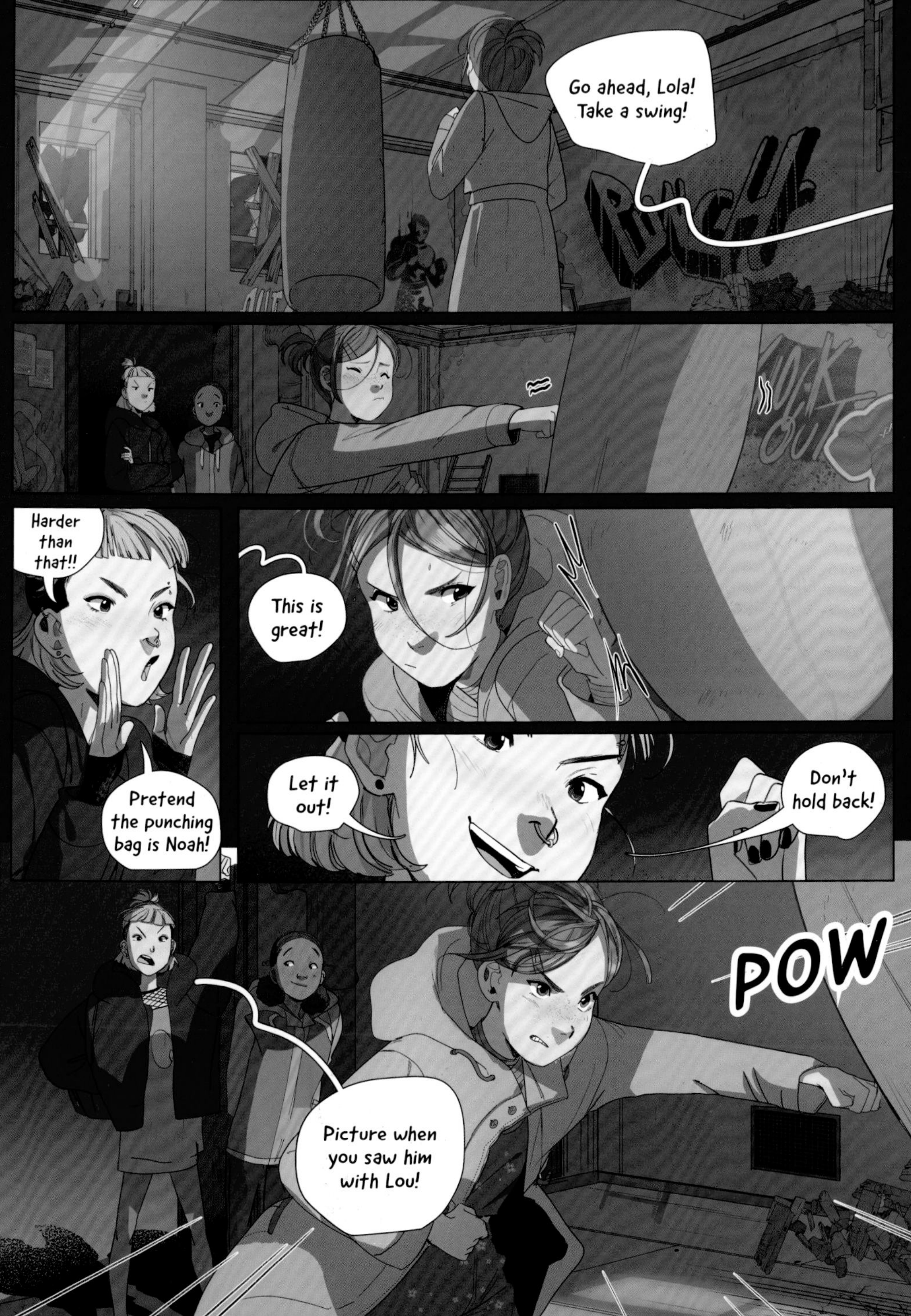
Go ahead, Lola! Take a swing!
PUNCH!
K.O.-K OUT
Harder than that!!
This is great!
Pretend the punching bag is Noah!
Let it out!
Don't hold back!
POW
Picture when you saw him with Lou!

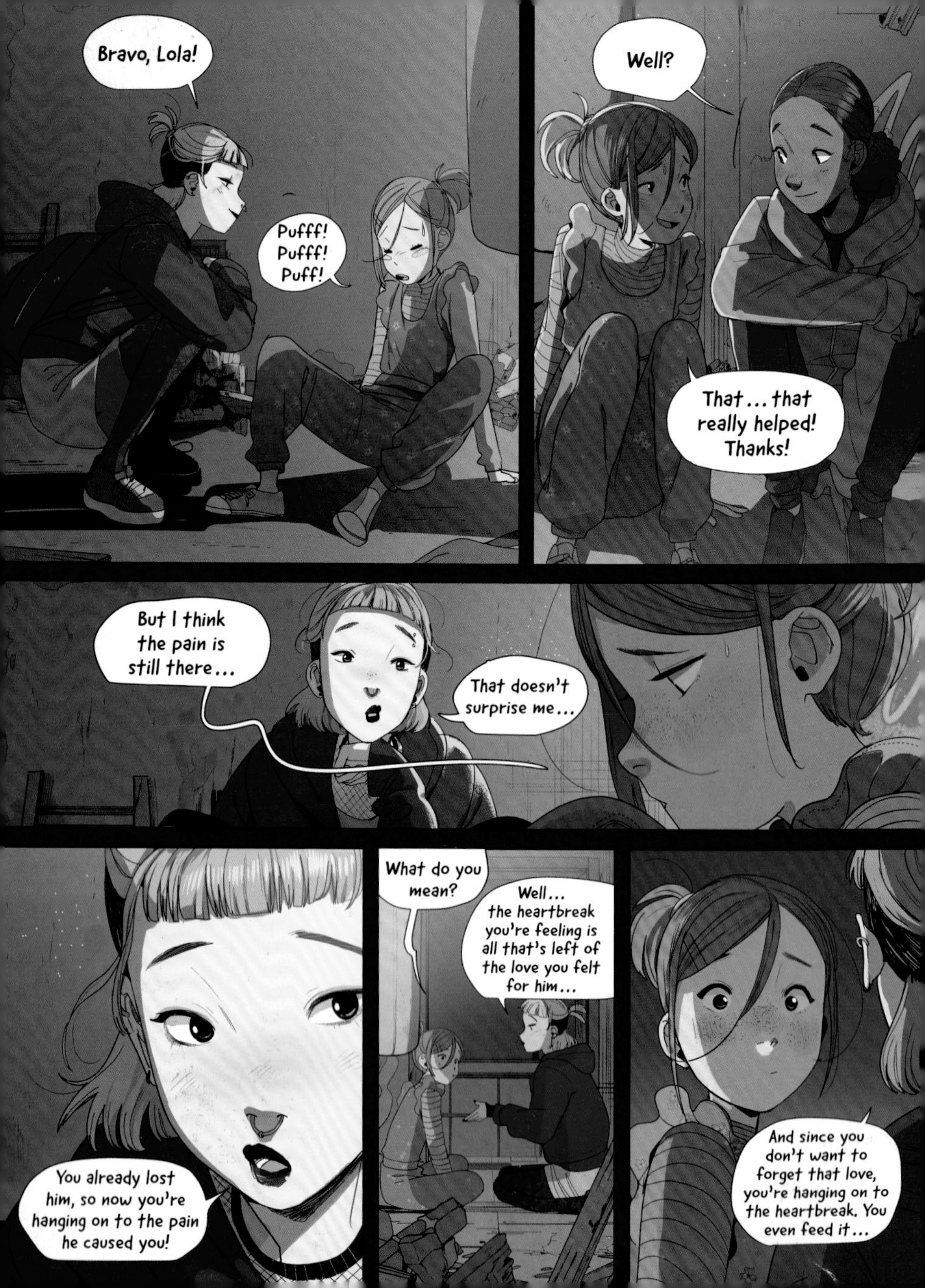

Bravo, Lola!
Pufff! Pufff! Puff!
Well?
That... that really helped! Thanks!
But I think the pain is still there...
That doesn't surprise me...
You already lost him, so now you're hanging on to the pain he caused you!
What do you mean?
Well... the heartbreak you're feeling is all that's left of the love you felt for him...
And since you don't want to forget that love, you're hanging on to the heartbreak. You even feed it...

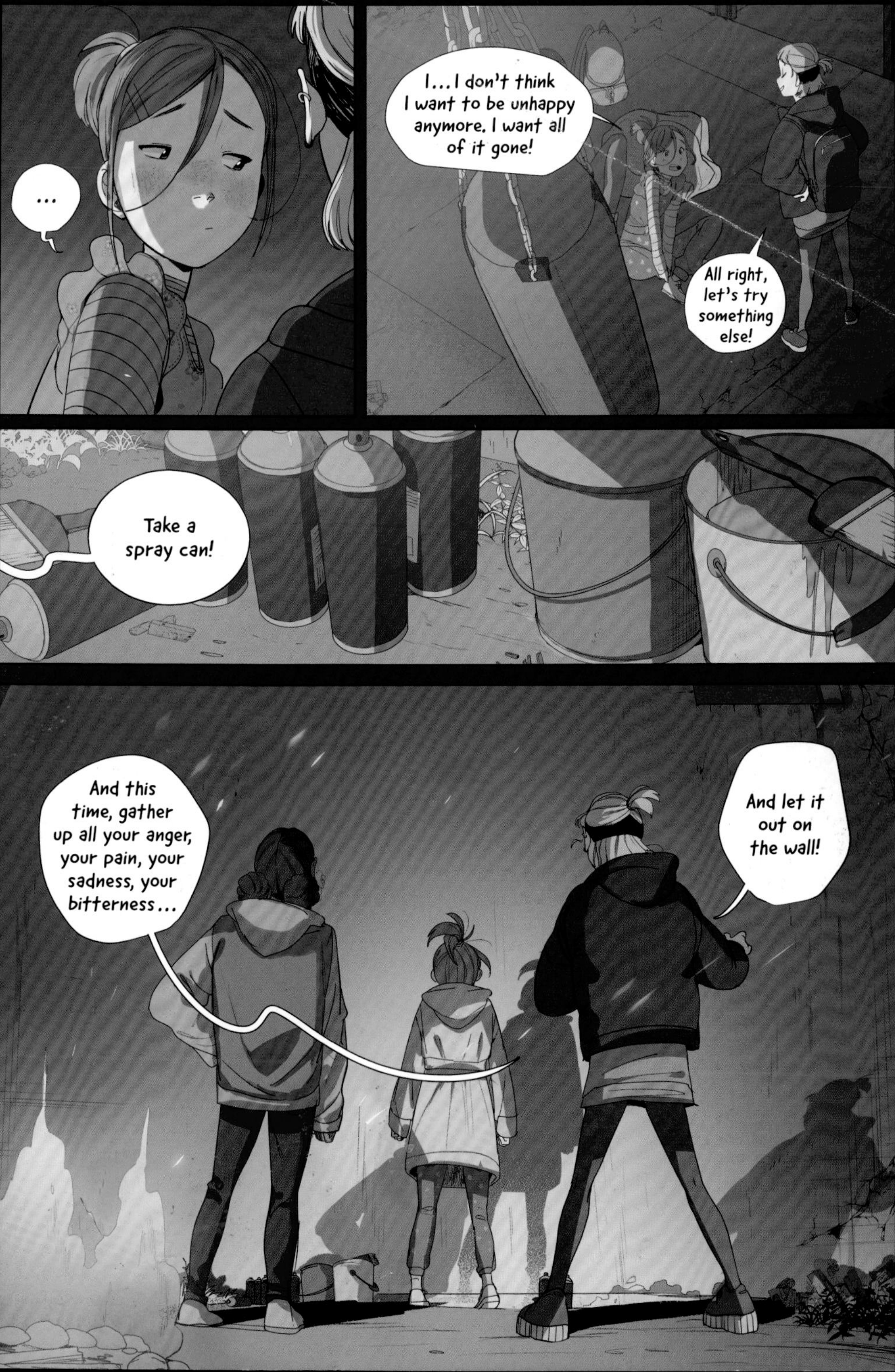
...
I...I don't think I want to be unhappy anymore. I want all of it gone!
All right, let's try something else!
Take a spray can!
And this time, gather up all your anger, your pain, your sadness, your bitterness...
And let it out on the wall!

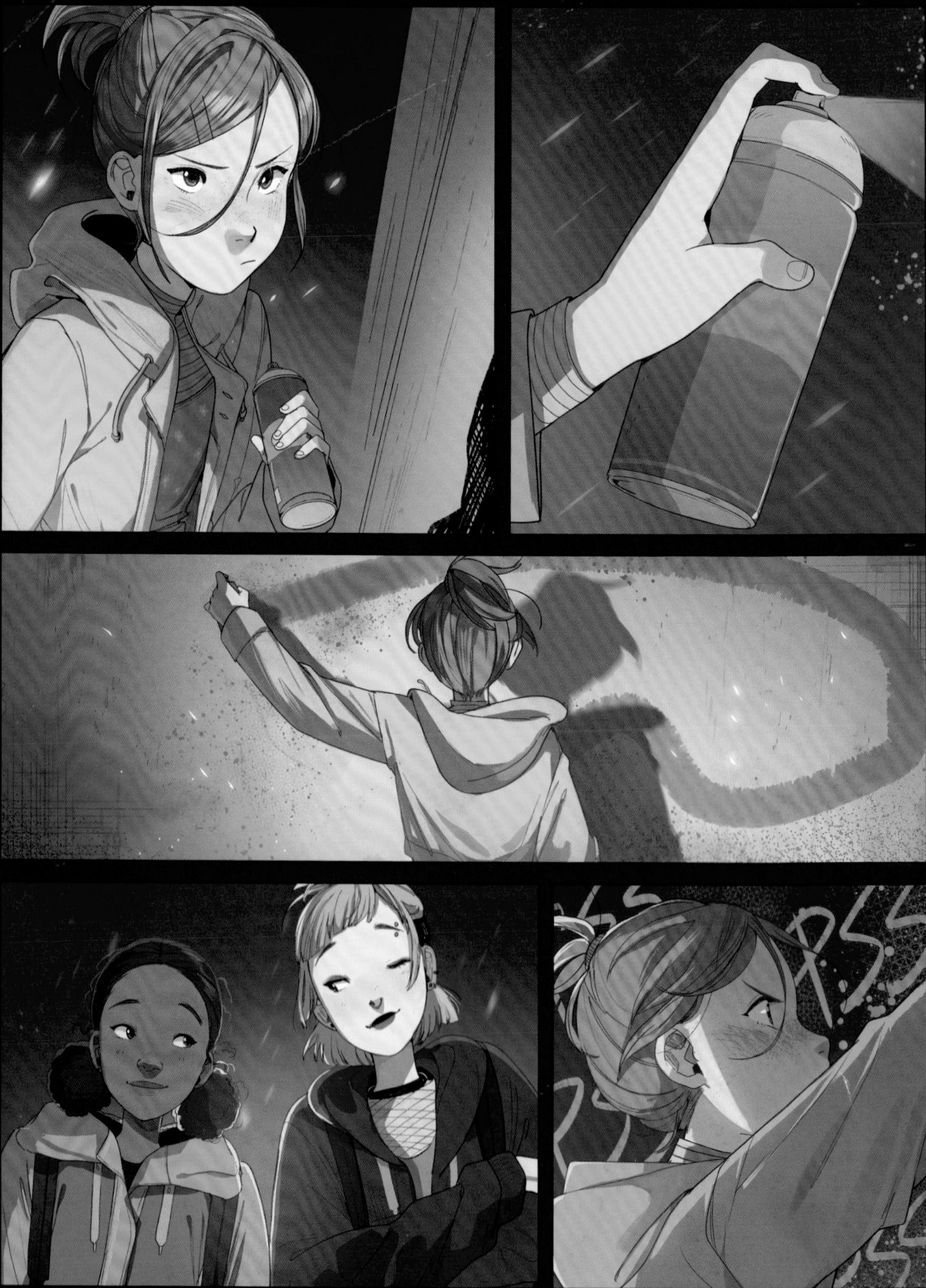
PSS

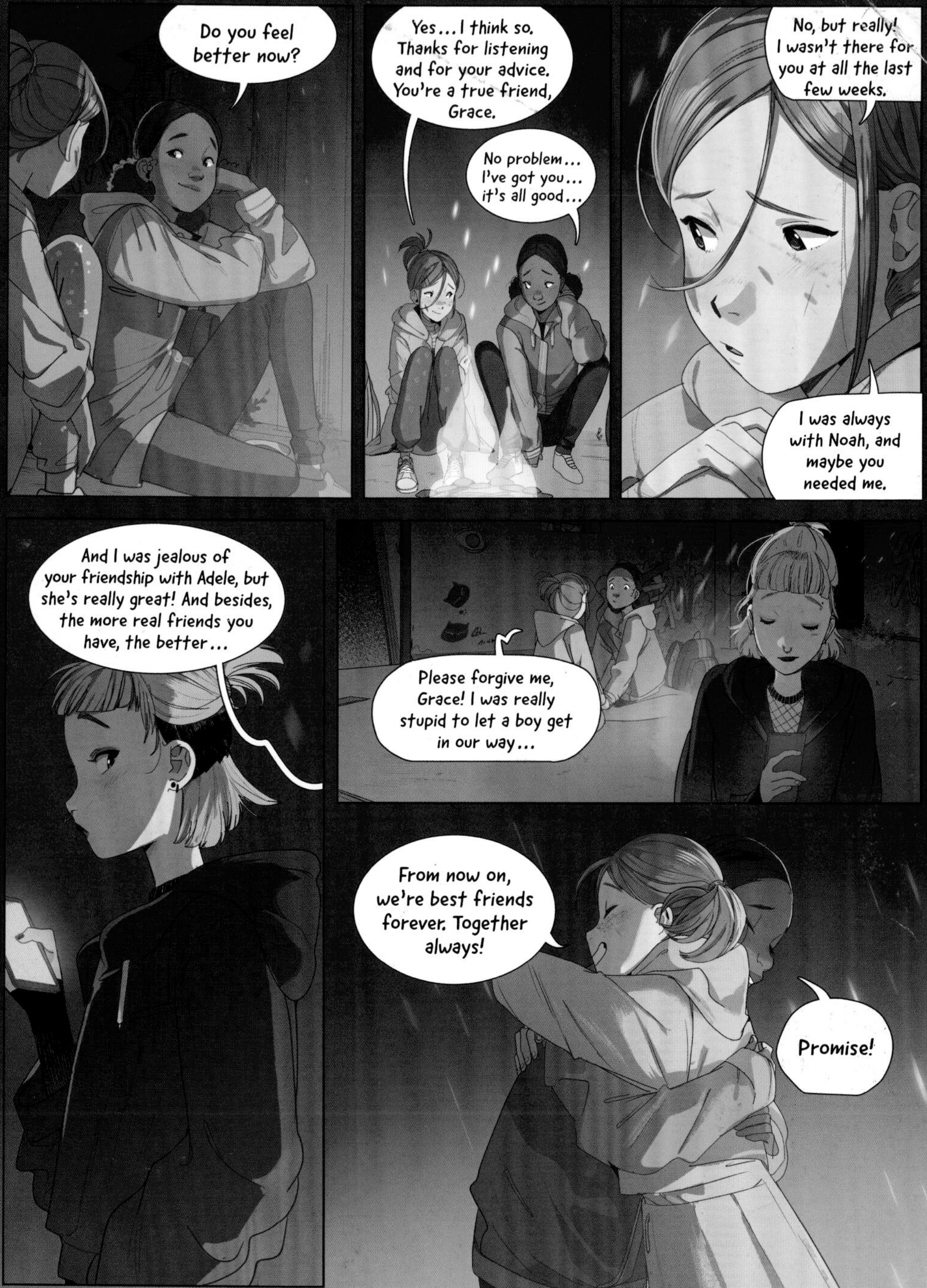
Do you feel better now?
Yes… I think so. Thanks for listening and for your advice. You're a true friend, Grace.
No problem… I've got you… it's all good…
No, but really! I wasn't there for you at all the last few weeks.
I was always with Noah, and maybe you needed me.
And I was jealous of your friendship with Adele, but she's really great! And besides, the more real friends you have, the better…
Please forgive me, Grace! I was really stupid to let a boy get in our way…
From now on, we're best friends forever. Together always!
Promise!

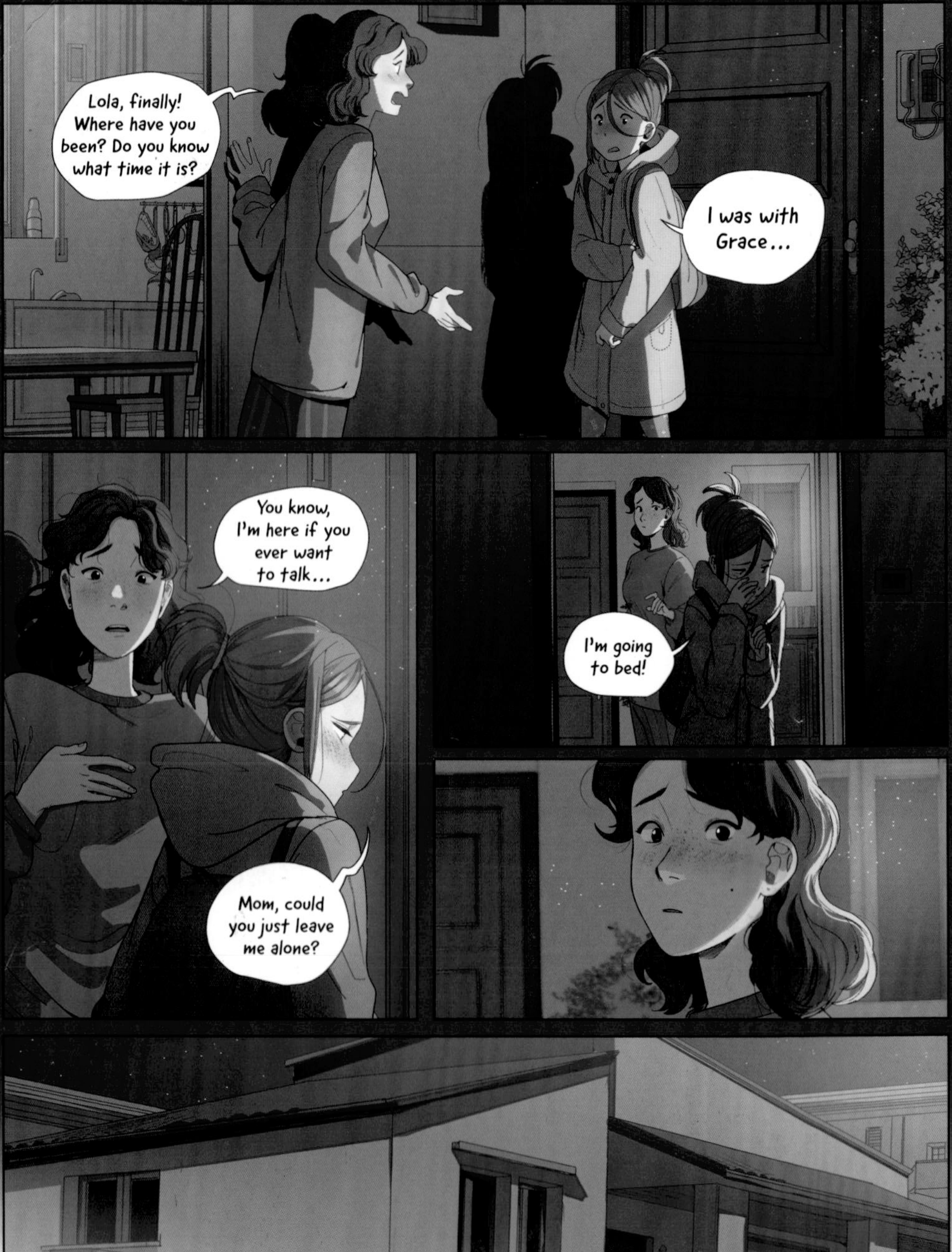
Lola, finally! Where have you been? Do you know what time it is?
I was with Grace...
You know, I'm here if you ever want to talk...
Mom, could you just leave me alone?
I'm going to bed!

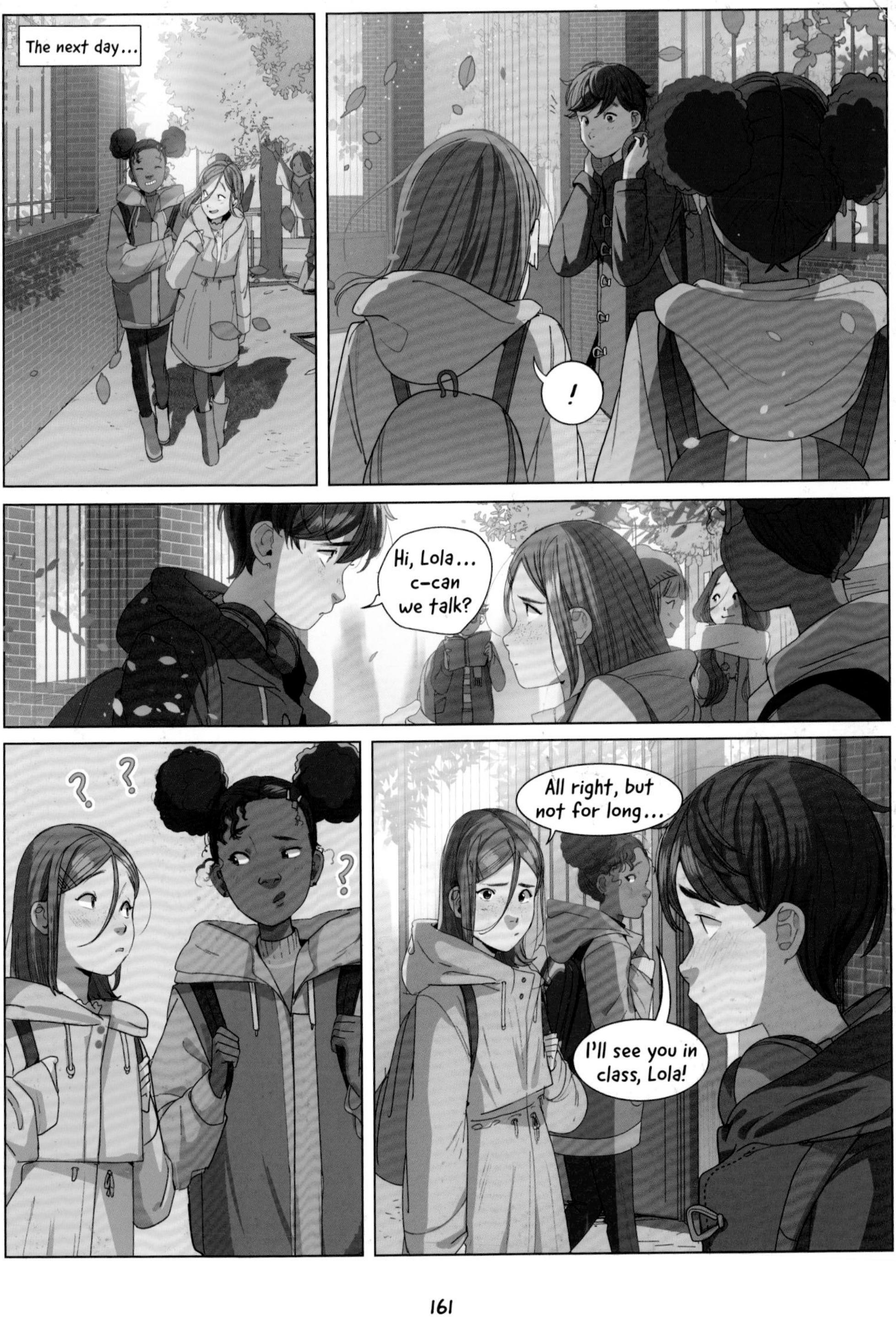
The next day...
!
Hi, Lola... c-can we talk?
All right, but not for long...
I'll see you in class, Lola!

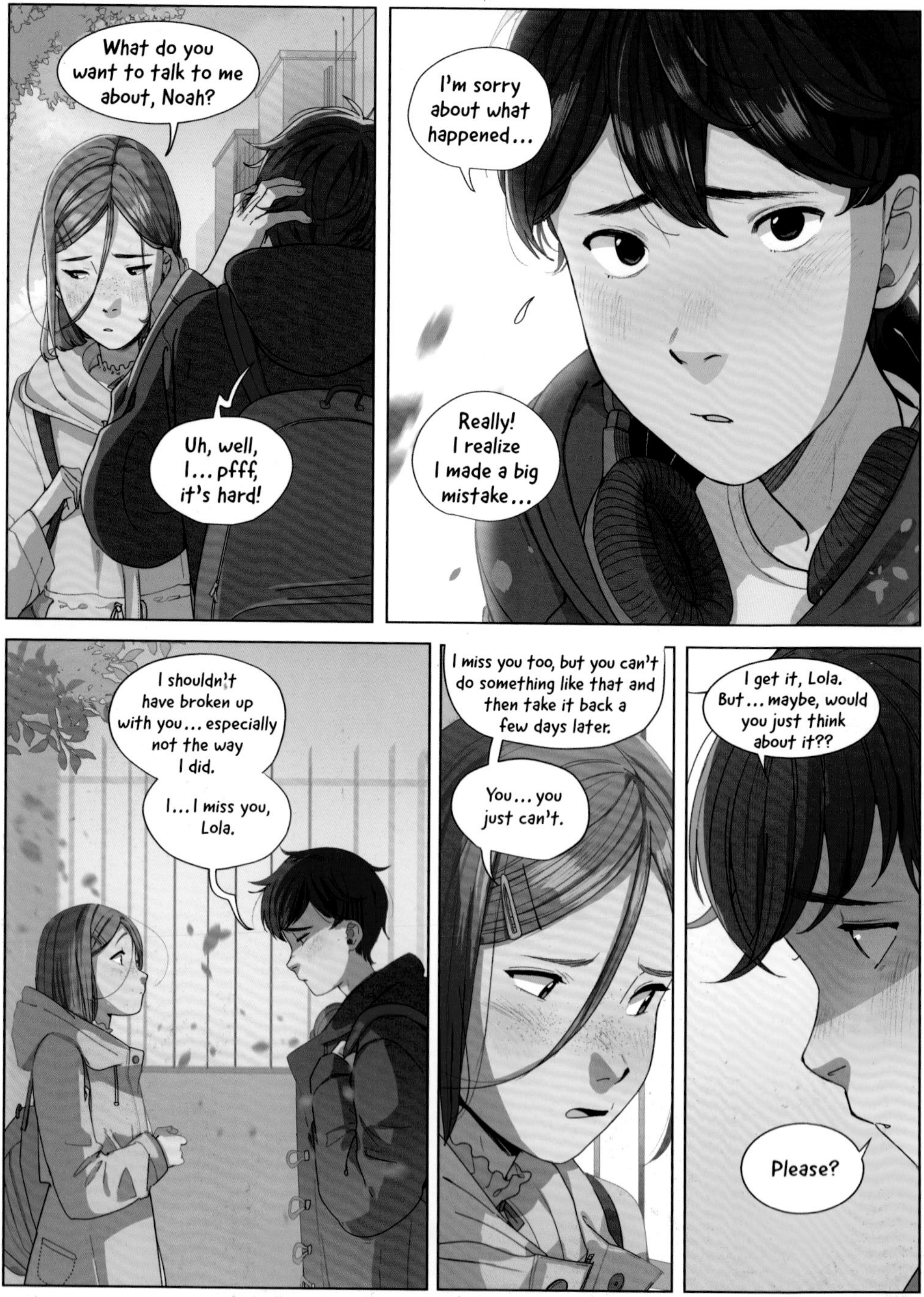
What do you want to talk to me about, Noah?
Uh, well, I... pfff, it's hard!
I'm sorry about what happened...
Really! I realize I made a big mistake...
I shouldn't have broken up with you... especially not the way I did.
I... I miss you, Lola.
I miss you too, but you can't do something like that and then take it back a few days later.
You... you just can't.
I get it, Lola. But... maybe, would you just think about it??
Please?

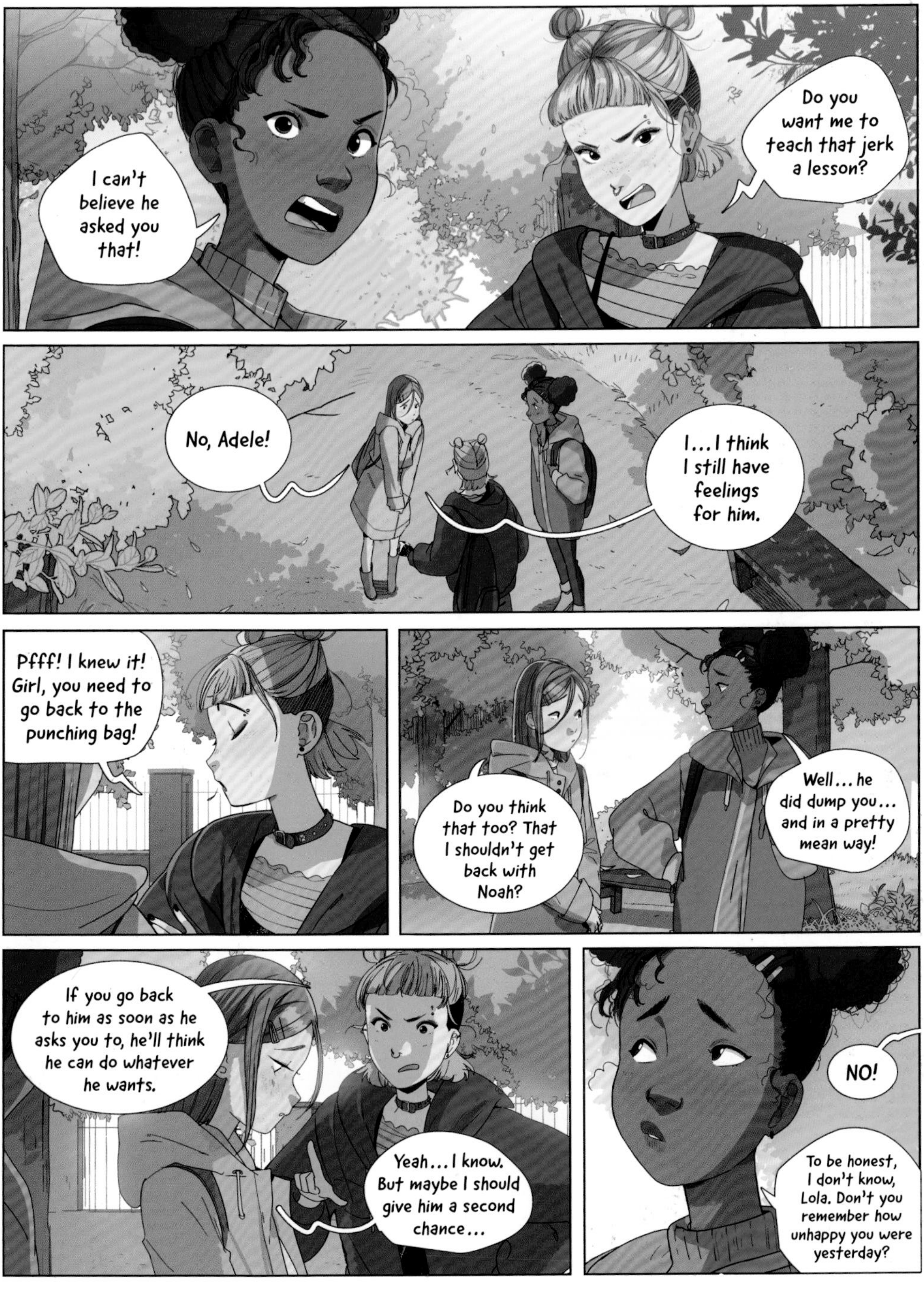
I can't believe he asked you that!
Do you want me to teach that jerk a lesson?
No, Adele!
I... I think I still have feelings for him.
Pfff! I knew it! Girl, you need to go back to the punching bag!
Do you think that too? That I shouldn't get back with Noah?
Well... he did dump you... and in a pretty mean way!
If you go back to him as soon as he asks you to, he'll think he can do whatever he wants.
Yeah... I know. But maybe I should give him a second chance...
NO!
To be honest, I don't know, Lola. Don't you remember how unhappy you were yesterday?

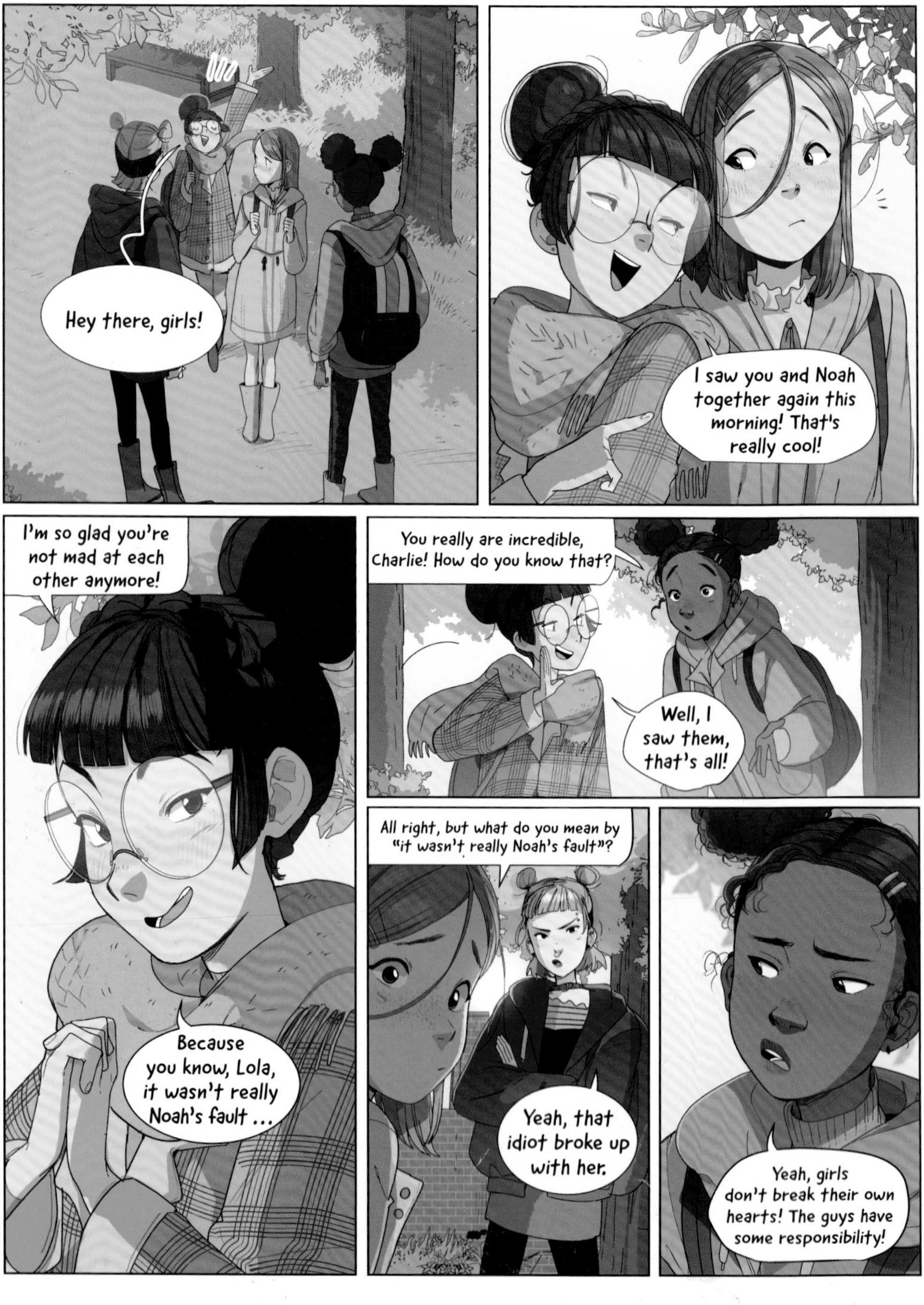
Hey there, girls!
I saw you and Noah together again this morning! That's really cool!
I'm so glad you're not mad at each other anymore!
Because you know, Lola, it wasn't really Noah's fault ...
You really are incredible, Charlie! How do you know that?
Well, I saw them, that's all!
All right, but what do you mean by "it wasn't really Noah's fault"?
Yeah, that idiot broke up with her.
Yeah, girls don't break their own hearts! The guys have some responsibility!

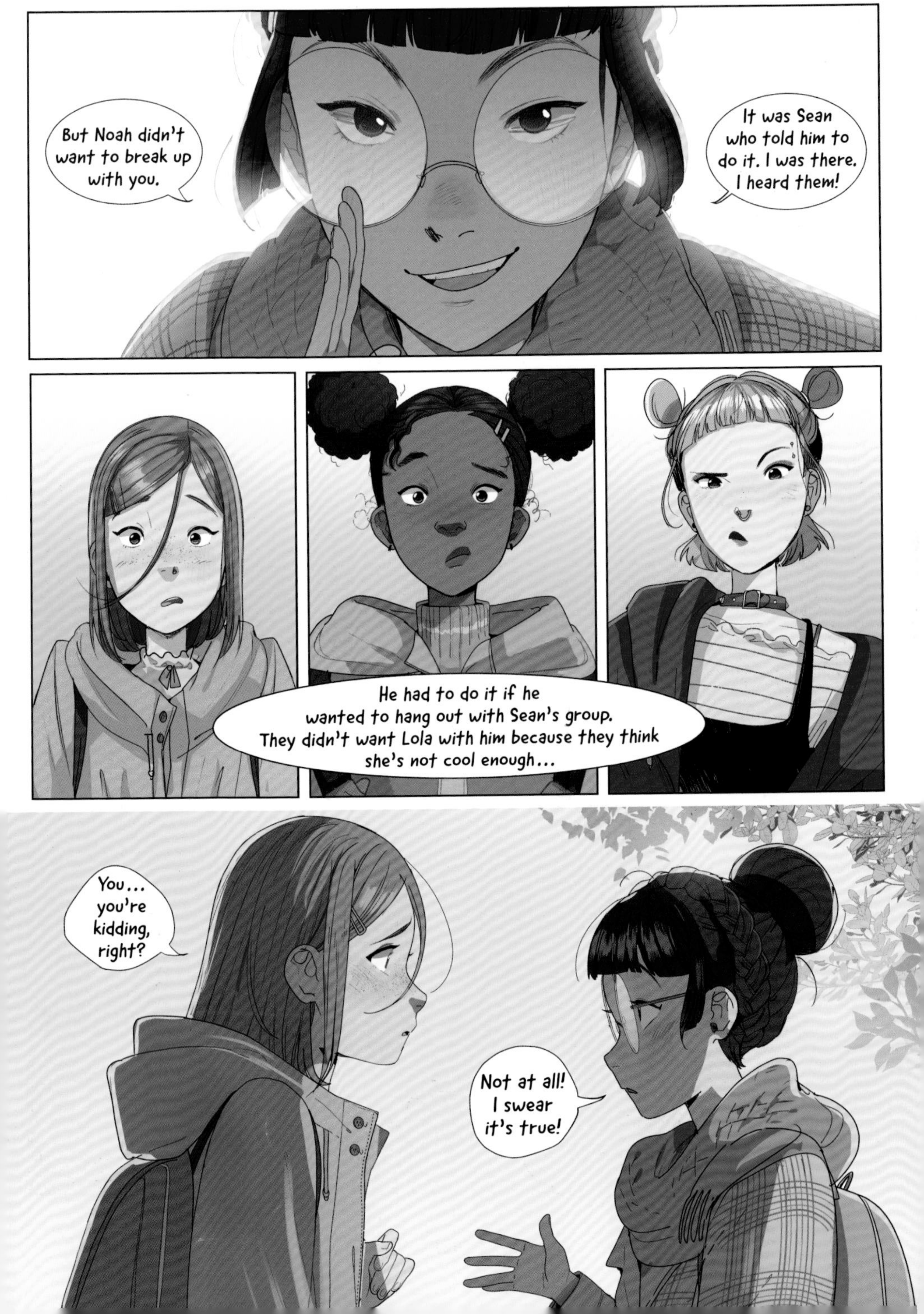

But Noah didn't want to break up with you.
It was Sean who told him to do it. I was there. I heard them!
He had to do it if he wanted to hang out with Sean's group. They didn't want Lola with him because they think she's not cool enough...
You... you're kidding, right?
Not at all! I swear it's true!

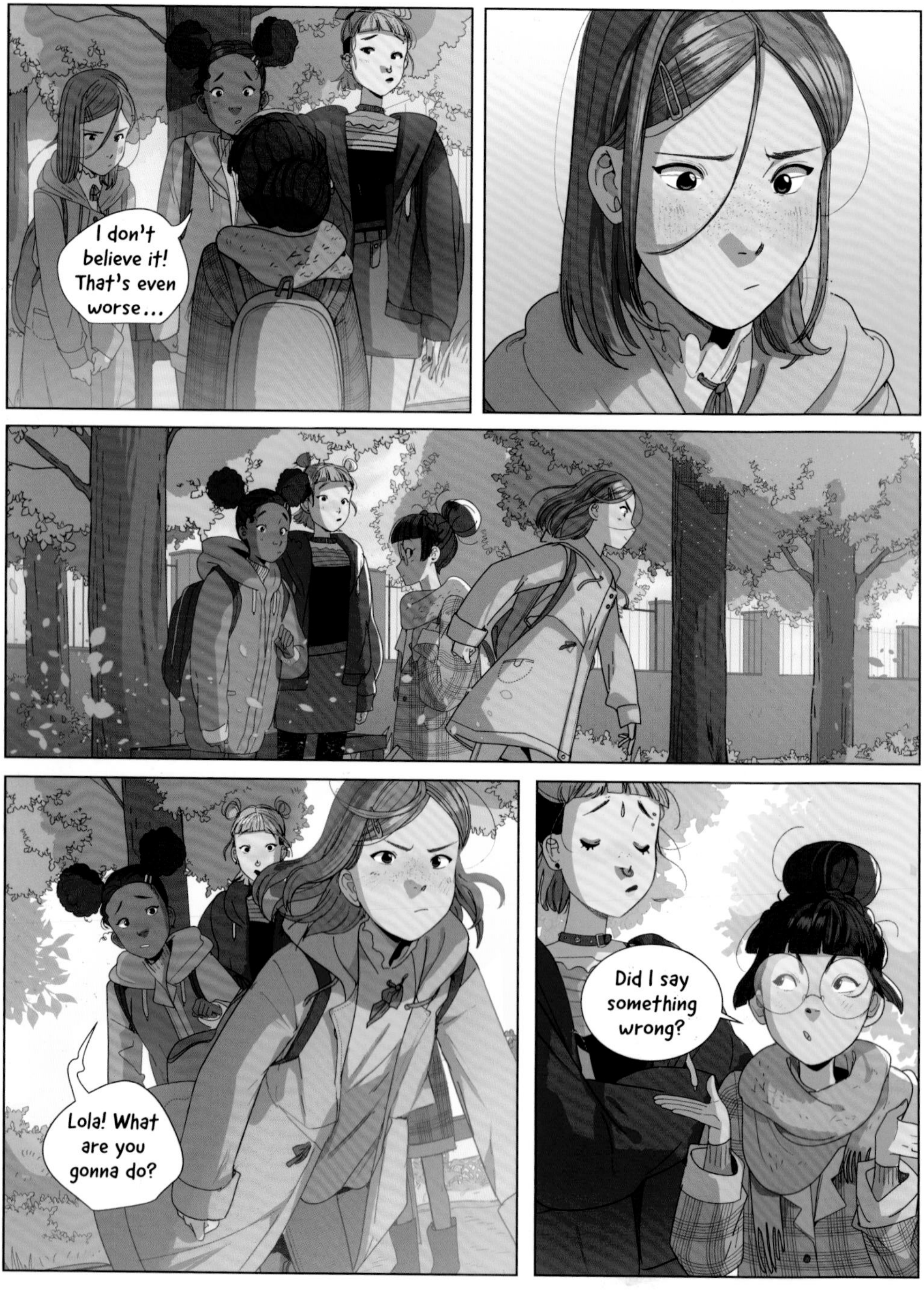
I don't believe it! That's even worse...
Lola! What are you gonna do?
Did I say something wrong?

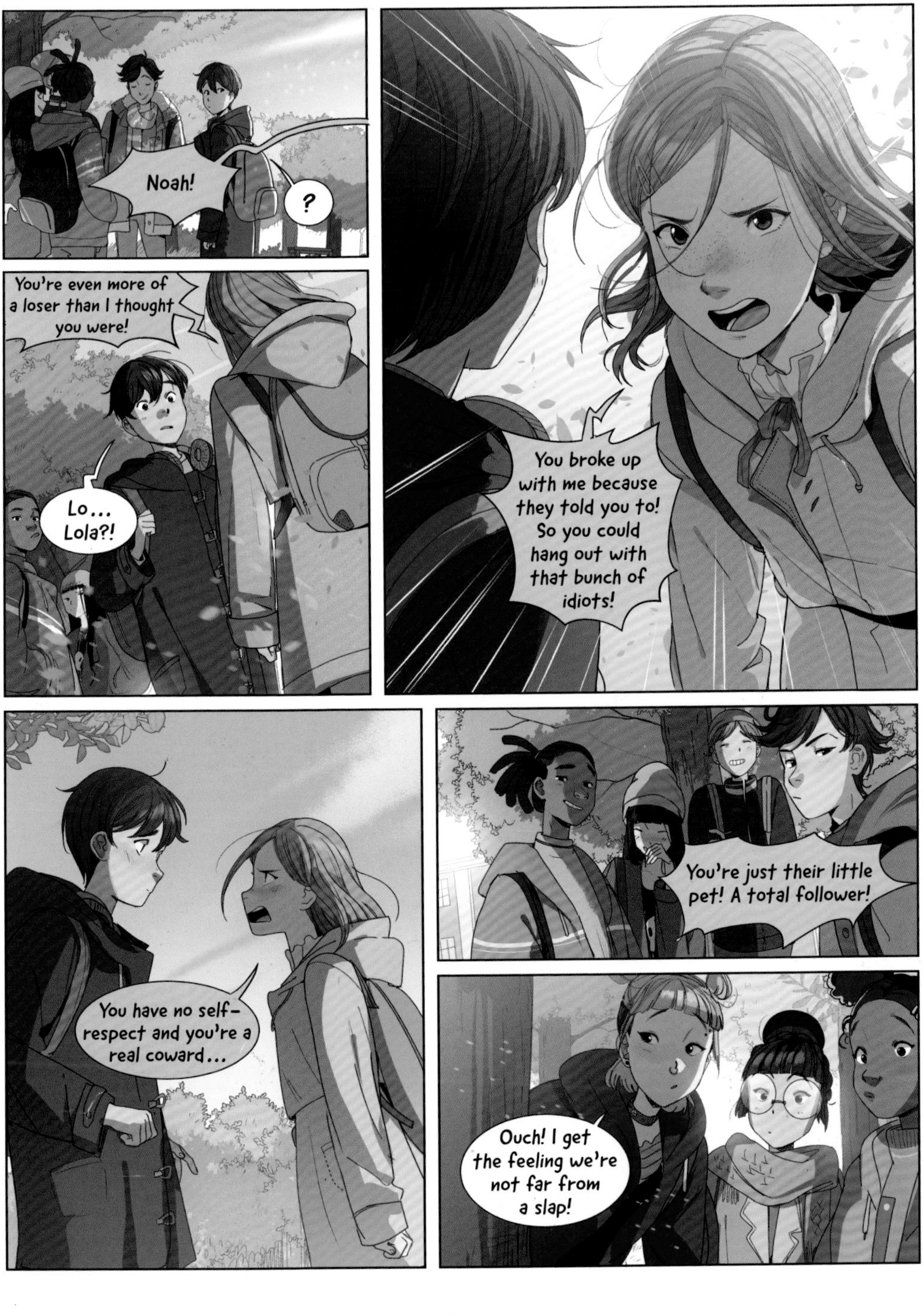
Noah!
?
You're even more of a loser than I thought you were!
Lo... Lola?!
You broke up with me because they told you to! So you could hang out with that bunch of idiots!
You have no self-respect and you're a real coward...
You're just their little pet! A total follower!
Ouch! I get the feeling we're not far from a slap!

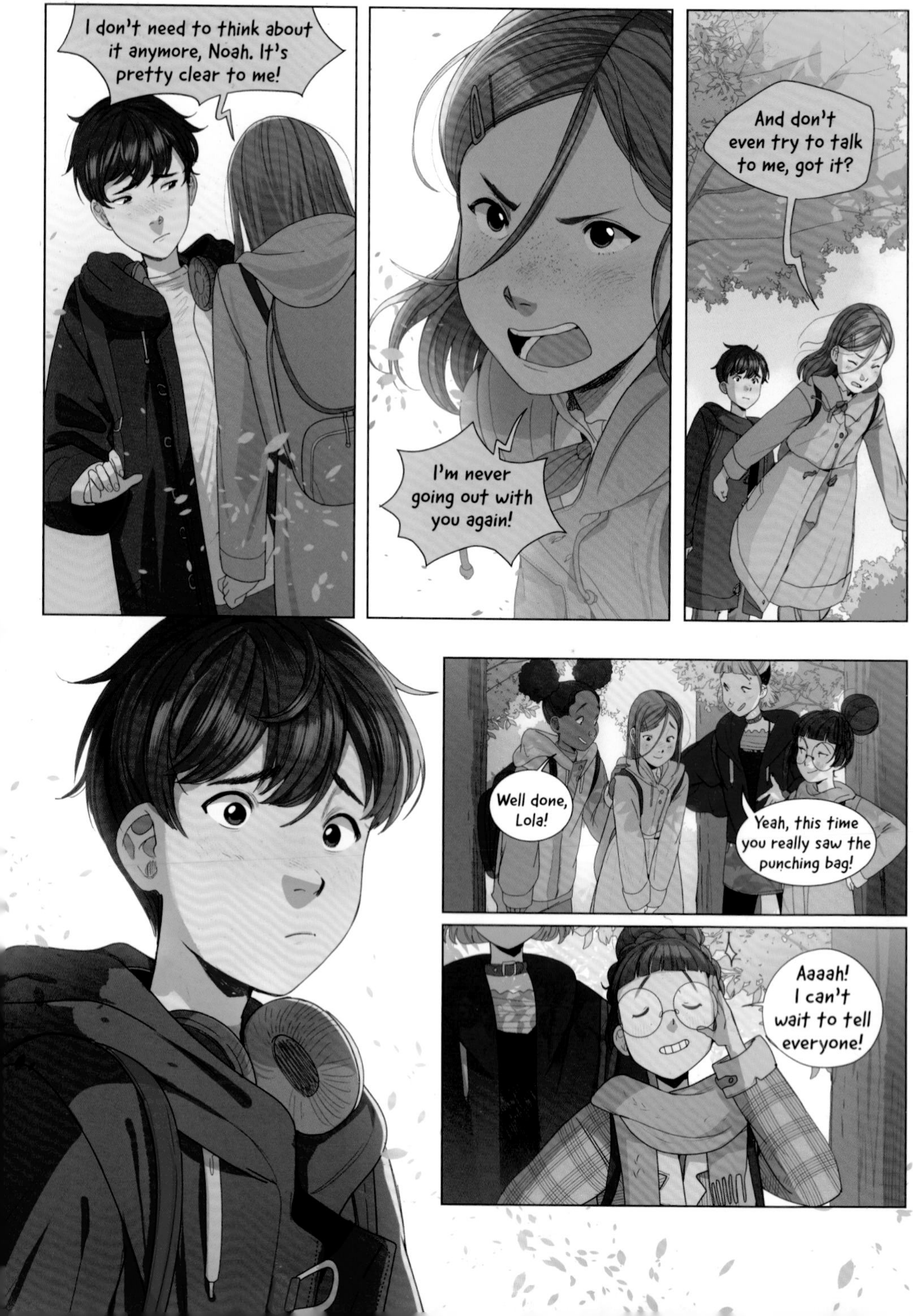
I don't need to think about it anymore, Noah. It's pretty clear to me!
I'm never going out with you again!
And don't even try to talk to me, got it?
Well done, Lola!
Yeah, this time you really saw the punching bag!
Aaaah! I can't wait to tell everyone!

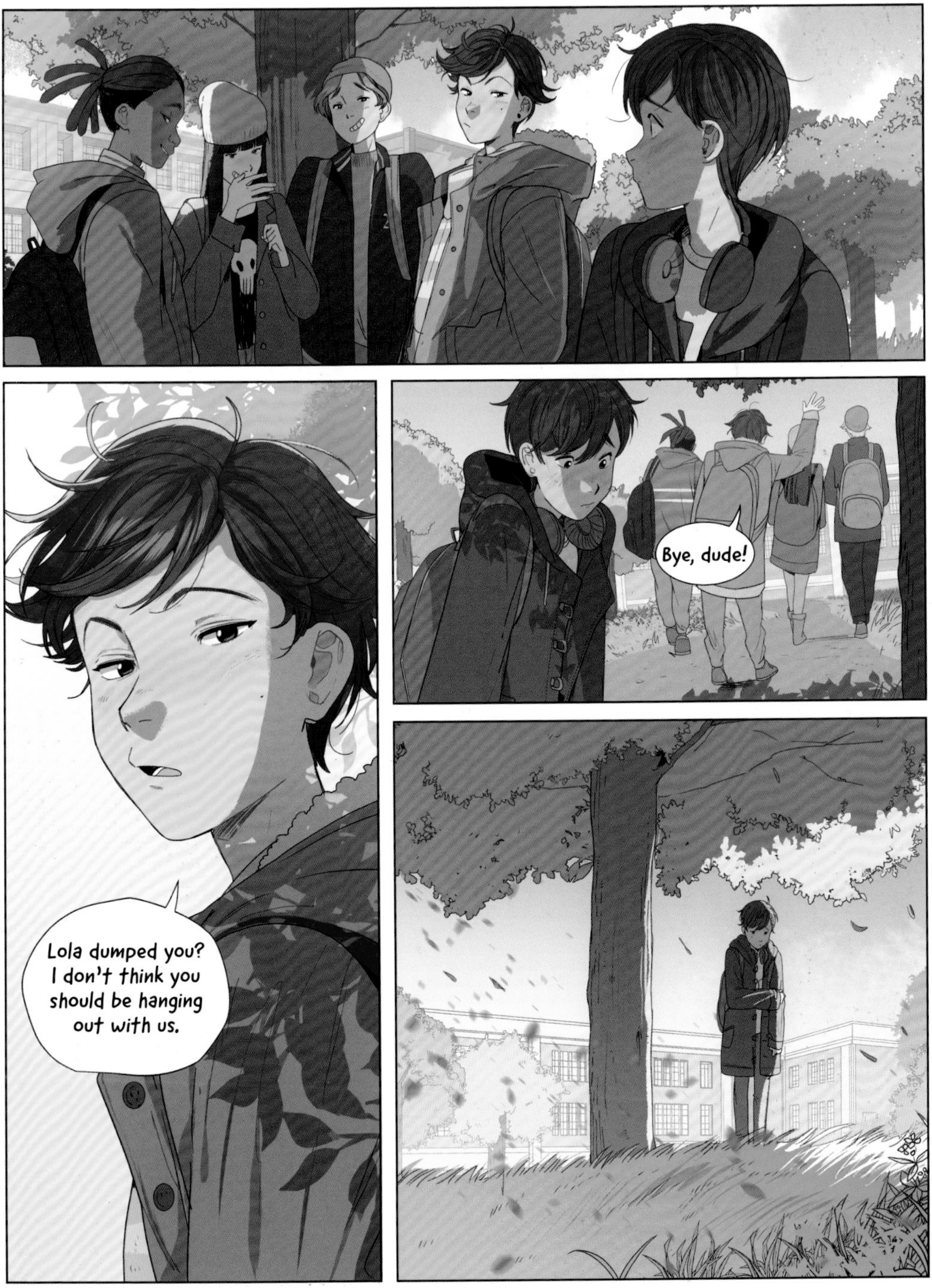
Lola dumped you? I don't think you should be hanging out with us.
Bye, dude!

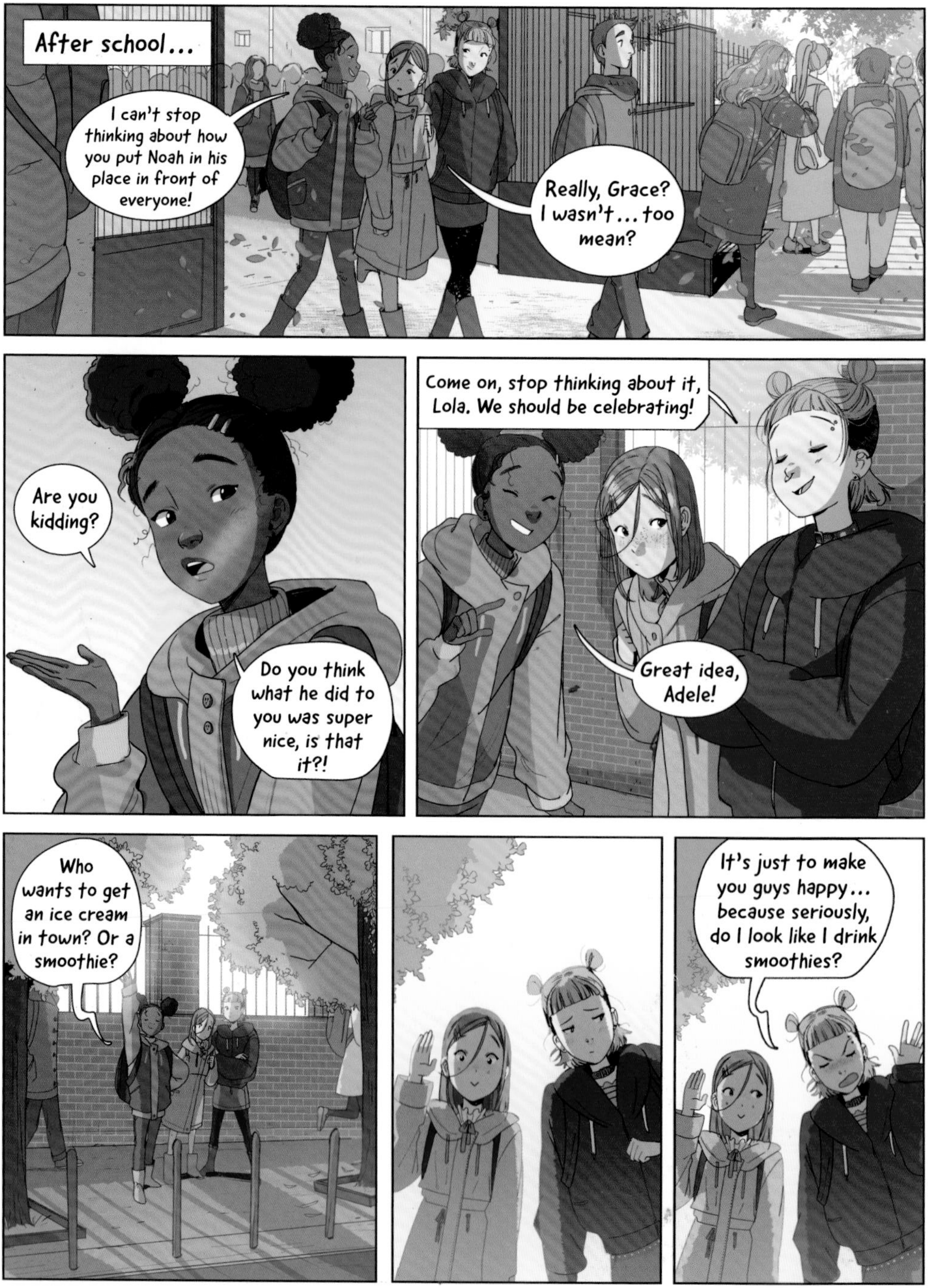
After school...
I can't stop thinking about how you put Noah in his place in front of everyone!
Really, Grace? I wasn't... too mean?
Are you kidding?
Do you think what he did to you was super nice, is that it?!
Come on, stop thinking about it, Lola. We should be celebrating!
Great idea, Adele!
Who wants to get an ice cream in town? Or a smoothie?
It's just to make you guys happy... because seriously, do I look like I drink smoothies?

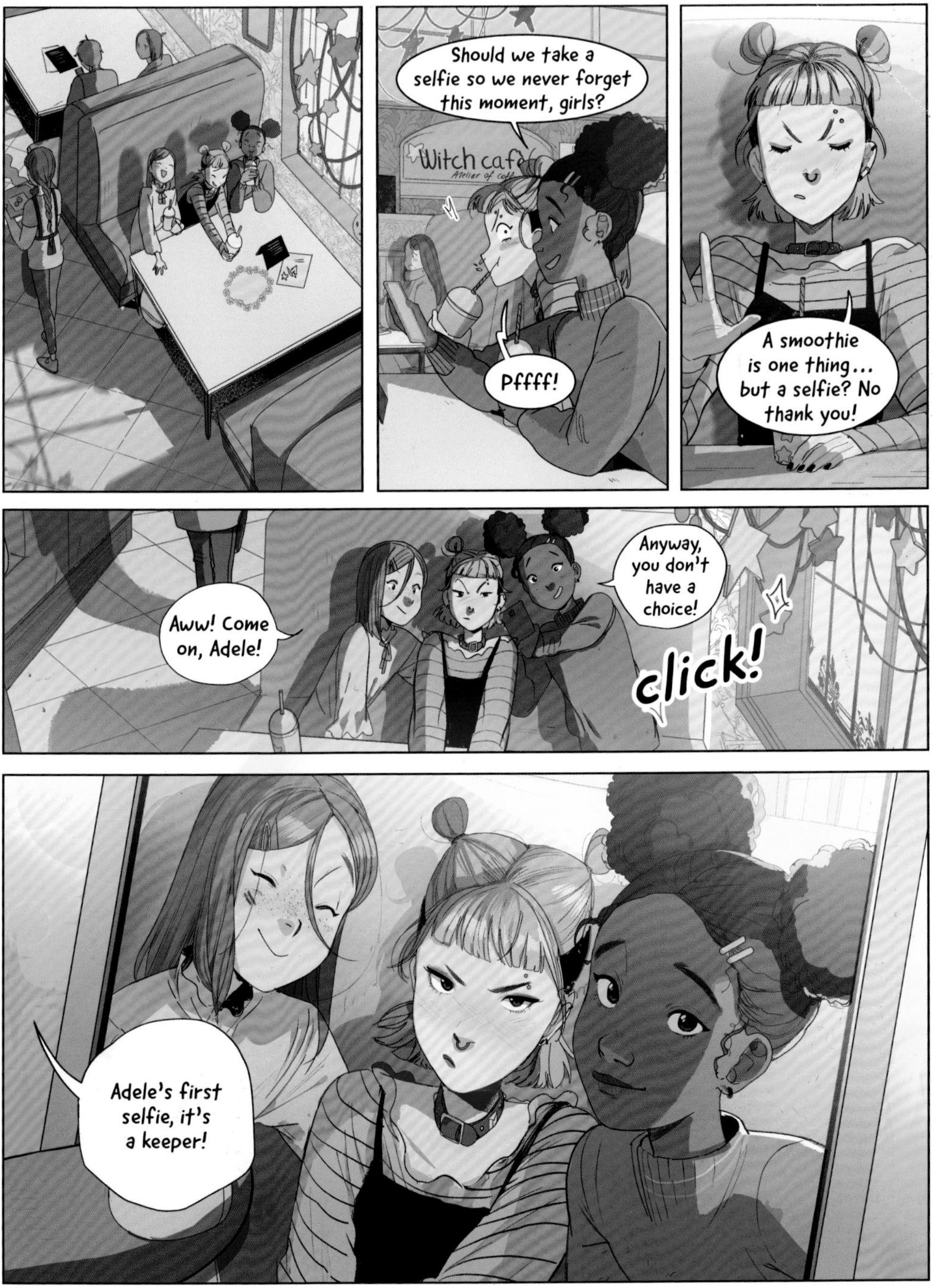
Should we take a selfie so we never forget this moment, girls?
Witch café
Pffff!
A smoothie is one thing... but a selfie? No thank you!
Aww! Come on, Adele!
Anyway, you don't have a choice!
click!
Adele's first selfie, it's a keeper!

!

Oh! I have another idea for how to give this day a happy ending!

Wait here!

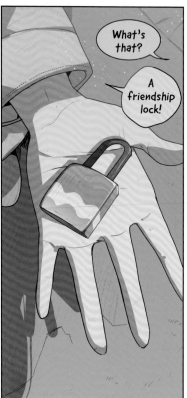

What's that?

A friendship lock!

We write our names on it and then lock it somewhere!

I can't believe this! This is even stupider than selfies!

And again, you don't have a choice!

Aaaah! Stop! I hate you!

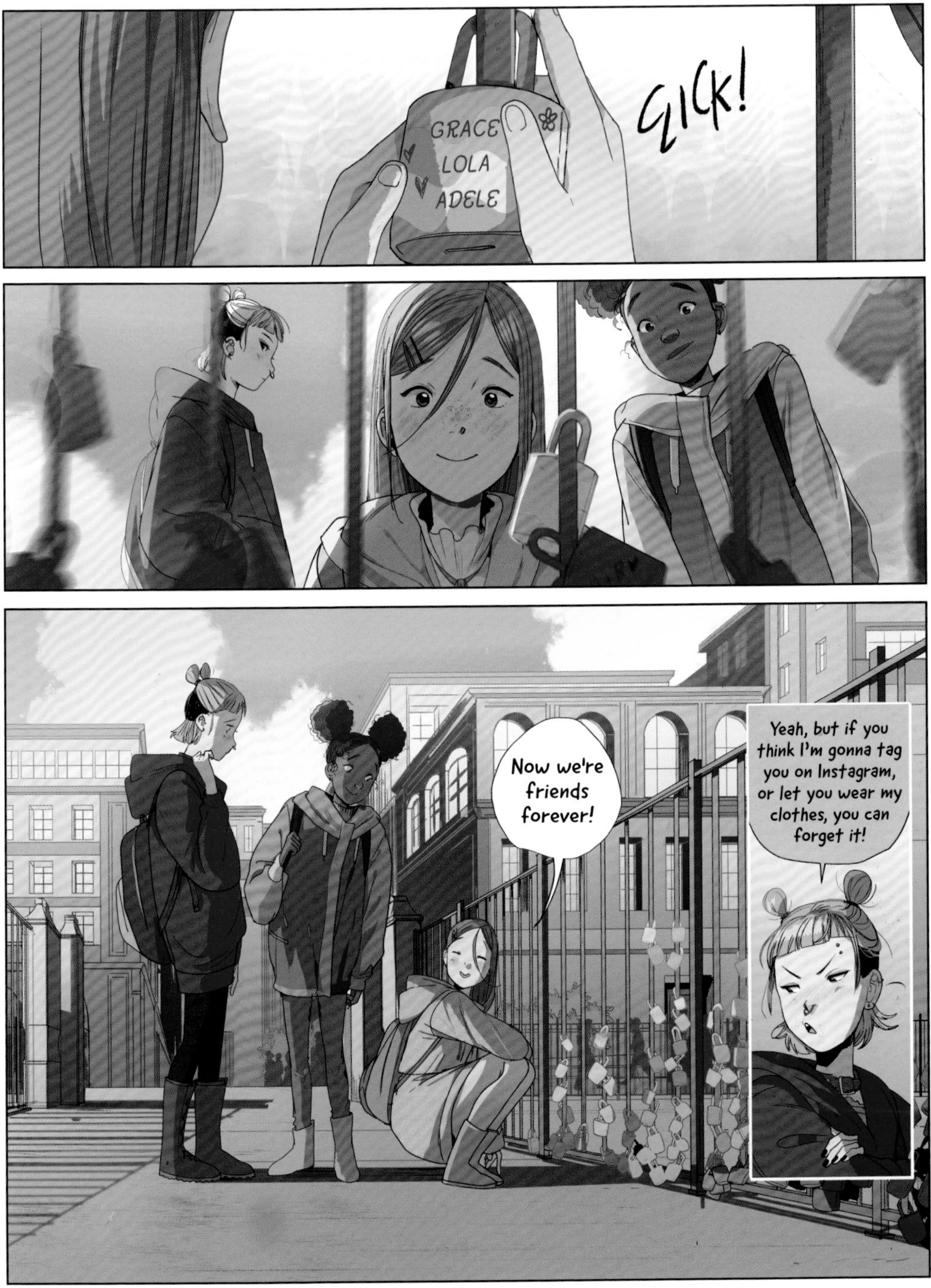
GRACE
LOLA
ADELE
CLICK!
Now we're friends forever!
Yeah, but if you think I'm gonna tag you on Instagram, or let you wear my clothes, you can forget it!

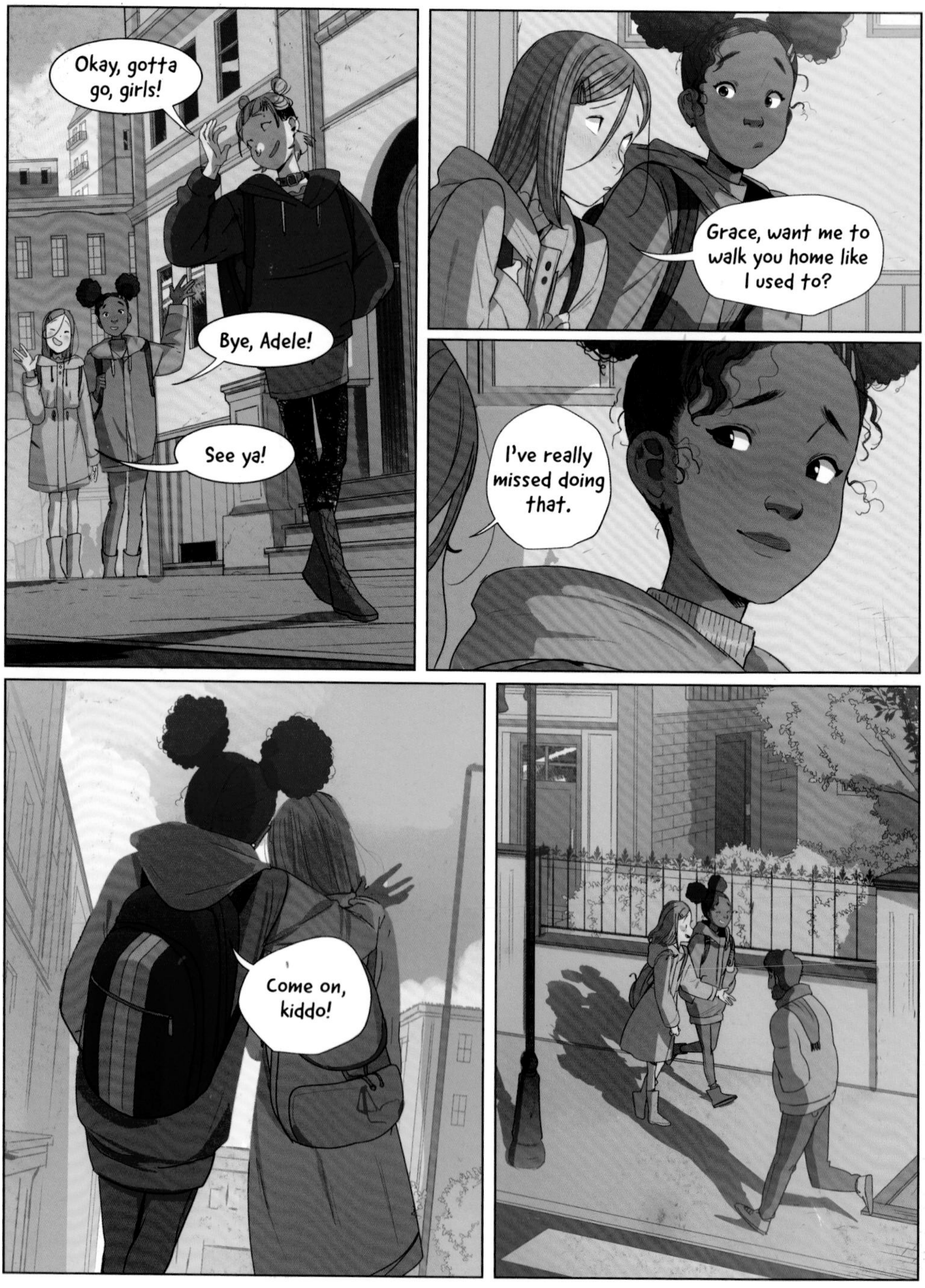
Okay, gotta go, girls!
Bye, Adele!
See ya!
Grace, want me to walk you home like I used to?
I've really missed doing that.
Come on, kiddo!

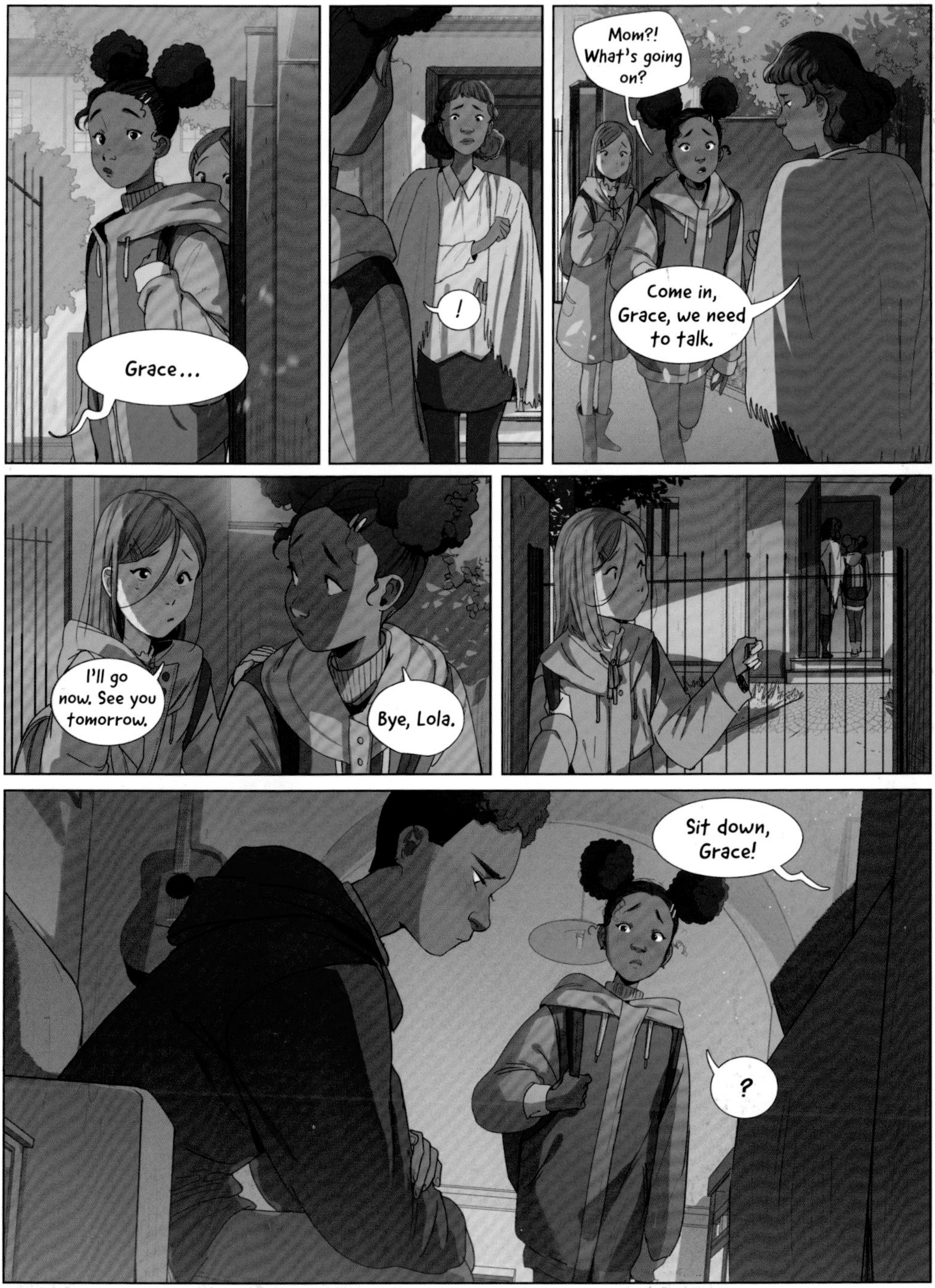
Grace...
!
Mom?! What's going on?
Come in, Grace, we need to talk.
I'll go now. See you tomorrow.
Bye, Lola.
Sit down, Grace!
?

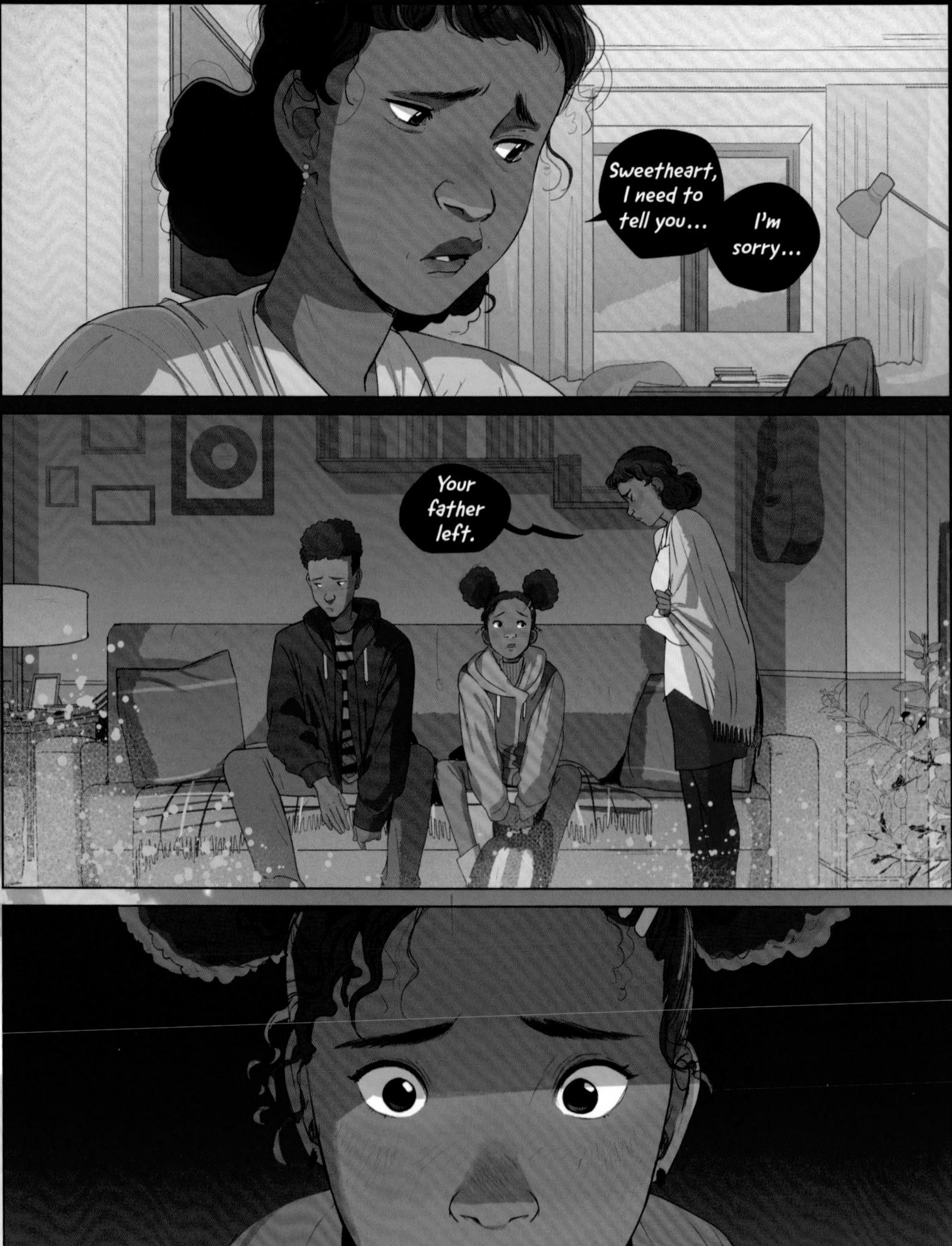
Sweetheart, I need to tell you...
I'm sorry...
Your father left.

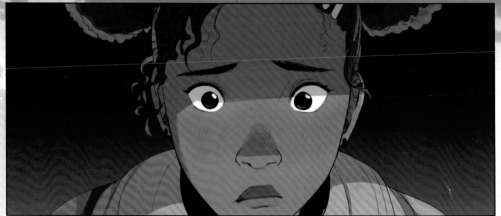

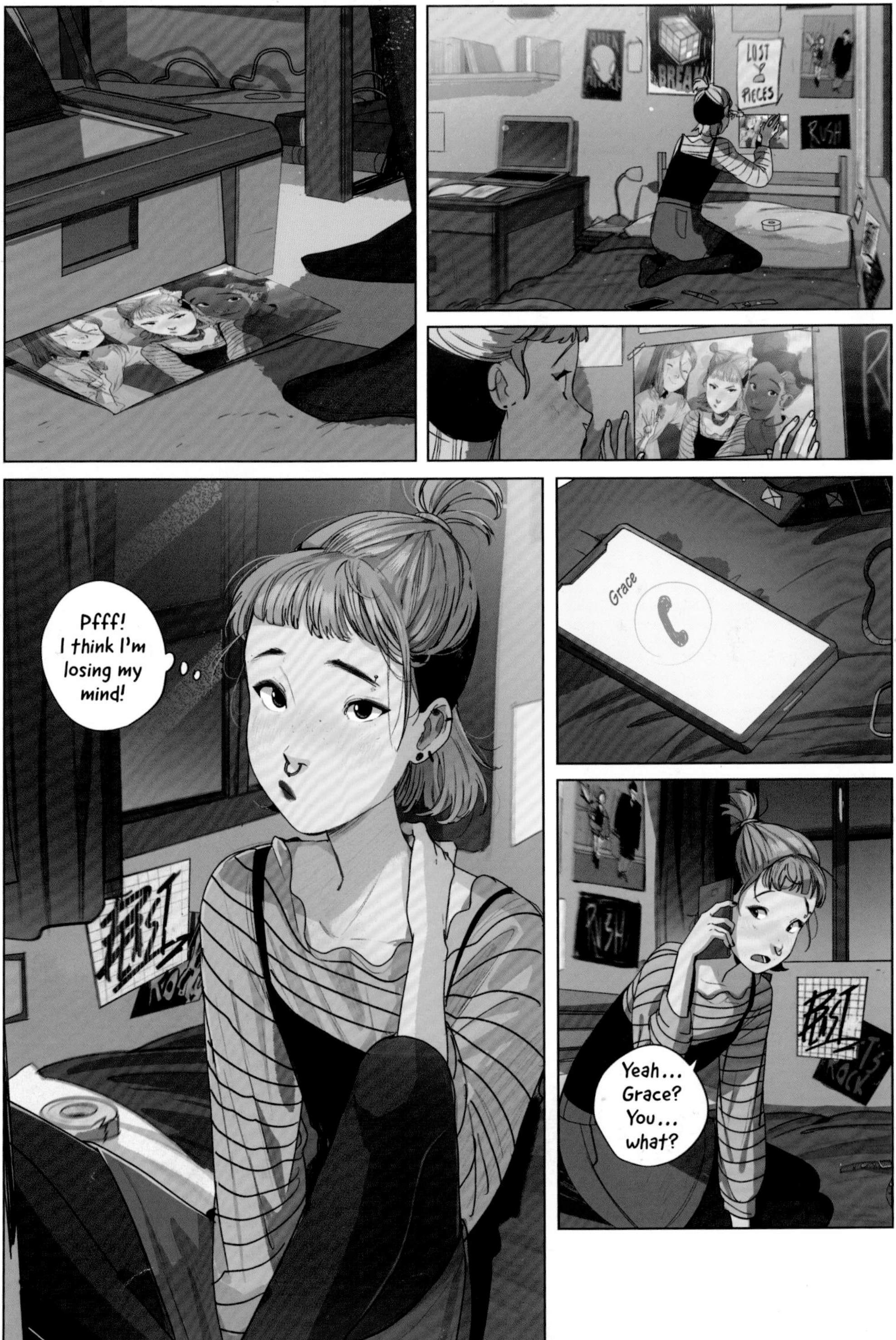
LOST PIECES
RUSH
Pfff! I think I'm losing my mind!
Grace
Yeah... Grace? You... what?

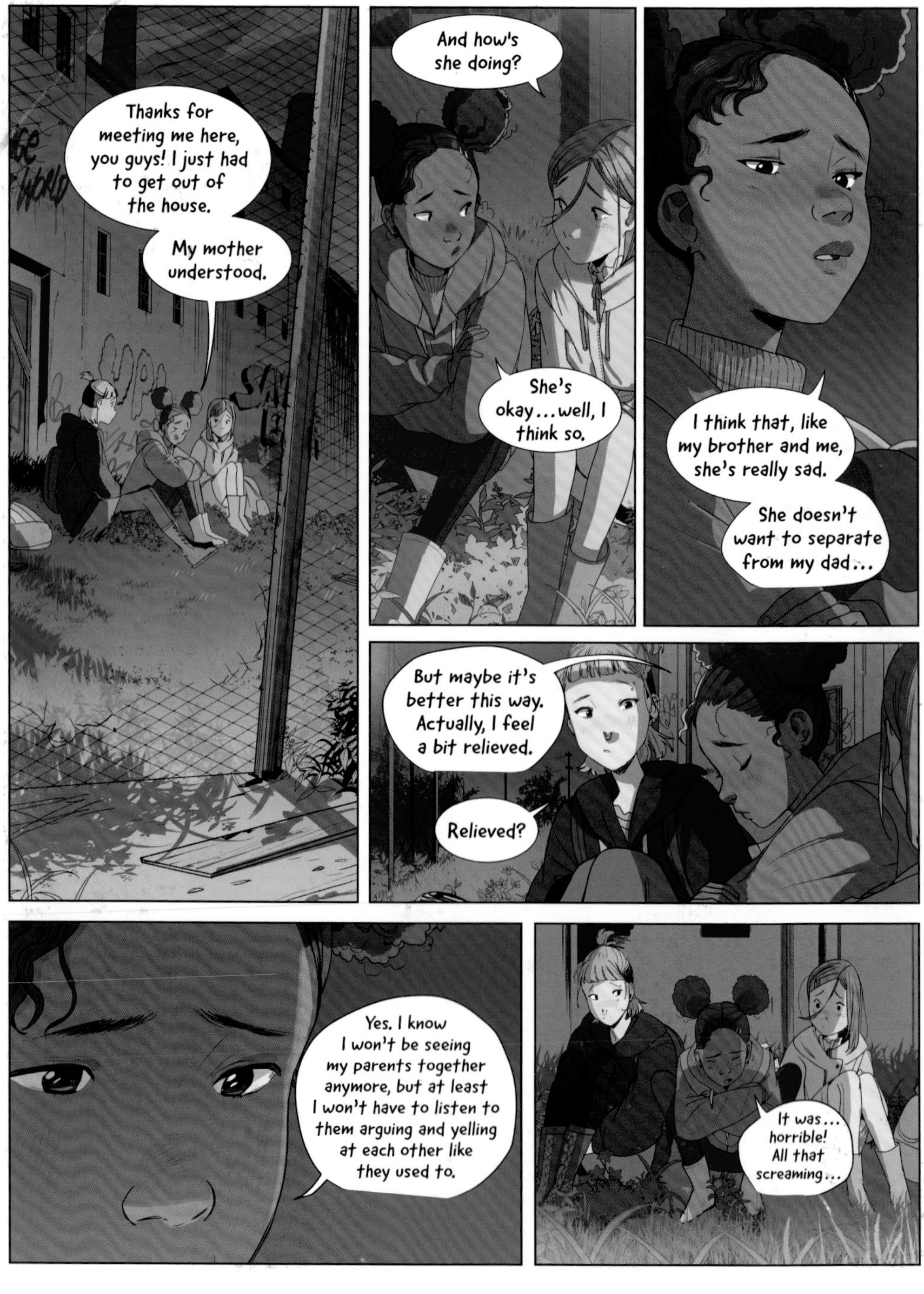
Thanks for meeting me here, you guys! I just had to get out of the house.
My mother understood.
And how's she doing?
She's okay...well, I think so.
I think that, like my brother and me, she's really sad.
She doesn't want to separate from my dad...
But maybe it's better this way. Actually, I feel a bit relieved.
Relieved?
Yes. I know I won't be seeing my parents together anymore, but at least I won't have to listen to them arguing and yelling at each other like they used to.
It was... horrible! All that screaming...

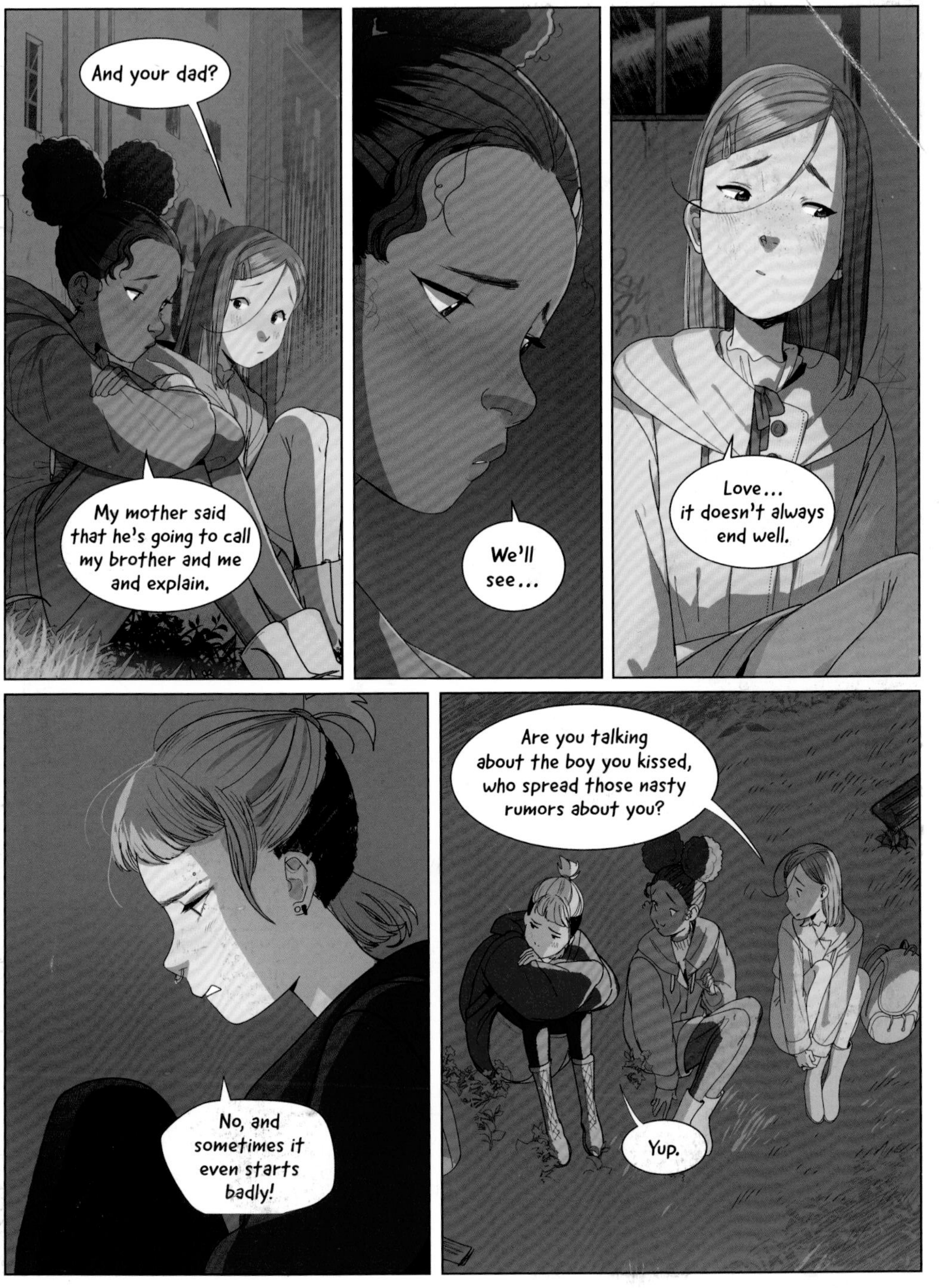
And your dad?
My mother said that he's going to call my brother and me and explain.
We'll see...
Love... it doesn't always end well.
No, and sometimes it even starts badly!
Are you talking about the boy you kissed, who spread those nasty rumors about you?
Yup.

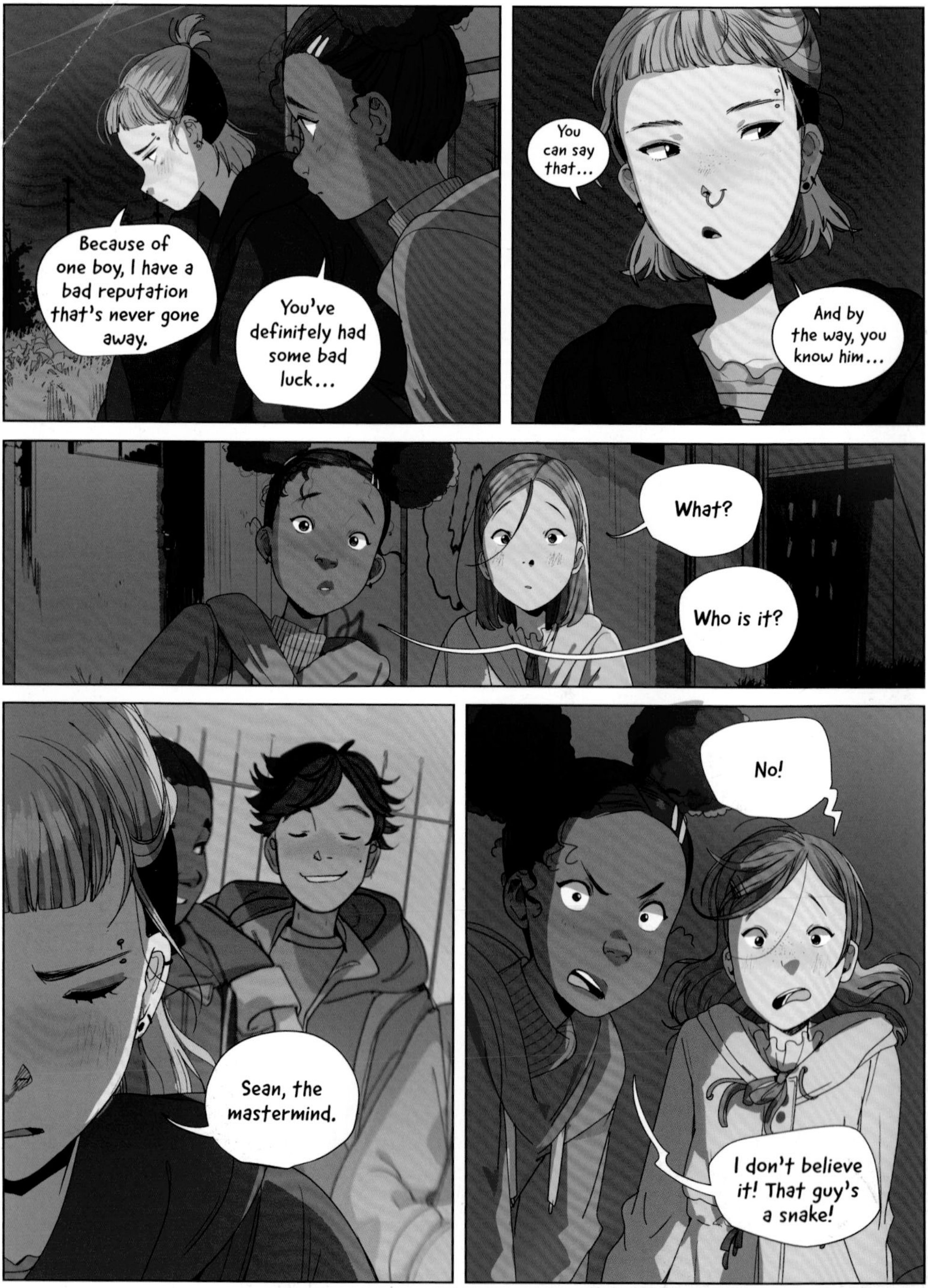
Because of one boy, I have a bad reputation that's never gone away.
You've definitely had some bad luck...
You can say that...
And by the way, you know him...
What?
Who is it?
Sean, the mastermind.
No!
I don't believe it! That guy's a snake!

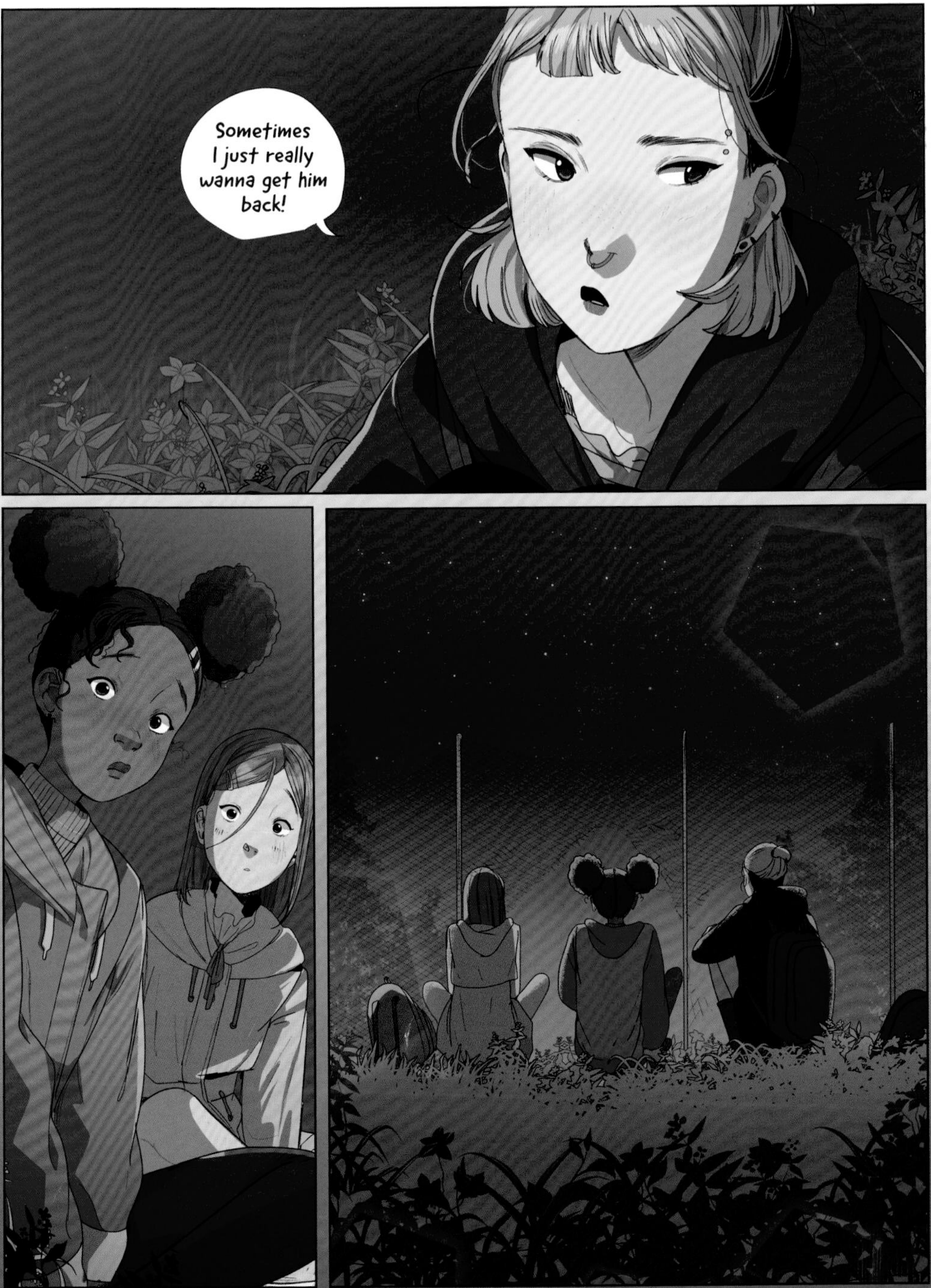
Sometimes I just really wanna get him back!

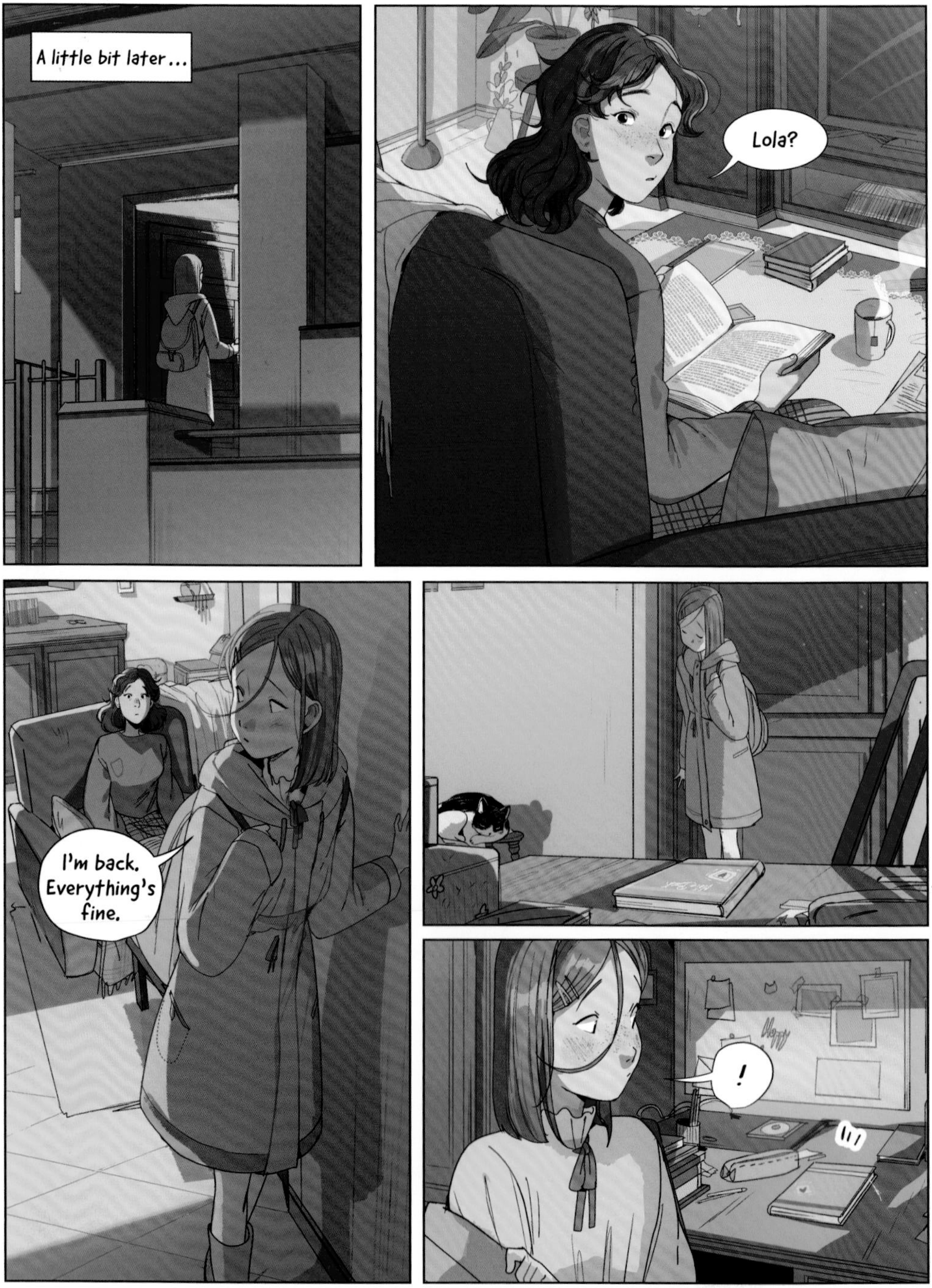
A little bit later...
Lola?
I'm back. Everything's fine.
!

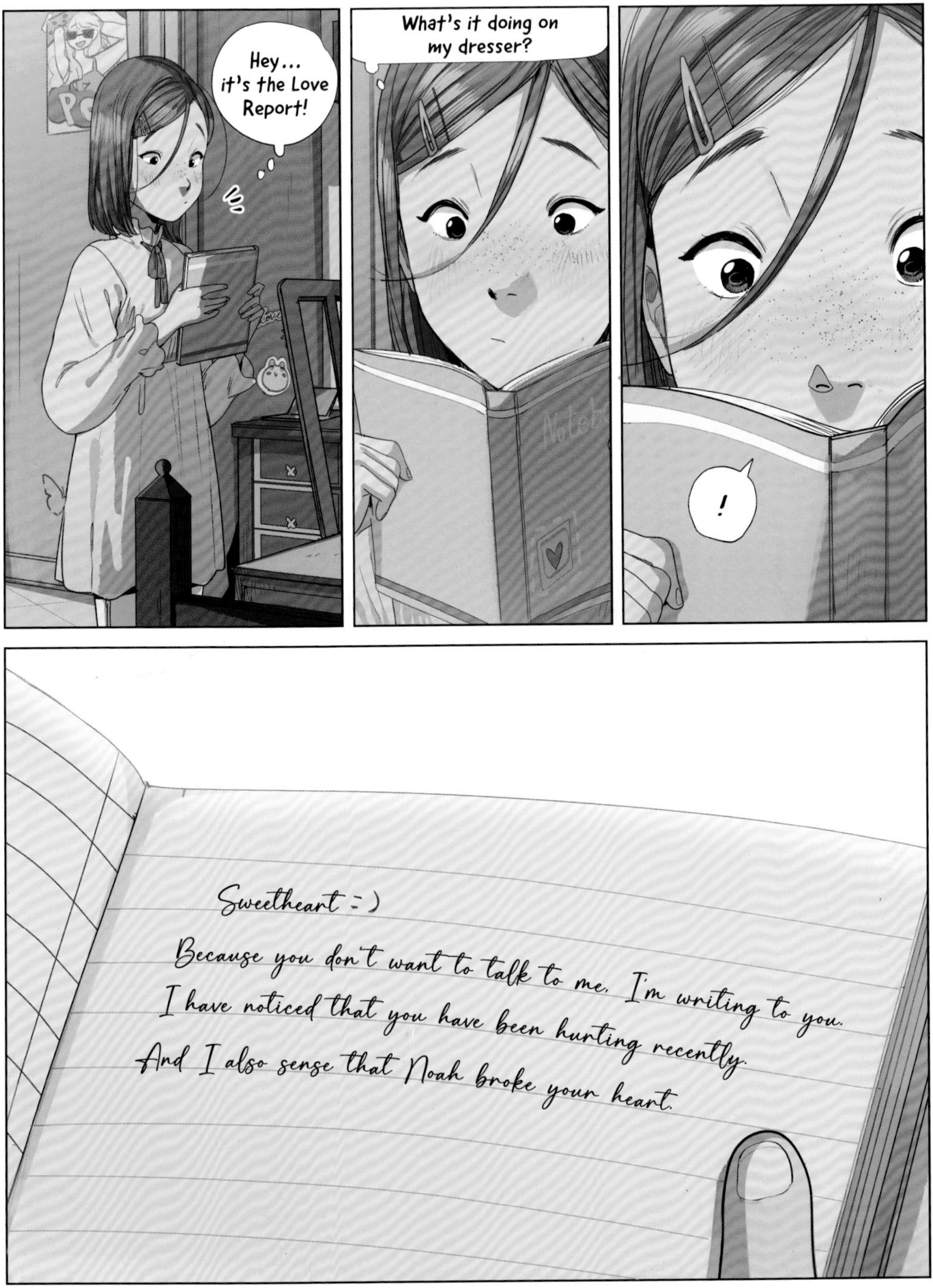

Hey... it's the Love Report!
What's it doing on my dresser?
!
Sweetheart =)
Because you don't want to talk to me, I'm writing to you.
I have noticed that you have been hurting recently.
And I also sense that Noah broke your heart.

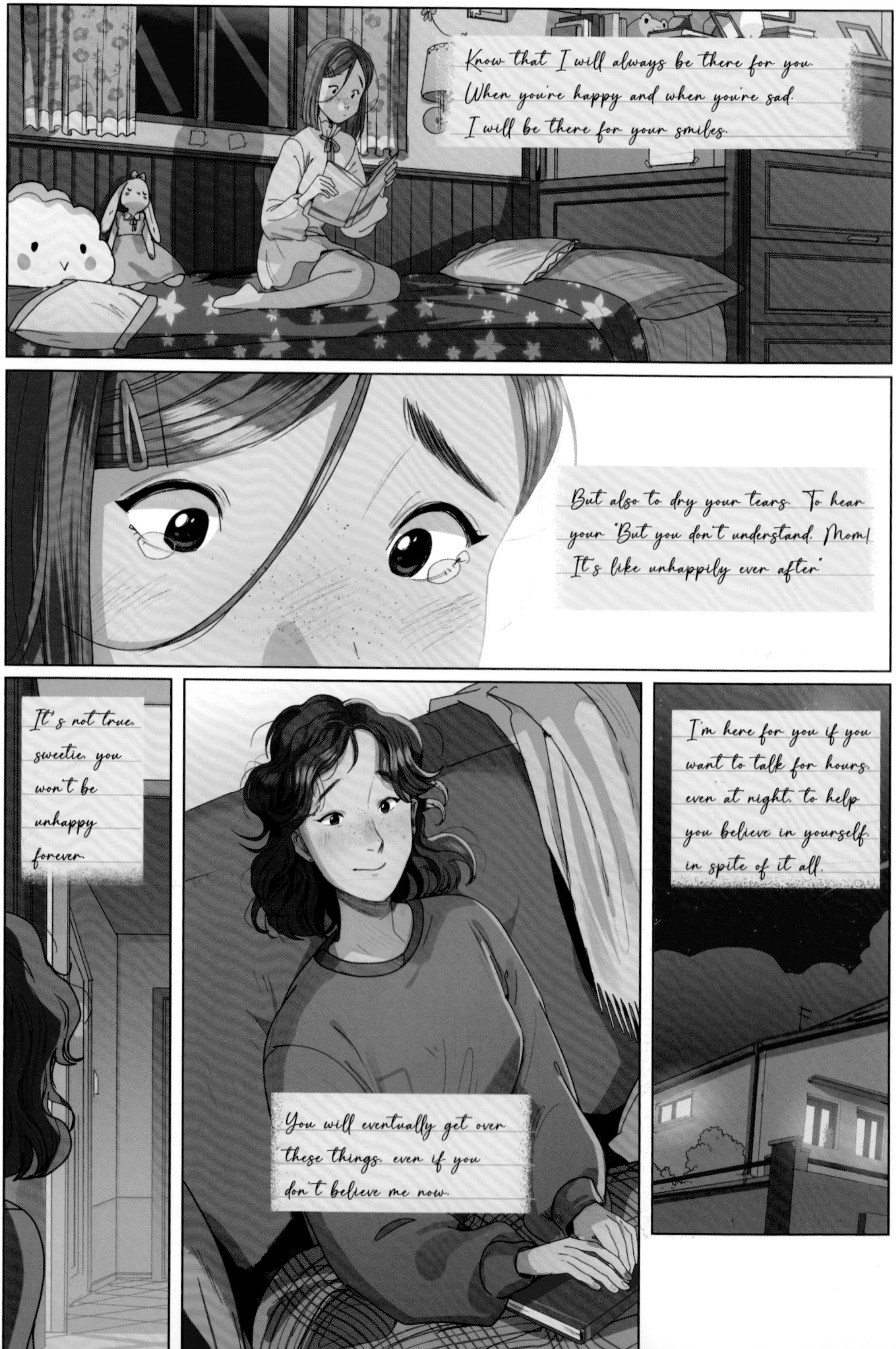
Know that I will always be there for you. When you're happy and when you're sad. I will be there for your smiles.
But also to dry your tears. To hear your "But you don't understand, Mom! It's like unhappily ever after"
It's not true, sweetie, you won't be unhappy forever.
You will eventually get over these things, even if you don't believe me now.
I'm here for you if you want to talk for hours, even at night, to help you believe in yourself, in spite of it all.

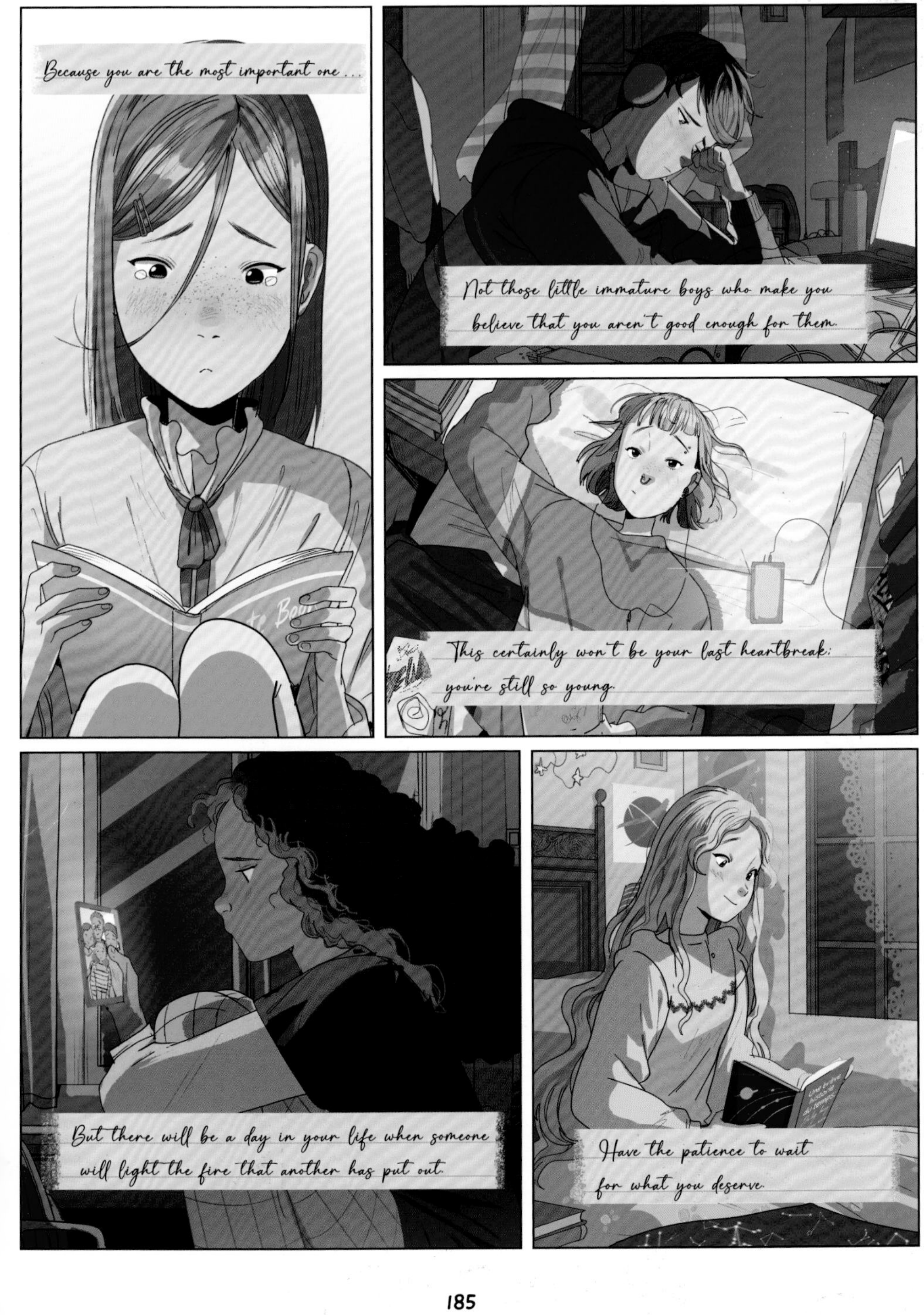

Because you are the most important one . . .
Not those little immature boys who make you believe that you aren't good enough for them.
This certainly won't be your last heartbreak: you're still so young.
But there will be a day in your life when someone will light the fire that another has put out.
Have the patience to wait for what you deserve.

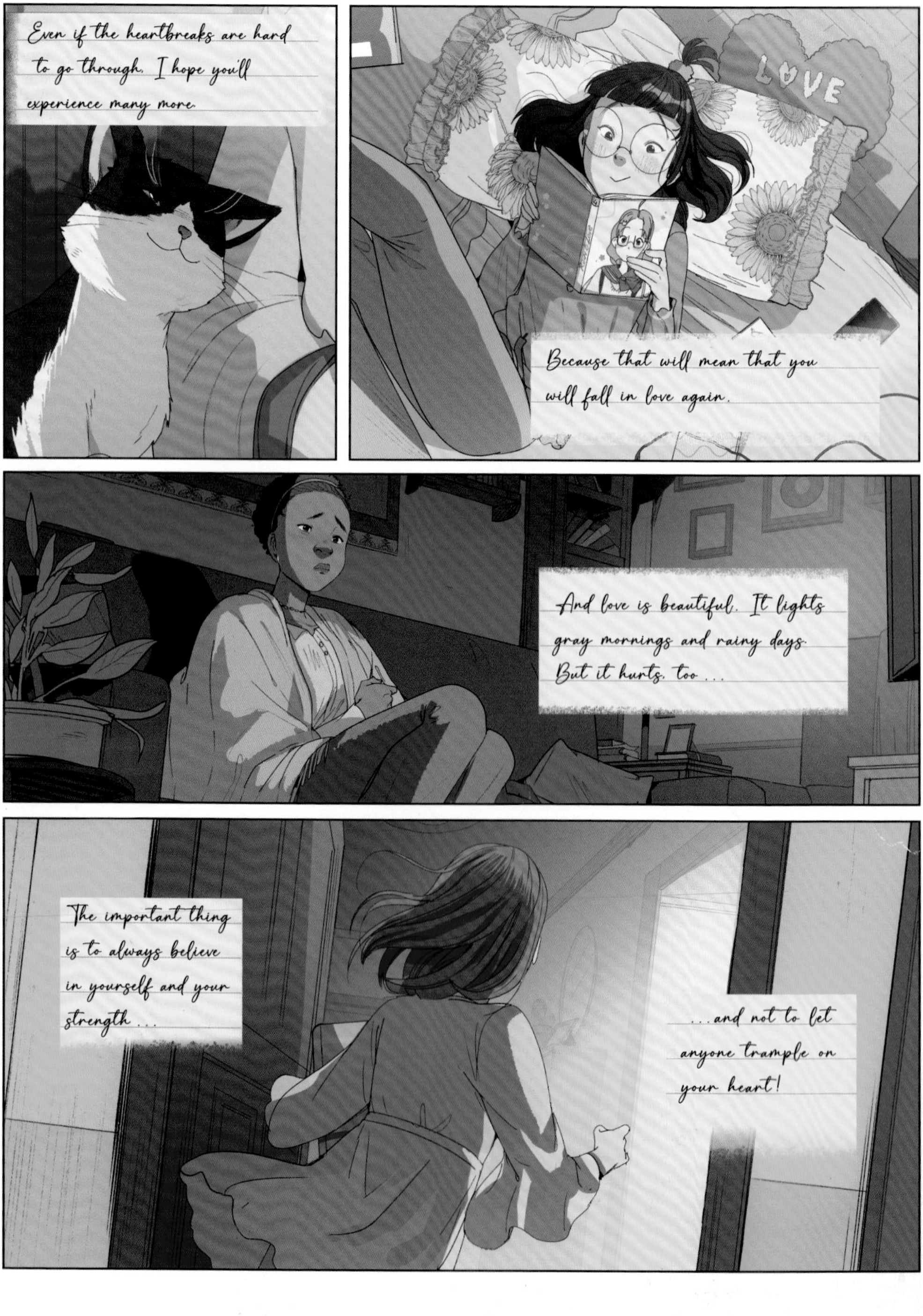
Even if the heartbreaks are hard to go through, I hope you'll experience many more.
Because that will mean that you will fall in love again.
LOVE
And love is beautiful. It lights gray mornings and rainy days. But it hurts, too . . .
The important thing is to always believe in yourself and your strength . . .
. . . and not to let anyone trample on your heart!

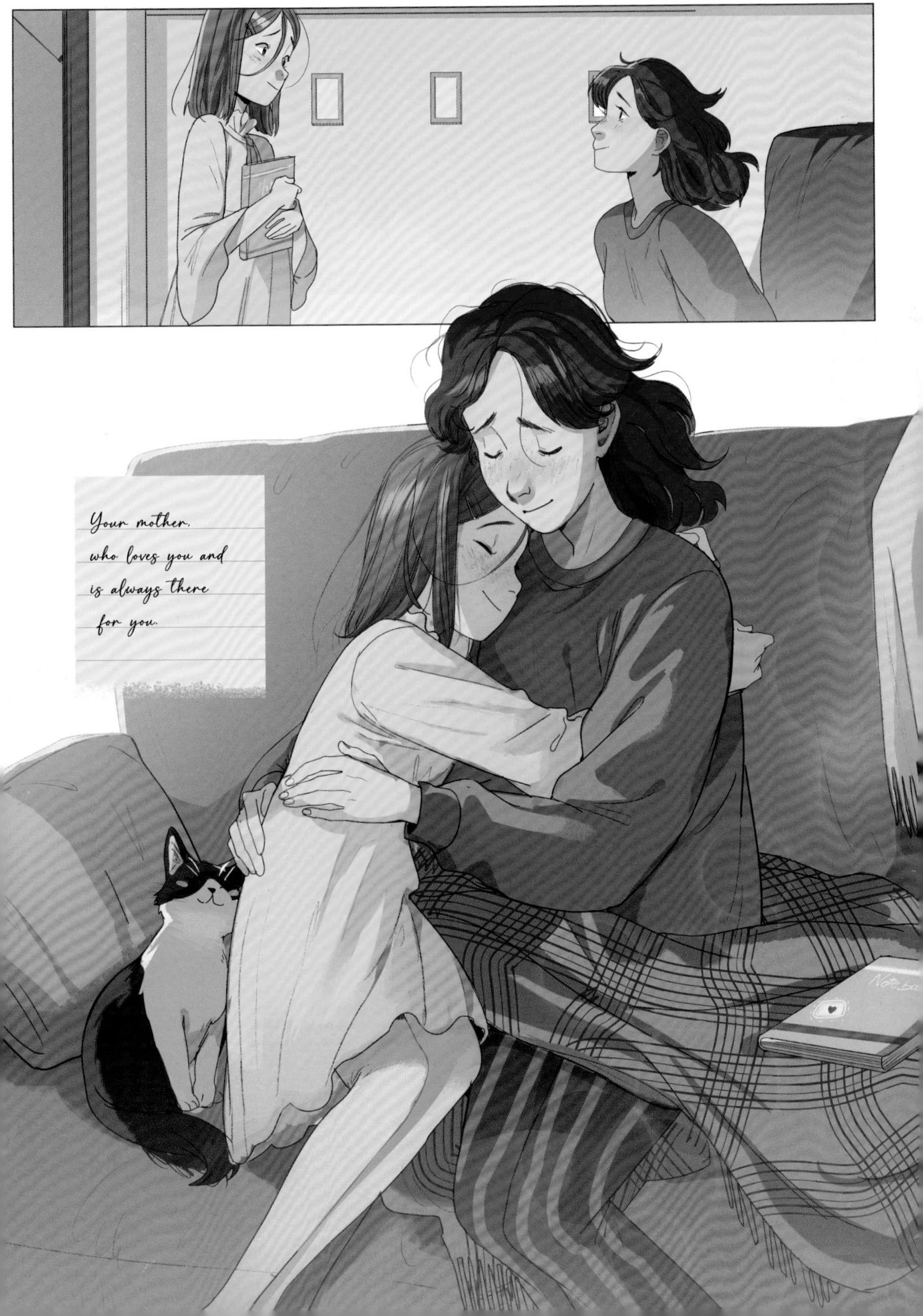
Your mother, who loves you and is always there for you.

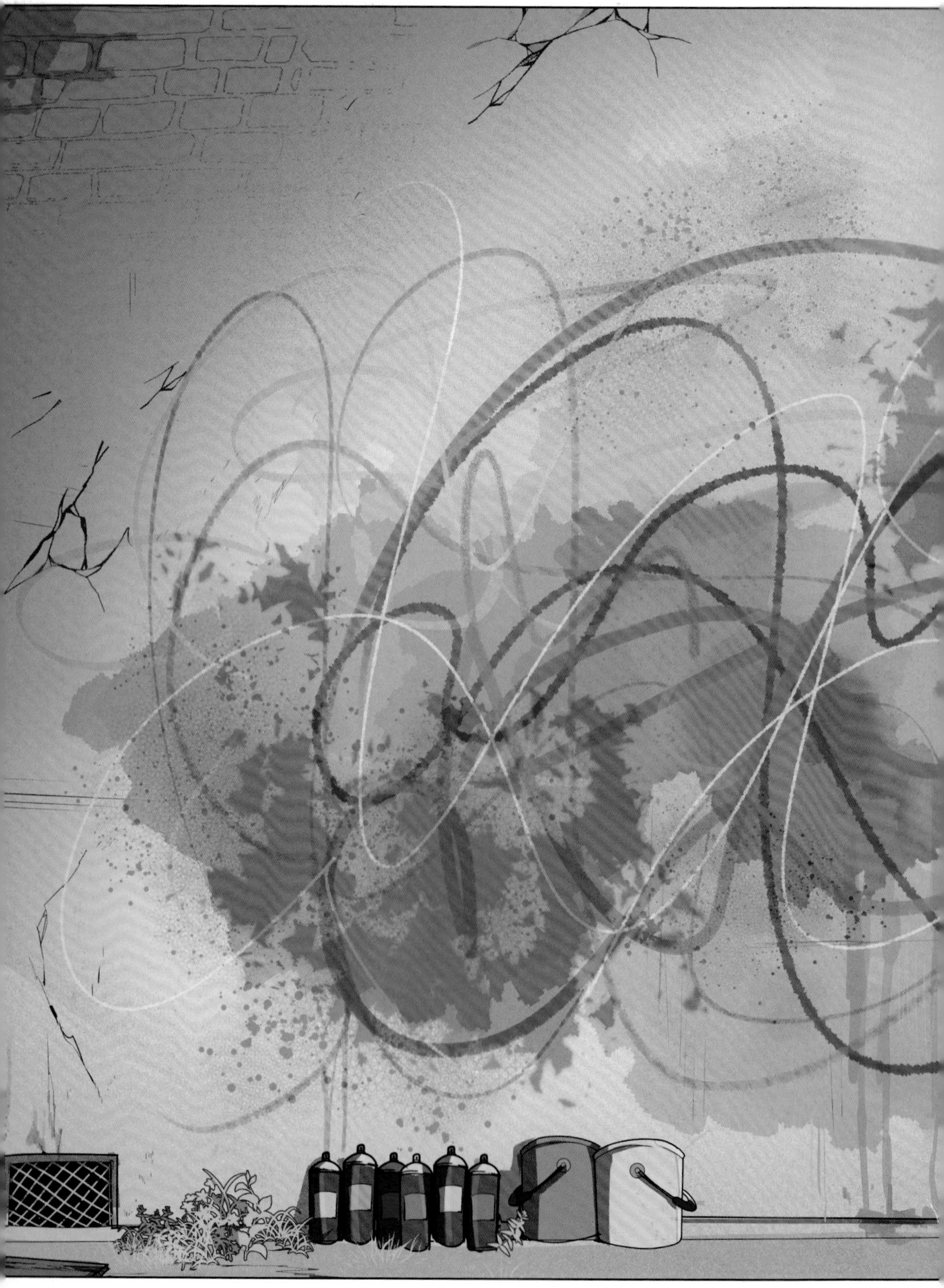

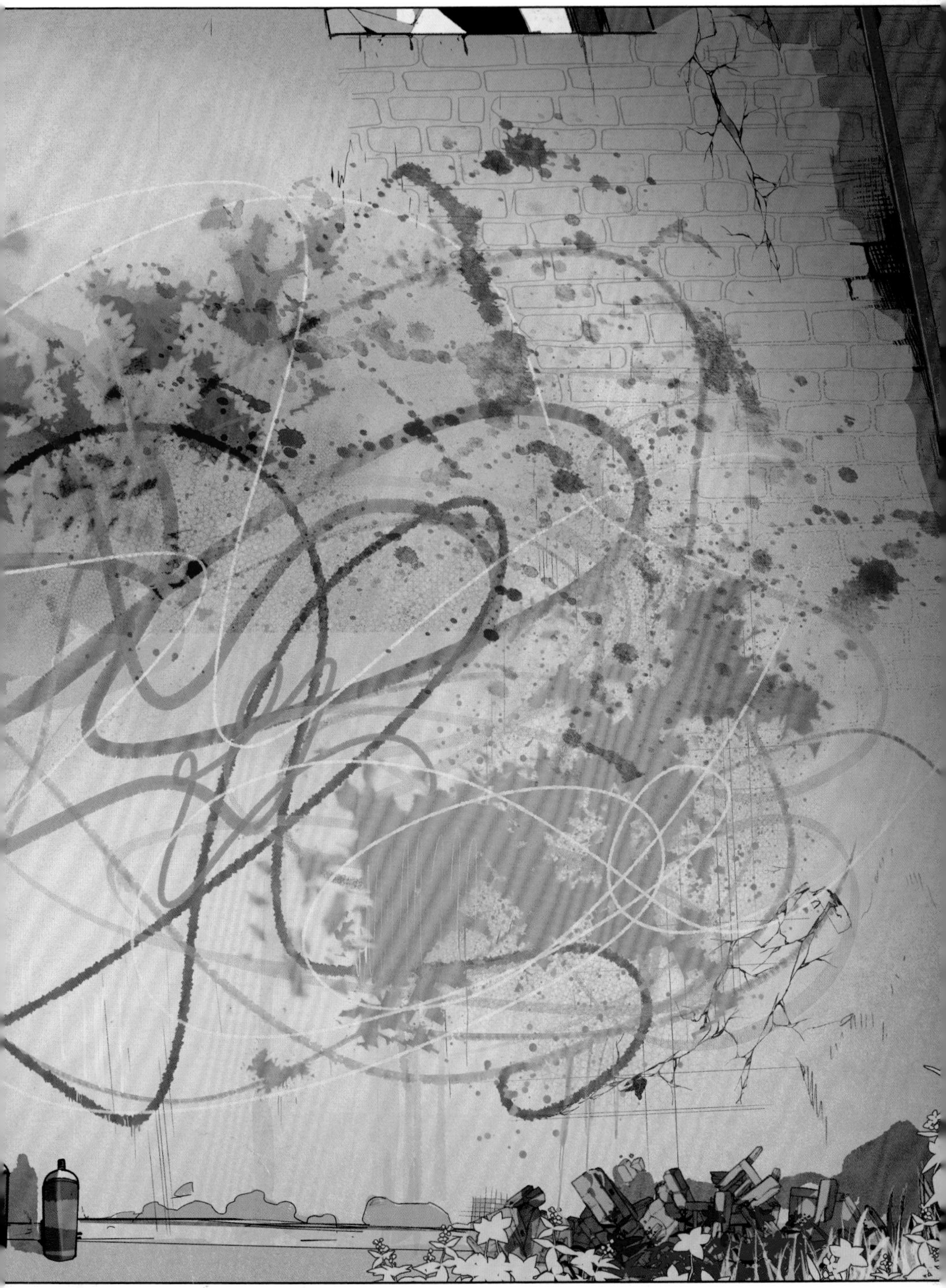

GRACE AND LOLA DISCOVERED MORE ABOUT
ROMANCE AND FRIENDSHIP
THAN EITHER EVER EXPECTED . . .

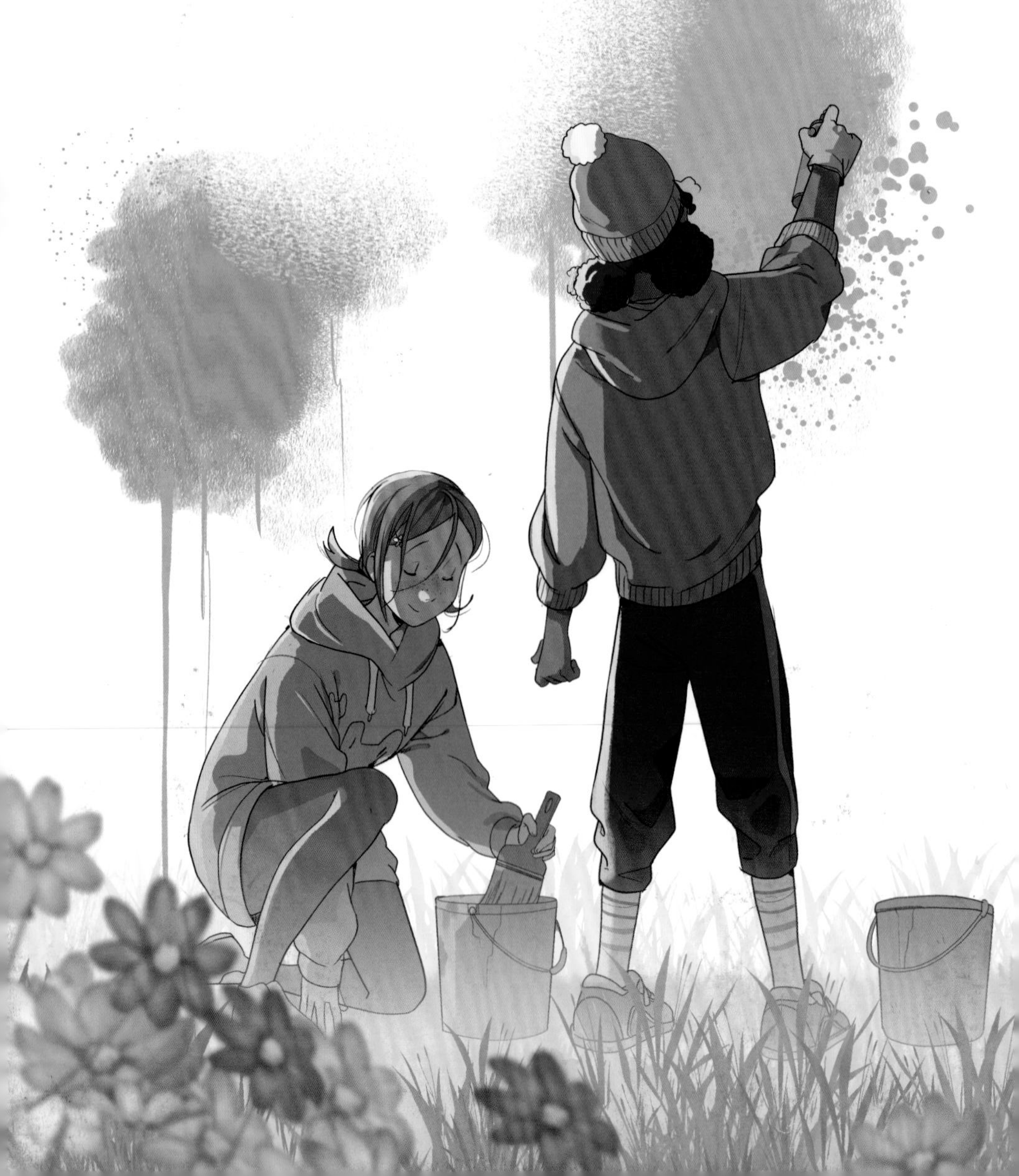

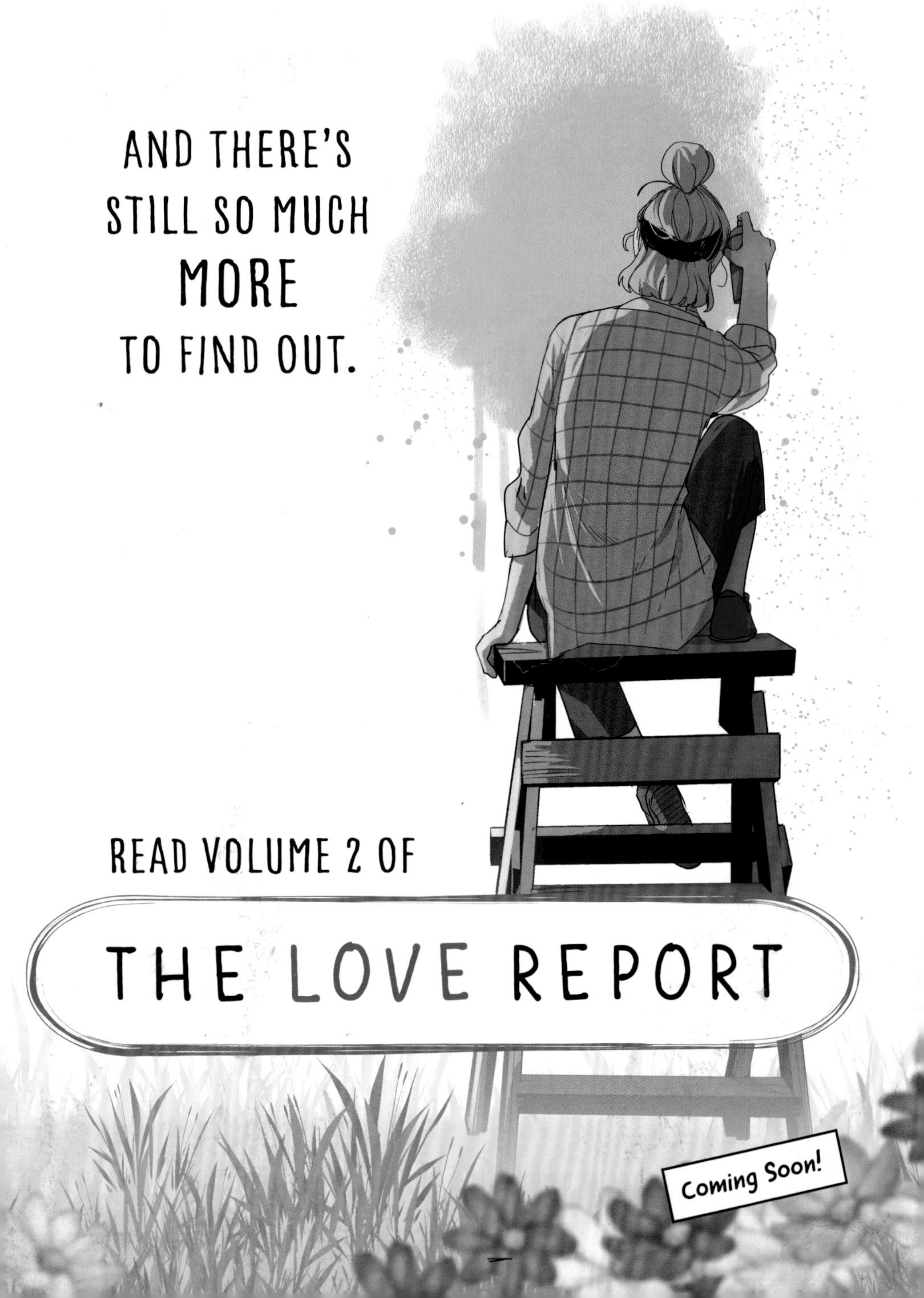
AND THERE'S
STILL SO MUCH
MORE
TO FIND OUT.
READ VOLUME 2 OF
THE LOVE REPORT
Coming Soon!

BeKa is the code name for a team of writers, Caroline Roque and Bertrand Escaich. They have worked together on several successful book series in their country, France, and are thrilled to bring Lola and Grace across the ocean.
Find BeKa at europecomics.com/author/beka.

Maya, whose real name is Martina Mura, is an Italian-born manga artist from the seaside town of Alghero, Sardinia. She attended the European Manga Academy, and her previous works include the graphic novel trilogy *In the Language of Flowers.*
Find Maya at europecomics.com/author/maya.

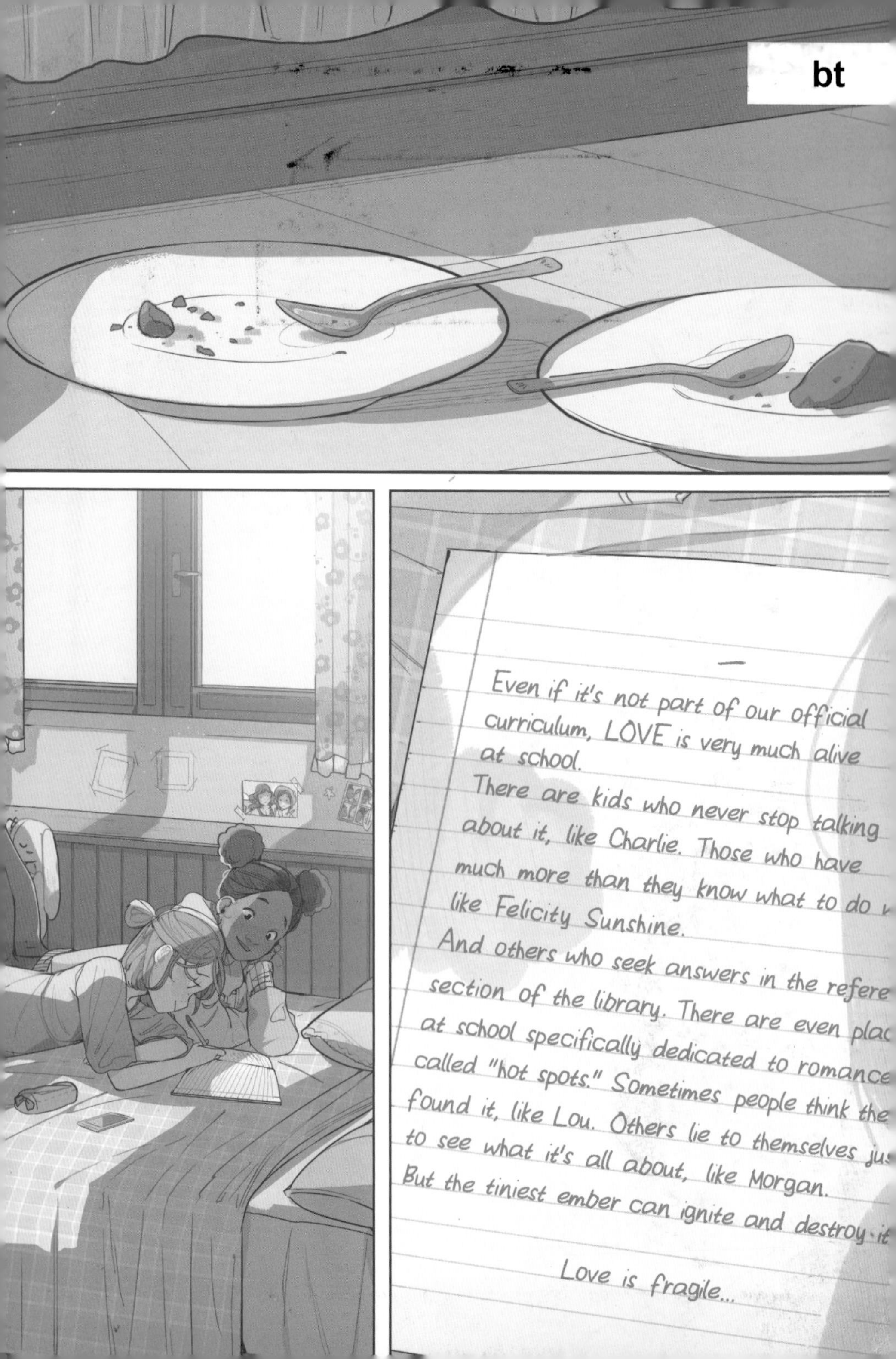

Even if it's not part of our official curriculum, LOVE is very much alive at school.
There are kids who never stop talking about it, like Charlie. Those who have much more than they know what to do
like Felicity Sunshine.
And others who seek answers in the refere
section of the library. There are even plac
at school specifically dedicated to romance
called "hot spots." Sometimes people think the
found it, like Lou. Others lie to themselves ju
to see what it's all about, like Morgan.
But the tiniest ember can ignite and destroy it
Love is fragile...